Somebody's
Sinning
in My Bed

Also by Pat G'Orge-Walker

Sister Betty! God's Calling You, Again!

Mother Eternal Ann Everlastin's Dead

Cruisin' on Desperation

Somewhat Saved

Somebody's Sinning in My Bed

Don't Blame the Devil

No Ordinary Noel

Holy Mayhem

Sister Betty Says I Do

Published by Kensington Publishing Corp.

Somebody's Sinning in My Bed

PAT G'ORGE-WALKER

Dafina Books

KENSINGTON PUBLISHING CORP.
http://www.kensingtonbooks.com

DAFINA BOOKS are published by

Kensington Publishing Corp.
119 West 40th Street
New York, NY 10018

All Kensington Titles, Imprints, and Distributed Lines are available at special quantity discounts for bulk purchases for sales promotion, premiums, fund-raising, educational, or institutional use. Special book excerpts or customized printings can also be created to fit specific needs. For details, write or phone the office of the Kensington special sales manager: Kensington Publishing Corp., 119 West 40th Street, New York, NY 10018, Attn. Special Sales Department. Phone: 1-800-221-2647.

Dafina and the Dafina logo Reg. U.S. Pat. & TM Off.

ISBN-13: 978-0-7582-3541-1
ISBN-10: 0-7582-3541-0
First Kensington Trade Edition: September 2009
First Kensington Mass Market Edition: August 2014

eISBN-13: 978-0-7582-9213-1
eISBN-10: 0-7582-9213-9
Kensington Electronic Edition: August 2014

10 9 8 7 6 5 4 3 2 1

Printed in the United States of America

CHYNA:

Sweet essence of you is gone
Love and trust long dead
Your lack of warmth testify
Somebody's sinning in my bed

JANELLE:

Heart to heart I loved you
My soul is yours, you said
Yet strange wrinkles in my sheets whisper to me
Somebody's sinning in my bed

ACKNOWLEDGMENTS

I thank God for His son, Jesus. Precious is the time He's given me and blessed am I to be counted among His own.

I'd like to thank my husband, Robert, my best friend and solid support. I thank my daughters, Gizel, Ingrid, and Marisa, all of my grandchildren and great-grand. In particular, I thank God for the little additions to the family who arrived in March 2008, one right behind the other: Pierce Logan Brewer, Jonnay Driver, and Raymond Ramseur, Jr.

In no particular order I'd like to thank the following for their prayers and support: Bishop John L. and Lady Laura L. Smith of the St. Paul's City of Lights Ministry, Reverend Stella Mercado and the Blanche Memorial Church family, and my close and extended family. I'd also like to thank Christian Comedians Brotha Smitty of NYC and Miss Vickie of Dallas, Texas.

Of course there would not be a book without the confidence and support of my editor, Selena James, along with the entire Dafina/Kensington family. I thank God for my longtime friend and attorney, Christopher R. Whent, Esq. (a pit bull with a British accent). I offer my most sincere gratitude to my publicist, Ella Curry (EDC Creations), Robin Caldwell of The J Standard, Debra Owsley, and Jacquelin Thomas (my rock). I also want to express my sincerest gratitude to the readers, the stores, the media, churches too numerous to mention, and all who have planted a seed in my career.

And finally, to President Barack and First Lady

Michelle Obama, I thank you and all the millions of United States of America citizens who, with faith in their hearts, votes in their hands, and a "righteous wind" at their backs made history. Oh yes, we did!

3. And the scribes and Pharisees brought unto him a woman taken in adultery; and when they had set her in the midst,

4. They say unto him, Master, this woman was taken in adultery, in the very act.

5. Now Moses in the law commanded us, that such should be stoned: but what saith thou?

6. This they said, tempting him that they might have to accuse him. But Jesus stooped down, and with his finger wrote on the ground, as though he heard them not.

7. So when they continued asking him, he lifted up himself, and said unto them. He that is without sin among you let him first cast a stone at her.

8. And again he stooped down, and wrote on the ground.

9. And they which heard it, being convicted by their own conscience, went out one by one, beginning at the eldest, even unto the last: and Jesus was left alone, and the woman standing in the midst.

10. When Jesus had lifted up himself, and saw none but the woman, he said unto her, Woman, where are those, thine accusers? Hath no man condemned thee?

11. She said, No man, Lord. And Jesus said unto her, neither do I condemn thee: go, and sin no more.

Chapter 1

Violent March winds swirled viciously along Brooklyn, New York's Linden Boulevard, showing little respect for a supposedly holy and consecrated Sunday night. From the second earth took its form, God set that seventh day aside for everything He'd created to praise His work. However, as if mocking God, the very winds He'd created angrily kicked around empty wine and liquor bottles along a small section of Linden Boulevard that struggled to hide its poverty. Small yet powerful wind funnels seemed to mock heaven as they propelled scraps of paper toward the night sky. In a blink of an eye, it then turned its anger on small colorful plastic crack vials, tossing them against the street curbs like dice.

And then, without a warning, evil shifted its shape and intention as it prepared to release its minions.

That night, chaos of another sort was about to visit Linden Boulevard and fierce gusts of winds and signs of poverty along that stretch were the least of its problems. That night, some folks would learn that what goes around certainly does come back around, bringing with it the proverbial flip-top can of vicious comeuppance.

Further down Linden Boulevard the distant purring of an automobile somehow reached through the howling wind to make its presence known. As if on cue, a nearby broken streetlight suddenly flickered, revealing a slow-moving powder-blue 2006 Mercedes.

The car's driver found a spot, parked, and slowly stepped out. The embers of a lit cigarette flickered as a figure of a man was outlined. He puffed once more before tossing it to the ground.

As if accepting the challenge to step up its evil, the wind suddenly changed its direction toward the Mercedes, abandoning its game of tossing about litter. Loud wooshing sounds accompanied its assault. It homed in on the rear flap of the man's expensive chocolate-brown trench coat, causing the material to fan rapidly.

The man suddenly stood still. With eyes narrowed and determined, he suddenly looked back toward his car. It was as though he were daring the wind to do its worst. He muttered, "Go to hell!"

He had dark, penetrating brown eyes that were set deep onto an extremely tawny-complexioned handsome face that hinted of a possible mixed heritage. Then he sucked in a deep breath of night air as though it were his last.

He'd only taken a few steps when one hand suddenly flew up and grabbed at the tan fedora about to fall off his head. He was too slow. The wind would not be denied and blew the expensive fedora over into the middle of the filthy street.

Through it all, he kept his eyes focused and determined. Without a word, he walked a few feet and retrieved the hat, placing it snug onto his head, and turned back to the sidewalk. He'd ignored the filth not so much from fear but almost as a reflex because of what he was about to do. With his hat now secured, he used the same hand to hold the front of his coat, not wanting anyone to see what he had hidden.

There was no turning back now.

Across the street there was a working streetlight. It burned bright on the man as he crossed the street as though to make up for those lights that didn't.

The man moved toward a two-story building nestled between a totally abandoned building and a closed Neighborhood Multi-Service Center. He came within a few feet of his destination and stopped. Despite the darkness, he could see clearly through a small square glass pane. He scowled briefly at a sleeping, obese man.

The portly man was supposed to be alert, but it was nighttime and sleep had claimed the bouncer for the Sweet Bush. Despite nodding off in a deep coma-like sleep and snoring like a bull with asthma, he somehow managed to keep from falling off a stool that was much too small for his wide girth.

The man was tempted to snatch off his unclean fedora, slap the bouncer, and stuff one of those disgusting snores back down his throat, but he needed to stick to the plan.

The man hugged his coat, again, against a body that had been well worked out and buffed. Being a bit of a health fanatic, he hadn't even started smoking until recently when it seemed as though his life was falling apart and brought him to where he now stood.

With one hand, he angrily pushed hard against the oak wood door. The door swung open and closed quickly. It almost nipped the hip of the man as he poured into the front room of the Sweet Bush Lounge.

Noise affected the bouncer much like a sleeping pill; with his barrel chest heaving slightly, he shifted his weight on the stool and continued sleeping soundly.

In a deep sleep, the bouncer would not be a problem.

Fool. The man suppressed a rising growl in his throat as he dismissed the bouncer as a threat. He chose, instead, to adjust his eyes to the dim lounge lights. While he slowed his heart to a manageable beat, he stood transfixed between the panels of a red velvet curtain and peered through a wall of love beads. His handsome face was stoic. With little effort he inhaled in the streams of thick, cloudy, cigarette and reefer smoke for what seemed like an eternity.

But it wasn't.

It'd only taken a moment before he fully understood that none of the other few patrons inside the dark smoky din of lust had paid particular attention to his entrance. Why should they? He wouldn't be the first, or hardly the last, to stumble through that door looking peaceful or angry, on the hunt for whatever was forbidden and getting it.

Chapter 2

The Sweet Bush was one of Brooklyn's worst-kept secrets. There were plenty of folks, young and old, rich and poor; the beautiful and the downright ugly, flooding in from miles around. They were unfulfilled souls who'd repeatedly risked reputations and relationships to freak nameless others. Full of denial and sex-driven demons, when they left at sunrise, they clung to a hope that their trysts stayed behind, hidden in condoms and disguised inside shot glasses.

The man pulled out the .357 Magnum from where he'd hidden it tucked in his waistband beneath his coat. With the gun now raised chest-high, his eyes searched. Side to side, his hypnotic gaze swept around the hall. With nothing and no one to stop him, he moved on.

As he inched closer to his destination, what moments before had been a purposeful gait suddenly became clumsy.

It'd been some time since he'd secretly visited the Sweet Bush. He'd visit the haunt usually after leaving his young wife crying in their king-size bed, less than satisfied and belittled. He reasoned his wife's hurt feelings and lack of sexual fulfillment were necessary collateral damage.

After all, he was the Right Reverend Grayson Young. He was the son of the renowned late Bishop Isaiah Young and the late First Lady Mildred Young. It was only natural that upon his father's death, ten years ago, every leader of faith anointed him Brooklyn's megachurch phenomenon.

With eyes still blazing, Reverend Young whispered, "One day I've got to ask God what He thinks about that." He snickered at the joke to which only he was privy as he took a quick glance around.

Inside the Sweet Bush, as well as in the Reverend Grayson's mind, it seemed nothing much had changed since he'd last visited. The laid-back, free-love, ambience of the place was the same, and the soft and jazzy music of Kool and the Gang's "Summer Madness" filled the lounge.

"Reverend Grayson Young." A bald, fat man called out to him. "Well suh, I can't believe someone like you, after all these months, would come back down here to get down. I still can't believe it's you preaching all that fire and brimstone from the pulpit of New Hope." He stopped and gave a conspiring wink. "I sometime catch the second service on television when I can't make it to my own church." He followed his revelation with laughter that sounded more like snorting as he extended a hand. "At least you don't have to worry about these others knowing who you really are. Trust me, none of them go or even think about church. Your secret has been and will be safe with me."

Reverend Young just stared in disgust. The weight of the gun lessened but his anger grew as he mumbled. "Who gives a damn who recognizes me? Just stick to the plan, Reverend. Just stick to the plan. She's waiting for you."

Reverend Young's head jerked suddenly and he looked back toward the entrance to the Sweet Bush. His ears picked up the taunting from the outside wind as it made a wooshing sound for his ears alone. "For God is not mocked," he heard the wind say.

He staggered slightly, placing his hand that held the gun behind him. He planned to harm any avenging angels should God decide to send them.

Reverend Grayson Young had played spiritual tag with his Heavenly Father one time too many. He'd preached one way and lived another. Year after year, Sunday after Sunday, he'd called upon his congregation to give up their evil ways. He'd condemned those who stepped out of the bounds of marriage to fulfill their lust, although he'd stepped out to the point of no longer wanting his wife.

That night all accounts needed settling. He'd discovered that for almost a year it was possible that his wife, First Lady Chyna, might've done just as much tipping as he. He'd had her followed one evening, and it seemed that she favored the Sweet Bush, too. And the reverend couldn't take that.

He set about lighting parts of the Sweet Bush afire with the lit candles that just moments before were ambience.

"I'm fired up and I've come to kill my wife!" the reverend yelled, waving his gun in the air, sending petrified Sweet Bush patrons looking for the exits.

Chapter 3

Inside a two-room suite at the Hilton hotel just a few miles off the New England Thruway in Tarrytown, New York, Chyna Young woke with a start. There was something deep within her spirit that suddenly felt, as the old folks would say, as though someone had stepped on her grave.

It took her a moment to realize she wasn't in her own bed and the sudden tug of an arm pulling her into an embrace calmed her.

Her long dark hair cascaded onto the queen-size pillow as she moved closer to inhale the scent from her current affair.

"Can I order something for us?" The man, young and willing with skin smooth and dark like shaven chocolate, arose. He was still naked and showed no apology, yet he moved in a way that offered her more of him if she'd wanted.

"Just tea for me," Chyna answered as she stretched and rose up on one elbow as she admired his physique. She loved a well-built man.

For a brief moment, a mask of sadness appeared upon Chyna's face as she remembered that at home she already had one. At least that was the way it was supposed to be. Her husband, the supposedly wonderful and heaven-bound reverend spent little time at home and even less in their bed. Early in their marriage, she'd spent more time crying in their bedroom than she did at the church. Once she discovered that the good reverend wasn't just *laying* hands at the church, but that he'd brought other women into their king-sized bed, where she'd caught him each time, she'd begun to seek satisfaction elsewhere.

"I'll turn on the television while I call down."

"Thank you," Chyna answered as she briefly enjoyed the touch from one of his powerful hands as he reached across her for the remote.

"Do you always look this beautiful?" he'd asked as though this weren't their second encounter.

Chyna smiled. This man made her laugh whereas her husband had stopped doing so long ago, and if for no other reason, she felt close to him. She loved that he'd asked with the enthusiasm of a teenager although he was hardly one. According to him, when they met a few weeks ago, he was still in his twenties, but married with a pregnant wife and a two-year-old. They'd met at a Christian club where the sanctity of faith was supposedly upheld and the chances of sinful encounters minimized.

"I'm freelancing on the weekends with different bands," he'd told her. "I guess you can tell by my long fingers that I can play one hell of an organ."

They hadn't even exchanged names yet, and the flirtation had already started. The club was in New Jersey, though neither of them knew much about the state.

Chyna was about to say something to him, but she was stopped cold by what she saw and heard on the television.

Chapter 4

Thirty minutes after she'd fled the hotel and left the remnants of her affair probably in chaos Chyna could barely keep to the speed limit. She struggled to navigate the winding parkway road before she turned off the Jackie Robinson Parkway. She scraped the front fender as she did. Despite the damage she was sure she'd done to the car, her small hands clutched the steering wheel. Letting go wasn't an option.

"Oh God, I'm sorry . . ." Chyna wanted to pray further, but couldn't. She'd promised God after several other trysts that she'd lean on Him and not seek revenge on Grayson. But she'd lied to herself and to God.

Her car skidded and came to an abrupt halt just in time to keep from rear-ending a school bus that had slowed down with the rest of the traffic.

Despite her belief that at that moment her God was in an unforgiving mood where she was concerned, there was a spiritual force that helped Chyna to keep her car on the road. Was it still His grace that kept her sanity as she alternated between trying to erase the image of Grayson's

Mercedes on television and her own sins, and the fact that if her husband was in the Sweet Bush he was now gone?

Finally Chyna pulled into the driveway of her expansive Highland Park home. She heaved violently from the car, all the way to the shrubs, trying to purge all that had happened.

Chyna had always appreciated living in a quiet and secure neighborhood but never more than she did at that moment. The only sounds heard or made were hers. Despite all the emotions that hopscotched about inside her head, which still looked disheveled, she had the presence of mind to leave the car window cracked before she'd bailed out. She'd attend to the mess later. She had bigger problems than a soiled car.

Chyna felt as though she were running on three legs. Every step she took was uncontrolled as she tripped, repeatedly. By the time she finally reached the stained-glass and oak door to her brick, three-story Tudor home, she had the strength of string.

"Alarm on. Please disarm immediately!" Chyna was startled by the robotic and unsympathetic voice blasting from the house alarm. Her body trembled, almost violently as she fought to remain on her feet.

"Oh God," she muttered. Ninety seconds hadn't passed. That was the maximum time she had to disarm before the police would be called. "Two-eight-six-three," she repeated the code, rearranging the order as she struggled to remember the code to disarm the alarm. With two seconds to go, she finally entered the correct code.

Stumbling through the front door, she managed to crack one of its glass panes with her elbow. Chyna couldn't stop had she wanted to. Finally, now almost crawling, she reached the hall stairway and surrendered to the support from its banister. Chyna became robotic, embracing a sense of safety.

For all her effort, Chyna made very little distance. She slumped down onto one of the wide marble stair steps, where she rocked and wept.

Minutes passed, or was it hours? How many? Chyna didn't know. Her legs felt stiff from not moving around and cold from the marble.

Although Chyna had no way of measuring the time, it seemed that every few minutes either the telephone or her cell phone rang. She ignored them. Deep inside she knew Grayson was gone, but she couldn't deal with it.

Suddenly tiredness clawed at her. She needed rest, but there was no time. All the dirt, physical and mental, from not only what she'd done that morning but also other times and all its effects made her skin crawl. She was as guilty as Grayson.

But she was alive. He obviously wasn't, if she was to believe the news report. Chyna looked toward her living room. She was tempted to go inside and turn on the television. She didn't.

"I need a drink." Chyna said angrily throwing open one of the glass doors to the liquor cabinet behind the mirrored bar in the den. Grayson usually kept a bottle or two of Hennessey and other spirits. It was for some of the deacons, who despite testifying against alcoholic spirits, still liked to "taste" every now and again.

She selected an expensive bottle of wine, guzzled from it, and waited on her sofa for the inevitable to arrive.

"New Hope Assembly deserved better than me and Grayson," Chyna murmured as she took another swig from the wine bottle.

But truth be told, she definitely knew that when she was cheating. Somehow she also preferred to believe that Grayson, as narcissistic as he was, would also admit the same thing, if he could.

Chyna was certain she'd need another bottle to numb

her pain, since she was still too ashamed to approach God. She was also certain that the hell from the fallout at the Sweet Bush would be nothing compared to what was sure to be waiting for her later if anyone found out she, too, was unfaithful.

But then later came sooner than Chyna expected.

Chapter 5

Chyna was still crumpled up on the sofa when she felt the burst of cold air followed by the sound of a hysterical voice calling out to her.

"Chyna, where are you?"

Chyna's reaction was swift and surprising being she was still in the throes of semiconsciousness and partially intoxicated. Her body shook. She wasn't certain whether or not she was back at in the arms of her earlier lover or was she imagining Grayson accusing and berating her. She tried to calm down, but the strong wine had quickly taken charge of her body. The best she could do was to coil back into a fetal position and shake.

"There you are. Why didn't you answer your phone?"

Chyna looked up, surprised to see her older sister, Janelle. The inside of her mouth felt like a cotton pallet soaking up any response she tried to give.

Chyna's older sister by two years, Janelle, had used a spare key to enter. Despite the age difference, the two could almost pass for twins. They each wore a size six and had the same long dark auburn hair fanning heart-shaped faces, same flawless mocha complexion covering their five-foot, six-inch frames. But that's where the similarity ended.

Chyna was Cristal to Janelle's Thunderbird. Janelle would order arugula and chitlins and then jump from a plane and think about a parachute on her way down. Chyna would've checked for a parachute first before being pushed. Although as in any sibling relationship, there'd been some hiccups—some more serious than others—along the way, there wasn't anything the sisters wouldn't do for one another, and they let the world know it.

"You had me scared to death," Janelle said. "I called a few places and no one had heard from you. You know when I heard that, I panicked."

Janelle quickly removed her black Russian mink coat. It was a recent Christmas gift from one of her several lovers. If anyone had asked her who gave it, she'd had to guess.

With a quick sweep of her hand, Janelle trivialized its worth and importance by tossing it aside instead of laying it down carefully. It was how she felt about most things and humans once she won them over. "I've been trying to reach you since early this morning."

"Sorry," Chyna finally said as she held her head in her hands. As much as she loved her sister, at that moment, she wished she hadn't given her that spare key or permission to use it whenever she wanted as long as Grayson was out of town. Again, she tried to respond further but couldn't while wishing Janelle would just shut up or at least talk softer.

If Janelle saw Chyna's discomfort, she didn't show it. "I heard what happened at the Sweet Bush overnight. You know, the first thing I thought was, 'damn, I'm sure glad that didn't happen when we was at the Sweet Bush for Cinnamon's bachelorette party last summer.' "

Janelle stopped just long enough to kick off her shoes before she started in again. She was used to Chyna letting her do her big-sister thing, so the silence didn't bother her.

"Which reminds me, did that heifer ever apologize for letting some fool spike your drink? If I was you I'd have dropped her quicker than a herpes diagnosis. She's a trifling piece of mess letting some man put you in all those poses. You know I'd have stepped in, but, hell, it looked like you had it handled and I didn't see anybody pull out a camera."

Janelle shut up just long enough to laugh before adding, "And then she didn't even marry the dude. You'd think she'd found out whether or not he was available before setting a wedding date and a damn stripper party."

Of course, Janelle didn't wait for a reply. She just kept on yapping. "The Sweet Bush burning down. That sounds like some kinda venereal disease, don't it?"

Chyna finally looked up at the second or third mention of the Sweet Bush as Janelle babbled.

". . . damn place burned completely down." Janelle continued in a more respectful tone, "It's a shame, too. I saw the fire engines, police cars, and Channel Seven news when I drove past there about one o'clock this morning. From what I heard none of those poor folks made it out. You know I don't like fire, and I wanted to call you when I got home, but I figured you were asleep. I didn't want that chauvinistic, uppity, hypocrite husband of yours answering the phone before he left to go to who-knows-where. I'm sure he'd have worked my last nerve with stupid questions. But then I remember you told me he said he was going out of town to preach someplace. So, here I am."

Janelle didn't try to hide the sneer as she mentioned

Grayson's name. ". . . still don't know why you ever married . . ."

Janelle's rant stopped as she finally sat down on the other side of the sofa next to the almost empty wine bottle. Despite the time of late morning, she poured the remainder of the wine into an empty glass and added a good amount of Hennessey to the mix. Downing it with one gulp, she continued rattling off the bad news.

"Oh Lord," Janelle suddenly belched and whispered, "I'm not trying to be cold hearted or nothing but can you imagine the embarrassment if we'd been caught up in there doing the nasty at Cinnamon's party? That damn hypocrite preacher husband of yours would've hauled us before the congregation and told everything except the abuse he does to you."

Janelle's rant was interrupted by another loud belch, of which she was not ashamed. She suddenly let out a nervous laugh, "I shouldn't judge. After all, he may be your husband number two but you're certainly set up a lot better than before. Too bad it had to be with this crazy son of a gun."

Janelle rose. She went over to the bar and adroitly opened a new bottle of Hennessey. She knew it would bother Grayson, so she filled the glass hoping to leave the bottle empty where he could see it. Janelle downed the hot-tasting liquid without a flinch.

Janelle's mouth was now into overdrive with no sign of slowing down, "but you're a reverend's wife; he's a lowlife reverend nonetheless, but you still need to get your freak on every now and then as long as you don't overdo it or get caught. I mean at least you and I ain't no skanks. We do have a little class."

Janelle poured a second glass and spoke while she drank, causing her words to slur a bit. "Of course, I still don't see how you gonna convince the Lord that your cheating was Grayson's fault, but you know God better than me."

Janelle swallowed the last of that glass, which seemed to sober her up but didn't stop her from babbling, "So, anyhow, you know when I called you earlier, I was worried when you didn't answer. I rushed over."

Janelle was starting to repeat herself, but it didn't stop her from refilling her glass. She stopped almost in mid-sentence and stared at Chyna as though finally seeing her for the first time. "You need to get it together, girl-friend. Here it is almost eleven o'clock and you look like crap . . ."

Chyna unfolded her legs and finally rose. Stumbling a bit, she walked out of the room toward the kitchen, try-ing to avoid any further bad news her sister would deliver.

Janelle followed Chyna with her mouth still in over-drive. After several cups of black coffee came a promise from Janelle: "Okay, I'm gonna shut my mouth 'cause it looks like you about to catch an attitude."

Chyna needed to tell it before it all came out in the news, first.

The tears poured, zigzagging, leaving streaks that re-sembled razor cuts along Chyna's smooth cheeks. The sordid and salty details stung as she whimpered. "—and then, I just left the hotel room without even saying g'bye. I heard the news report, saw Grayson's Mercedes, and just left. If Grayson was in that place and he's dead, I don't know what I'm gonna do. What I did was so wrong, too. I know there's gonna be hell to pay when this gets out."

Janelle's jaw dropped hard. It was hard enough for the pain to shoot up through her cheek and immediately numb her tongue. She placed her cup down gently, which was how she wanted to console her sister. With arms stretched open, still unable to voice her shock, Janelle navigated her way through her own painful maze of emotions. She strolled across the room to rescue Chyna in an embrace.

The silence was momentary but seemed much longer.

"I'm sorry to put this on you," Chyna offered as Janelle cradled her in her arms.

And then the awkwardness of that moment broke. Janelle's chameleon ability to push unpleasant things aside took over. "It's almost noon. You might want to think about how you're gonna act when the police or whoever brings you the bad news shows up. 'Cause if that sorry piece of an evil spirit is really dead, then you'll need to show the proper grief."

"How should I do that? He was still my husband and the church's pastor." Chyna couldn't argue with Janelle's description even if she'd wanted. She'd often felt the same way about Grayson and probably still did.

Janelle lifted Chyna's chin. She kissed her sister on the cheek and said sharply, "You'd better be prepared to show your arse."

Janelle did what most fearless big sisters were supposed to do. She went into overprotection mode, which almost always led to more trouble.

Dismissing the perplexed look on Chyna's face, Janelle continued, "I'm gonna call Cinnamon. She can be your alibi, too, if you need someone other than me. She ain't a classy heifer, but she's a ride-or-die sista, and she's your girl. As for me, I'll just stay here with you until somebody comes by or calls you about Grayson."

"Cinnamon's away on a cruise," Chyna replied in a matter-of-fact manner.

"She's away on a cruise, damn. I hope she took that jailbird son of hers, Hard Life, with her. Lord knows Brooklyn would be a lot safer if she did." Janelle quickly placed a hand over her mouth to hide a grin before adding, "I'm sorry. I hadn't meant to say that out loud, but you still don't need a lot of folks in your business. I'm just sayin' that's all."

With compassion slowly settling in, Janelle didn't wait for Chyna to respond. She suddenly truly wanted to cry for her sister. She couldn't, at least not then. She blinked and willed back the tears from her large brown eyes. Letting out a sigh, she let go of Chyna's shoulders and picked her mink off the floor.

Looking at the mink, Janelle quipped, "I've got to update my wardrobe." Janelle knew what she'd just said didn't make a bit of sense. She was chattering nonsense as she grappled with lowering her soaring blood pressure, trying to formulate a plan she was certainly going to need. She glanced over and decided that she needed to get Chyna cleaned up. "You need to get it together," Janelle blurted. "You looking scraggly is distracting and it's messing up my scheming."

Chyna tried to smile. She failed.

"Let's get you cleaned up and make sure you brush your teeth before the police come knocking. Of course, if it's those churchy folks that sweep in first I don't care what your breath smells like."

"Janelle, please." The dark circles widening around Chyna's swollen eyes completed the plea.

"Okay," Janelle replied, "When you get back to praying, just pray for me. I don't know when I'll ever be able to deal with them folks."

That time it was Chyna's turn to make a move. She willed her arms to wrap around her neck. "I know."

And Chyna did know. She knew that when her sister needed the church that some of the holier-than-thou folks attacked her. Janelle had innocently gotten involved with a church deacon,

and not just any deacon, but one that was mar-
ried to a well-known evangelist. Her sister had
barely turned twenty-two when the affair was
discovered. It was no different than when the bib-
lical adulterous woman was found in the very
act; Janelle took the punishment of ridicule and
public humiliation. The deacon minimized his
part, and with the aid of his famous wife and
their church, Janelle's road to salvation was tor-
pedoed. That was several years ago, at another
time and in another city.

"I guess I should shower." Chyna said softly pushing history aside as she allowed Janelle to wriggle free from her embrace.

"Yeah, you go and do that. I'll go through your closet and try to find something that's a cross between a First Lady and a dutiful housewife, slash, recent widow."

"I think I've got a black dress with a silver neckline. There should be a soft red jacket that can go with it."

"Damn, what are you trying to look like?

"What's wrong now?"

"You gonna look like a ladybug."

And for the first time since Janelle arrived, she got her sister to laugh. It only lasted a few seconds, but it was a start.

It took almost two hours and several wardrobe changes before Chyna, fresh from a shower, looked a bit more presentable.

Of course, whatever she'd picked out still hadn't met with Janelle's expectations. "Is that the best you can do?" Janelle has asked.

Chyna would just stand like a statue and take whatever Janelle verbally doled out. Of course, Janelle played the big-sister role to the hilt. She'd roll her eyes and shake her head while uttering an impatient "uh-huh" to make her point at the various outfits.

Janelle continued to protest about trivial coordinated designer outfits adequate enough to display a worthy amount of surprised grief. Although armed with her arsenal of rabid rants primed and ready to fire, she stopped in mid-sentence. The sounds of a car pulling into the driveway and the slamming of its doors put a stop to it.

"Who's that?" Janelle rushed past a frightened Chyna, stopping just long enough to quickly turn on the radio and blast its volume. Leave it to Janelle to turn on a radio station blasting the Ohio Players's "Fire."

Almost tripping over an ottoman Janelle managed to peek through the brocade living room curtains. She'd barely closed them before the xylophone-toned door chimes rang. It was too late for them to finalize their plotting.

It was showtime. Janelle was ready for a starring role. Chyna, still rooted in her same spot, looked stricken.

Janelle swung open the door like the B-list diva she was. "Yes," she said sweetly, "Can I help you gentlemen?"

Chapter 6

From the moment the two police detectives from Brooklyn's seventy-ninth precinct arrived at Chyna's door, she mentally removed herself from the scene. Chyna sat in a chair over in a corner, with her hands folded, her eyes transfixed, as though she were watching a movie, one that could only end badly.

The downward spiral started with Chyna watching Janelle take over. As soon as Janelle placed one of her hands on her hourglass-shaped hip and started acting like she was at the door of a local Chicken Ranch inviting in a customer, Chyna's blood pressure shot up. As much as she was glad her sister was taking over, angst plucked at her nerves and wasn't stopping.

With Janelle's help things went south, first in slow motion and then at warp speed.

And she hadn't even closed the door behind the detectives yet.

In her shocked state, Chyna's mind lagged a few minutes behind the reality of what was happening. It was only when she finally realized that the detectives had displayed their badges identifying them as a Detective Lavin and a Detective Gonzalez that something snapped in Chyna's head.

Suddenly the reality of what could happen to her freedom and her reputation if she didn't play her part sent her psyche soaring into survival mode.

Little became much as to Chyna. Just the sight of their holstered guns and in particular the handcuffs did what Janelle couldn't. So, for that moment, whatever happened in Chyna and Grayson's failed marriage, their adulteries, and their deceptions had to take a backseat.

Detective Lavin was of average height and looked about forty, dark skinned. His lips were double thick with teeth so yellow his mouth looked like the butt of a bumblebee. He was Mutt.

The other Detective, Gonzalez, was tall, fair-skinned, and thin. He was also about the same age as his partner. Although Gonzalez wore the typical police-issued winter wear tan-colored, thermal-lined all-weather coat, his looks were deceiving. He appeared to perhaps once been very athletic. He was the Jeff of the duo.

Now facing the two detectives, both Chyna and Janelle set about to win a ghetto Oscar. Silently, the mental curtains rose as they signaled to one another. Janelle tilted her head slightly and Chyna smiled. It was a sign they'd used, when in collusion, since childhood.

The seasoned detectives had no clue that they were about to be tag-teamed and slammed by the skillful feminine wit of Chyna and Janelle.

The detectives had barely walked over the threshold before Janelle started her routine from a chair where she'd just sat down. "Would you care to sit down, too?" She'd directed the seemingly innocent question toward one of the detectives.

The two detectives glanced at each other quickly and before they could respond, Janelle began act two.

"Gonzalez, is it?" Janelle purred, "Are you sure we can't offer you a cup of coffee?" Janelle asked still smiling. She kept her eyes glued to the detective.

Not waiting for an answer, Janelle attempted to rise from her seat, allowing the split in her skirt to fall open and show a creamy-colored hint of one of her best assets. "Do you prefer cream and sugar?" She asked slowly ignoring the fact that neither detective had answered. She allowed the rhythm of her words to perform a striptease through barely opened teeth. With her eyes penetrating any defense she felt was hidden by the man, she took her time pulling the split back together revealing the other perfectly shaped thigh, before she'd innocently pulled the split apart again.

"I've got tea if you'd prefer that instead," Chyna offered as she joined the show. Her voice was soft and in some respects robotic. She hadn't offered a show of skin, but her voice carried the same effect.

"We're fine." Gonzalez replied, haltingly. He'd tried to exude command over the moment, but his stammering and the way he suddenly tried to avoid Janelle's eyes said otherwise.

"Just offering," Janelle said, coyly.

Chyna and Janelle continued in sync, showing pretend nervousness and surprise, as the detectives lay out the reasons for their appearance.

"Well, Ms. Young. I imagine you haven't watched the television or turned on a radio this morning." Detective Lavin said slowly, examining her face for any sign that she had.

"We've come to inform you that around one o'clock this morning your husband was one of the fatalities at the Sweet Bush in Brooklyn, New York. It's a sex club over on Linden Boulevard." Detective Gonzalez didn't feel the same need for caution. After all, the man was inside the Sweet Bush with a beautiful wife at home. He hoped the fool suffered.

"According to one eyewitness . . ."

Janelle and Chyna gave each other a quick glance. Each sister automatically knew what the other was thinking. Eyewitness, what eyewitness? Didn't everyone die in the fire?

Chyna and Janelle turned their attention back to Detective Lavin, who had continued speaking, "One of the bouncers had fled about the same time your husband was in the throes of killing his third victim . . ."

"What do you mean my husband is dead?" Chyna wailed on cue.

"There's got to be some kind of mistake," Janelle blurted, "there's no way my brother-in-law would do such a thing. He was a man of God. He didn't have a murderous bone in his body. How could he? He was a preacher, a famous preacher."

Janelle was going for the gold. By the time she finished immortalizing Grayson she wasn't quite sure if he wasn't all she'd just claimed. She was too caught up in the pretense.

While the detectives offered apologies and condolences, the sisters went for the gusto. In keeping up their act, with another slight head tilt they'd suddenly turn serious. The sisters gave quick answers. They would then in turn ask questions, for which they'd already known the answers.

"I can't talk anymore." Chyna finally blurted, with tears streaming down her face. She was so good she even had her nose running.

It'd taken almost thirty minutes for the sisters to disarm the detectives. Finally, more for their own relief than for the women both detectives prepared to bring their questioning to an end.

"Mrs. Young," Detective Lavin said as he closed his pad and rose, "will you please let us know if you can think of any reason why your husband would take his own life or take the lives of others?" Detective Lavin had spoken in a rehearsed sort of sympathetic voice as he then pressed his business card in Chyna's hand. Then he smiled, sort of.

Janelle couldn't let the detectives leave without getting a few more answers or licks in.

"You said that the place burned down and practically all the bodies were burned beyond recognition. I still don't understand how you are so certain that my brother-in-law was definitely there, other than some words out of the mouth of a bouncer?" Janelle asked as seriously as she could without letting a smile appear. "You've really upset my sister and just because Grayson never came home last night doesn't mean he'd be at such a place."

Another quiet sob came from the corner where Chyna now sat dabbing at her invisible tears while she rotated the detective's business card in her free hand.

"Ma'am . . ." the Mutt-looking Detective Lavin answered. He was caught off guard. "I understand that you and Mrs. Young are probably in shock. Let me explain it again."

"Let me try." The other detective, Gonzalez said turning to Chyna instead of answering Janelle. However, Gonzalez appeared out of sync. His steps didn't seem that confident as he almost tripped walking over to where Chyna remained seated. It was an awkward move. With him, professionalism suddenly took a backseat as he appraised Chyna. Without shame, he'd openly showed lustful appreciation for every bit of her femininity, from head to toe, despite her crying.

When Gonzalez finally spoke, his voice was slow and deliberate as he continued to ogle Chyna. "There were two bodies whose identifications had not been consumed by fire. We cannot tell you the identity of the other."

His eyes locked on to hers, Gonzalez bent over and offered her a handkerchief he'd magically pulled from his coat pocket before continuing, "but we are 100 percent certain that the coroner gave us the correct information when it came to identifying the other bodies."

"Excuse me," Chyna finally said after pushing aside the detective's handkerchief. So as not to offend, she did so gently, "Could you please make it clearer?"

"Of course, the coroner's office has already located your dentist. The coroner knows his job." Gonzalez answered while returning the handkerchief to his pocket. He stopped and looked over to Lavin as if to prove his point, "What was the dentist's name?"

Lavin, eager to show that he, too, was still a part of the investigation, answered quickly and with authority. "Dr. Kevon Jackson in St. Albans, Queens." Lavin said and then quickly added, "The dental records were a match. We'd not come here if we weren't certain."

"Thanks," Gonzalez said hurriedly before turning around and softening his voice toward Chyna. "We can't reveal much more since it's treated as a crime," the detective added.

Almost as an afterthought and to not bring the conversation to an end without his additional input, Lavin, still leering, said, "We've yet to determine if the place had a security camera . . ." He stopped in mid-sentence more from a gut reaction than anything more.

Lavin could feel his partner's eyes burning into the back of his head, so he quickly added, "But then I can't see why a place like that would risk losing customers with a camera in the place," Lavin shrugged trying to downplay what he'd learned in Detective 101, "but then it wasn't the type of place I'd frequent. So what do I know?"

Knowing they then had the detectives off stride and possibly ready to disagree about small things between themselves, Janelle tilted her head and that time threw a look of concern toward Chyna.

Despite all that was going down, Chyna knew Janelle's look was saying. *Just keep your mouth shut! You were miles away doing your own thing.*

"And, of course, we'll see that you get back the Mercedes registered to your husband when we're done going through it." Gonzalez suddenly offered his hand to Chyna as though she needed help to stand.

And that's when everything done in the dark came to the light.

"Okay, Carlos Gonzalez," Janelle suddenly blurted out while blocking the detective's view, "If my sister can think of anything *I'll* be certain to call you. Or better yet, I'll just tell Bianca tomorrow night, if I see her at the spades game."

Janelle took a step forward before continuing. "You know I'd hate to have to see your wife arrested for cutting you."

"You'll never change, will you, Janelle?" The detective smiled nervously. No one had been as shocked as he when he'd discovered his wife played the game of spades at the same place as Janelle.

Lavin, who'd started toward the front door, stopped and pivoted toward his partner and Janelle now locked in a silent mind battle. "Excuse me," he said, "you two already know one another?"

Detective Lavin was so shocked he never saw the look of confusion now on Chyna's face.

"Damn, Janelle," Carlos fumed, "this is a police investigation. I need to keep it professional. You didn't think I'd treat it differently because we know each other?"

"Then respect this house!" Janelle barked. *That's my sister. Keep your eyes to yourself.* She was sure he'd read her look and knew exactly what she meant because he immediately backed down.

"I'm sorry, Mrs. Young," Gonzalez said, flatly to Chyna without explaining what he was sorry for.

Neither Detective Carlos Gonzalez nor Janelle had wanted that little bit of information about their knowing one another out there.

However, Janelle was about to explode with anger at the way he'd leered at Chyna. He'd been one of a few virile men with good-paying jobs with whom she'd slept. He was also one of several who'd never said that they were married before tearing up the bedsheets. For someone who'd never married, it seemed she was always committing uninformed adultery.

The atmosphere had turned toxic. Five minutes later, the detectives left with the option to return if necessary. The detectives had barely made it to their car before Chyna had collapsed into tears.

"What if anyone finds out I was at the Hilton in Tarrytown?" Chyna didn't try to hide the panic behind the question.

"How many times did you meet with that young man?"

"It was only once. It'd been months since I'd stepped out on Grayson."

"That's another thing I'll never understand, but back to the present. Does this young man know your real name and is he married?

"No. I'd never use my real name and, yes, he said he was married." Chyna's mind began to race. Despite the

32 *Pat G'Orge-Walker*

coolness Janelle displayed, she was certain, deep inside, that her sister was now a wreck, too.

"Let's not borrow trouble. You had sex. You didn't kill anybody other than your pristine reputation. It was good, right?"

She was trying to put a different spin on things for Chyna's sake. It didn't take much for Janelle to quickly decide what she would do. There was no way she'd leave Chyna alone. She didn't quite view sex like Chyna. She didn't use sex as a way of payback. She used sex to hide pain, sex to express happiness, and mostly sex to deal with loneliness.

Although neither sister wanted to watch the news on television, they did. There wasn't much reported that the detectives hadn't shared. Of course, there was always the unanswered question asked at the end of each segment. "Why would such a prominent man, a preacher no less, commit such a crime?"

And then, as they knew would happen, there were the news vans gathered at the mouth of her driveway. She'd not responded when they rang her bell, and she wouldn't allow Janelle to answer. Janelle would've certainly cussed them out.

But then this was just day one.

Chapter 7

The next morning the deluge continued at Chyna's home and she was glad Janelle had stayed the night. It seemed that the neighbors and the media took turns either ringing her bell or calling her phone. When several of the church board members finally called, Chyna permitted Janelle to speak on her behalf, hoping she'd keep the craziness to a minimum.

"No, I'm sorry, she's unable to come to the telephone." Janelle said as calmly as she could when one of the churchy folks, as she called them, telephoned. "I'll let the First Lady know that you'll be praying for her."

Janelle kept pretty much to the script whenever a church or board member telephoned. She was proud of herself for not telling them off.

Several of the callers were the same folks from New Hope Assembly who'd refused to forgive her a few years back when they found out about her infidelity with the prominent deacon. It certainly didn't help nor matter that she was the sister of their First Lady. She was always certain that Grayson probably had something to do with it.

But she couldn't prove it and didn't attend that church or any other to try.

"Janelle," Chyna finally whispered. She was coming around from her self-imposed silence. "What time is it?"

"It's almost five o'clock." Janelle answered slowly. She could almost read her sister's mind and she floundered trying to find an excuse to tell her, "no."

"It's getting late." Chyna said rising off the sofa. "We might as well get it over with."

"Are you sure?" Janelle asked, "It's not like he's going anywhere."

"Now's not the time to get cold-blooded." Chyna answered. Somewhere in the deep recesses of her mind and heart she was starting to grieve or at least show some semblance of grieving. She was certain that if she didn't move at that moment, she didn't know when she could.

Janelle peered through the drapes. There was still a news van idling at the corner trying to appear nonintrusive. As if on cue, a police car appeared and parked at the mouth of Chyna's driveway. It was blocking the view of the news van.

"I gotta remember to give Gonzalez a special thank-you when I see him." Janelle told Chyna. "I'm glad he's good for something. He said he'd make sure we could leave without being followed."

"Well then, let's go." Chyna had produced two pair of sunglasses for her and Janelle. It had started to drizzle and that was a good excuse to hide behind head wraps and raincoats.

Chapter 8

Nothing could have prepared Chyna and Janelle for planning Grayson's memorial. Although Grayson had died two days ago, it would be several more before the event could take place. After all, he was the Most Eminent Reverend Doctor Grayson Young.

Apparently even a crime of murder and suicide hadn't diminished his name to the degree it should have. Chyna was almost certain that she'd never be treated the same. Janelle knew for certain she wouldn't.

Neither woman particularly cared to deal with death and all the ceremonies that went along with it. They were young when their mother died from an undiagnosed and rapidly malignant breast cancer. A year later their father died from grief. Both sets of grandparents outlived their only children. Since Janelle and Chyna were barely into their teens, their grandparents had to put their grief aside to twice make all the funeral arrangements. They'd lost their only children and in their seventies they took over the care of their only grandchildren.

Years later, when death returned for the grandparents,

Janelle and Chyna had no one but themselves. They were
on their own; Chyna had been eighteen and Janelle
twenty.

It took little more than perhaps an hour, but Chyna finally wrapped up the details.

"Okay, let's go and get it over with," Chyna said as
Janelle narrowly missed hitting one of the cars as she
pulled out of the funeral parlor's parking lot. That little
near-mishap told Chyna perhaps she'd better pull it together. Obviously she was putting too much on Janelle.

"Get what over with?" Janelle asked with an arched
eyebrow.

"I need to go to the church and get things started. I'm
still New Hope's First Lady, and I'd better hurry up and
show up."

"I'm sure they can give you another night of peace."

"I know these members. If I don't stop by there
tonight the grievance committee and probably the church
board will come by tomorrow."

"I see. Well let's go and get it over with. I'm sure if
they come by your house that before they leave they'll
have me emptying the liquor cabinet."

Chyna began to call upon an inner strength to fight
the nagging guilt pangs so she could handle her church
business. She still couldn't confront God. Another bit of
hypocrisy on her part. Were she to counsel someone in
her same predicament she'd have glued them to the altar
until they got a breakthrough.

The weight of her adulterous guilt became too overwhelming. If ever there was a time when she needed to go
to God, it was at that very moment. Sin had sapped her
strength and blocked her entry to the mercy seat.

And yet she was still going to church to do the work
of a grieving First Lady with her spiritual fuel tank on
empty.

An hour later they arrived at the church.

"You didn't say I had to go inside." Janelle was angry enough to bite a bear's butt and dare it to holler.

Chyna had to almost drag Janelle out of the car kicking and screaming.

March hadn't given an inch to the thought of spring so it was still dark. It was barely eight o'clock and only a single floodlight lit their way as they entered the side door that led directly to the pastor's study.

"This ain't normal for me!" Janelle protested struggling against Chyna's firm grip on her coat. "I'd probably set off the water sprinklers in this church with my hellish ways. You know I ain't ready to give them up. I don't know if I'll ever be ready to do that."

"Wasn't it you that said we had to act as normal as possible?" Chyna asked. She continued taking command because Janelle was acting like a child going to the dentist.

Janelle would've continued her protest, but as they approached the door they could hear muffled sounds coming from the pastor's study.

"Sounds like a pack of demons have invaded this church," Janelle said as she suddenly tiptoed toward the door. "I believe you would call them congregation members."

"This is still God's house, Janelle." Chyna felt like a hypocrite reprimanding her sister but she didn't have time to doubt her decision to come there.

"Church or Sweet Bush," Janelle shot back in a low voice. With an impish grin spreading across her face, she whispered, "I can't tell much difference. You know there's probably some in here that were going there on nights for a little special service."

"Not now, Janelle."

Chyna knew it was futile trying to convince her sister

that despite her own lukewarm religion practices, God did exist, even if at that moment she and He weren't on speaking terms. But she knew that Janelle would never accept reasoning that perhaps it was God that spared Chyna's life during their marriage. After all, only God could've prevented Grayson from easily taking it during the times when he'd beat her before going into the pulpit to preach. Other times he did it just for the fun of it.

Despite knowing that there was obviously someone inside Grayson's study, which should've been locked, Chyna slowly opened the door.

"In your name, Jesus, we ask for your healing and deliverance for our churches—"

It was the sounds of women praying and moaning. The pastor's aid committee had taken over the study. They were the last people she needed to see at that moment.

It was too late.

"Come on in, First Lady," Sister Eartha Blackstone whispered. She remained standing with her hands stretched out as though she'd not received enough of a blessing from God.

The coffee-colored, fluffy-haired, senior member of the pastor's aid committee peered over rimless eyeglasses supported by a huge nose. Never one to pray with both eyes shut, the self-proclaimed Saved, Sanctified, and Fire-Baptized old woman saw Chyna and Janelle when they entered.

From a first look at Sister Blackstone, it was hard to tell if she were seventy or eighty. She often wore dark wigs and when she didn't she kept her hair dyed black. No one knew exactly how old she was because she was willing to testify truthfully about everything but that. However, black hair or not, she thought most highly of herself and didn't mind browbeating others into thinking the same.

The prayerful outcry to God came to an abrupt halt. One by one Sister Blackstone and three other women approached Chyna. Instead of looking prayerful, each looked nervous, like they'd raided the church's collection box. Shaking her head in a show of disbelief and grief, Sister Blackstone continued, "We're sorry we didn't come to your home immediately, yesterday, to see about you."

"We were so shocked." One of the other women said quickly and then added, "I heard it over the news yesterday and much of the day before that. So I immediately called the pastor's aid committee together to come together and pray for you, our First Lady."

The other Bible-toting women, all appearing to be in their sixties, dressed in floor-length white linen dresses and matching knitted napkin-shaped scarves, in stark contrast to the expensive outfits worn by Chyna and Janelle, bobbed their heads in agreement.

"This is the second time we've come together," Sister Blackstone added, quickly. Even if the others couldn't add, even she knew the difference between yesterday and today. She needed to give an excuse for them being in the pastor's study at that particular moment.

"Now that you're here, we can take over any plans you've made, including having the proper programs created. We want you to have time to yourself so that you can grieve properly. We'll have no problem working side by side with the grievance committee."

"The truth be told," one of the other women said with a voice sweet enough to make sap taste bitter, "We believe that you should just let us handle everything. You don't need to confront all the lies and accusations flying about blaming you for the reverend's downfall. Besides we know it's gonna take a lot of finesse to minimize the damage done to the church's reputation."

A collective hush fell upon the room. Janelle, however, wasn't about to let the slight go unchallenged.

"Since when do church folks care about what other folks say if it ain't the truth?" Janelle's voice rose. "The real truth be told is that ya'll acting like it was my sister that was caught doing the nasty and now y'all wanna take her out and stone her and let the real culprit go!"

"Sister Young," Sister Blackstone said quickly, "I don't expect your sister to understand. It's obvious her Bible lessons never took hold."

Sister Blackstone took Chyna by the hand, "Like I said, we can take care of things. That way no more gossip can be added by you trying to run around and handle things yourself." She turned and was about to lead Chyna back to the door without waiting for a reply.

"That's enough," Janelle interjected, "you can turn her hand loose. I can take care of my own sister." Janelle hissed through her perfectly aligned clenched teeth. She knew insincerity when she heard it. She'd given off the vibe often enough. With both hands on her hips, she stood her ground, prepared to slap away the old woman's hand if it came to that. Refusing to blink, she glared trying to intimidate the supposedly heaven-bound witches into disappearing.

But this was the pastor's aid committee. They'd seen bigger and better demons than Janelle in Sunday school. So only an act of God could stop the staunch old women from being involved in their beloved pastor's funeral or whatever service was planned and keeping the First Lady's involvement from bringing more shame to New Hope.

"Please don't take this the wrong way," Sister Blackstone, meeting Janelle's glare, said firmly, "But you don't come to church often enough, if ever, to know what to do in a situation like this. This *was* a church of holiness."

"Well," Janelle hissed, "Sisters, you can take this any way you want to . . ."

"Janelle," Chyna interrupted, "I'm all right." As off to center as Chyna felt at that moment, the last thing she needed was a fight between Janelle and Sister Blackstone. Short of killing the old woman, Janelle would lose.

"Thank you so much, First Lady," Sister Blackstone said, smiling as she took Chyna's hand in hers. She'd barely gotten the sweet words out before she turned and rebuked Janelle with a glare strong enough to wilt steel.

Janelle moved quickly. She dislodged Chyna from Sister Blackstone's grip. She wasn't giving up that easy. "Whatever. Y'all can leave it to my sister to handle things. This is a family matter as much as it is a church one. My sister needs to take care of business in here." Janelle let one hand whirl about the pastor's study before adding, "All up in here, so you and the rest of your coven need to step off."

Again, Sister Blackstone showed her old school cred. She moved past Janelle, allowing one of her wide hips to bump her, and addressed Chyna directly. "One other thing," she said with a look of concern, "Despite what Channel Seven is reporting about some 'apparent murder,' we know that the reverend was at that den of iniquity trying to save souls and was probably shot by one of those reprobates." Sister Blackstone dropped her head on cue, as did the other women. "That's the story that needs to be told among all the other mess they're spouting."

Janelle wanted to spit, but instead she took a tissue from atop the desk and wiped the same spot on her dress where Sister Blackstone had touched it. She watched in disgust as the old women even had their supposed expressions and motions of grief synchronized. Under other circumstances she might've had some appreciation for their unified hypocrisy.

"Okay, that's really enough this time," Janelle said as she rushed to open the door. "If we need anything," she said with authority, "we'll call on the bereavement committee."

Chyna's head shot up. *What in the world would Janelle know about a bereavement committee?*

As if reading everyone's minds, including Chyna's, Janelle said with a forced smile, "Y'all be surprised at what I know about church without frequently going inside one. Church is supposed to be in the heart, right?"

As if Sister Blackstone's words were prophetic, Chyna and Janelle stopped at a local Chinese restaurant for takeout. Neither had eaten a meal of substance in the last few days.

"That's that crazy preacher's wife." One of the customers said as he paid for his order. He tilted his head quickly toward Chyna.

Chyna recognized the young man as one of New Hope's choir members. Just his few words alone were enough to take her appetite. "Let's go."

It was a rare time that day that Janelle agreed. Even she was savvy enough to know that those words of scorn were only the beginning.

Chapter 9

A few days later and after keeping Sister Blackstone and the other women out of her business, Chyna held the memorial service for her husband.

Leave it to fate to intervene and throw grade-A fuel on the chaotic fire. Media coverage was crazy. Every channel had both footage and opinions regarding the "Murderous Reverend Grayson Young."

If Grayson's funeral was fodder for the media, it was a banquet for all the religious bigwigs. There were many women, some who cried just a little too much to have not had the hands of Grayson laid upon them, and an equal amount of men wearing their collars backward who attended.

There were several women pastors draped in congregation-purchased expensive furs and hats. Many of the megachurch pastors arrived with their cherry-wood walking sticks and diamond-encrusted pinky rings. Each tried to outdo the others in style, dress, and speeches. Standing behind a huge picture of Grayson on an easel beside the coffin, they compared him to everyone from Martin Luther King to Mahatma Gandhi. Not a single word was said or read about what happened at the Sweet Bush. Anyone not up on the news would've thought he'd died doing God's work.

Twisting and turning slightly in her seat, on the front pew, and from behind her large dark shades, Chyna looked around. She scanned the church's huge auditorium and two-tier overflow balcony. Chyna tried, in vain, to see who they were talking about.

Leave it to Janelle to put it out there. She asked Chyna, "Who the hell are they talking about?" in a loud voice that showed no reverence for the occasion or the place it was held. Fidgeting in her seat more from dullness of the memorial than from being overdressed in a hot mink coat, she continued complaining. "Grayson killed people and they're trying to make him seem like he wasn't responsible for nothing."

Janelle didn't care that she'd not been to church in years and certainly hadn't boned up on the protocol for funerals, memorials, or regular services. She glared back at those who dared glare at her.

Chyna didn't nudge or rebuke Janelle. Truth was truth, no matter where it was told.

The service couldn't end soon enough for Chyna. She'd already made the arrangements for Grayson's ashes to be delivered into her care at a later date.

"We'll call on you real soon." One of the deacons said after the service once the receiving line had lessened and he could get Chyna's attention. He spoke softly as if his small words of dishonesty would fool Chyna.

They couldn't.

Chyna had never known the church board to go underground or cooperate when there was the tiniest of holes for them to grab control. They wouldn't approve a woman to preach in their pulpit and so she didn't stand a chance of holding much authority. Grayson's death left a hole in the chain of command as wide as an ocean and all she could do was wait for the attack from the sharks wearing wide hats and pinky rings. Of course, each shark would come carrying his own Bible.

Chapter 10

Despite Janelle's promise to keep hers and Detective Gonzalez's affair a secret forever if he'd go easy on bothering Chyna, Detectives Lavin and Gonzalez had reappeared. They had questioned Chyna four times since Grayson's memorial. They'd also hit a dead end, it seemed.

"I'm sorry to have to be the one to tell you this," Detective Lavin said as officially as possible, "but apparently, your husband went to the Sweet Bush for the same reasons that the other patrons had. He was into alternative sex."

As usual, feeling the need at that moment to contribute and not be upstaged by his partner, Gonzalez broke in and added, "No one who'd been able to give an explanation as to what went wrong survived beside the bouncer, and he's taken a lie detector test. He passed."

Detective Lavin indicated for Chyna to take a seat, even though he was standing in her living room. He watched her as she slowly did as he requested, never taking her eyes off him.

"There's one other thing. It hasn't been leaked to the news and it's not our job to do so." Detective Lavin seemed to suddenly flounder as he searched for the words.

"Would you please get on with it?" Janelle snapped. She could feel hers and Chyna's nerves almost vibrating and coming out of their skins.

"I'm trying," Detective Lavin explained, "The only conclusion reached, with any finality, was that the Reverend Grayson Young took his own life after killing others." He gave a quick nervous grin toward Janelle that the others didn't notice. "We may never find out why he'd killed the others," Lavin conceded.

"You mean there was no videotape from any security camera?" Janelle asked, innocently.

"Well, there's always that." Lavin responded, "But we doubt it."

Again, the detectives gave their belated condolences and promised to update her should any new information come about.

At that moment Janelle truly appreciated Gonzalez and his decision not to throw Chyna to the media wolves. She'd also decided to keep her word about not telling his wife about their affair. All she needed to do was to destroy the letter she'd written and, with any luck, hadn't mailed.

Chyna barely had time to fret over whether it was discovered that she, too, had extramarital affairs because she had another serious problem.

"I know what you're thinking," Janelle said after a few minutes of silence. "You think it's your fault that crazy husband of yours took his own life."

"No, that's not it." Chyna went to the window and just stared with her arms folded. The color of her face looked dull and she looked much older than her thirty-two years.

"Then what is it?"

"He took his life," Chyna said softly.

"Okay, we've known that for about ten minutes already. What's the big deal? You certainly didn't think he was going to heaven whether he committed suicide or not. At least if you believe the Word like you say you do."

"He did more than take his life." Chyna said, turning to face Janelle. "He took mine, too."

"What do you mean?" Janelle's face became a mask of concern, "how could he take your life?" Janelle suddenly laughed, "Come to think of it, with all the money you'll get, you can buy a new life."

"Insurance policy won't pay off on a suicide."

That time it was Janelle's turn to take a gut punch. "Oh, damn."

Chapter 11

Barely two weeks had passed before Chyna learned to what extent things could go from bad to worse.

In a short period of time, she learned it was a bigger hit than she could've imagined. Apparently Grayson, secretly, had them living high on the hog in a very expensive pen. Bills poured in like a flood from all his expensive vacations, failed investments, and so on. It didn't take long for Chyna to realize that she would need to sell the house and perhaps give up even more of their belongings.

And then "giving up even more" came banging on her door toting Bibles and a reality check.

It'd only taken a few minutes of suffocated boasting from four of the men on the trustee board to present Chyna with that reality check.

Chyna was shocked to learn that practically everything except her house belonged to the church. The two cars, including the Mercedes, much of her jewelry, as well as Grayson's, and even some of the furniture, were on loan or bought by the church.

"We'd love to let you keep most of these things," one

of the trustees said as sadly as he could manage, "but we must either return or sell the property to keep losses to a minimum." So under the guise of helping her to help the church to defray costs and without even asking Chyna if she'd like to buy the items, they set about taking an inventory to repossess the church property.

"That cheap son-of-a-snake," Janelle said loudly after boldly listening in to the conversation, "I betcha he never told you that all of this was from New Hope Assembly Church rent-a-center." Janelle bounced from the room and returned just as quick. She took a pen when no one looked and started putting little nicks in the furniture. It marred the furniture, but she felt better.

Apparently the church board, in a backroom conference, had agreed with Grayson when he decided that he needed to look and act the part of a megapastor.

"I didn't know any of this, but you want me to go along with whatever the trustees decide." Chyna's eyes grew wide as she wrung her hands to keep from punching something or someone.

"So if I understand correctly," Janelle said to a trustee who stood about a foot taller than she and just as wide, "you can come in here and repossess all the furniture and cars, but you can't take away her position as First Lady because another pastor hasn't been voted in as yet. And until one is, you still have to provide a small subsidy for her until the entire church votes otherwise?"

The trustee didn't budge. He simply looked down and basically spoke to the top of her head, "That's pretty much it."

Janelle took a step back and purposely stepped on the trustee's foot as she did. With no apology given, she turned to Chyna and with her best Cheshire-cat grin asked. "Well, don't you have a good relationship with the church members?"

"Church members are wonderful people, but they have limited power." *The church board just lets them think they have more than they really do.*

"Well go ahead and do the Christian thing," Janelle snapped, "Y'all all big and Christlike, take this damn furniture and shove it . . ."

"Janelle!" Chyna quickly interrupted, "It's okay."

Janelle was beyond angry. She picked up a vase that she thought might've belonged to the church and accidentally, on purpose, dropped it."

"That didn't belong to the church," Chyna said. "But it was expensive."

Yet, Chyna was no fool. She wasn't entirely without a cushion. If she played her cards right, she could end up sitting quite lovely.

Chapter 12

Janelle put her spare key in Chyna's front door a little after nine o'clock the next morning. And despite arriving there wearing a skintight fuchsia-colored pantsuit and her latest expensive fur, she looked like she hadn't gotten much sleep.

"Hey Chyna," Janelle called out, "Sorry I'm a bit late. I forgot to remind you that I had a doctor's appointment this morning that I cancelled."

Janelle could hear Chyna moving about in the kitchen even before Chyna responded.

"I'm in the kitchen."

"Want a cup of coffee?" Chyna asked, "You look like you could use it."

"Okay, and why are you so chipper? Have you been eating coffee straight out the can?"

"No, besides you know I prefer caffeine-free tea."

Janelle, with her usual flair, tossed her fur onto an empty kitchen chair and claimed a seat.

"Glad to see that those churchy folks at least left you

a table to nibble a slice of bread on." Janelle could feel the anger return.

"Why did you cancel a doctor's appointment? You don't have to babysit me. If you need to see a doctor, you should go. And why do you need to see one?"

Ignoring Chyna, Janelle quickly changed the subject. "I have to tell you that I'm glad to see that you're beginning to come back to normal." Janelle took a piece of toast from the toaster and began to spread some butter. "I'm still gonna keep my eye on you. If you're anything like me you might snap and . . . never mind." Janelle stopped speaking when she realized that it was what had happened to Grayson. She was sure her sister didn't need a reminder.

"You played the part last evening pretty good." Chyna told Janelle, ignoring her sister's reference to her sanity as she poured a cup of coffee. "But you still owe me for that Tiffany vase."

"I'm not paying full price for it, because I didn't use it to crack that ugly trustee's head." Janelle laughed at the thought of standing on a stool to knock the man out.

"Well, I've got to take care of a little business today." Chyna said, "They're supposed to bring Grayson's ashes around today."

"I'd forgotten about that. In fact, I thought they were supposed to do that yesterday morning?"

"They tried," Chyna said. "I just didn't answer the door and you were taking a shower."

"Now you wrong for that?

"I wasn't wrong, I was just intuitive. I was right, too. There was nowhere to set the urn. The church ended up taking the armoire."

The sisters continued chewing and chatting about

nothing and everything. With the kitchen tidied and their energy renewed for the moment, it was time to plan.

"Follow me," Chyna said as she turned off the coffeepot and walked out of her kitchen. "It's time for me to raid the nest."

"What are you talking about?" Janelle asked slowly. "You ain't about to trip out again, are you?"

"No, I'm not trippin'. But I am going to send you on one."

"Oh, really," Janelle replied, "and where would that be?"

"There's a large picture on the living room wall. You need to go there."

A look of contentment spread across Janelle's face as she walked toward the living room. She understood exactly what Chyna was getting at.

"I'm proud of you. You took my advice and hoarded a few pennies. That's what you gotta do when you can't trust your man." She looked around the nearly furniture-free living room before she quickly added, "Do you have all the paperwork handy?"

"It's in the same place it's always been." Chyna said as she headed toward the bathroom. "Can you please get it for me?"

"Sure," Janelle said as she moved toward a picture on another wall. She put two fingers behind the frame and removed a small key. "Sure, why not."

Chyna had showed her the spot a couple of years before. "Just in case something should happen and you need to take charge." Chyna had said, "Even if Grayson should survive me, he doesn't need to know about anything in the envelope."

While Chyna gathered her wits and dressed in the bathroom, Janelle got busy and removed a slender envelope from a deep slot in the wall behind the picture frame. Without really thinking about it, or perhaps it was just her second nature, Janelle opened the envelope. She let a sly smile cross her face as she thought about how it was the one place, her sister's wedding photograph, that Grayson would've never thought to look. Chyna had been smart to hide all her personal papers there. Grayson was entirely too controlling.

By the time Janelle had gone through the papers, her mood had changed. What started off as happiness that her sister had pulled one over on Grayson suddenly changed.

Janelle was certain Chyna had probably forgotten about all that was inside the envelope. But what she held took her breath away. The picture now in her hand was one of a man she'd never forget. She allowed her fingers to trace the outlines of the man's face and then down his body clad only in a pair of swimming trunks. There was a smile on his face that rivaled sunshine.

"Cordell," Janelle whispered, "Cordell."

"I'll be out in a moment," Chyna yelled from the bathroom. Her voice carried through the hallway and stunned Janelle back to the moment.

"I'm not going anywhere," Janelle said, sharply. She wasn't sure if her sister could hear the change in her voice or not. Janelle didn't care. Instead, she took another look at the picture in her hand and then placed it back between the folds of a small address book. She put them both back inside the envelope.

"Cordell," Janelle repeated his name as though saying it would make him appear and take the pain of losing him away.

Cordell DeWitt was not only Chyna's ex-husband but also had been Janelle's first and only true love. Her soul mate, she'd thought at the time. Actually, she hadn't changed her mind about that. He was still that. She'd chased her lost love for him from bed to bed since he'd left her for Chyna.

Never finding what she'd had with Cordell made Janelle wild. She wore infidelity almost like a badge of honor every time she'd committed adultery with someone's husband or stole a man. She was doing to other women what she'd felt her sister had done to her. She'd kept up her reckless behavior even after months of pleading for forgiveness from Chyna. Eventually she'd finally forgiven Chyna for marrying Cordell, her Cordell. Or perhaps she hadn't.

However, Janelle had never forgiven him, nor would she, not even when Chyna had left him for Grayson. Chyna's second marriage only gave Janelle two men to hate; Cordell for cheating on her with her sister and Grayson on principle.

Janelle felt a chill as if someone had shoved ice down her back. She took one hand and massaged her temple until she got control. Not willing to retrace her steps back through bad memories, Janelle placed the envelope on the sofa and poured a drink. Forty minutes later, when Chyna finally returned to the living room, Janelle was almost drunk.

"Almost drunk" would never deter Janelle from doing what needed to be done. She gulped a glass of lemon-flavored water with egg yolk and got ready for battle.

"You might want to change into something a little more appropriate for visiting a stockbroker," Chyna said, chastising her sister as she pulled her from the chair. "You look like you struck gold on Wall Street. Are you sure you can handle doing this with me?"

"Sure," Janelle slurred her answer. The memory of Chyna still secretly hanging on to Cordell's picture among important papers was too fresh. The alcohol had not diminished her funky mood at all. Janelle suddenly started humming Chaka Khan's hit, "I'm Every Woman," because with her mood swings, she was.

"Listen, I need to get my emergency bag from my trunk," Janelle said when she finished singing one verse of the song. "I'll be back in a moment." Her words were now stronger, which made her determined to fix another drink when she returned.

Janelle's emergency bag was a joke between the sisters. She always kept the bag packed with a little something extra in case she either ran into someone she wanted to spend the night with or if she needed to get out of town in a hurry. It was mostly the latter.

Walking out the door, Janelle's feelings were all over the map. She went from anger at Chyna to anger at Cordell to anger at church folks. Hatred for Grayson was still constant.

"Damn vultures!" Janelle murmured as she glanced back over her shoulders at the living room, which was nearly devoid of furniture. It was so hard for her to believe that her sister's house was ransacked by the church and it was all Grayson's fault.

Of course, thinking about Grayson brought back thoughts of Cordell. Janelle quickly dismissed them, preferring to concentrate on her hatred of Grayson as she walked cautiously down the front steps to the pathway. Janelle didn't like Grayson from first sight and definitely couldn't stand him because of his hypocrisy and mistreatment of her sister. However, in a moment of letting down her defenses she had to admit that she didn't want him to go out like that, and leave her sister to get caught up in the mess.

By the time Janelle reached the beginning of the pathway she suddenly remembered her part in enabling Chyna to feel comfortable about combining her Christianity and her sexuality outside the marriage. "You know Grayson is a freak with everyone but you," she'd told Chyna. "If he can get up and preach souls to heaven on Sunday, you can certainly get your little piece of heaven, too, on whatever day you can."

That was almost eighteen months ago. Janelle would've never thought things would turn out this bad.

But bad was about to get worse.

Then in true Janelle style, her mood changed, and she became angry again before she'd barely passed by the side patio when she found herself muttering. "I still can't believe that fool put a bullet through his own brain." Janelle continued ranting as she hurried toward her car at the mouth of the long driveway. "It looks like he is gonna be just as much a pain in the arse dead as he was alive."

Reproving and signifying, inwardly, as she prodded down the path, mentally mired in real and imagined mess, she'd barely touched the car's remote control before its trunk flew open. Two inches closer and it would've almost snatched off her blond wig.

"Instead of spending money on an expensive memorial, Chyna should've hired a couple of mimes to do the doggone eulogy and found a cracked, topless mayonnaise jar for his sorry ashes; the dumb ashhole." Janelle hissed as she moved things around inside the trunk of her car.

Suddenly the thought of a cracked mayonnaise jar for Grayson's ashes, broke through Janelle's anger, replacing it with a mischievous grin. And then just that quick the moment of levity disappeared as thoughts of the gravity of Chyna's predicament returned.

Think, Janelle, think! Selling her stocks won't keep her outta the poorhouse forever. "Calm down," Janelle whispered as she took a deep breath. "And for Pete's sake get that triflin' Cordell outta your mind."

"Hi there." A voice called out.

The interruption jarred her. Janelle jumped, bringing her head up and almost hitting the roof of the trunk.

There was a slight laughter. "I'm sorry, Janelle, I didn't mean for you to bump your head."

"Huh?" Janelle hadn't heard a car pull up or footsteps approach the driveway. Nervous and without thinking, she snatched the bag from the trunk and slammed down the lid.

Her eyes grew large as she fingered the wig, which had become slanted. Was it déjà vu or just her bad karma coming back for seconds?

Chapter 13

Janelle straightened her wig with an air that signified that losing one's wig was no big deal. "Cordell Dewitt?" She asked, "What in the world are you doing here?" She could hear surprise in her own voice, but was he really outside in Chyna's driveway? Was it the alcohol?

"Calm down. Yes, it's me."

Janelle didn't like surprises. Especially surprises that caused her wig to flip.

But this surprise was different. This was her Cordell DeWitt. She'd only seen him twice since he'd left her for Chyna. The second time was when she stalked him outside one of his conferences. Her plan was to throw a jar of honey and rat feces on him.

She couldn't go through with the dastardly deed then and with her heart fluttering, she certainly couldn't stay mad now. There he was standing in front of her looking every bit as handsome and tantalizing in his forties as he was when they were all younger. He certainly looked as good as he had about an hour ago when she'd held his picture in her hands.

"Janelle?"

Hearing his heavy voice, Janelle accepted that she hadn't lost her mind. She took a step forward. As if she hadn't seen him in a few days instead of years, she hugged Cordell harder and longer than necessary before continuing, "What's a world-famous 'make folks happy' speaker like you doing here?" She was inhaling every bit of him. She could've sopped him with a biscuit.

"You didn't know I was coming to Brooklyn?" Cordell looked down at Janelle, who still had him in a viselike grip. He tried to look sad, but he was much too good looking and couldn't pull it off. "I'm offended." Yet, he didn't try to pull away.

Wait a moment. Janelle thought. *I'm angry with you. I've been angry with you for years. I can't stand your guts. I want you to shrivel and die. . . .* She pushed him away, suddenly appearing distant, forgetting that just seconds before she'd tried to hug him until she reached a climax.

"I'm guessing that from wherever you were, you heard what happened to Grayson," Janelle said in an even tone. It was more of a rebuke that he'd stayed away so long than anything else.

"I was in Los Angeles when the news broke several weeks ago with the sordid details. I must admit I was shocked, so I wasn't sure if I should've come or stayed away. I chose to stay where I was."

"Then why have you come now?"

"Grayson had scheduled a conference for this week. Everything's been confirmed and your church asked if I'd step in."

"My church—?"

Cordell let out a small chuckle before correcting himself. "Sorry, I forgot about you and your relationship, or lack of one, with churches."

"I still don't have much use for those folks." Janelle said with disdain before adding, "Of course, present company excluded."

Cordell pulled his coat collar up around his neck. There was a slight tremor as he continued, "I can't get used to this cold weather. We don't have much use for snow in Los Angeles."

Somehow watching Cordell shiver from the cold didn't bother Janelle as much as thinking about him going inside and seeing Chyna.

"So why did you come here to Chyna's house?" Janelle asked. A nuclear bomb blast couldn't have taken Janelle's attention away. Her eyes scanned Cordell's body, again, for the umpteenth time. She was certain there probably wasn't an ounce of fat under his Brooks Brothers deep-blue wool coat. She felt a familiar longing to find out for sure.

You look so good, Janelle thought. She'd almost given up on having those sorts of feelings when Cordell had left her for her sister. She'd had many men since him, including Gonzalez, who showed a lot of potential when they weren't lying face-to-face, but, at that moment, those men seemed insignificant and lacking.

"If I didn't say so," Janelle said suddenly as they started to walk up the path to the house, "it's truly good seeing you again."

"It's good to see you again, too," Cordell said with a sudden smile stretching across complexion the color of caramel—sweet caramel. It might've been a few years since he'd spoken to or seen Janelle, but he still knew her flirtation moves. "You haven't changed at all."

"I'm glad you remember." Janelle knew what he'd meant. She was sure he'd known what she'd meant, too. "So, why did you say you came here?" She needed to change the subject. She needed to do it quickly.

Cordell stopped. He took the bag from one of Janelle's hands and held her other as he spoke, "The kept woman conference starts soon."

"Oh, really now—?"

"Yes," Cordell answered. "I want you to attend. Chyna should attend, too, as the First Lady if she's up to it."

"Why would the three of us want to occupy the same space, especially in a church?"

"We've all moved on," Cordell answered, "I know I have. Grayson's unexpected death should've taught us something."

"What?" Janelle asked, "That we shouldn't play with fire while we're out getting our freak on?"

Janelle let go of Cordell's hand. With just a hint of hesitation, she asked aloud what they were both thinking. "With everything that went down with you, my sister, and especially with Grayson's sorry ashes fresh in a mayonnaise jar . . ."

"Say what?" Cordell was speechless as Janelle continued her rant.

". . . do you think it's smart to come here alone? Isn't that playing with fire?" Janelle was fuming and still stuck on wishing Grayson's ashes were really mixed with mayonnaise.

Finally able to get a word in, Cordell replied, "I'll say it again. I've moved on, Janelle. It's a conference and I thought it would be good if we could all get together. It's nothing more and nothing less. You'd be surprised at how much you can get over in ten years."

"Really," Janelle said, again, "you mean that there are no residual feelings? There's no hot lust for my sister who's also your ex-wife?"

"Excuse me?" Cordell asked quickly. He moved a few feet away, showing he was truly offended that time.

"Do you think I'm playing when I bring forth God's word? This is no game for me and you have no shame."

The hurt look suddenly etched upon Janelle's face caused Cordell to cut her some slack. "I gotcha—!" He came closer and took her hand again as he watched her smile return as they walked up the path to Chyna's front door.

Chapter 14

It seemed Janelle had been gone much too long and Chyna grew more nervous by the minute. *Come on, Janelle. What's taking you so long?* She'd already put on her coat and was beginning to feel overheated.

Chyna barely lifted her head and looked out the living room window when she'd suddenly wanted to scream, again. Could she be losing her mind? Dumbstruck, she looked over from where she stood and watched intently, again, through the living room's wide picture window.

Janelle wasn't alone.

Arriving at the front of the house, Janelle threw open the front door and practically tossed Cordell into the living room. Not bothering to see if Cordell landed on his head or feet, she stood back to watch the show begin.

Ignoring the erratic behavior of her sister, Chyna's blank stare moved over to where Cordell luckily landed on his feet.

All Chyna could do was look at Cordell as he stared back. Everything seemed surreal. Why not? The past thirty days or so couldn't have possibly happened, could it?

"Cordell, is that you?" Chyna asked. Her question, even to her, seemed a little crazy. Of course, it was him. She'd know her ex-husband anywhere.

Thoughts of more payback coming her way, crossed Chyna's mind. She'd made Cordell's life a living hell, so why would he be standing, innocently, in her living room, in the house she'd shared with his old college roommate, her late husband, Grayson?

Chyna sat down without beckoning Cordell to do the same. She looked past him as if she were seeing what they once were. Much like everything in her life appeared beyond her control, Chyna's mind embraced a flashback.

Like Grayson, Cordell, her first husband, had the good looks along with the street charm. Even back then, Grayson's voice was definitely suited to preaching the gospel. But he wasn't a preacher. He was a local radio jock with a deep radio-ready drop-those-panties bass voice. Whenever he spoke it was as though her ears were tasting vocal nectar and his powerful, yet gentle, voice became her undoing.

He'd courted Chyna with it and he'd used it to paralyze her common sense as he escorted her down a path of lies.

Cordell lied when he'd told her he loved her. He lied about his finances, making her believe that radio jocks swam in money. She soon discovered that his lying was about the only thing truthful about him and all she could depend upon.

Yet, the most hurtful lie of all was the one left unspoken. Chyna had slept with Cordell not knowing that he'd also held her sister's heart a prisoner. He'd courted Chyna on purpose. He did not hold regard for the damage he'd done to the close-knit sisters; neither for Janelle, whose heart he'd broken, nor for Chyna, whose heart he'd not wanted. And it was all because he'd believed a lie that Janelle had cheated on him.

Cordell's plan backfired. It seemed that no sooner had they started sleeping together Chyna become pregnant. And then, no sooner than they'd said, "I do," she'd miscarried, but it was too late. The damage to the relationship with her sister had been done. It took quite some time to make Janelle understand what happened and receive her forgiveness.

As bad as their marriage was, it was a mystery as to why Chyna and Cordell remained together for another five years. It was a time that brought out the worst in one another. A time that created the opportunity to unlock the door to adultery, and Grayson Young was the key.

Grayson showed up, unexpected, with Cordell at her job where she worked as an administrative assistant to one of the vice presidents. She and Cordell were supposed to have dinner out alone after she finished her day at Salomon Brothers on Wall Street. She couldn't say that she was disappointed in not having advance notice, because she'd found the almost-thirty Minister Grayson Young extremely handsome.

Chyna was spellbound at first sight. It wasn't too long before her carnal desire grew by leaps and bounds when she learned he was the pride of his church. She wasn't particularly spiritual, at that time, but she did love a strong man that everyone else loved, too. Power was a dangerous and relentless aphrodisiac.

While Chyna was mentally stalking Grayson, he'd done the same except he'd already claimed victory long before she knew what was happening.

Chyna was ripe for the picking, and Grayson conquered her before she had time to let out a second breath. She ignored a gut warning reminding her that she was still a married woman and she'd been at that place in her life before.

Chyna covered caution with layers of excuses. "I'm not getting what I need at home," was one excuse and used the most often. So a month later in Grayson's arms, overtaken by his relentless need to exploit her body, she soon erased the shame of her adultery. Over the next several months, in countless hotels, they'd given fake names, as if using her real one would add to her shame. With each lingering shower taken, after their trysts, she'd mentally chosen to scrub away any reminders of déjà vu.

Déjà vu would've reminded her that she'd fallen for Cordell with that same intensity.

So when it was all said and done, when that slight opportunity for love arrived on her job's doorstep it wasn't hard, in her mind, for Chyna to put everything aside, again. That time she'd upgraded. Instead of falling for her sister's boyfriend, she'd fallen for Grayson, her husband's college friend.

Chyna hadn't realized she'd tuned everyone out until Janelle spoke to—or rather snapped at—her.

"Chyna, stop acting like you don't know how to speak." Janelle's warning was apparent. She didn't need Chyna going off the deep end at that moment if there was one. She shook her head at Chyna and went to look at the window, but not without throwing a warning look at Cordell.

With Janelle off to one side and Cordell now standing with full confusion etched on his face, Chyna suddenly let out a sigh of frustration. "My Lord," she muttered as though they were somehow interfering with her memories, which they had. "I'm sorry," Chyna said softly, "Just give me a moment, please." She pulled a tissue from her purse and began to dab at her face. Chyna needed a reason to avoid the present, because her mind hadn't let go of the memories she was experiencing.

Chyna remembered the exact words Grayson used to begin his conquest.

> *"Now I know how David must've felt when he looked at Bathsheba for the first time,"* Grayson had said when he'd stopped by her home with Cordell that same evening on the day they'd met. His eyes widened as he gently took her hand and kissed it. *"You put the Queen of Sheba, Esther, and the other biblical beauties to shame."* He grinned as though he'd just announced that he'd killed that big bad Goliath.
>
> Too bad she hadn't taken into consideration that Grayson whispered those words within seconds of Cordell leaving their living room to hang up Grayson's coat.
>
> But at that time Cordell wasn't even close to God and in debt so deep that their marriage and the bills had bankruptcy written all over them.

Chapter 15

Cordell glanced over at the clock on Chyna's living room wall. It was almost noon, although probably only a few minutes had passed since he'd arrived. As he waited for Chyna to respond, it seemed a lot longer.

"Ahem," Cordell said as though he were tired of waiting for Chyna to get it together. "Chyna, did I catch you at a bad time?" Cordell asked, fully realizing how foolish the question sounded. Even though they'd not seen each other in several years, he imagined she was acting like a recent widow would with just a tad bit extra weird added. His question, albeit stupid, put them on even ground.

When Chyna didn't answer, Cordell removed his coat instead of retreating. All the time, he never took his eyes off Chyna. They were in the same room, but he could tell her mind was miles away.

He finally glanced over his shoulder and saw Janelle still at the window. Her beauty hadn't diminished one bit. He wanted to continue looking at Janelle, but he felt the pull of whatever was on Chyna's mind. Was it the same thing that he was beginning to think? Was she remembering the bad times?

Cordell let out a sigh. The truth was that it didn't matter what was on her mind. They were now in the same space and time and Cordell felt he'd made the right decision by coming there. He truly no longer felt the anger he'd always thought he would if he ever saw Chyna again.

Yet a pang of guilt tugged at Cordell. He saw her now as a bit more fragile, but even if she weren't, he couldn't judge her. Back then, he was just as guilty as Chyna.

Back then he didn't know God.

Chyna still hadn't said anything more and the tissue she used as an excuse to avoid him was tattered. She finally looked up at Cordell. She'd expected him to say something more, but he didn't.

It'd only been a few minutes, but the time Janelle spent watching the strange nonactions between Chyna and Cordell seemed an eternity.

Somewhere, someone must've been praying for her, Chyna thought as her mind struggled for clarity. She lifted her head, again, and looked at Cordell. She straightened her posture, almost regally, as though finally acknowledging a subject for the first time standing in her living room.

"Cordell, is it you?" Chyna said, again. That time there was a hint of suspicion that quickly turned into an appreciation.

"I know this must be a shock," Cordell said, coyly. He would've said more, but nothing had prepared him. Chyna looked every bit as beautiful as the last time he'd seen her. Both sisters had aged very well. "It has been quite some time."

"I'm not good with pretenses," Cordell said, "I haven't seen you since you and Grayson were in front of

the courthouse on the Grand Concourse in the Bronx
after our divorce.

"You mean when you took the money from Grayson
to divorce me?"

"Yes. I'm not proud of that, and I'll never be able to
undo what I did to you."

"Ahem!"

"Neither what I did to you, Janelle. Especially, what I
did to you."

"Okay, enough with all the greetings, what's in the
past should stay there." Janelle interrupted. "Chyna and I
were just about to leave and take care of *her* business."
Janelle's hands fidgeted with a handmade doily she'd
absentmindedly taken off a left-behind cocktail table.

"Well then, I guess it was okay that I took off,"
Cordell told Janelle while his eyes stayed locked upon
Chyna. He could almost feel the animosity Janelle emitted. *Lord, just let me say what I need to say and get out of
here.*

Janelle might've missed their earlier actions as both
Chyna and Cordell revisited the past, but her home-girl
instincts homed right in on what *wasn't* being said. And
none of it was a surprise.

"Well now, ain't this cozy?" Janelle said with just a
hint of jealousy in her tone. She was torn. She needed to
protect her sister from what was sure to be a hot mess, but
she also remembered that Chyna had stolen her man, the
only man she'd ever loved. But then she also wanted to
snatch the razor she kept hidden in her side pocket and go
to work on Cordell. A moment of sadness engulfed her as
she tried to hide the pain of what the two people she loved
the most had done to her.

"Never mind," Janelle told Cordell. With a wave of
her hand, she dismissed what she wanted to say, "go

ahead with whatever you were about to say." She turned back to look out the window at the nothingness that mirrored how she felt at that moment.

Janelle listened with sadness as Cordell prodded and encouraged Chyna with Bible verses and several friendly hugs. It didn't take long before Chyna fell into the rhythm of telling him everything—almost. She'd shared reluctantly her financial woes and the hope that what she'd saved would see her through until better times came.

As if Janelle had been an insignificant fly on the wall, she watched and listened, as her beloved adulteress sister, accepted a surprise offer from Cordell to purchase her home.

"I'm pretty much solvent, financially," Cordell said. "I can give you a fair offer for this house and you can still remain in your home."

It wasn't what Cordell had meant to say, but before he could think he'd said it. Perhaps God was prodding him, but usually the Holy Spirit gave him a "heads up."

Just like that, Chyna felt a burden lifted. Perhaps she could have an ex-husband as a friend. She could only hope that Janelle was over him and wouldn't be jealous.

Even as she thought it Chyna knew how foolish and far-fetched her wish was. She could only hope that she hadn't just tossed aside all the time she spent asking Janelle for forgiveness.

"Thank you, Cordell."

"It's no problem. I know God would want me to help you, or he wouldn't have had me come by." Cordell spoke as soft as one could with a deep voice. "God loves you."

"You see, Chyna," Janelle interjected, "God does love you. It looks like you just got love just dripping and waiting to touch you." She didn't even try to keep the venom at a minimum.

Cordell started to say something but thought better of it. "I must be going," he said as he rose and reached for his coat. "I'll call soon and get the paperwork started."

"I bet you can't wait to start something." Janelle hissed. Even as she let the jealousy take over, she knew it was wrong. She didn't care. Not at that moment when the man—the only man she'd ever loved—had just offered to buy her sister, his ex-wife, a house.

Chapter 16

Cordell had barely been gone long enough to allow his cologne to dissipate when hell came a-knocking.

Sometimes when one won't go to hell it will come on its own.

On the other side of Chyna's front door, tapping her foot and shifting her large pocketbook from one hand to the other, Sister Blackstone waited, impatiently. Normally she'd have admired the well-kept grounds of Chyna's home. Not today. There was a sense of urgency that almost seemed surreal. She fought to maintain her composure as she tapped her foot fast enough to almost dig a hole in the dirt.

Sister Blackstone wasn't prepared for Janelle to answer the door. Once she saw that she'd not be alone with Chyna, it only took a second to put on her "church face" full of serenity, ready to do God's work.

"Praise the Lord, Ms. Pierce," Sister Blackstone said, as sweetly as possible. "I've come by to see Sister Young."

Janelle's spirit became disturbed, but she didn't know if it was because she didn't like the old woman or her kind, or if she was just being overprotective of Chyna. Either way, it was still Chyna's house.

"Come in," Janelle said as she opened the door wide enough for Sister Blackstone's hefty body to enter. "Wait here, I'll get my sister."

Janelle didn't bother to wait and see if Sister Blackstone obeyed. Instead, again, she sped down the hallway and found Chyna.

"Come on and pull it together," Janelle whispered with as much compassion as she could muster as she shook Chyna, who'd decided to visit her stockbroker at some other time and opted for a nap. "You've got company."

But Sister Blackstone never obeyed anyone. Even God had to come at her in a certain manner before she'd obey Him. She'd barely waited two seconds before she'd followed Janelle on into Chyna's bedroom.

Sister Blackstone saw everything she thought she needed to see when she saw Chyna's condition and went into action.

"In the name of Jesus, I need you to move, Lord." Sister Blackstone pulled a bottle of blessed oil from her large pocketbook and was moving toward where Chyna still sat on the side of her bed. "Cancel out every demon from Hell," she added before deliberately sprinkling some of the blessed oil onto Janelle, who stood next to Chyna.

"What tha—&#%%&!" Janelle swore with new cuss words. "Do you know how much this outfit cost?" she snapped at Sister Blackstone before dashing out the room to find a bottle of seltzer water to take care of the stain.

"Your sister is something else!" Sister Blackstone said with as much indignation as she could. "I came by to give you my condolences again and to speak to you about some of the sinful things starting to take place at New Hope. But I want you to know that God don't want adulteresses around His good people. I've heard from very reliable sources about your sister's husband-stealing ways."

Sister Blackstone stopped just long enough to point her finger back at herself just in case Chyna thought she was fortunate enough to be included among God's good people.

"And I don't know too many, with the exception of a wife or two, who don't know about her and that Spanish detective from the Seventy-ninth Precinct."

Sister Blackstone would've rolled out Janelle's entire sordid-affair resume, but she managed to stop a moment to see if her accusation caused Chyna to react. When it didn't, she continued as though what she said was not out of line. "Too bad your kind of salvation wasn't enough to bring her into righteousness."

And that's when the old Chyna, the brazen woman, who'd in her pre-Cordell DeWitt and Grayson Young days, used a straight razor on a couple of foul-acting folks, reared its head through her mourning. She got up enough nerve to get rid of not only the throbbing headache that held her a prisoner on the side of her bed but also the pesky headache in an oversized church hat and pocketbook.

"Get out of my house right now before I forget who you think you are," Chyna threatened as she leaped toward Sister Blackstone. Before she could control her anger she was hustling the old woman down the hallway by her flabby arm.

"Get outta my house."

Sister Blackstone's face was as hardened as her heart. She glared back at Chyna and without another word walked out the door in a huff.

"No one, not even the head of the pastor's aid committee, walks in my house and starts signifying about my sister." Chyna yelled and added, "Now go run tell that!"

Back inside the kitchen Janelle heard the front door slam like someone had thrown a ball against it. Then she heard the commotion in the living room and raced back. She made it just in time to see Chyna slam the screen door so hard the door handle shook.

Not knowing what to do next, Janelle almost knocked Chyna down when she passed by her. She made it to the front door just in time to catch a glimpse of the back of Sister Blackstone lumbering down the pathway. The old woman's hefty hips were sideswiping the bushes and her large pocketbook decapitated some early blooms on the flowers.

"Chyna, what happened?" Janelle turned and asked, "You look like you could churn butter with your lips quivering so fast."

"They can all go to hell!" Chyna burst past Janelle and raced back down the hallway to her bedroom.

Janelle stood speechless as she watched the old woman lumber down the pathway.

Sister Blackstone might've been old, but when push came to shove, she'd put her old orthopedic shoes in high gear and huffed it. She had her hat sideways, pocketbook with flower petals clinging to it like magnets as it hung from her wrist. "Heathens," she barked, "devils."

Chapter 17

"Just hurry up and write the dang ticket," Sister Blackstone snapped. Her brash demeanor was in stark contrast to the motherly and churchy look she presented when the New York state trooper pulled her over. She'd done almost eighty miles per hour on the winding and turning curves of the Jackie Robinson Expressway.

"Please be careful," the state trooper said while trying to maintain an air of authority. "No sense in you having an accident or causing one for somebody else."

The trooper absentmindedly pushed his wide-brimmed caramel-colored hat away from his brow. He could almost feel the heat coming out of the car through its window and it wasn't from the car's heater.

Sister Blackstone snatched the ticket from the hands of the state trooper.

"Lord, help me to keep my testimony," Sister Blackstone prayed. "You know Father God that I was only trying to help poor Pastor Young's memory. And that woman wouldn't let me."

She careened away at almost ninety miles per hour

that time. The only reason she didn't get another ticket or
spend a night in jail was because the state trooper had already pulled off. He was already on his way to interrupt
someone else's day.

As angry as Sister Blackstone was, she finally calmed
down enough to drive within reason—that was, until she
was caught up in traffic. She was on the Grand Central
Parkway, trapped. The entire four lanes were congested
and became a parking lot. No one was going anywhere.
She saw flashing red lights far ahead. "Lord, can this day
get any worse?" She muttered. "Can it, Lord?"

There was nothing she could do but sit idly in her car
just like the other drivers. To save gas, she turned the engine off and laid her head back against the neck rest. She
hadn't meant to, but Sister Blackstone began to recall
how more than a year ago, she'd made a move that would
change not only her life but several around her.

> *One day, without Pastor Young's knowledge,
> she made a spare key to Pastor's Young's private
> file cabinet. She'd gone ahead and had it made
> after an episode where Pastor Young almost
> seemed on the verge of a nervous breakdown
> when he thought he'd lost the key. By accident,
> she'd actually found the key after he'd left his
> study and already gone home. The next day she
> had a spare made. She also called him and with-
> out telling him what she'd done simply said
> where he could find the key.*
>
> *"Thank you, Sister Blackstone," Pastor
> Young had said with a sigh of relief. "I've got
> God's business in there, and you well know that
> God's business is my business and nobody else's
> business."*

A few cars started blasting their horns, causing Sister Blackstone's heart to lurch forward. She looked about her and saw that she was still trapped in traffic. With her head lying, again, against the headrest, she closed her eyes.

She recalled, further, the feeling of uneasiness that enveloped her when he'd specified that God's business was his business alone. She'd let it go, because if he'd ever misplaced or lost the key to "God's business," again, she'd simply come to his rescue with her spare key. If anything, rather than become angry at what she'd done behind his back, he'd thank her. The way she saw it, a pastor's aide was there to help.

How was she to know a year later, he'd be dead?

And then several weeks ago she felt it was time for her to finally put her grief aside. Without any of the other committee members along, one evening after the last Sunday service, she finally got around to using the spare key. Since Pastor Young had intimated that he'd kept God's business inside the cabinet, Sister Blackstone felt it her business to make the reverend's and God's business her business.

Nothing could've prepared the old woman. She'd not seen such filth in all her sixty-plus years. Her beloved Pastor Young had pictures of a naked woman. Each photograph showed the young woman in various stages of ecstasy, in what Sister Blackstone could only describe as sodomy and satanic sex.

She'd dropped the file to the floor as if it were on fire. It was only after Sister Blackstone had prayed and anointed her face and particularly around her eyes with blessed oil that she finally got over the shock. She slowly realized the woman, whose face was a bit hazy in the picture, had to be New Hope's First Lady. However, that shock paled in comparison to the one she'd soon have when the other photographs revealed her beloved Pastor Young doing much of the same; and none of it with his wife.

Inside that office that afternoon Sister Blackstone's emotion swept from shock to anger at her discovery. Although she'd never married or been particularly interested in sex once she was past the age of twenty-five, she was disappointed in the both of them. But at that moment she admitted inwardly that she was even more disappointed in her pastor, whom she'd thought of and treated like a son she would've wanted to have.

Why would he keep this filth in this sanctified place? She'd thought as she took a napkin to handle and replaced the items back inside the envelope. And then in another moment of clarity she became enraged, again. With teeth grinding and bile boiling because upon second thought, her pastor shouldn't have kept those demonic images anywhere, but he had.

And he'd also kept a journal inside the envelope. Sister Blackstone felt a need to read it in as much as she'd already seen the photographs. Though not as shocking as the photographs, she was surprised at the revelation.

. Although many in the congregation knew that the First Lady was a divorcée, no one ever questioned the reasons behind the divorce. So when she read the journal and discovered Pastor

Young's deceitful part in bringing it about as well as the history and involvement of Minister Cordell DeWitt, she was beyond disturbed. She was livid.

By the time Sister Blackstone finished reading entries that dated back almost ten years earlier, she wasn't sure if she'd ever truly known her beloved Pastor Young.

The mighty Reverend Grayson Young had made a fool of them all. What damage had the man of God done to New Hope Assembly?

After much prayer and fasting Sister Blackstone had come to the conclusion that she could only reveal but so much to the board. She remembered how much David disappointed God time after time, but God always forgave David.

Yes, David was forgiven, but Bathsheba was punished with the death of their child.

Sister Blackstone was angry and disappointed, but she knew she'd have to forgive her pastor. After all, he'd only been a man doing what most men did. Because she'd held him in such high esteem, it was her belief that Satan had worked overtime to bring him down. She wasn't going to let it happen and take New Hope Assembly down with it unless it became necessary.

However, Sister Blackstone felt that Chyna's involvement was different. The First Lady should've been able to resist the enemy. Chyna used her body like a human sperm receptacle and looked quite happy to be on the receiving end of the devilish acts.

Sister Blackstone couldn't offer the First Lady the same compassion as the reverend. In her self-righteous mind, Chyna Young needed to be treated like Bathsheba; she needed to be punished for not treating her body like a temple.

Two weeks later and under the guise of being protective of her church, Sister Blackstone finally showed two of the scandalous photographs, minus the ones with Pastor Young and the journal, to Deacons Athens and Pillar.

Deacon Earl Athens, a seventy-plus man just two ounces short of being obese, had coffee-colored and snow white hair that covered only the perimeter of his head. He was one of the oldest members in the church and the pushiest member on the board.

"Oh my God," Deacon Athens had cried out. It wasn't lost on her and Deacon Pillar that he'd seemed to examine one picture longer than necessary. "Can a human stand it to be done in such a manner?" He'd asked the question aloud, although she was certain he hadn't meant to do it.

Deacon Thurgood Pillar was a different matter. He was a man a little older than she but seemed in excellent health compared to some of the others. He was a dark-skinned man with sparse hair that he still wore in a conk.

Deacon Pillar also had a weird way of analyzing situations by taking a route through fantasy land before arriving at reality. He never minced words, although the words he used sometimes seemed alien to most. Even before he'd found Jesus he was a bit weird. People on the street used to call him, "Pillar the Killer." When he finally embraced salvation he never explained his street name. But few had to guess its meaning.

*"Okay," Deacon Pillar said as he snatched
the photo from Deacon Athens's grip and placed
them among several others. "This is an outrage,"
Deacon Pillar said as his dull brown eyes leaped
from photo to photo. "She's talented, though,
nasty but very talented."*

*It was agreed that although each photo-
graph was as disturbing as the next there was
another matter that needed their immediate attention. A revival to return to the old morality
was needed and it was up to the three of them to
force the board to bring it about.*

Out of the corner of Sister Blackstone's eye she saw
several cars begin to inch forward. She sat upright, turned
on the ignition, and began her crawl toward the church for
the board meeting. She'd hoped to arrive there before
they decided to do something stupid, but it wasn't likely.
A few minutes later the traffic opened up and she placed
her foot heavily on the accelerator. She raced along the
Van Wyck Expressway. Her speedometer was just a notch
or two below eighty miles per hour and Sister Blackstone
didn't care.

Chapter 18

Pounding raindrops pelted the windows of Chyna's now-rented house. It caused a slapping sound that jolted Janelle from a much-needed deep sleep. For the past month, since Cordell's surprise arrival she'd felt tortured even when she'd slept in her own home. She'd ridden a mental pendulum that swung between love and hate. That thin line applied to both Chyna and Cordell.

A clap of thunder caused Janelle to jerk. In one swift movement she sat up in the bed. She'd perspired heavily and her damp clothes clung to her like a second skin. Janelle adjusted her eyes to the dark. A sudden chill caused her to pull the covers around her shoulders. She looked around the room and imagined shadows dancing on the wall. Several shadows appeared illuminated by stubborn moonbeams that looked like outlines of swaying branches. In her semiconscious mind, those shadows swung back and forth, pushed and taunted by a reluctant April wind.

She'd finally moved in with Chyna about a week ago. She'd decided she needed to keep an eye on Chyna, who seemed to swing between joy and sadness all too frequently. And as close as she felt to her sister, she couldn't help imagining that Chyna was holding something back. Or was it someone?

Janelle moving in with Chyna seemed like a good idea at the time. She'd come to spend so much time there and, of course, she could protect Chyna from Cordell, or vice versa.

Janelle knew a thing or two about blocking.

Yet before and even since she'd moved in, Janelle's concern about Chyna's mental health wasn't without merit. Chyna, instead of showing security in Janelle's presence, had started displaying all kinds of craziness.

During Janelle's daily visits to see about Chyna, she witnessed the frequent calls from the church board members. Those cryptic calls certainly didn't seem to help Chyna's situation. Whenever Chyna needed to meet with the deacons or the wretched Sister Blackstone, she'd ask her sister not to come.

"You don't get along with the church folks and I can handle things."

And yet, whether Chyna was inside the house or running about trying to do errands, she'd always imagine fingers pointing at her. Of course, then she'd call Janelle if Janelle wasn't with her. "I know people are talking about me," Chyna would complain, "Why can't they just leave me alone?"

"Who's pointing the finger at you now?" Janelle asked, not even trying to hide her annoyance. "If it's one of those churchy folks, they can't throw stones."

But in the end Janelle always ended up at Chyna's house with her just-in-case bag in tow. However, it was when Janelle caught Chyna trying to set fire to some of Grayson's belongings that she knew Chyna was perched on the ledge of insanity. "Grayson wants me to burn up everything and he's upset because I'm not dead." Chyna once said. "He told me in a dream and he meant it."

Janelle also knew crazy when she saw it and Chyna was becoming crazy's poster child. Janelle had to step in.

However, things didn't change that much once Janelle moved in. Chyna's mood swings and her need to accept responsibility and confess to cheating kept Janelle on her toes.

"I need to do it for the church's sake and mine." Chyna would insist.

Janelle knew her sister and didn't believe most of what Chyna revealed. Something more was going on, and if Chyna wasn't confiding in *her*, then who could she confide in?

A strong gust of wind pushed its way through a small hole in Janelle's bedroom window. The cold strokes of wind across her face now made her fully awake. "Damn," Janelle said as she shivered. However, wind or not, no matter how many reasons Janelle created, real and imagined, she'd also have to admit that her lack of any real sleep was also or even more in part due to the return of her deep-rooted jealousy, mixed in with her real love for her sister.

"It's Cordell's fault." Janelle yanked the covers up higher, almost covering her head.

Why did Cordell have to insist on sticking around? She threw off the covers. "Why couldn't he just go away?" she mumbled. But if he had, she'd eventually complain, "Why did he go away?"

A slight pain tugged at Janelle's bosom, interrupting any further demonizing of Cordell. It wasn't the first time she'd felt that burning sensation in her breast. It'd begun about six months ago, but she'd ignored it. Lately with all that had happened, the pain seemed to worsen and come more often. She also had to admit that her need to appear just as healthy as, if not more than, Chyna had a part in her not seeing her gynecologist even though she'd made and cancelled several appointments.

"I love my sister," Janelle whispered as she finally swung her legs over the side of the bed and slipped her feet into her house shoes. "Damn Cordell." The pain hit her again as if her words were chastising her with a hot fork in her chest.

Janelle didn't want to turn on a light and chance waking Chyna, too, even if Chyna's bedroom was further down the hall. She needed some real alone time; a time away from babysitting her sister. Much-needed time away from trying to douse that reckless fire that burned deep within the very pit of her being. It seemed every time she heard or saw Cordell, her drawers caught fire.

Janelle fumbled around in the dark until she found her pocketbook with a pack of cigarettes. She'd quit twice before. But with all that had happened within the last several months, she'd started puffing again. "Here they are," she whispered. Like a junkie, longing for a hit, Janelle's hands shook as she took one from the pack. She lit it, inhaling deep enough to make her cheeks appear sunken.

Normally, she'd have opened a window when she lit up. Chyna couldn't stand the smell of cigarette smoke or even have ashes or an ashtray in her house. Not tonight. Janelle needed to have things her way. Tucked away in a room feeling alone, she would.

Janelle's erratic thoughts continued sparring with the reality that she felt evaded her sister. So she puffed away as she debated.

I should've been glad that Cordell agreed to buy Chyna's house. That's what a friend with plenty of money would do if he found out his ex-wife had financial problems. So how come I'm not glad? It was but one of many questions that plagued Janelle as she tried to relax.

Since the time Janelle had moved into Chyna's home, Cordell had returned to California twice.

Even thousands of miles away, he fared no better than Janelle in trying to confront his feelings. Each time he returned to Brooklyn he spent more time at Chyna's than he needed to. He could've returned home to California anytime he'd wanted. But he didn't want to, especially after Chyna secretly shared that the New Hope Church Board wanted her proxy vote and ultimately her resignation as the First Lady.

"The church hasn't even started looking for a permanent pastor," Cordell had said, "so why the urgency to force your resignation?"

"I can't say anything more." Chyna had said as she held back tears. "I just can't, and you must promise that you won't say anything about this to Janelle."

So he'd found one excuse after another to fly back and forth to Los Angeles, and ultimately Brooklyn became his second base of operations.

Whether it was for his own ego or man's definition of karma, while being around Chyna and Janelle, Cordell had slipped into the role of ex-husband and ex-lover quite comfortably.

Now it was Thursday, and as became his habit, Cordell was preparing to return to Brooklyn. As he packed, he pondered, as he had begun to do more and more lately, if what he was doing was God's will.

"Double-minded folks will make twice the amount of mistakes." He'd taught that lesson at so many of his conferences and yet, here he was somewhat torn between his need to protect the two women he'd harmed before he knew God; one from an unknown, the other from his own feelings. And he was working overtime to avoid common sense.

Cordell, on the flight back to New York, had a chance

to think about his conferences. They were a gift from God after he'd fallen so low in life. He'd been at the very door of success in radio when one slip, of accepting a gift under the table to play tracks from a major record label, caused his firing. He'd never told Chyna the truth and he'd allowed their finances to dwindle. When Grayson appeared with the money and the means for him to divorce a wife he'd never loved, he'd taken it. He'd sold his dignity, but little did he know that Christ had already paid the price for his redemption.

"Would you like your drink refreshed, sir?" The offer came from one of the male flight attendants in first class.

"I'm fine, thank you," Cordell replied with a smile. He hoped his face hadn't betrayed his conflict.

Cordell thought again about the ministry doors God had opened for him. Only God could've picked him up, cleaned him off, and used him to help heal relationships. At first he'd taken it as a joke. Why would God choose him for this? Wasn't he the one who broke hearts, lied to get what he wanted, and walked away with little remorse?

"Ladies and gentlemen, this is your captain. Please buckle your seat belts. We will begin our descent into New York's JFK Airport. We are due to land in about fifteen minutes."

Cordell buckled his seat belt and watched as the same flight attendant went through his first class cabin collecting whatever wasn't needed. He pulled out his schedule book to see if at least his ministry agenda was in order.

No matter how things went, he couldn't abandon his ministry. It was his life. Without a doubt he always believed that God placed him in one of the singles classes at his home church, Crenshaw Christian Center in California. He'd gone for almost two years before the ministry leader and the pastor confirmed what he'd come to believe. Indeed, God had called him for relationship ministry.

After looking over his schedule, Cordell realized that he'd forgotten to reconfirm one of his upcoming appointments. *I've got to do better than this,* Cordell thought. His life and ministry schedule couldn't be significantly changed despite the chaos he'd stepped into with Chyna and Janelle.

"Will you be flying with us next week?" The flight attendant asked. "I read the books you gave me. It is really helping me and my wife." The flight attendant smiled and handed Cordell his briefcase. "Have a good day, Mr. De-Witt."

Cordell returned the smile before he left the plane. It seemed that during his frequent flights in and out of town he'd quite regularly have the same flight attendants. He'd come to know the JFK airport like the back of his hands, and his frequent flyer miles increased dramatically.

Cordell picked up his rental car and started his drive to Brooklyn. With no prodding Janelle came to mind. He had to admit he missed her and really couldn't wait to see her.

It was only a week since he'd seen Janelle. During this past week he had been committed to a telethon in California with the taping schedule of twelve-hour days. Yet Cordell and Janelle made sure to keep in touch.

Their pattern of calling one another with frivolous excuses to do so was fast becoming an inside joke. Yet they knew any wrong moves or perceptions would not bring laughter. However, either out of a need to complete unfinished business or lust, their conversation soon turned to very little about Chyna's situation and more about them. He welcomed it because he couldn't reveal Chyna's predicament, anyway, and he really wasn't sure what it was. He could only offer Chyna an ear and a shoulder. For Janelle, he wanted to offer more, but resisted mainly because some of their conversations were becoming a bit strange. He recalled one in particular.

"So, why would Chyna care if someone thought she might've committed adultery or not?" Cordell had asked the question because it seemed as though Janelle was dropping hints along those lines.

"I never said she was," Janelle replied, "I'm just saying that the way those church folks act when they stop by or call that they're looking down their noses at Chyna. You'd think she'd done something to provoke Grayson's stupidity. I don't know how you got adultery out of that."

"I can't speak for them," Cordell said slowly, "but we're still pretty much good friends, right?"

"Yes." Janelle said quickly, although she wasn't quite sure where he was going with the question. "I thought everything was going as well as it could in our situation."

"It is," Cordell agreed, "but I don't want to discuss further what I'm thinking about over the phone. Can I come by when I return tomorrow? It may be a little late."

Janelle took her time responding. She could hear bells and whistles going off in her head. She just wasn't sure what melody they played. "Okay," she finally answered, "Come on by." Almost as an afterthought, she added, "Chyna probably won't be here. She's supposed to meet with Sister Blackstone and those other old biddies."

"Not a problem," Cordell said trying to ignore Janelle's attempt at degrading the church women. He smiled, anyway, although he couldn't ignore the dis and added, "Janelle, biddies belong in a chicken coop, not the church."

He was foolish enough to think that he'd chastised her.

"Exactly," Janelle shot back, "None of those old chickens belong in a church."

The conversation went on for a while longer. They played word tag with no end in sight because neither truly wanted to hang up.

So now Cordell was keeping his promise. He did return later the next day, by mid morning, to Brooklyn. He'd managed to reschedule one of his conferences and taped two television appearances. He'd taken the red eye from Los Angeles back to New York. He pulled into the hotel parking lot. He wanted to freshen up and drop off his bags.

Cordell also felt the need to pray and meditate. Whatever battle he was entering, he knew it was not against man but principalities. Battles with or against church folks were never ordinary.

Chapter 19

After gathering his thoughts after prayer and meditation and before leaving his hotel, Cordell called Chyna to let her know he would stop by.

Twenty minutes later, Chyna answered the door when Cordell rang the bell. "You don't have to ring, you're the landlord," she teased and then returned to silence.

"I'll never be your landlord," Cordell replied. He was happy that her mood seemed a bit lighter than as of late, but it wasn't by much. She still didn't look like her old self and she hadn't replied to what he said.

Cordell threw his coat over the back of one of the chairs in the living room and started following her toward the kitchen. "After the three-digit heat in Los Angeles, I'm glad to come back and feel a little May warmth in the air."

Chyna still didn't respond.

Seeing as she didn't seem to want to discuss the weather, Cordell let it go. "I see Janelle is up and at it." He could hear her moving about in the kitchen. He really didn't need to mention it, but the silence coming from Chyna, as usual, unnerved him.

Since arriving back into her life it was disheartening for Cordell to see Chyna use mourning as a crutch while she fought the church board at the same time. Neither she nor Janelle actually mentioned Grayson's name too often. However, he'd gathered from snatches of not-meant-to-be-heard conversation between the sisters that Grayson's bad memory still haunted them.

"It wasn't like you'd put that damn gun in his hand!" He'd heard Janelle argue when he wasn't supposed to.

"I might as well have," Chyna then replied, "I wasn't where I was supposed to be."

Had he misunderstood? Why would Chyna feel guilty about Grayson's suicide or perhaps the murders? Cordell dismissed the conversation and put it as far back into his mind as he could. He'd determined that he must not have heard what he heard.

No sooner had they approached the kitchen when Chyna announced in a matter-of-fact manner, "Cordell's here."

"Glad she said my name, Cordell. A minute ago, she called me 'landlord,' " Cordell teased.

Teasing or not, he had to admit he was often a bit conflicted when he was in Chyna's presence. Grayson had taken his wife; no, not taken her, Grayson paid for her at a time when Cordell was deep in debt. Now, Cordell had returned in time to prevent Chyna from declaring bankruptcy by purchasing her house. One day God would explain things to him.

"Hello, Janelle," Cordell said, entering the kitchen behind Chyna. He walked over and gave her a quick peck on her cheek. He pulled back and whistled, "You look good."

Janelle quickly closed her robe, denying him the eye

candy her perfect breasts presented. She threw him a teasing glare and replied, "As opposed to what?"

Janelle trained her eyes on him—all of him. It was becoming harder to look at Cordell. He always looked and smelled so good. It was even harder being around him without remembering that he'd taken her virginity, at a time when most women her age tossed theirs to and fro and to whomever at will. No matter how many men she'd had since then, none ever compared to Cordell.

Leaning against the kitchen counter Janelle also thought about what she imagined happened when Cordell and Chyna were married. Without realizing it, she'd balled up a napkin and tossed it aside in anger. She turned her head slightly toward her sister. She couldn't help but glare at Chyna who'd, fortunately, already turned around.

Janelle was about to say something nasty when the pain in her breast returned. Was it her nerves? It seemed that every time she became anxious or upset the pain followed.

Cordell couldn't understand Janelle's mood swing from just yesterday. "*. . . As opposed to what—?*" She'd hissed. Maybe he was becoming too accustomed to being around Chyna and Janelle. Perhaps he needed to reassess his judgment. Both women had issues he hadn't seen a few years ago. At times, they made him feel like he was living moment to moment with potential killers, both hormonally driven.

"Janelle, what are you going to do with that balled-up wad of tissue, resurrect your basketball skills?" Cordell gave a nervous laugh and stepped back a few inches. She looked pained, so without saying anything more he began to pray inwardly. And that time with fervor.

"Tell me again how you became so famous?" Janelle asked, interrupting whatever Cordell was thinking about as she rammed the wad of tissue into her pocket. Her eyes were piercing as she wondered, *is he thinking about Chyna.*

Swinging mentally between a state of anxiety and the pain in her bosom, Janelle began to slowly tap the side of a now-empty napkin holder. The question was directed at Cordell, but her eyes were trained on Chyna's back. Chyna was filling the dishwasher and never joined their conversation.

Janelle returned her attention to Cordell. "It must be wonderful to be as well off as you've become," she said with her eyes suddenly lighting up. "You could've knocked me over with a flower petal when you up and bought this house without blinking."

"I've been blessed," Cordell replied. He'd already gone to the counter and poured two cups of coffee. He took one and seemed to pause as if trying to decide whether to offer the other to Janelle, who'd obviously already had one, probably spiked, or to Chyna first.

Cordell wasn't certain of what was on Janelle's mind at that moment. He needed to tread lightly. Since he'd left Brooklyn and went back on the road, almost immediately, after putting into motion the purchasing of Chyna's house he'd begun to think about and *notice* Janelle. It was a little too much *notice* for him, and not the kind he really needed.

"Well, let me see," Cordell said as he offered the second cup to Janelle. He'd also noticed that Chyna had already walked out of the kitchen as though neither he nor Janelle were there.

"Like I told you before, Christ knocked at the door of my heart after I had been attending a relationship class for a couple of years. I opened it. I let Christ do a new work, and so on and so on." He smiled and winked. He hadn't meant to wink, but he surely couldn't take it back.

"Oh, I know about the so on and so on," Janelle said.

I've seen you and Chyna with your heads glued together.
She laughed loud, trying to distract him from noticing
that her sister had walked out of the room just in case he
hadn't.

Not saying anything didn't mean Chyna hadn't noticed what was happening before she walked out of the
kitchen.

Chyna walked into the living room, which was still
filled with memorabilia of her life with Grayson including the urn filled with his ashes. Everywhere she turned
she saw something. She'd already removed so much of
what they'd shared, and the church so much more, and yet
there was so much left behind that wasn't tangible.

Chyna found one of the remaining chairs in the living
room. Even with Cordell purchasing the house, she'd
been careful spending money. Furniture was not a priority
especially since what Janelle had given was adequate.

With her Wall Street background, she could probably
take a few classes and get back to work.

Chyna wasn't ready to return to a job even if the
money she'd made and spent from her stocks said differently.

With the uncommonly warm weather filtering through
the window and acting as a balm for her body, Chyna allowed her head to fall back against the headrest of the recliner. The movement allowed for a relaxing and rippling
effect to claim her body.

"Thank you, Jesus." The praise rolled off her lips as
though she'd been saying it constantly since that night
Grayson took his life and others at the Sweet Bush. But
she hadn't. She'd avoided praising or asking God for anything. Feeling unworthy and guilty had taken its toll on
her spirituality. At least she was honest about it. She'd not
returned to the church for a service for many weeks.

And yet, she now sat with her small Bible clutched in her hand.

Deep laughter from Cordell and girlish giggles from Janelle drifted in from the kitchen. Chyna closed the Bible, though she'd barely opened it.

"Oh, I guess it's okay to look, if you ain't gonna buy?" Chyna heard Janelle say loudly.

Chyna couldn't make out Cordell's response, but she did hear him laugh. It was that deep bass-sounding laughter that made him so endearing. But she also knew that laughter was never meant for her. He'd always loved Janelle. He hadn't said he still did, but Chyna knew it deep down in her soul.

Chyna shut her eyes, but she couldn't shut her ears to their laughter as she again pulled the lever on the recliner and let her head and body recline further back.

"Chyna, are you still going to the church today?" The question from Janelle hit Chyna hard as though her sister had asked from a few feet away instead of yelling it from the kitchen.

"Yes," Chyna replied as loud as she could without straining her voice. "I'm going alone. You stay here with Cordell if he's not leaving soon."

She let her head fall back, which somehow caused the pins holding her hair pinned back to loosen. Her long hair fanned about the back of the recliner. "I should tell Janelle the whole truth." Chyna mumbled. But she knew she couldn't or she would've already. The fact that she hadn't been completely honest when she told Janelle that she was going to confront Sister Blackstone and the board about her status tugged at her conscience.

From the time they'd called her, reaching her at a time when she'd answered the phone, unexpectedly things got ugly. Face-to-face they'd issued threats, and made insinuations about her character, their insistence that she resign or support their plans to take the church in a direction that was no longer relevant. Yet, never did any of them say a word about the shame Grayson's actions brought to the church.

However, she'd finally made up her mind. Today, when she saw them, if they didn't produce whatever shameful evidence they claimed they had about her, she was going to denounce them in front of the entire congregation and the diocese if necessary.

A brief moment of peace continued to claim its hold on Chyna. She'd almost smiled when she'd repeated the praise, "Thank you, Lord."

When it, the moment of the ability to praise God happened, Chyna didn't know. She certainly wasn't aware of her hands fingering the cover of a small Bible. Had she done it while whispering God's praises? The Bible was a small one she'd always kept by the telephone in a red velvet tote bag.

The feeling that she was not alone suddenly came upon her. She looked up to see Janelle and Cordell looking at her as though they'd caught her with her hand in a cookie jar.

"Glad to see you giving God the glory." Cordell said smiling. "Prayer does change a lot of things."

"So it's praying for my sister that you've been doing?" Janelle asked the question with innocence that was believable to only her.

When Cordell just looked at her with a smile that remained plastered upon his face, Janelle let whatever she was about to start, go. Instead, she handed Cordell his coat and turned to Chyna.

"Cordell has a quick errand to run for me." Janelle said as though his doing so was a prize. "I already told him that you'd probably be gone before he returned."

"Okay," Chyna answered. She knew Janelle wanted

her to say something more, but she didn't feel up to the game.

"Listen, ladies," Cordell said as he walked to the door, "I'll see you later." He stopped and for no real reason he looked at Janelle and added, "Except for you. I know you've got me on a timer for these crabs."

"That's right." Janelle replied, "You owe it to me. I never had crabs until I met you."

The color almost drained from Cordell's face, and it was enough to cause both Chyna and Janelle to suddenly burst out laughing.

"You two need some serious help." Chyna said as she rose to leave the room. "I have to get dressed."

"Don't worry," Janelle teased, "Chyna knows you took me out for my first seafood dinner and we had crab legs."

"Glad you cleared that up." Cordell looked at Janelle and shook his head. "Girl, if you only knew."

"Only knew what?" Janelle asked, "Only knew what?"

"Aha, you know two can play the game." Cordell winked on purpose that time and walked out the door.

Janelle closed the living room curtain just as Chyna returned dressed and ready to leave.

"You look fashionable," Janelle teased. "Of course, if I were going with you," she added, "you'd have to hike that skirt up a bit. You know I have the four inch rule."

"I know you need to quit teasing me about my so-called matronly manner of dressing—"

"Speaking of which," Janelle interrupted as she sat down on the sofa. "I need to ask you something that's been on my mind. And seeing how we share so much, I just need to understand something."

Chyna had only gotten one arm through her coat

sleeve and knew it was useless to try to delay any conversations with Janelle. "Okay, let's have it."

Janelle's obvious snide remarks, here and there since
Cordell's arrival might as well be brought out into the
open. Any wrestling with Janelle would only arm Chyna
for the real bout when she got together, later, with the
church board.

"Don't get all uptight," Janelle said softly, "I'm not
one of your needy congregation members calling for a
consultation. I'm your sister."

"I wasn't," Chyna had begun to say.

"Please stop. I know you, so let's just keep this real.
It's only us two. Just like it's always been."

"Okay."

"Our two is becoming a threesome." Janelle said as
she showed three fingers on one of her hands. "What are
we gonna do about it?"

Chapter 20

The softness of the recliner seat, in her living room, suddenly felt like being trapped in a thorny bush as Chyna reeled from the implication of Janelle's offhanded accusation. Chyna wanted to speak and found she couldn't.

"I guess I can guess by your silence that there's some leftover feelings for Cordell." Janelle had tried to speak with authority, but the apparent sadness was too strong to ignore.

"I don't love or even care for Cordell the way you think." Chyna finally admitted. "You should know better."

"If you say so," Janelle got up and walked out the room mumbling, "You must think I'm a damn fool."

"Stop it, Janelle." Chyna jumped up. "He doesn't love me. He's just trying to help me!"

Janelle reeled around and rushed toward Chyna. "Help you with what, Chyna?"

"What is wrong with you, Janelle? One minute you're for me and just as soon as a pair of pants that you used to jump shows up, you turn on me."

"A pair of pants, that's what you thought he was?"

"Janelle, I'm sorry. I didn't mean it like that!"

From somewhere deep within her, Chyna started screaming uncontrollably.

"Chyna, wake up!"

Cordell shook Chyna harder than he would most men twice her size. He had to do it. She was screaming and locked somewhere in a mental hell struggling to get out.

"Move," Janelle said as she shoved Cordell aside, "I've got this. She's having another nightmare."

Cordell moved a few feet away and watched with his arms folded. "She's having another nightmare?" That was something Chyna had not shared and he couldn't figure out why. What she'd already told him was already crazy enough.

What Cordell wasn't certain of was whether or not to get involved any further.

The urgent reverberations of the doorbell and persistent knocks at the door cut through the silence at the same time.

Janelle let Chyna's head slide from her hands as she rose to answer. Passing by Cordell, she said quickly, "Just leave her alone until I see who's at the door." She'd acted as though he weren't capable of doing a simple thing like answering a doorbell. When Janelle was in control, she left nothing to chance.

"Never mind, you stay with her. I'll see who's at the door." Cordell gently turned Janelle around so she could return to Chyna's side.

Cordell saw the UPS driver rushing away just as he opened the front door.

The UPS envelope had landed atop a small patch of annuals by the front door and the driver had already taken off by the time he picked it up.

Cordell's eyes fell upon the return address. New Hope Assembly Church in big bold letters leapt out at him. "I guess the mountain came to Muhammad." He was certain it was what Chyna needed and yet feared.

Cordell didn't know when Janelle came outside. He was about to place the envelope under his shirt when he felt her tug on his shirtsleeve.

"I've got her calmed down." Janelle said, "What's in your hand?"

Whatever Janelle was saying escaped Cordell. He was too busy trying to wrap his mind around what he could do to keep it from her until he could give it to Chyna. It was up to her to decide whether to share it with Janelle.

But nothing much could ever pass by Janelle's eagle eyes. Cordell was taller than her, but that didn't stop her from trying to see closer what was in his hands. She stood on her toes trying to look over his shoulders. That's when Janelle yelled out, "Damn!"

At the same time, Janelle reached out for Cordell's arm. He barely had time enough to place the envelope under one arm and catch her.

"Janelle," Cordell said, quickly, "What's wrong with you?"

Janelle wanted to say something. She couldn't. The pain in her breast came like ocean waves. Hammering away with its burning intensity, the pain became unbearable.

Chapter 21

It was almost four o'clock and the board meeting had finally begun.

The New Hope Assembly church board was a mixture of nine men and three women ranging in ages from fifty to about seventy-five. They were the most vocal and conniving forces behind the customized interpretation of the church's bylaws and other ideology. The board usually met on a quarterly basis, unless there was an emergency or if certain cliques didn't come together secretively; which was exactly what Blackstone, Athens, and Pillar had recently done.

The women, Sister Blackstone not included, were placed on the board for decoration and to make a statement as to the church's tolerance of having them on the board but not in the pulpit. Several of the members inherited their seats from family members and perhaps one or two were actually voted in by the will of the congregation.

Before this emergency meeting, the board had recently met for a second time, which was unusual, to decide upon several urgent issues facing the church. Supposedly they were to put together the calendar indicating the names of visiting preachers and when they would preach. Since the Reverend Young's untimely death, it had become an urgent matter. They also had to decide what monies to offer so as not to offend.

But today was set aside for a special meeting. This day their meeting would finally deal with the real issue of the church and its return to respectability. And they would also be two members short on purpose. Several days before the other ten members, including Sister Blackstone, held a secret meeting. It was determined after a unanimous and secret vote not to invite the other two women. This was serious business.

"You know they can't be trusted to keep their big mouths shut." Sister Blackstone had insisted at that meeting. "They don't know how to tell only two or three people. That's how rumors get started."

The clock read ten minutes after four. All formality was tossed aside and it was time for several of the professional hypocrites to throw one another under buses, left and right.

"We should've stuck to our guns," one of the board members reprimanded, "We took our eyes off the prize."

The others nodded in agreement, because the hypocrite was right.

They discussed how it was only several years before that Reverend Young became the pastor of New Hope Assembly their church enjoyed and boasted a reputation of one of the holiest of congregations in Brooklyn. However, time, liberalism, and loosely applied church beliefs caused it to backslide.

"We should have used our power when we saw that decency and accountability no longer attended our New Hope Assembly church," another hypocrite added.

They opined about the men who often came to morning service in nothing more than a wrinkled shirt and dress pants. Teenage and young adult men arrived with colorfully coordinated pants hanging low and exposing underwear and more.

The women, according to a few of the other old church relics at the meeting, were seen as worse. "Look at how many young and single women were either pregnant or had already given birth," someone observed.

"You're right," another added. "They have no shame. Back in my day they'd have gone on long vacations or just disappeared. Now they just give birth and then have the audacity to have their illegitimate bastard children christened."

"And how many times did the baby's daddy show up? Not many, I can tell you that." Someone else added their two cents' worth of hypocrisy to the discussion.

The board's observations weren't totally without merit. There was a lot of work needed among the congregation members, but what church was perfect?

Shameless women wore revealing low-cut dresses or blouses. The hems were almost always above the knees. Unlike the elderly or stauncher female church members who used modesty cloths, to cover their ankles, bare knees, and upper legs, the "brazen" females did not. There was no shame coming from a majority of the ladies, who exposed their bare arms and liberally applied lipstick, brightly colored nail polish, and over-made-up eyes.

"What we should've done was to just veto the Reverend Young and his accommodating ways," someone hissed. That time, the declaration caused the others to look his way. It came from the mouth of another board member, Deacon Duke Brown.

Duke Brown, one of the few white members on the board, looked about fifty. He was lean and somewhat unkempt compared to the others. His five o'clock shadow seemed too dark to be just that.

"Y'all remember what the reverend always said whenever a complaint was voiced, he'd ask for patience," Deacon Brown said slowly. He looked around to see if anyone would follow his accusation with further testimony.

One did. "I remember it, too," said a fellow board member.

And the Reverend Grayson Young had responded in such a manner. "I promise to only make enough progressive changes to keep up with the other megachurches," he'd say calmly while fingering the Bible he most often used as his prop during a negotiation. "I'll slowly return New Hope Assembly back to its former promise of holiness. Remember, we're supposed to be fishers of men. Let God clean them with conviction after we take up the collection."

And now the Reverend Grayson Young has committed murder and suicide with not one promise fulfilled. And months ago, the void created a huge problem for the board.

At that time the consensus among the board members was that something drastic needed to happen after the Sweet Bush scandal. They'd spent a great deal of their quarterly church budget hiring a publicist to downplay the horrific and unseemly, not to mention criminal, acts of Pastor Grayson. One after another of the biggest names in the church community were prodded into giving glowing endorsements of his spiritual and community works.

The board finally got the whole mess down to a manageable rumor and stopped the flood of members who left or threatened to leave. Now the photos of who they believed to be the first lady had surfaced and added to Deacon Pillar, Deacon Athens, and Sister Blackstone's angst.

They knew another scandal could bring the church down for good. Keeping the photos from the public was a nonissue for Sister Blackstone and the other two deacons.

Though it wasn't voiced aloud, there were other considerations. Everything done on behalf of the church hadn't exactly been reputable or legal. There were some issues that didn't involve the Sweet Bush that would surely bring down their nonprofit status and lead to an IRS investigation. Having the IRS involved would open the floodgates. The Reverend Young had made it his business to have each of the board members involved with some deal or another.

In the past, each board member had a secret *itch* for something or another. Even though the Reverend Young would use methods more resembling a sickle than a feather, to scratch their itches, he expected complete loyalty when it was time for payback. Almost no one on the church board was exempt.

"Has anyone heard from Sister Blackstone?" Deacon Athens finally said. He'd grown tired of listening to complaints and walks back down memory lane.

"I ain't heard a word from her," Deacon Pillar answered.

"Well if anyone needs to be here on time, it should've been her." Deacon Athens said, exasperated. "She truly needs to be here." But then he and Deacon Pillar knew things that the others didn't and couldn't know. Sister Blackstone's participation in the meeting was crucial for more than one reason.

Some time ago, in her zealousness to please and gain influence with the Reverend Young, Sister Blackstone's hands became the dirtiest of them all. She'd signed off on proposals and other schemes, thinking that the reverend's explanations of using "progressive" thinking made it all right. She somehow knew it probably wasn't, but he was her pastor; and she was his aide.

Of course, she also felt there were other reasons to go along. Like the time when she'd asked him to place one of her nieces at the head of the list for the church's new housing. Her forty-year-old niece had finally left an abusive marriage and with three children in tow had no place to go. Sister Blackstone had an extra bedroom, but she was used to living alone. Reverend Young hadn't hesitated. He'd simply said, "No problem, Sister Blackstone. On our way to the bank with the papers you signed, we'll stop by the housing office."

Sister Blackstone had yet to sign any papers, but she knew she would. That was how Pastor Young operated.

So despite the other important matters the board members discussed at the meeting, the real question in Athens's and Pillars's mind became: was the Reverend Young as careless in keeping those dealings safe as he was with those photographs?

The problem was that Athens, Pillar, and Blackstone could not avoid implication if the dirty deeds were exposed. So that's why they concocted the scheme that Sister Blackstone would confront Sister Young. They figured that if Sister Young was confronted with the photographs, if she did discover any of their little improprieties, she'd keep her mouth shut. If she wouldn't, then out of embarrassment she'd just step aside.

Deacon Athens looked over at Deacon Pillar. There was no doubt that each man's mind was on the same thing and it wasn't what was discussed at the meeting.

It was almost an hour later before Sister Blackstone finally arrived at the New Hope Assembly Church. She almost did a wheelie as she drove her car quickly into the church's parking lot. She was still so outdone that she had to send the photograph through UPS and that she'd forgotten to make the copies, she parked at a ninety-degree angle instead of parallel parking. She slammed the door hard enough to rattle the front windshield when she got out. Still angry, she grabbed the sideview mirror from the car she'd just sideswiped that landed by her front tire, and tossed it into a trash can.

"They can't play with this woman of God." Sister Blackstone said to herself, "Not today, and never!" She was still muttering angry words as she walked quickly inside and down the hallway to the church's boardroom.

The New Hope Assembly's church board meeting had already finished about fifteen minutes before Sister Blackstone arrived.

The "real" meeting had started and hypocrisy was still in charge.

"Okay, let's get down to brass tacks." Deacon Athens announced as he crushed the butt of one of his trademark Newport cigarettes in a piece of aluminum foil he carried. "The others are gone, but we can't wait for Eartha Blackstone all day."

Deacon Pillar said, "Those idiots were no help at all. But we've got bigger fish to fry. I guess it's up to the two of us now."

Deacon Athens didn't respond to the remark. Instead, he clasped his hands, which made the swivel chair he sat in almost tilt from his weight. Yet it was a move that meant he wasn't in the mood for tomfoolery.

"Enough with all these mime dancers and young girls in short skirts and tights pretending to be dancing for the Lord." Deacon Athens punctuated his distaste by pounding the table. "If the First Lady don't know about her husband's sordid church business, then we've got to either get her on board with the new program, or set her down. Either way, this church is coming back to holiness!"

Deacon Athens, showing off how offended he was at

the young people's unholy behavior, shamelessly lit another cigarette. "So, let's hear some of your ideas."

Deacon Pillar didn't have a chance to answer, because that's when Sister Blackstone came barreling through the door.

"Did you get it done?" Deacon Athens asked. He dispensed with the formality of a welcome as he scratched a hair-free spot on his head.

"Does that adulterin' she-hussy in a church hat see the proof about her wanton ways? Do she know that we've found her out yet? Do she know that we done found out about her?" Deacon Pillar butted in and asked.

"Gimme a chance to catch my breath," Sister Blackstone snapped as she tossed her bag onto a nearby table.

"Well?" Deacon Athens asked. He felt that a second was long enough, since they'd waited more than an hour for her to arrive. He added cautiously, "Between you and me, we must've spoken with her more than a dozen times since Reverend Grayson died. Even with subtle intimidations from me and the Board confiscating her furniture and such, I still couldn't tell if we're getting through."

"That's the part I don't understand," Deacon Pillar added with furrowed brow as he cracked a few of his gnarly knuckles. "Why wouldn't she want the church to go back to true Holiness? I mean we all done sinned at some time, although her kind of sinning might've caused a few more of us to return for a quick taste."

"Can you please get your mind outta the gutter long enough for us to stay on track?" Deacon Athens spun his chair around to face Sister Blackstone without waiting or caring what Deacon Pillar thought about the chastisement.

"Eartha, yes or no, does she know anything about church business and our involvements?"

"I messed up," Sister Blackstone finally said.

"What?" The question was chorused by the two men.

"I gave the envelope to the UPS for delivery," Sister Blackstone said, sadly. "But I didn't make copies. I was too mad and I forgot."

After begrudgingly taking a smattering of rebukes from the deacons, including a reminder that they'd not asked how she came into possession of the evidence, Sister Blackstone reminded them of what had gone down at Chyna's before and that she'd still not had a chance to confront the First Lady. What she didn't tell the deacons was that it didn't matter. She hadn't been entirely forthcoming when she'd said she'd messed up.

The journal was still in her possession. Was it God's plan for all the players to now be in one place at one time? The very prominent Minister Cordell DeWitt, First Lady Chyna, and her heathen sister, Janelle; it couldn't be a coincidence.

"Well then," Deacon Athens snapped, "I guess this has been for nothing. I could've left with the others had I known you'd make such a mess of things."

"You need to fix this, Eartha," Deacon Pillar added. He rose to accompany Deacon Athens. "Don't you take too long in doing it, either. I've got my mind made up to bring this nonsense to an end."

"I've got my mind made up, too," Deacon Athens said as he and Deacon Pillar started to walk out the door. "And you know that when I make up my mind about something—"

"Like a tree that's planted by the river of Jordan," Deacon Pillar interjected, "We shall not be moved." He stopped and allowed Deacon Athens to go before him. "And you know God loves a made-up mind."

Sister Blackstone said nothing as the two men left the room. She remained for a few minutes more seated in a wicker chair over in the corner. She was already ahead of the game and saw no reason at that moment to invite them to play. Sister Blackstone was no amateur hypocrite. She had a mind set in concrete and just as mixed up.

Later that evening in the comfort of her home Sister Blackstone sat in its quietness. She allowed her mind to retrace certain other conversations and things she'd observed while serving Pastor Young. There was a lot she couldn't remember clearly. She wasn't certain whether it was due to her age or her refusal to believe that Pastor Grayson would deliberately lead them astray.

Chapter 22

Cordell's perfectly fitting dark, expensive, blue Jos. A. Bank suit was a pattern of crisscross wrinkles. All of the debonair was gone from his demeanor and dress. He was a mess. Earlier he'd driven his 2006 Honda Accord, alone, erratically, trying to keep up with the ambulance that rushed Janelle to the Downstate Medical Center in Flatbush, Brooklyn. Chyna had insisted on riding along inside the ambulance.

Hours after Janelle had been admitted, Cordell and Chyna entered her room. On their way in two doctors were coming out. Neither doctor looked happy.

Chyna tried to suppress her emotions at seeing her sister hooked up to an IV stand with tubes running from several bags into Janelle's arms and chest. There was almost a bluish-purple discoloration to Janelle's lips and it contrasted deeply with her cream-colored complexion.

"I would ask how you're feeling," Cordell finally said. How had she been so sick and neither he nor Chyna saw it?

"I feel like a pincushion," Janelle answered. Her

voice was raspy, and it was apparent she was struggling against the medicine to remain conscious.

Chyna walked around to the other side of the bed. She stopped and closed the venetian blind as though she didn't want the world looking in on her sister.

"Have they said anything?" Chyna asked. She tried to read the labels on the various IV bags, but she hadn't recognized any of the medicines.

"Yeah, but they wanna run tests." Janelle's voice began to trail off, indicating she wasn't able to hold a conversation much longer.

Just then one of the nurses entered. With just a hint of a Caribbean dialect, the nurse directed her question at Chyna.

"You be Ms. Young?" she asked while using her pen to scribble something on the clipboard she held. Not waiting for Chyna to answer, she continued. "I need a little information from you."

Chyna stepped away from the bed. Janelle had finally drifted off and Cordell remained at the foot of her bed like a deer caught in headlights.

"How long and when Ms. Pierce start seeing her nipples leaking and feeling the pain under her left armpit?" The nurse stopped writing and with an impatient look she stared at Chyna. "The pain in Ms. Pierce's chest and breasts, can you tell me when she feeling it?"

Chyna felt completely useless as she struggled to explain that her sister's independent nature had probably kept her from sharing her illness and that she'd dumped all her problems upon Janelle with no thought to her sister's health. Having the nurse suck her teeth and switch away as though Chyna were someone of a lower class certainly didn't help.

As Chyna picked up the hospital-issued plastic bag containing Janelle's clothes and belongings, she took another glance toward her sister's bed. Despite the severity of the situation, Chyna was angry with Janelle. The anger only lasted a moment or two, because in truth Chyna was angrier with herself. *Janelle was too caught up in my mess to take care of herself.*

Getting Cordell to leave Janelle's side took a bit of doing. Chyna had to almost drag him from the room. He'd not said much, but Chyna felt a sudden emotional distance coming from him every time she'd tried to speak. When he would answer it would be a quick one-word response. *If I didn't know better, I'd think Cordell was angry with me. Maybe Janelle being here is my fault.*

Finally, after getting Janelle completely settled, Chyna and Cordell reluctantly left. There was plenty to see and hear as Cordell and Chyna rode along Kings Highway from the Downstate Medical Center. Loud music flowed freely, with both secular and religious vying for control. There were colorful hand-painted signs and drawings on homes urging folks to try the owner's skills claiming cheap labor at everything from African hair braiding to flat-tire fixes. At another time perhaps they'd have commented or even laughed at the changing Jewish neighborhood.

There were no neighborhood observations or comparisons that night. Cordell couldn't look at Chyna as the image of Janelle collapsing into his arms tugged at his heart.

Meanwhile, Chyna's thoughts had also returned to Janelle. In one day the chaos in their lives elevated. Chyna had gone from a recluse to fighting with the church board and now Janelle was hooked up to an IV.

Locked in their own thoughts, neither Chyna nor Cordell could wrap their minds around what had gone down in their lives.

Chyna's chin was propped up in the small of her

hand. Her jaw as set as her face gave way to small twitches. *Why didn't Janelle say something to me?* Chyna's face turned into a mask of scowls as she, again, silently berated herself for not having the answers for the nurse.

It hadn't been said aloud, but she recognized that the question regarding any history of breast cancer in her family could've meant but one thing. *Why didn't they just say it? They think Janelle might have breast cancer like our mother.*

Cordell's finger tapped with no particular rhythm on the steering wheel. Although unfamiliar with the route and refusing to ask for help from Chyna, he drove and prayed. For the past few months nothing seemed to make sense. Had God caused him to return into these women's lives just to observe their meltdown? Where was all his sound biblical advice concerning weathering storms and allowing God to try His people with fire? And with everything, at that moment that poured through his mind, what truly saddened him was that the only woman he'd ever truly loved now lay sick in a hospital bed.

Taking a quick glance in Chyna's direction offered no relief. She sat rigid in the passenger seat. Cordell was certain she'd retreated and gone to a place, mentally, to be alone. The look on her face read "do not disturb."

The silence in the car became deafening and yet, he couldn't discuss his feelings. He wanted—no, he needed— to hear something—anything. Yet, with the still-fresh image of Chyna entering a sex den, the same place where Grayson killed and committed suicide, caused him to take his eye off the road. He swerved and regained control quickly. "Sorry."

The apology was automatic. It wasn't what he'd wanted to say. But how could he possibly discuss his deep love for Janelle to Chyna, his ex-wife and Janelle's sister?

He could no more do that than reveal to Chyna his new-found information.

Cordell was in his own hell, and too many people were holding matches and vying to light the first fire.

Reaching the end of her driveway, Cordell took another look over at Chyna before shutting off the engine. "We're here." He finally announced before exiting the car. "Do you want to talk about Janelle later?" he asked. But she didn't answer.

Even when he went around the side of the car to help Chyna out, she still wouldn't speak. Any hope of her returning to the feisty and strong woman he'd once married appeared diminished, even though she'd shown a little of it earlier. He secretly hoped she wasn't having another meltdown. Now was not the time.

Less than thirty minutes later, after making sure Chyna was situated and okay with being alone, Cordell was again on the road back to his hotel. He'd needed a shower since before they'd rushed Janelle to the hospital. At that moment, a lot of water was needed to clear his head and clean his body.

Somewhat refreshed from the shower, Cordell ordered room service. While waiting he took the envelope from atop the coffee table and opened it. He felt guilty and intrusive, but since the church apparently was now blackmailing souls instead of saving them, he needed to protect Chyna. And if he knew what he was really dealing with then he could help her better.

Two minutes later he could feel his heart race, as he scanned every inch of the photo.

He'd seen enough fraudulent material from his days as a radio jock and even as a conference leader to know the photo was real and untouched. *But this isn't the Chyna I married. What was she thinking?*

An hour had passed since he'd found a magnifying glass to look over the photos again. The shots were a bit grainy, but there was no mistake. It was Chyna and she was apparently someplace where there was stripping going on. There was a half naked man just off to her side and next to him was a high backed wicker chair covered with some sort of decorations. *It must've been some type of party,* he thought.

And then Janelle came to mind. He was almost certain she hadn't seen the photograph because she'd passed out at the same time he'd closed the envelope. *I can't let Janelle know about this. She'd be devastated.*

He quickly put the envelope down and walked over to the window. He wasn't up to examining his returning feelings for Janelle; particularly since he was certain they'd never left. He knew it was a losing battle.

Looking out, he noticed a plane taking off from La-Guardia Airport. Initially since in the past several months he'd spent so much time in Brooklyn, he thought it was a good idea to stay close to an airport. It was not unusual for him to keep a hotel room handy by each airport. Now he wished he'd been able to stay closer to downtown Brooklyn, which was nearer to Janelle.

There's something happening with Janelle, physically and mentally. I can feel it.

Earlier, when he'd dropped Chyna off at her home he'd told her that he would look in on her. "I still have to prepare for the upcoming conference at New Hope. It's in a few days. You can attend it with me and it will make it easier for me to help you handle the board if they see we're close. I'd like to see how tough they'd be with a man."

He hadn't meant to offer, but he'd said it and couldn't

take it back. "If you don't want to and rather stay with Janelle, I'll certainly understand."

"Let me think about it." Chyna responded. "Too much is going on."

"Like I told you," Cordell said with measured words, "I truly do understand all you're facing."

Chyna had turned to face him and it was the one time she'd smiled since they'd returned from the hospital. "At least I don't have to worry about Sister Blackstone or those deacons from the board."

"Why not?"

"I forgot to tell you when I shared the other craziness they were dropping on me."

"Go ahead and tell me," Cordell said, "What could they have possibly done to make you suddenly smile?"

"I told those hypocrites that if they had any evidence of their accusations as far as me bringing more shame to the church when they wanted to go in a more holier direction, then they should show it to me."

"You told them that?"

"I most certainly did. I couldn't say anything to Janelle and it was only so much I could tell you. But that was a few days ago. Believe me, I'm not complaining, but since they've been so adamant in calling and threatening me, I figured if they had anything, I'd have seen it by now."

The weight of Cordell's guilt almost glued him to the sidewalk. Apparently, the church board members had met Chyna's challenge and he was holding their "proof."

"These women are taking over my life. I've got to re-focus. God's gonna work it out," Cordell murmured as he rose and took his briefcase from the closet. He was far behind in his research and reading. That was something he'd never allowed to happen before. Yet in reality what he really wanted to do was to confront Sister Blackstone since she seemed to be the proverbial stone in Chyna's spiritual shoe.

As much as he wanted to go over everything for the conference, he couldn't. There was too much on his mind, Janelle in the hospital hooked up to an IV, sick with what he didn't know. Of course, the images of Chyna's graphic and pornographic pictures were competing.

Chapter 23

Sister Blackstone lived in the Bed-Stuy area of Brooklyn, on Putnam Avenue. It was a neighborhood known for its beautiful rows of two- and three-story brownstones. It was also known that Sister Blackstone in all her rigidity and self-righteousness always stood guard at her front and side windows. Come rain or shine, she always looked out and butted in where she wasn't wanted.

It also seemed that the borough of Brooklyn, New York, was also blanketed with members from New Hope Assembly. Janelle's medical bracelet was hardly clamped around her wrist before the telephone in Sister Blackstone's small living room rang.

"Praise the Lord," she'd answered. It was the only greeting Sister Blackstone used. It was partially because she wanted to show she was always in "praise" mode, and partially to disarm any creditors or hawkish salespeople who'd called to harass her.

That time the call was from one of the choir members, a young man named Graham. He worked as an orderly in Downstate. "I wanted to let you know that First Lady's sister, Janelle Pierce, is up on the tenth floor. She's hooked up to all sorts of IVs and stuff." Graham gushed.

"I figured you'd want to know so you could place her name on the prayer list. Although praying for right now wouldn't be a bad thing. I'm sure First Lady might be feeling a little overwhelmed with Pastor Grayson being less than a year deceased and all . . ."

He continued with his explanations of how he saw things, hoping Sister Blackstone would be impressed with his spiritual growth.

Even after the young man hung up, he would never know how wrong he was. She'd hung up before he'd finished speaking not really caring about Janelle or her situation. And, since the First Lady had abruptly dismissed her earlier, she wasn't in the mood to be charitable toward her, either.

Sister Blackstone sat on a cushioned seat, looking out of her large bay window at the starless night. Before taking her seat at her post at the window, she'd been in the living room rereading Pastor Young's journal. She'd noticed nothing unusual going on in the neighborhood, so she'd returned to her living room to read. Sister Blackstone had barely begun to turn more pages when she was interrupted with a loud knock on her front door.

Sister Blackstone tiptoed softly to her door. She'd already dressed for bed in a long plaid flannel nightgown and a stocking cap fitted tightly on her head. It was too late to have visitors, although the time of night had little to do with her wanting any.

She managed to push aside the metal cover to the door's peephole.

"Open up, Sister Blackstone, I see you peeping out."

Brother DeWitt, she thought, *Should I let him in? What is he doing at my door?*

Without responding, Sister Blackstone opened a door just a few inches.

Cordell opened it the rest of the way before he barged inside. "Sorry to bother you. But we need to talk," Cordell apologized as he dismissed the annoyed look on her face.

He'd not known what to expect when he arrived. He waited for her to close the door behind him and looked around the room. Cordell was taken in by her mahogany princess writing desk. It was an expensive piece of furniture that looked completely out of place in her sparse living room.

While Cordell stood, seemingly admiring the piece of furniture, Sister Blackstone sat down and carefully placed the journal under a sofa pillow. She continued looking at him without an ounce of emotion but pounds of annoyance.

"Can I sit down?" Cordell asked, finally. He'd waited for her to offer, but it didn't seem she would.

Basking in her sense of power, Sister Blackstone finally pointed to one of the most uncomfortable seats in her living room. It was actually a wooden stool that earlier in the day had held an indoor philodendron pot.

"I guess you're here to discuss the First Lady?" Sister Blackstone said as she leaned forward. It was another power move she always used when needing to keep the upper hand. "I know you've spent quite a bit of time there with her and that sister of hers."

"I can't imagine that you'd think I wouldn't want to discuss *it*," Cordell said. His voice was steady despite trying to retain his balance on the uncomfortable stool. The fact that she hadn't fastened the top button to her ugly flannel gown was also a distraction. *Is there anywhere on her that isn't wrinkled?* he thought.

"I'm not going to pretend that I don't know to what extent you and the board have gone to in ousting the First Lady. I must say that for a church who claims it wants nothing but Holiness to abide, it uses some pretty low and unholy methods to get there."

"I'm not apologizing nor am I gonna sit here in my own living room and pretend I don't know what you're talking about. It's apparent that the disgraced Sister Young has shared more than a bed and a baby with you."

"Excuse me."

"I'll get to your relationship with her sister later. But since you felt the need to barge into my home to defend what's indefensible, let's get down to it."

"Sure," he said angrily, "Why not get down to it. Particularly since you seem to think that you know so much about my relationship with the two Pierce sisters."

Sister Blackstone inched her body forward just enough to make her appear larger than she was. "Where do you want to start?"

"The authenticity of what you sent through UPS. I am still at a loss as to why you felt the need to do this," he added as he retrieved the envelope from an inside coat pocket.

"Whatever," Sister Blackstone replied without emotion, "before I answer is there anything more you need butt in about?"

As Cordell rattled off his list of concerns and conclusions, Sister Blackstone folded her hands and kept her eyes trained upon him.

It appeared she was listening, intently, to every word Cordell spoke. She wasn't. Her mind was on Reverend Young.

If what Pastor Young wrote in his journal was true, then there was a lot more improprieties going on than the board knew. The more she'd read, the lower her opinion of Minister DeWitt sunk.

"What do you think of the First Lady's sister, Janelle?" Sister Blackstone said, suddenly. Whether her question had anything to do with what he'd been saying didn't matter. Her question had more to do with the revelation of him previously being with Janelle, whom she'd never liked or ever could, than anything. And she could care less about Chyna losing a baby. What kind of mother would she have been anyhow?

"Whatever friendship I had with Chyna and Janelle has nothing to do with the underhanded things the church board is trying to use on Chyna."

"You call it friendship. According to what I know, and, trust me, you'd be surprised at what I know," Sister Blackstone hissed, "whatever we're doing to make sure our church takes advantage of bringing it back to its former standing before the Reverend Young crushed our reputation, brick by brick, is nothing compared to what you did to those women."

"What in the hell are you talking about?" Cordell hadn't meant to speak that way, but he had.

"Glad you mentioned hell. That's exactly where you, Chyna, and that slut of a sister of hers belong."

Cordell and Sister Blackstone went round and around, with neither giving an inch. They'd assigned blame and refused to accept responsibility for anything. Their meeting was a total waste of time.

Cordell stormed out the door pretty much in the same foul mood he'd arrived in.

"Ain't none of y'all getting away with nothing." Sister Blackstone promised, "Y'all ain't worth the precious dirt it took to create ya."

In Sister Blackstone's opinionated world, God wasn't picky enough when it came to judging.

Chapter 24

Within the next two weeks Janelle began to improve. During that entire time Chyna was practically glued to Janelle's bedside and gave little thought to her own situation with the church.

She alternated between offering sisterly love and peppering Janelle with questions. "We're supposed to look after each other," Chyna chastised. "You don't have to be so doggone stubborn. I could've helped to take care of you."

During one of Chyna's visits she finally broke through to Janelle. Chyna's constant harassment and a little help from megadoses of a strong painkiller, Percocet, did the trick. The medication turned into Janelle's truth serum.

Alternately between fighting drowsiness while trying to still maintain her position of big sister, Janelle explained. "It's been about six months since I noticed a little leakage and a burning sensation. I didn't wanna bother you," Janelle stated while trying to muffle a laugh.

"Six months!" Chyna shot back. She stopped and clasped her hands as if doing so would also give her more patience or keep her from slapping her sister.

"I should've known these perky twins would revolt one day." Janelle stopped and cupped one of her bandaged breasts. "They did a couple of biopsies and took a little fluid out, but you and I both know that they're just too perfect to be cancerous."

Janelle suddenly leaned forward forcing herself to smile. She pointed her finger at Chyna and added, "And I know that's the case, despite what you're probably thinking. It's most likely a mild infection." Falling back, Janelle's head almost missed her pillow as she grimaced in pain.

"Janelle, just stop it," Chyna threatened, unimpressed by Janelle's false bravado. "If you don't get it together, I'll call the church and tell them to send over a prayer posse."

The threat of a visit from a bunch of old prayer warriors did for Janelle what all the antibiotics, fine-needle aspiration biopsy and other remedies didn't—it caused her color to return, the pain to diminish, and, later, a cooperation with the doctors quite unbecoming her stubborn trait.

Finally released and armed with a bag full of prescription medication, Janelle's trip back to Chyna's house was for the most part uneventful. She was truly grateful to have Chyna pick her up, but Janelle had hoped that Cordell would've been there, too.

"Just in case you're wondering," Chyna teased, "I had to talk Cordell out of coming. He's been preoccupied with us and not handling his conference business."

"What are you talking about?" Janelle asked. She

tried to make her question sound as matter-of-fact as possible. More like she only responded because it was polite to do so.

"He'd postponed the conference at New Hope for as long as he could, it's scheduled to begin, hopefully, next week."

"I see," Janelle interrupted. She really didn't want to hear anything about church, not even if it included Cordell. She hadn't quite figured out how she'd ever be able to fit into that part of his world.

"He needed to prepare," Chyna said and added, "I knew you'd understand."

"I see." It was Janelle's only response.

"But he did cook his famous homemade chicken noodle soup. He sent over a big container of it and told me not to touch it."

"Why not?" Janelle asked warily. "It's not like we both don't know that he could cook almost as good as he could do his radio disc jockey thing."

Janelle hadn't meant to say anything that would fuel the awkwardness that accompanied any discussion they'd have about Cordell, but she had.

Dismissing Janelle's obvious meaning, Chyna said with a pretend sadness, "He told me not to take one spoon full. He said it was only for you to taste and enjoy."

I wish I could put him in a pot to taste and enjoy. Janelle smiled and again shifted her head on the car's neck rest.

Much like the ride Chyna had taken when she'd returned home with Cordell when Janelle was first admitted, this ride was done in silence.

Janelle seemed to enjoy the buzz of street activity as though seeing it for the first time. Two weeks ago she wasn't certain she'd live out the day she was admitted. A wave of nausea swept over her, reminding her that not a lot had changed.

After arriving home and seeing that Janelle was made comfortable in her old bedroom, Chyna called Cordell to let him know that the pickup was uneventful. "I told you I could do it alone," Chyna said, cheerfully, "Now finish doing whatever you're doing. You can visit Janelle later."

From the small table beside her bed Janelle eased the telephone receiver off its hook and hit the mute button. It was painful trying to raise her arm, but she was determined to listen. From what she could gather, Cordell would stop by later.

With that Janelle took one of her painkillers to fight the onset of the tightness in her breasts. She needed to be fresh and appealing for the visit.

Down the hall Chyna buzzed around the kitchen preparing something light for Janelle. It seemed that having her sister return home from the hospital as quickly as she had resurrected a peace and a hope Chyna thought was lost, or that Grayson had stolen.

Chyna rummaged through cabinets to see what was available, since she'd not really shopped in a while. It took another moment before she remembered Cordell's soup for Janelle was in the refrigerator.

Smiling, she found herself humming one of the praise songs she loved, "He's an On Time God." Just repeating the words seemed to add a little zip to her step along with a smile.

Her slow road back to redemption had begun during the time Janelle was hospitalized. To her amazement and surprise Chyna had begun to pray again. She'd whisper a word of praise, here and there, and never asked for anything. The praises that started to roll off her tongue began while she performed mundane tasks: tighten the corner of a bedsheet and mutter, "thank you, Father," or she'd get up in the middle of the night and murmur, "thank you, Lord."

"Heal her, please Lord," Chyna persistently prayed. "I'll live and work for You, Lord." Her love for her sister was never clearer and more urgent than at the thought of losing her.

Chyna knew better than to make promises to God that she probably couldn't or wouldn't keep, but she did it. And she'd done it hoping that at that time she could keep her word.

While Chyna bustled around the kitchen Janelle had fallen asleep in her bedroom, but the nap was short.

The coolness of the bedsheets embraced Janelle. For a moment the comfort and the medication held her on the verge of consciousness. "Hmmmm—" She moaned through the haze, which momentarily captured her as she heard Chyna moving about down in the kitchen. But it was the smell of something cooking that finally woke her.

"What in the world is that woman doing now?" She was alone in her room but asked the question anyhow.

At some other time Janelle would've laughed and teased Chyna for acting so domesticated and ready to serve. Instead, an image of Cordell and Chyna rushed to her mind. Suddenly she propped up on her pillow and wondered how much time Chyna and Cordell had spent together while she was hospitalized.

Janelle wrestled with the image embedded in jealousy. *This is so stupid.* Denying it was useless, because it was still there slowly claiming space in her head and she had to head it off.

Negative thoughts were not what Janelle needed. It was shallow bravado she'd used to discuss her illness with Chyna, "I'm just worn down and anemic." She'd lied to the only person she'd die for despite the fact that she knew she was the one now dying.

"Cancer," Janelle suddenly blurted angrily. "The Big C, the body's cancellator." It was already in its second stage and the last thing she needed was to be distracted by her jealousy if she were to beat it.

Janelle thought she'd heard footsteps near her door and before she could move an inch her bedroom door opened.

"Here's lunch," Chyna announced. She'd bounced into the room balancing a large tray and a small stack of fashion magazines. "I warmed this soup for you and brought you something to read."

"Thank you," Janelle replied, dryly. Without changing her expression she carefully balanced the tray on her lap and added, "You look a mess. Shouldn't you change clothes or fix up before some of those churchy folks drop by unannounced to harass you again? Or Cordell might stop by unannounced, too?" she added, slowly. Keeping her jealousy in check wasn't easy.

Between the times Chyna hung up from speaking with Cordell and fixing lunch for Janelle, more company, the uninvited kind, dropped by. That time it was Deacons Athens and Pillar. Apparently Janelle had overheard them.

"I don't have time to discuss church reformation or anything else." Chyna told them, "Come by at some other time and while you're at it," she added, "Next time do what Jesus would do, please call."

"You're not acting like a true Christian," Janelle

heard one of the church folks snap. They didn't seem too pleased to be dismissed. And, of course, had perhaps one of them offered prayer Chyna might've acted differently.

Chyna saw the pensive look upon Janelle's face. That wasn't a good sign. "Don't worry about them," Chyna scolded, as she fluffed Janelle's top pillow, "You eat your soup." She was fighting hard to keep up appearances of being in charge.

Janelle laid her head back, welcoming the coolness of the newly fluffed pillow. Her eyes followed Chyna as the tinny sound of her spoon scraped the bottom of the bowl as she stirred. "Well, are you going to fix yourself up or what?" Janelle made a painful effort to turn toward Chyna. "Ouch!" Janelle blurted as she dropped the spoon onto the tray.

The back of Janelle's hand began to redden as she shook it trying to cool it off. It wouldn't have happened if she'd not tried to eat the soup without looking at the bowl. She was too busy focusing on any effect her words might've had on Chyna.

When Janelle didn't get the response she wanted from Chyna, she inexplicably blurted, "Okay, enough with the pretense. I've got breast cancer."

If Chyna was shocked, she didn't show it. Instead, she walked over and gently sat on the edge of Janelle's bed. "I know," Chyna said softly, "I know."

"How do you know?" Janelle asked. She was confused. Everything she'd said and done was to keep her condition a secret.

"I remember mama," Chyna confided, "I remember how mama was when she had it."

"Mama died," Janelle replied shoving away the tray and causing everything to spill on the bed covers as she begun to weep.

Chapter 25

Miles away from Chyna's posh neighborhood and on the other side of town, where the air was almost stifling in her living room, Sister Blackstone sat stone-faced. Although each time she'd said it was the last, after hissing and threatening Cordell into returning several times to her home, she'd finally determined it was.

Cordell had taken his time that afternoon in coming to see Sister Blackstone. He was more than a few hours late.

They'd dispensed with the small talk and Christian pleasantries.

Several minutes later, her composure came apart. With her hands folded, her lips now tightened into a scowl, Sister Blackstone spewed forth the venom she'd harbored.

If Cordell thought he'd heard it all before, he was wrong.

"I've got copies of her doing worse," Sister Blackstone threatened. "If Sister Young won't go along with our reforms or completely step down I'll see that those

trashy photos are shown. You've only seen the one of her
inside the Sweet Bush party with her eyes looking like
she was taking drugs. I've got others of her doing un-
thinkable acts, elsewhere." Her brow furrowed as she
tried to maintain the upper hand with her empty threat
and lies. She was certain God would forgive her. After all,
she was all about doing His business the best way she
knew how.

Cordell countered trying to keep the upper hand.
"That's the place where your so-called beloved pastor
killed people and committed suicide. You think it's wise
to remind the congregation and the whole of Brooklyn
about that?"

It was the first time she'd intimated that there were
other women involved. He'd not been prepared for that.

"Everyone knows that treacherous woman drove him
to do whatever it was that he done. And everybody knows
he didn't commit suicide. He'd go to hell for that."

"And now you're God's judge and jury? Are you that
evil?" Cordell knew she was.

She continued mumbling, her words becoming erratic
as she spoke. "He was a good man. All three were . . ."

"Three, what three are you talking about?" Cordell
wasn't sure if he'd heard right.

Ignoring his question she shot forward in her seat. It
was an action to add power to her words. "You call it evil.
I call it doing God's business."

Cordell rose slowly. This wasn't his house and under
normal circumstances, he'd show respect. This wasn't
normal.

"I've seen all kinds of fake Christians—" Cordell
said, cutting off his words as he came off the stool.

"Who are you calling a fake?"

"A fake, a fraud, that's what you are," Cordell repeated. "Trying to make God's house into what you think

it should be; based upon what? Your custom-made idea of church is nowhere near where God wants His people."

"You would know that how?" In a show of defiance, Sister Blackstone's hands clamped tight on her Bible.

"Read that book!" Cordell could almost feel the heat coming off his forehead, he was just that angry. "Read the book of Hebrews, Corinthians, and see what the Word says about your contempt and judgment!"

The sniping continued and the accusations flew. Even as he spoke and his anger rose, Cordell's conscience urged him to remember all the lessons he'd taught to caution others when it came to rightly divining God's word.

Almost toe-to-toe they argued and neither would change the others' mind.

Cordell finally had enough and rushed to grab his coat, knocking over a picture of what at a quick glance he figured was a younger Eartha Blackstone. Angered, he almost broke the picture placing it back. There was no doubt left as to what she was prepared to do.

Chapter 26

For the next several weeks after Janelle received her diagnosis of breast cancer and finally shared it, Cordell's world was divided. He'd constantly phoned Chyna to get updates on Janelle and sought God as to what he should do about Chyna.

"Do you want to speak with Janelle?" Chyna would eventually ask, before they hung up.

"Perhaps at some other time; things are hectic." He'd always pretend to either be going or coming from somewhere that did not allow him to drop by. He knew his actions probably caused some confusion to Janelle.

After Sister Blackstone's insinuation that there were other photographs, more explicit ones, than just what he'd seen, he couldn't face Chyna. And that was his dilemma. Cordell was praying for God to help him and lying to Chyna at the same time.

Cordell never spoke directly to Janelle. He couldn't trust that Janelle wouldn't pick up on his distant demeanor if he faced her. At that time, he was the very thing he'd taught against. He was a coward. He felt guilty and somewhat angry. A woman he loved so dearly was facing a possible death sentence and he was too much of a coward to get beyond what he was hiding from Chyna.

If Cordell's feelings were inconsistent, they paled in comparison to Janelle's emotional journey.

Janelle struggled, too. She'd struggled as she constantly looked in the mirror. She fought tears and fears as she allowed images of a body possibly without breasts to invade her mind.

She remembered the words from her oncologist from her last visit. "We are here to make sure that every ounce of medical and emotional support is available to you."

The oncologist, a woman named Dr. Ruthee-Lu Bayer, who had survived her own bout with breast cancer, promised as she took Janelle's hand. "I know what you're going through. You have my cellular service number; use it whenever you feel the need."

At first, Janelle insisted upon speaking with her doctor alone. When she was satisfied her medical business would remain private, that was when she'd allowed Chyna to join in the discussion. "If there's anything more than what Chyna already knows, it will be my decision to tell," Janelle threatened.

"How are you feeling?" Chyna entered Janelle's bedroom without a sound. "You may not feel like eating, but you really should."

Janelle said nothing as she stood facing a wall mirror. Instead, she pointed to the nightstand where Chyna could place the tray. "Just leave it."

Chyna by that time knew that it was nothing personal. Janelle was in crisis. They both were.

Chyna, as become her custom, opened the drapes to allow the sunshine to bring a little light and warmth into

the coldness. Just as she turned to leave, Janelle's words
stopped her cold in her tracks.

"So tell me something," Janelle ordered. She quickly
tied the satin belt holding her purple robe in place as she
walked back from the mirror toward her bed.

Janelle turned back the top sheet before she continued. "I heard you praying last night while you were on the
telephone," Janelle said in what seemed like an accusatory
manner. "It was late, at least about eleven o'clock. Is that
what you and Cordell do now when you chat late at night,
pray?"

Chyna measured her response. There was something
she'd noticed, days ago, about Janelle's mood swings. She
assumed it had something to do with the sudden barrage
of the chemo and the radiation intravenous cocktails.
Janelle's weakness from the treatment was expected, but
her emotions were becoming more erratic, particularly
since Chyna knew she hadn't been on the telephone praying with anyone. Praying alone in her room, yes, she'd
done that. *Why would she think I was praying with
Cordell? What does he have to do with me?*

Janelle didn't care if her food grew cold. She wasn't
hungry anyway. She wanted to stand beside the bed for a
moment more to confront Chyna, but her legs felt like
two pieces of string, her mouth was like cotton, and her
stomach churned. The light coming from the bedside
lamp began to hurt her eyes. "Whatever——," Janelle whispered.

Readjusting the pink silk scarf she wore to cover her
unkempt and thinning hair, Janelle got in the bed. She
laid her head back on the pillow. Without saying another
word, she then turned her head away, facing the window.
It was a signal she no longer wanted company.

It was impossible for Chyna to misunderstand Janelle's snub. Yet, she decided that in comparison to what her sister faced, it was nothing.

"I'll come back later for the tray," Chyna said, softly backing away toward the door. And then for some unknown reason, her voice laced with compassion, she added, "I have been praying a little more lately. But I prayed alone last night. Cordell has called, but he's not been by in the past couple of weeks."

Because Chyna was trying to gather her thoughts and convey her love and sympathy without patronizing Janelle, she'd not seen what Janelle had.

And Janelle hadn't heard anything Chyna said. Her focus was on the man coming up the walkway. *Cordell. Chyna said he hadn't visited in two weeks. She's such a liar.*

Janelle turned around and caught a glimpse of Chyna leaving the room and as had became her habit, she began to tear up at the thought of their betrayal. *Of course, they weren't praying on the telephone. Cordell's been sneaking in . . .*

Janelle tried to muffle her whimper by burrowing her head in her pillow. At that moment she'd almost hoped for death's visit because deep down she knew that the closeness between the two people she loved most was hurting her. Despite the promise she'd made to herself to do what was best for her to beat the cancer, her jealousy grew faster than the cancer. That defeating emotion trumped any of the agonizing pain felt in her breast.

Janelle's strength was sapped. Yet she somehow managed to get out of the bed. She tugged and pulled at the bed until it was bare, with the sheets and blankets piled on the floor.

Inching toward the recliner, Janelle fought to remain standing as she tried to kick the pile of bedding out of her way. Gently, she lowered her body onto the cushion while she glared over at the naked bed.

"I can almost smell them," Janelle whispered. "I'm such a fool." She cradled her head in her hands and wept. "First Lady, the hell she is. She's been sinning in my bed."

Chapter 27

The incoming May spring weather was unusually warm outside New Hope Assembly church on Friday's young people's night. The lack of vehicles in the church's parking lot didn't mean the church wasn't packed, because it was; and those young folks were not happy.

"Why can't we get him to speak?" The question was repeated during the last two meetings held between the church board and the young adults' auxiliary. "We want someone who connects to the young people in this church."

"Amen." The voice seemed very tinny despite coming from one of the larger of the teenage men in the room.

"That's right," another one of the young ladies agreed. "Everything we want to do since Pastor Young passed away the board always shuts down."

"Believe that," said another one of the young men. "I ain't had nothing to do but get in trouble before I came here. Now ya'll wanna take away any chance of us young people coming together to praise God instead of robbing somebody."

"I pay tithes, too." One of the other young men shot forward. Even though he tried to keep his words respectful, it wasn't easy.

"We can't have a Christian comedy night, we can't have a bowling night, we can't even have young peoples fellowship anymore, and I've been coming here since birth. I know that was long before Reverend Grayson came."

"Listen up real good, young people, and especially you, Brother Brooks. I know you've been here probably longer than most of these young people and we don't need you or these others to remind us of what was done before Reverend Grayson."

Deacon Athens rose and shut one of the windows hard as though the move signaled what he would do if he wasn't obeyed. He'd shut it down.

"It is up to this board to approve anyone espousing the Word of God from this church's pulpit," Deacon Athens continued. Somehow he kept appointing himself as the spokesman despite the presence of the other board members. "We keep the order and ordinances of this church," he said harshly before remembering, he'd just snuffed out a cigarette before entering the church. In one quick move he covered his mouth as he spoke. He was mindful that the young adults would smell the smoke on his breath. That might diminish his piousness.

Sister Blackstone sat a short distance away and observed Deacon Athens. *What a hypocrite.* Other times she'd try to show patience with him, but it was getting harder each time. So she turned her head while he got all preachy with the young people and started to read the different plaques on the wall. But even doing that couldn't make her feel comfortable.

Although he wouldn't say anything directly to her,

his smirk throughout the years at New Hope Assembly always kept her in check because she knew he knew something about some of her not-so-holy deeds. She just didn't know how much and which ones.

After Sister Young, I'm coming after you. Sister Blackstone's practiced stony-faced demeanor hid her thoughts as she retrained her eyes upon Deacon Athens and several of the other spineless board members.

Sister Blackstone continued to watch, determined not to butt in unless it appeared the board would give in and allow Cordell DeWitt access to *her* pulpit. The thought of her last conversation with the young Cordell popped into her mind. She'd not received a definite response from him, even with him thinking she held more debasing photos of Chyna. Yet she was also pleased that he'd not said anything about the photograph he'd knocked over. She was certain had he been more observant he'd have seen the resemblance between her, as a young woman, and Janelle.

Sister Blackstone noticed their common and yet uncanny resemblance and character from the moment she'd laid eyes on Janelle a while back. The Youngs had barely been installed as Pastor and First Lady when Janelle showed up at one of the church functions. Friends and family day was a day of celebration and hope, and Janelle spoiled it.

"Y'all know that's real wine served at that communion, right? And those wafer things are loaded with calories?" Janelle obviously had been drinking and her mouth lit a fire every time she'd opened it. And then Janelle-the-fraud had the nerve to say grace before she ate.

Sister Blackstone took offense at the disgraceful accusation of the church's Communion practice and instantly disliked Janelle. She had a good reason to continue to hate

Janelle. Janelle's flirty, smug, and conceited ways were a constant reminder to Sister Blackstone that she, too, was once an unrepentant and adulterous Christian.

However, unlike most Christians, Sister Blackstone didn't forgive and she certainly didn't forget. Her religious beliefs resembled a Rubik's Cube and were just as complicated.

Yet, in Sister Blackstone's mind, she, unlike Janelle, had finally come around to repenting. Now she was about doing God's work as she imagined He'd want it done.

The debate in the room continued and despite trying to dismiss bad memories once more, Sister Blackstone's mood grew darker. She strained to keep tears from flowing as her attention was drawn to an inscription on one of the several wall plaques.

Presented to New Hope Assembly and the Reverend Grayson Young; the 1998 Grammys Spoken Word Award Album of the Year, Out of Egypt.

That album sold more than two million copies and thrust New Hope Assembly into the limelight. Along with the fame came a change, a change Sister Blackstone and the church board didn't like and weren't prepared for.

But what could the board do? The youth and young adult membership grew tremendously fast. They had to have two morning services because it seemed the entire neighborhood started attending. Everyone wanted to hear and be near the good-looking preacher. One who could skillfully and rhythmically, orate the word well enough to get a Grammy.

Of course, the financial increase was welcomed and they'd earned back every penny spent in producing the album. Then there was the Reverend Young, who'd remind them, constantly, about their refusal to initially get involved in something so worldly, so why should it be the

church that got the greater reward when it came to settling accounts?

According to the board's observation, their church
started backsliding as more secular things were added
and accepted. The fellowship hall was turned into "gospel
supper club," and the youth started having bowling and
skating parties. And when the church started bringing
laughter through the doors with appearances by Brotha
Smitty from Manhattan, New York, and Miss Vickie out
of Dallas, that ripped a hole in the board's collective
drawers. As far as the old bulwarks of the church were
concerned and despite what the Bible taught, laughter in
the church, no matter how holy the subject matter was not
acceptable. It was a downright disgrace and contempt for
the Cross.

Despite it all, the Reverend was having his way and
the church was going to pay for it. The old order was
shoved aside for a new one. The Reverend was loved and
the First Lady Chyna was simply adored.

The Reverend was now dead and it was up to Sister
Blackstone and some of the others to kill Chyna's reputation if she wouldn't leave New Hope. The offer to the
First Lady to participate in reforming the church was off
the table in Sister Blackstone's mind. She was convinced
that every time Sister Young showed up in a church hat,
bad memories and disgrace would attend with her.

"Do you have anything to add, Sister Blackstone?"
One of the other board members asked in deference to her
lack of participation.

"Not at this time," she answered. The interruption
was welcomed as she was about to veer off the path she'd
taken that day. There was a purpose to her attending the
meeting.

She'd done something a little different that day. She'd

arrived at the church wearing her white lace communion gloves, the pair she used when separating herself from the other pastor's aid committee members on communion day. So with her hands folded as though in prayer, and with the chaos in the room heightening, she watched knowing that her long-held view of what God wanted for New Hope would certainly happen. It would all come together under her watch.

Sister Blackstone held a winning hand that would whip all the board members except perhaps Deacon Athens and Deacon Pillar into submission. They'd lean her way and they'd back her when she told them she was prepared to out Sister Young, their precious First Lady.

Chapter 28

Cordell took his time walking up the pathway to Chyna's front door, hugging the envelope close to his chest was like plunging a dagger into his own heart. In the two months since he'd learned about the possibility of evidence of Chyna's supposed extracurricular activities, he felt he'd aged quickly. There were bags under his eyes and earlier when he shaved he noticed his shoulders appeared to have slumped over.

Despite the many debates he'd mentally held he knew there was but one way to handle things, or at least he hoped so. With several days of fasting behind him and the constant praying, he still hadn't received a word from God.

He was reminded of a sermon he'd heard by a well-known preacher back in California. "You had to go through it," the man preached. "If you didn't you'd just keep trying to avoid it, you'd try and go around it and you wouldn't learn a thing."

"You had to go through it," he echoed as he realized the trial of faith was just as much for him as it was for

Chyna and even Janelle. He took a moment to stop and embrace the sun's warmth. With a new resolve he continued up the walkway to her front door. "What a mess." Cordell knew there was no stopping Sister Blackstone, but he could warn Chyna of the coming storm.

Janelle turned away from the window. She was nauseous, but she fought it. Nonchalantly, she cupped one breast and quickly caught a glimpse of Cordell as he turned the corner of the house.

She grimaced as the thought of a mastectomy entered her mind. She swung her head in denial. *No man wants a woman without breasts!* Janelle began to squeeze her hands around the breast, causing the discoloration from the biopsy to deepen. Despite the searing pain and the greenish-colored liquid leaking from the nipple, she continued squeezing until the sight of her fingerprints embedded in her flesh stopped her cold. *Oh God, what is wrong with me?*

As Janelle suffered and fought the demons of her disease, down the hall Chyna sought a moment of peace inside the bathroom. Chyna looked at her reflection in the bathroom mirror. Frowning, she used a wet washcloth to dab at her face. She'd lost weight and the gauntness made her look much older than she was.

The past public humiliation still left invisible scars and the media, both print and television, for several weeks after Grayson's death, seemed to delight in picking at her mental scabs.

True, the police had the word of the bouncer at the Sweet Bush, who claimed to know firsthand what'd happened, but nothing seemed resolved. She was also bothered by the way the media continued to revisit the crime from time to time. They'd cough up sensationalized spins that lately turned into small hiccups when the news cycle was slow. As if on cue, her stomach let out a small growl.

It was a reminder surely because she couldn't remember the last time she'd eaten a full meal despite how often she'd cooked something for Janelle.

Thinking that perhaps she needed to go into the kitchen and try to fix something, her plans were interrupted. Instead, hearing the doorbell brought Chyna rushing from the bathroom. If Janelle was sleeping, she didn't want her to wake up.

"Cordell, I'm surprised to see you." Chyna said softly as he stepped through the door. She'd chastised him about acting like a landlord. They compromised and he agreed to ring the bell before entering.

Chyna clutched her robe. She hadn't expected company and it was unfastened, revealing a pink brassiere and way too much cleavage. It was mid afternoon and she still had not dressed.

Cordell entered, giving Chyna a quick peck on her cheek, acting as though he'd not seen even more than when they were married.

However, Janelle had seen more than she'd care to. She'd gotten up expecting Cordell to ring the doorbell after he'd disappeared around the corner of the house. Not knowing her sister had been in the hallway bathroom, she'd watched Chyna race to the door with her robe billowing out behind her. *I knew Chyna was lying. Look at her. Whore! She can't even close her robe she wants him so bad.*

Janelle again gave in to her delusions. She quickly and silently closed the bedroom door. She snatched away the scarf she'd so carefully tied about her hair, causing strands to fall like snowflakes onto her shoulders.

In an act of pure determination and defiance Janelle resisted the pain and allowed her back to straighten. The sprinkling of fallen hairs caught her attention, but she remained resolute. She then pursed her lips and snatched a lip-liner pencil from among several above the basin and began to paint around her lips. She repeated the lip lines; not one upon the other, but each circling the other. "Chyna don't get him without a fight," Janelle hissed. "If God don't punish that sinner, then I will!"

Because of the unpredictable and pent-up jealousy, the progressive chemotherapy and the radiation treatments, and the multidrug cocktails, Janelle was losing her hair and her mind, one just as fast as the other.

Suddenly Janelle stopped ranting. Her head was held high and her chin angled with the air of someone who'd just won a beauty contest. She dropped her head slightly and smiled at her reflection. Janelle had applied a brownish-colored lip-liner in a fashion that made it look as though stitches had been sewn around her mouth. Her eyes were devoid of makeup and the whites of her eyes looked almost gray. She still had not retied her scarf, allowing tousled patches of baldness and thinning hair to appear. She thought she looked fabulous. "Chyna wished she looked this good," Janelle whispered. Her whisper was followed by a quick wince, but she decided not to take her pain medication. She needed to be sober for her lover.

Down the hallway, Cordell and Chyna stood in the living room.

"I'm sorry I didn't call first," Cordell said, as he absent-mindedly fingered the envelope. "I don't have a lot of time, but we need to talk."

"Why do so many folks want to talk?" Chyna asked. She really hadn't meant to say out loud what she'd thought. She pointed to the sofa. "Have a seat."

"Perhaps I should come back if you're expecting company," Cordell said, as he hesitated to sit. "I can just visit Janelle, if you don't mind, for a few moments and then I'll leave."

"There's no need for that." That time Chyna gently

took him by one of his elbows and led him to the sofa. "Sister Blackstone called a little while ago. I'm sure it's just some leftover church business." Chyna gave Cordell a wink, knowing he'd understand her real meaning.

Chyna would've continued speaking, but she noticed a brief scowl on Cordell's face at the mention of Sister Blackstone. Had the old woman planted herself on his bad side as she'd done with most others?

"Ahem," Janelle said, coarsely. "I see we have company." She was leaning on the hallway wall inching the last few feet into the living room.

Janelle dismissed the shocked looks on Chyna and Cordell's faces for guilt. A sardonic smile flashed across Janelle's face and then quickly disappeared. Without giving a hint to what she was truly thinking and feeling, she plopped onto the nearby love seat.

My God! Cordell thought as he took in every inch of the woman he'd loved for so long. Never in his wildest imagination would he think she could look this bad. *What has this cancer done to her?*

It took every ounce of willpower not to run to her and just hold her. He'd counseled enough to know and see the signs of how powerful and healing acts of love could be.

Why won't he come to me? Janelle thought before turning to Chyna. Her eyes blazed a hole through Chyna as Chyna stood shocked. "Chyna," Janelle finally said, "I've been calling you from the bedroom for quite some time. I guess you couldn't hear me."

Chyna imagined her mouth speaking. She couldn't say a word.

Coming to Chyna's rescue, as well as his own, Cordell spoke up quickly, "Janelle, I stopped by without calling you. I hope it is okay." His words weren't nearly as direct as the penetrating look he gave her.

Chyna finally spoke up. "I'll leave you two alone.
I've got a load of laundry in the machine."

She didn't, but she could think of nothing else.

Janelle listened, almost bemused, to Chyna's childish
excuse to leave. She waited until Chyna was completely
gone before she started to say something. Just as she
started to move her lips, the metallic taste from her medicines, along with a dry, cottony sensation attacked her
mouth. Those symptoms seemed to always appear when
least wanted—as though they ever were wanted. Saying
nothing, she extended one hand toward Cordell, indicating he should come nearer.

Without thinking, Cordell placed the envelope on the
coffee table and walked slowly to where Janelle sat. Despite trying not to stare, he couldn't move his eyes away
from the cracked, dry skin hanging almost lifeless off
Janelle's wrist. *She's wasting away.*

"I am truly sorry for not coming around," Cordell
said, as he maneuvered his way beside her, trying not to
crowd her space. "I did call as often as I could," he added
hoping it would soften whatever mood she was in.

"I know," Janelle finally said as she purposefully slid
closer to him. *He can't even stand to be near me.*

Janelle probably would've held on to her anger
longer if she hadn't seen the sadness in Cordell's eyes.
For some reason she didn't see it as pity. She saw it for
what she'd longed it to be for so many years, caring.
Janelle, for that one moment saw Cordell truly did care
for her. And, for that she was grateful.

He hadn't meant to do it, but Cordell took one of
Janelle's hands. Using his free hand, he swept away a tear
on his face. He'd hoped she hadn't seen it. Since returning
to New York and coming back into Chyna and Janelle's
lives, he'd learned just as much about himself as he had
about the sisters.

"Janelle." Cordell said her name with such softness that he wasn't at all sure she heard him, so he repeated it, "Janelle."

Janelle fought a sudden wave of nausea. The way he'd just said her name. He was so careful and with more tenderness than she'd experienced in quite some time. His show of affection caused alarm, because at the same time she'd felt that foreign tenderness she longed for since he'd left her years ago, she'd also looked over and caught a glimpse of her reflection in the wall mirror that hung over the sofa. It was sobering.

With strength found deep within, Janelle yanked her hand from Cordell's. Instead of making one of her usual awkward attempts at standing, she propelled herself off the love seat and fled the living room.

Cordell couldn't get it together. *What did I do now?*

Chapter 29

Despite the mental storm brewing and swirling in the minds inside Chyna's home, outside that afternoon, the sun shone at its brightest.

Yet sunshine had to take a backseat, as usual, when inside the New Hope Assembly Church's study room Deacons Athens and Pillar and Sister Blackstone met, again, in secret with two of the other board members. The two other board members were both two months older than dirt; one couldn't hold a thought and the other couldn't hold his water.

They'd already gone through their normal back-and-forth schemes and personality attacks. They did it in darkness that thwarted any attempt by the light of Jesus to enter.

It was Sister Blackstone that time who sat behind the large pastor's desk fuming. She'd thought she would have more power if she suggested taking the two attending board members along when she planned to confront Chyna.

She'd arrived at their present meeting with her Bible

in one hand and the journal in her other. She was singing, off key, at the top of her lungs, "Power, Holy Ghost Power."

Deacon Athens had already briefed the other two board members about the photos.

"Oh, no," one of the board members named Lucius protested. "I'll not have anything to do with that. I thought we were going about the business of restoration with decency and order."

"You can count me out, too." The other man, Adam, who just happened to be the first man's younger brother, followed suit.

The look of shock and disgust upon the brothers' faces might've caused any other Christian to rethink what they were doing. But these were New Hope Assembly's board members. Thinking wasn't on the menu.

Sister Blackstone didn't protest or acknowledge the brothers' disappointment. Instead, she hummed a little more of her song, "Power, Power, Holy Ghost Power," and said with authority, "Y'all better get ready, get ready, hallelujah! Get ready . . . I'm about to bind up the devil in here."

"Well, you just make sure you brought enough rope to start binding up them demons you carry around," the older of the two brothers barked. "Come on, Adam," he then ordered. "They've lost their minds."

The brothers rose quickly and left, lest the devil make them change their minds.

"They aren't fit for God's army," Sister Blackstone said to the shocked expressions on Deacons Athens and Pillar's faces. "God don't need no unmarried, sissified, wimps."

"Eartha Blackstone," Deacon Athens barked, "You gotta lot of nerve. You ain't ever been married, either. Does that make you a sissy?"

"She can't be a sissy," Deacon Pillar as usual chimed in, "She'd have to be one of those lesbian women. Come to think of it—" Deacon Pillar and Deacon Athens turned and gave Eartha the once-over and scowled.

"Both of y'all going to hell!" Sister Blackstone said, as her face took on the look of disdain.

"Well if we do, you'll be there giving the welcome address." Deacon Pillar shot back.

"Look at what you've done, Eartha Blackstone," Deacon Athens said as he ignored any further interruptions, "You gonna have those two blabbermouths going back telling half of what they think they know and bringing shame to us."

"That's right," Deacon Pillar chimed in, "And you know we ain't got no shame."

Both Deacon Athens and Sister Blackstone decided it was best not to correct Deacon Pillar. It would've been useless.

"Like I started to say," Sister Blackstone continued. "In my hands I have something that will make the loss of those photographs really trivial."

"And what would that be?" Deacon Athens asked slowly. In all the years he'd known Eartha Blackstone, he'd never really trusted her, and it was no different at that moment.

"Pick up your jaws and tighten your drawers," Sister Blackstone said. "I'm about to read a little bedtime story to the two of you."

About fifteen minutes later when she finally finished reading bits and pieces of the Reverend Grayson's journal, the men's jaws dropped harder than a sledgehammer on a block of cement.

Ten minutes later, fully expecting the ultimate respect and a "job well done," she couldn't be more disappointed. The last thing Sister Blackstone expected was a more aggressive push back from Deacons Athens and Pillar. It'd seemed that since their previous discussions and before she'd arrived the two men had developed "religion."

Deacon Athens went to the study door and peeped out. He wanted to make sure no one was lurking around, even though he hadn't bothered to do so before Sister Blackstone read from the journal.

"Eartha Blackstone," he barked, as he stubbed out the remainders of a cigarette, "Have you lost your ever-loving mind?" Deacon Athens's shoulders and chest seemed to grow as he fumed. "We discussed getting the First Lady to leave or sit down. We didn't agree to destroy New Hope along the way."

"That's my understanding," Deacon Pillar chimed in. He sucked his teeth in disdain to show he was just as deeply offended. "What is the purpose of restoring the church back to holiness if we end up destroying it?"

"It's what God would want." Sister Blackstone said sharply. "Are you going to back down from His plan?"

"Yes," Deacon Athens shot back.

"Best believe it," Deacon Pillar added.

Sister Blackstone repeatedly urged them to back her. It was only when she'd threatened to go ahead without them that she realized she'd stepped over the line.

"I wish you'd try it!" Deacon Athens's face grimaced and although he was slightly stooped from age, he didn't flinch. "You ain't exactly clean—"

Interjecting and still determined to have his say, Deacon Pillar added, "Oh, I know about you and the deacon here." He stepped in front of Deacon Athens and continued, "Your imagined stellar and holy reputation can be shut down, too."

"Say wha—?"

"That's right. It's only because we're true Christians

that none of us didn't out you as soon as the deacon here told us about your scandalous ways. For years there's been a few of us that kept our mouths shut about your nasty habits and affairs."

Sister Blackstone, for the first time in a very long time, was stunned beyond words. Her body almost missed the chair as she moved backward and sat down.

"You two would do that to me?"

"Damn right!" Deacon Athens spat. "We're gonna get this church back to holiness, but we ain't gonna tear it down brick by brick just so you can claim a victory."

"You'd better be real careful about who you cross, Eartha." Deacon Athens reached for his sweater without taking his eyes off her.

"We got more days behind us than in front. You do the math." Deacon Pillar moved toward the door, opening it for Deacon Athens to exit first.

The dark pupils of Sister Blackstone's eyes seemed darker than normal; they were almost pitch black. She wanted to move, but couldn't.

"Oh, we're going back to the old ways and days," she murmured and began to pray. "Father, I'm about Your Will and Your ways. Help me to take them down." Sudden laughter came from down the church's hallway, filtering into the study where Sister Blackstone remained rooted in the chair.

"You young heathens go ahead and have your comedy night. Just go ahead and laugh now. We'll see who'll be laughing later."

She pounded the journal and set it next to the shopping bag she'd carried it in. "Oh yes, God's gonna get the glory out of this!"

Chapter 30

Janelle's sudden breakdown earlier that evening had Chyna and Cordell beside themselves. They didn't know what was wrong and what part, if any, they might've played.

Cordell had raced down the hallway after Janelle's sudden dash back to her bedroom.

Chyna milled about in the kitchen. She finally fixed a small snack but couldn't eat. She was still stunned by Janelle's appearance and stranger-than-usual behavior. She'd also called Doctor Bayer's service and left a message. Something was not right. Things hadn't been right for weeks, but this time Janelle had her truly scared.

Chyna hadn't meant to listen through the cracked kitchen door, but she had. The conversation between Janelle and Cordell, before, was a bit muffled, but the silence now was clear and she took it as a good sign. Whatever needed to be healed between Cordell and Janelle probably had started.

Or so she'd thought. Chyna had barely stepped into the hallway when Janelle opened the living room door.

Janelle sped past so fast it took Chyna's mind a few seconds to catch up with what she'd just seen.

Chyna was torn. Should she run after Janelle, who was obviously upset, or should she go inside to find out from Cordell what happened? She hastily looked inside Janelle's bedroom and took a quick glance at Cordell. He just sat with his hands stretched out in surrender with a questioning and sad expression on his face.

Cordell looked up in time to see Chyna turn around, obviously to rush after Janelle. Still stunned, he decided to leave.

He could see the outlines of Janelle and Chyna as he passed the den. Without hesitation Cordell left and didn't say good-bye.

Cordell didn't bother to close the front door behind him as he raced down the pathway to his car. And most importantly, Cordell hadn't picked up the envelope containing the picture of Chyna from the coffee table. He was already on the highway and minutes away from his hotel room before he realized that he left it and where.

"Just leave me the hell alone, Chyna." Janelle's hands kept reaching for a pair of scissors that lay on a bookshelf in the den. "I don't need and damn sure don't want no sympathy from you or your lover."

Not giving Chyna a chance to protest, Janelle knocked the scissors to the floor and fled.

Inside her bedroom, Janelle's mind raced, and her thoughts were too far ahead for her to catch up. Back and forth, retracing her steps, she walked, from one end of the bed to the other.

By the time Chyna reached Janelle's bedroom, she was standing stripped as naked as her bed. She was pounding the flesh between her breasts with one hand. With her other hand she snatched at precious remaining hair that fell, limp, from her scalp.

And before Chyna could reach Janelle, to stop her before she did herself more harm, Janelle fell to the floor.

"Help me, Father God," Janelle suddenly wept. As if the barrier she'd built between her and God had fallen away, Janelle's tears poured. Each drop that fell to the carpet carried a plea to the Throne of Grace.

Rather than interrupt and instead of joining her sister, Chyna retreated from the room to give Janelle privacy. Janelle and God had some catching up to do.

When she was midway between Janelle's room and the living room, Chyna heard her front door open. She hadn't heard a bell, but someone was definitely entering.

Chapter 31

Nothing and no one had cooled down inside New Hope Assembly. In one part of the church, the young people were holding a praise party. The sounds of Kirk Franklin, Hezekiah Walker, and a group of young men called Commissioned poured through the closed doors. The youngsters seemed a bit too energetic to most of the elderly members, who were trying to hold a semblance of a prayer meeting on the other side of the church.

"There they go again," said one of the senior choir members. "They're playing that hippity hop music in God's holy place."

It was pretty much the consensus of those trying to craft and repeat prayers long and repetitive enough to make the most sanctimonious Pharisee proud.

However, back in the pastor's study, Deacons Pillar and Athens had returned and came face-to-face with Sister Blackstone. She was still planted where they'd left her earlier.

"Oh Lord, woman, I can't believe you still here."

Deacon Athens slammed the door shut behind him, almost slapping Deacon Pillar, who seemed attached to his side.

Deacon Pillar hadn't said anything. He sure felt like pulling out his conked hair, but conking was expensive. He was still so upset with Sister Blackstone that he wanted to punch her and told her so. "If I wasn't a saved man I'd wanna knock you into next Sunday."

To add to the mayhem, because he wasn't one to back down, either, Deacon Athens made her a promise. "You can stay in that seat until the Rapture, but you'd still remain after it'd come and gone."

"You just worry about how you'll spend eternity in a crowded hell." Sister Blackstone hissed.

"You need to just go on home. Instead of plotting to have the First Lady removed, you need to be concerned about yourself. All I gotta do is call for a vote to have you removed. You've teed off enough folks to have it seconded and passed in no time.

"Try us," Deacon Athens threatened, "it ain't nothing but a phone call and the church bus to get the board members over here."

Sister Blackstone's mind raced. She knew both men were capable of doing much worse than having her removed, if provoked.

"I'm not afraid of either of you," Sister Blackstone sucked her teeth and then in the next breath added sweetly, "But we'd better come up with something before this church descends into the pits of degradation."

As if it were trying to get in on the nefarious plan, the words and rhythm from "I ain't Gonna Hurt Nobody" performed by the turned-his-life-around Chris Martin from Kid 'n Play filtered into the study from the young adults' program.

Deacon Pillar inched toward the door and opened it about an inch or so. He laughed a little and then turned to Deacon Athens. "Young people . . ."

"Can we please get back down to business?" Sister Blackstone threw up her white-gloved hands, denying the deacon a chance to finish his thought.

"Hold your tongue, Eartha." Deacon Pillar didn't bother looking her way. He knew he didn't have to.

"I guess you wouldn't have hung around all afternoon if you didn't have something biting at your left knee."

"The two of you knew I wasn't going nowhere until I finished having my say. I don't know why y'all always gotta play your stupid games when it comes to the Lords' work. I swear if I wasn't as saved and sanctified as I am . . ."

The two deacons stiffened and were ready to react, if the need arose. They then traded nods and winks with one another. In effect, at that moment, they decided not to argue any further with the immovable senior citizen, warily accepting Sister Blackstone's blasé tone of defeat.

Moments later, with a cease-fire implied, they began to discuss other ways to restore "pure holiness" to their precious church's reputation.

Thirty minutes later they were no closer to coming to an agreement on a sensible plan than they were earlier in the day.

Wringing his hands, and with the wrinkles on his face seeming to double from anger, Deacon Pillar looked at his watch. "It's getting late. I need to go downstairs to the fellowship hall and see if I can calm down the young adult auxiliary. It sounds like their program is over."

"I think you probably should," Deacon Athens said. "I'm sure they're confused as to why they can't invite Brother Cordell to speak when he's been here so often since the reverend's death."

"I'm gonna try my best." Deacon Pillar said. "Those poor young'uns been lied to so much about the reverends' death. It's a shame the church don't really know what went down."

"Of course, they don't." Deacon Athens replied, "Heck, we just found out ourselves not that long ago."

"Just be careful what you tell folks," Sister Blackstone said. "You don't want to stray too far from the official story."

Of course, she'd remember the official story. She was a part of creating it, along with the media publicist they'd hired.

A sudden death was the only official description given of Grayson Young's suicide; that and the total decimation of the bouncer's credibility. It'd taken several months for the clamor to die down. Of course, there were a few whispers by those who came not to worship but to gawk at the regular members. Even some who'd belonged to New Hope Assembly for years and even several multi-generation members had begun to look differently at one another. Under the guise of just being friendly, there were, of course, a few who tried to discern if there was the possibility of a sex demon roaming the church aisles and pews. Innocent or not, the reverend was still inside the Sweet Bush.

Finally, the questions and comments started dying down and then almost to the point when the "pastor disaster at the Sweet Bush" was seldom mentioned. After all, it wasn't good church policy. Of course, a great deal of credit went to the First Lady for "having the common decency to stay away."

"Well what are you waiting on?" Sister Blackstone snapped. When Deacon Pillar didn't leave like he said he would, she became angrier.

"I don't know what is wrong with you," Sister Blackstone snapped. "I can get this done." She stopped, and with poison dripping from her tongue, she hissed. "And you, Thur-No-good Pillar, everyone knows you couldn't find a plan on your own behind with radar!"

"Go to hell," Deacon Pillar snapped. Quickly, he nodded his good-bye to Deacon Athens, and then said as he ambled past Sister Blackstone, "You need a lot of prayer, Eartha. I've known you for years and I'd thought by now that you'd have learned something. At the very least, I'd thought you embraced salvation."

"Hypocrite . . ." Sister Blackstone tossed back. "Learn this and see who's in control." She refused to move from his path and forced the deacon to go around her and her middle finger.

"Watch her, Deacon Athens," Deacon Pillar warned, looking over his shoulder, "she's out of control. It'll be like sending a bull into a china shop. She'll have the media and every other church around looking down on us and revisiting that mess."

Without missing a beat, Deacon Pillar nodded his good-bye, again, toward Deacon Athens. With eyes still blazing in her direction, he slammed the door behind him, and by doing so gave his last word to Sister Blackstone.

"The Devil is a liar!" Sister Blackstone barked as she made her way across the room. Angry and focused on gathering her possessions, with her hands trembling, Sister Blackstone was just about to lay her shopping bag against one of the upholstered chairs.

Using the agility of a young boy, Deacon Athens, in less than five steps, cleverly snatched the shopping bag from her clutches before she could place it against the chair. It wasn't lost upon him that she'd already placed the journal and some other items back inside the bag.

"Have you lost your mind?" Sister Blackstone yelled as she lunged at the deacon.

"I'll hold on to this," Deacon Athens replied standing resolute as he held the bag high and out of her reach. He felt a lot better with the evidence in his possession. He could only hope that she didn't have copies.

"Either you give me my bag back, or I will take down this church and just move my membership," Sister Blackstone threatened as she repeatedly reached for her bag.

"Go ahead," Deacon Athens replied. "Won't no other church have you. You must've forgotten that God said that His house would be a house of prayer."

She moved toward him again and she brought a kick with her.

Deacon Athens was a bit quicker than Sister Blackstone. He'd avoided a kick that would've resulted in the need for surgery. "I'm sure you didn't share everything in this journal," he argued. "I think I'll read what the good Reverend Grayson had in mind." *I'd also like to read what he wrote about me.*

"Gimme back my bag!" Sister Blackstone's voice grew louder. It wasn't easy, but Deacon Athens managed to keep his manhood and the shopping bag out of her reach.

She'd never seen it coming. Again, Deacon Athens sidestepped one of her unsteady moves and made it to the door. Without a word he'd opened and slammed it hard behind him.

"Damn." Sister Blackstone's back was against the wall, and that wasn't good for anyone.

Chapter 32

Chyna, upon hearing a strange noise, crept into her living room and found Cordell standing beside her coffee table.

"Cordell, thank God it's you. Come quick." Chyna said. She'd worry about his returning later.

Down the hall the walls inside Janelle's bedroom felt as though they were closing in and nothing made sense to her.

Her eyes were shut tight enough to cause a streak of pain to zip through her skull, but she dared not open them. And then Janelle thought she felt Cordell's touch against her naked, dry skin, which was almost paper-thin, but that was impossible. Not even his smell, a mixture of pure soap and lavender lotion, seemed real. And there was no way his kneeling beside her was real. After all, she wasn't the praying kind, so why was she on her knees?

Despite what she'd thought was real or not she couldn't fight what was happening, as her strength was spent. So Janelle permitted Cordell, or whoever it was in her room, to pick her gently off the floor.

"In the name of Jesus," Cordell whispered. "In the blessed name of Jesus," he repeated. He then moved aside a stray wisp of her hair and kissed her forehead.

"Jesus." Janelle whispered finding some strength and solace in hearing the Savior's name. She wanted to say more, and she really tried to do so, but her mouth felt like it was filled with a wad of cotton.

Janelle's sparse, now dark brown hair, matted with foul-smelling sweat and tears, clung to Cordell's blue cotton shirt. He didn't care. As though he carried a sleeping baby, he laid her upon the bed and stepped away.

Janelle's red, and somewhat sunken eyes watched Cordell. She felt like she was bravely watching her own body and his from a distance. Her eyes still didn't blink as she lay motionless watching his every move and yet she dared not trust what she saw or felt. There was nothing real about what had happened in the last half hour. Had she prayed real prayers in that room? Had God heard them? Was there a real urgency and yet a tenderness to Cordell's touch?

Was she truly naked? As had become her custom, Janelle touched her breast. It had a warm feeling. Where she'd at any other time felt the need to punish her cancer-ridden body, at that moment she hadn't.

Clarity returned slowly to Janelle, dragging feelings of shame along. Shame covered her because she'd just talked to God about what she'd done to enable her sister to sin against what was surely not God's plan for her. She'd asked God for His forgiveness because she'd shamelessly done so knowing that her sister was the first lady of a church. But then she'd had no relationship with God and until an hour ago thought little about what it meant.

When Janelle summed up what she'd done and where she was at that moment, she began to whimper softly. It was the same shame she imagined Eve felt and caused her to gird a fig leaf about her. She was naked in more ways than she imagined.

"How do you feel now?" Cordell asked. That wasn't the only question he had, but he was hampered by the image of him covering her nakedness without her permission. The boundaries between them were still muddled.

Janelle didn't answer. She extended her hand cautiously, showing a bit of pain was still present. She did it in a way that not only confirmed her gratitude but also dispelled any questions of how she felt about him. However, her shame and breast cancer still remained, and she now accepted it as punishment.

"I'm going to leave you two alone, again." Chyna said as she tried to muster a smile. At that moment, she was relieved that Cordell had returned.

Janelle's earlier prayers were not the only ones pled that afternoon. As soon as Chyna left Cordell and Janelle, she'd gone into her room. Because no one, not even Janelle, entered her room, she'd felt free to leave the evidence of her repentance.

As relieved as Chyna felt she also felt a little apprehensive. She couldn't shake the feeling that the day's troubles were far from over. She walked over to her bedroom lamp and turned it on.

Chyna's Bibles, some printed and some audio, were strewn about the nightstand. During the past few months when one challenge grew larger than the last, she felt almost pushed by life into prayer. She removed her shoes and sat in a chair by her window, where she fingered a white woven cross she had crocheted as a child and kept from childhood. Even now, somehow, as far as she'd fallen from the Cross, her woven one gave her comfort. Did she mock God by putting more faith in something she could feel? She'd always have that question in her heart.

Chyna knew that the mercy seat was always available, but she couldn't accept its unconditional cover of God's forgiveness; she also needed forgiveness from her church for what she saw as her part in Grayson's demise.

But how could she go to the church without going through an unforgiving church board?

Just as she was about to rise from the chair because she'd grown tired of rehashing the reasons why she hadn't accepted forgiveness, she heard the doorbell ring. There wasn't time to do anything about the shabby clothes she still wore or to comb her hair. She didn't want Cordell or Janelle disturbed, so she rushed to answer it.

One of hell's hardest workers waited on the other side of Chyna's door.

The heat radiated by Sister Blackstone's anger would've set bushes on fire. She was just that livid. She hadn't quite made up her mind by the time she arrived at Chyna's. So there she was shuffling from side to side, determined to bring holiness back to New Hope by any means possible. *No adulteress or deacon is gonna stop my ministry.*

Perhaps Sister Blackstone had not developed a plan, but she was convinced that retribution was actually her ministry.

Chyna's bare feet slapped the carpet as she raced to the front door. Swinging it open, she was surprised to see Sister Blackstone and even more surprised to see Deacon Athens racing up her walkway, too.

"Hold up," Deacon Athens hollered. His footing

seemed a bit unsteady as he pushed his aging body up Chyna's walkway. "Sister Blackstone," he continued, "you left your shopping bag behind."

Chyna wasn't certain what was going on because she noticed, immediately, that the deacon didn't have a shopping bag with him.

Sister Blackstone noticed the same thing Chyna had. However, unlike Chyna, she knew that if the deacon didn't have her shopping bag on him, it was still in his possession. She'd hoped to have started baiting Chyna and see where it went. Even without a plan, she still believed that things would go her way.

"You followed me here to tell me about a shopping bag?" Sister Blackstone said. There was no denying the agitation in her voice or manner. She'd turned away from Chyna without having said the first word and slowly moved in the deacon's direction.

"Sorry to barge in on you like this, First Lady," Deacon Athens said, smiling and trying to catch his breath. "I figured Sister Blackstone might be coming this way."

"You did?" Chyna replied. She was about to ask how he would know Sister Blackstone's business, and more importantly, why would she come there, especially since Chyna had challenged them to show her proof of anything that would embarrass her and the church or leave her alone. So far the only thing that showed up was them.

Before Chyna could complete her thought and Deacon Athens could drag Sister Blackstone away, Cordell's voice rang out. There was no denying the urgency.

"Chyna!" Cordell hollered. "Oh God, please come here. Hurry!"

Chyna turned away and started down the hallway. She

hadn't realized that both Deacon Athens and Sister Black-stone had entered and followed.

Nothing could've prepared any of them for what they saw. Even the sight of Janelle lying partially covered on the bed, her complexion, a ghastly bluish color, stopped them cold.

Chapter 33

Calling for an ambulance was the last thing Cordell thought about. He'd hurriedly placed Janelle, who was wrapped in a blanket and little else, in the backseat of his car. She was sandwiched between Sister Blackstone and Deacon Athens. Chyna was in the front seat with her cell phone to her ear literally screaming for help to the 911 operator.

"Is she breathing?" the 911 operator repeated. She'd asked several times in between giving instructions to Chyna to keep Janelle from going into shock.

Each time Chyna called out, "Is she breathing?" it was Deacon Athens who'd replied. He'd looked over at Sister Blackstone for assistance, but the old woman just sat still with her hands clenched. She, too, was completely in shock.

At that time of the evening there should've been heavy traffic on Kings Highway and Cortelyou Road, but the lights were on Cordell's side. Not only was there not much traffic, but he'd only caught about three red lights as he lay on the horn announcing his urgency. By the time he'd reached about three blocks from Downstate Medical Center, two police cars with sirens blasting escorted him to the front of the hospital.

How Cordell navigated the narrow driveway leading to the emergency room without flipping over his car was another miracle.

The emergency room at Downstate Medical was bedlam at its worse. Two hours had passed since they'd arrived. Cordell tried to remain calm while also trying to reassure Chyna. While they huddled off to the side of the emergency room, Deacon Athens had Sister Blackstone cornered not too far away.

"Feeling any better now?" Deacon Athens snapped. He was frustrated and angry, but there was a smile plastered on his public face should anyone think otherwise. "I told you there was another way to get this done!"

"How was I supposed to know that trollop had cancer?" Sister Blackstone replied in a tone that made it seem as though she was the one misunderstood.

Deacon Athens and Sister Blackstone went back and forth with their sniping. Somehow during the discussion, which had begun to calm down, they both began to show a little concern for Janelle.

While they spoke—or rather argued—neither Deacon Athens nor Sister Blackstone bothered to mention the involvement of Cordell with the sisters. It was as though each were waiting to see who would bring it up first. Sister Blackstone in particular was anxious because she didn't know if Deacon Athens had a chance to read the journal beyond what she'd shared.

Deacon Athens did read a little of the journal and what he'd read propelled him to find Sister Blackstone. He'd discovered within the pages of that journal the unorthodox relationship between Sister Blackstone and Pastor Young. He'd also read other tidbits that would definitely bring down the church harder than the walls of Jericho. He was determined that Sister Blackstone would not be a Joshua.

And although there was little Christianity in the conversation between Deacon Athens and Sister Blackstone, there were other discussions that were toxic in that emergency room.

". . . One moment she was clinging to me and I was about to pray for her and the next . . ." Cordell's voice trailed off. There was so much self-recrimination in his words.

Cordell couldn't complete the sentence. He looked about as though groping for help and from whom could he get it?

The sick and the infirm were strewn about the hospital emergency room. And inside that room, four supposed-to-know-God people: Cordell, Chyna, Earl Athens, and Eartha Blackstone, all diseased with retribution, recrimination, and secrecy, stood in their own way of helping Janelle.

Each of them knew God was not pleased.

Chapter 34

Dr. Bayer rushed through the emergency room doors. The heavyset woman seemed light on her feet and swept past Chyna and the others through the automatic doors without saying a word. As the doors closed quickly behind her, she'd barked orders into her radio pager too low for Chyna to understand.

When Dr. Bayer finally reached the floor housing the Don Monti Oncology Center, she found Janelle in almost total distress. She immediately went to work. The medicines she ordered waited on the cart attended by one of the floor nurses. She rewashed her hands, and in a measured way she quickly retook Janelle's vitals and when she was assured that no mistakes were made, she hurried along.

Thirty minutes later, Doctor Bayer exited Janelle's room. During the time she'd worked on Janelle, Chyna and the others were permitted to wait in the waiting room opposite Janelle's room.

"Heavenly Father, please help her." Chyna repeated while Deacon Athens and Cordell chorused amen.

Cordell tried to read the doctor's expression as she approached. Although he'd not given much thought to either Deacon Athens or Sister Blackstone since they'd arrived, he was thankful that Sister Blackstone had gone to the bathroom and had not returned.

Chyna immediately rose when she saw Doctor Bayer enter the waiting room. She'd been crying and her eyes were swollen, causing her to look a lot older than she was. Her appearance was the last thing on her mind as she rushed to meet the doctor halfway.

"How's Janelle?" The way Chyna asked the question sounded almost as if she were asking, *Is Janelle dead?*

Doctor Bayer looked at Cordell and Deacon Athens before steering Chyna to a nearby corner for privacy.

Cordell wanted to scream. He needed to hear firsthand about Janelle and he'd been shoved aside like a stranger.

Within seconds, or so it seemed, Cordell watched Chyna collapse into a nearby chair. The color was drained from her face even as the expression on the doctor's face remained stoic and professional.

Cordell's eyes were locked onto every movement made in that corner. A lack of bionic ears or sight did not deter his determination to try and glean any information.

He continued to concentrate and just as the doctor was about to say something more to Chyna, she hesitated. Cordell followed the doctor's gaze and saw that it fell upon Sister Blackstone, who had just entered. It was the only time Cordell saw the expression on the doctor's face change.

"Miss Blackstone?" Doctor Bayer said, not trying to hide her surprise. "I haven't seen you in quite some time. How have you been?"

The only faces that looked more surprised than the

doctor's belonged to Chyna and Cordell. Deacon Athens didn't seem surprised at all.

Without responding, Sister Blackstone backed quickly out the door and raced down the hallway toward the bank of elevators.

"I'll be back," Deacon Athens said, quickly. He snatched his coat and fled the room. He'd left little doubt that he was going after Sister Blackstone.

Without seeming to give what'd just happened a second thought the doctor proceeded to speak to Chyna.

Cordell didn't know why he did it, but he had. While the doctor and Chyna were distracted by whatever they were discussing, he'd left the room, too. He needed to see Janelle. Cordell headed in one direction and caught a glimpse of the deacon running the opposite way.

Sister Blackstone hadn't moved that fast in years. Not even when she shouted in church had her body felt as though it levitated.

"Eartha," Deacon Athens shouted as loud as permitted on the hospital floor. "Wait!" His breath was starting to come in spurts as he fought passing out. "Wait, Eartha!"

Sister Blackstone rounded the corner without giving any hint of acknowledging the deacon's plea.

She pounded on the elevator button. The small white knitted cap she wore over her black hair looked like a piece of tattered cloth as she clawed at it with a free hand.

"Eartha, wait!"

Sister Blackstone could hear the deacon's voice closing in on her. She pounded on the closed elevator door with enough force to almost break her fragile wrist.

"What is wrong with you? You didn't have to run off like that" Deacon Athens hissed because as he gulped for air he could do little else.

"Have mercy, Jesus," Sister Blackstone pleaded. She began to mumble as the elevator finally arrived.

Hospitals being as busy as they generally were became a blessing in disguise. As people filed off, focused on their own destinations, none paid attention to the crying old woman or the pleading old man.

Chapter 35

Cordell's eyes darted around Janelle's hospital room. He wasn't prepared for what he saw. The color was now definitely gone from her face and yet, there seemed a peace about her.

He turned and peeked out the door and saw that Chyna and the doctor were still in conversation. Cordell took that opportunity to get closer to Janelle. He washed his hands in the small sink, donned a gown, cap, and a pair of gloves, and went to her.

Cordell looked at Janelle. His eyes scanned her entire body. "Baby, you look even frailer than when I lifted you earlier."

His nerves were becoming raw and he stood for a moment and just seemed to rock. *Where'd that come from? I haven't called her "baby" since she was twenty years old.*

Yet despite what he saw, he moved closer to her bed as he continued to speak. "I can't be angry with you because you didn't feel secure enough to tell me what was wrong. It's all my fault."

He continued trying to encourage her, praying that whatever he said, she'd respond instead of just lying there.

"Hi, baby." Cordell repeated in a whisper. "I wish you could see what I see. You look beautiful." As quietly as possible, he pulled a nearby chair closer to her bed and sat. He fought to look past all the machines and gadgets that he knew nothing about and settle back in on talking to her.

"Hey girl," Cordell said sweetly. "You remember when we danced?" *Stupid. Why would I say something so stupid? Get it together, Cordell.*

He was about to quickly follow up what he'd just said with something more when she stirred. It wasn't a big movement, but he knew she moved. Could she really hear him? Did she remember the dance?

"You knew you had me going and that's why you drew me closer in Ned Lake's old dingy basement." Cordell stopped to see if there'd be any reaction.

Janelle stirred again. She'd said nothing, but she definitely moved. Cordell was encouraged and started saying whatever came to his mind and his heart.

"Ned almost lost his mind when he saw us dancing so close. I bet there wasn't room enough between our bodies for a thin sheet of paper to pass. Oh, and I remember Cinnamon was there, too. Remember how she thought she was too hot and wouldn't give Ned the time of day? It was so funny to see him almost beg."

Cordell saw the squiggly lines on one of the machines connected to her heart. The lines seemed to squiggle more. He assumed it was a good sign, so he continued.

"Janelle, I've heard all kinds of music since we parted." His voice became emotional to the point of almost tearing as he continued, "But, baby, I've never danced the same. I've heard the music but I haven't danced a real dance since I danced with you."

Cordell was about to say something more when he heard the door open behind him.

"Cordell, I didn't know you'd come in here," Chyna said. She wasn't angry as much as she was surprised. She didn't want to admit that she thought that he'd again abandoned her sister as when he'd left earlier without saying anything.

"I need to speak with you," Chyna added. "They'll be coming for Janelle shortly, and before they do, I need to tell you something."

Chyna and Cordell quickly moved over to the window. Their heads nodded and their bodies seemed tense, all at the same time. It was apparent that they were deep into a discussion meant only for their ears to hear. At least that's what Janelle thought as she watched them while she fought her way back to consciousness.

In another part of the hospital, Sister Blackstone wished she were the one that was unconscious. The elevator seemed to take forever to reach the first floor. On the way down she was too upset to have an intelligent conversation and didn't try.

It was Deacon Athens who watched her reactions and finally put two and two together. It only took four floors for him to do it.

"I thought I remembered that doctor's name when I heard the First Lady say it," Deacon Athens's tone was still angry, although not as angry, as he'd wanted it to be. "She's the same oncologist you had about ten years ago. Isn't she?"

Sister Blackstone wiped away a tear hard enough to erase an eyeball. She didn't respond, preferring, instead, to glare at the deacon.

Deflecting her evil eye with one of his own, the deacon continued. There was no sympathy in what he was about to say.

"Eartha Blackstone, I know you might not have known before what kind of illness Janelle Pierce had, but you do now. You've had cancer, and God gave you a second chance. He gave you a healing."

Sister Blackstone was moving her hand across her chest as if she were trying to avoid a vampire's bite. But she said nothing.

"I told you before we can return the church to where it should be without tearing it down first. But now I'm not sure if it's going to be worth rehashing things with the First Lady. She's got too much on her plate to deal with."

Sister Blackstone started to walk away. Her steps were slow at first. However, as the deacon continued to chastise her, she sped up as best she could. She finally reached the front door and walked quickly to the sidewalk. Deacon Athens was only two steps behind her.

With gnarly fingers, Deacon Athens clutched her shoulder, preventing Sister Blackstone from stepping off the curb.

"Those two women have no one but each other. I'll not be a part of this. God didn't reveal this to us for us to use it against them."

"The hell He didn't," Sister Blackstone had finally found her voice. Unlike the others who saw some redemption in Janelle's situation, she hadn't.

Yes, God had healed her, but not without exacting a price. She'd lost a breast. The way she'd accepted her punishment for her illicit affairs, while she'd masqueraded as a Christian, had fueled and colored everything about her life. Missing a breast did not humble her. Instead, its absence was a constant reminder of what happens when God is displeased.

Sister Blackstone was all about pleasing her God, and she couldn't care less if Chyna and Janelle were hurt. "All healing got some pain involved."

Chapter 36

"I'm sorry I had to give all this information to you at once," Doctor Bayer told Chyna.

"I'm just glad someone finally did."

"I've got to put a rush on the lab, but I'll still be around the hospital should you need me."

"Thank you."

"Oh, another thing, I see Miss Blackstone is with all of you. That's good. I'm happy that she has some support. I haven't seen her return to my clinic in quite some time."

Before Chyna could digest what the doctor said about Sister Blackstone, she'd left.

Chyna remember that she had been momentarily distracted by Sister Blackstone's reaction to having seen Doctor Bayer. Yet, what the doctor had just said about Sister Blackstone couldn't compare with what she'd revealed regarding Janelle. Chyna hung on to every word the doctor had said.

Your sister is in a strange place emotionally and in a very serious place, physically. I cannot

stress enough how one element impacts the other,
both negatively and positively. Two weeks ago, I'd
taken Janelle off the experimental trial medica-
tions. Her bloodwork was unchanged as regarding
her cancer. Also, her counselor-related interviews
showed a possible break with reality, which was
a known side effect from the medication. All in
all, Janelle's stats proved that she was not a good
candidate for this particular trial. Apparently,
she chose to disregard my instructions. She also
wasn't up to date on her bloodwork. Had I not been
away last week I probably would've caught it . . .

The bottom line was that Janelle had lied, and Chyna
hadn't picked up on it.

Cordell looked over at Janelle. She still appeared to
be under the medication. He then lowered his head to continue speaking with Chyna. "What are we going to do?"
Cordell asked after Chyna shared what the doctor told her.
They were still huddled in the corner of Janelle's hospital
room, but it seemed as though Chyna's mind wandered. "I
think . . ." He stopped and tapped Chyna on the shoulder
to make sure he had her full attention.

"You think what?" Chyna asked. She tried to pay attention, but the doctor's words kept haunting her and it
only added to her guilt. Seeing dried tear lines on
Cordell's face unnerved her a bit. It seemed that the confident man she'd known for so many years was weakening
before her very eyes.

"I think Janelle needs to know the entire truth about us."

"Why?" Chyna's interest peaked. "Why now? Why
here?" She stopped and nodded toward Janelle's bed.
"Does she look like she needs to hear any more bad news?"

"I'm tired of holding things in. How can I instruct

others and not take my own advice? It's not right what she's going through."

"I don't care what you've told others to do," Chyna's voice began to rise. "Where's all this Christian love you're supposed to have? How could you endanger my sister's well-being because you need to clear your conscience about helping me?"

"It's not easy," Cordell insisted. "But look at her. She knows something. I can just feel it."

"Try feeling some sympathy," Chyna ranted. "Janelle needs our strength, not our weakness."

"It's not like I didn't try . . ." Cordell stopped speaking when he heard a movement coming from Janelle's direction.

"Ouch. Dammit," Janelle winced. She tried to move. One of the microthin needles that carried medication implanted on her side caused her skin to sting.

Chyna raced to her sister's bedside. "Janelle," she said tenderly. "Please stop moving about—I'm afraid you might pull something out."

Janelle's smile was controlled. The pain subsided to a point where it was bearable. Her mind returned sharp and there was no longer a feeling of being an onlooker in her own body.

"I'll let you two talk in private," Cordell said as he started for the door. He hadn't told Chyna exactly what he'd done earlier, but at that moment, Janelle needed her sister. His revelation could wait. Cordell's eyes were still misty and he wasn't trying to do the manly thing by hiding his feelings. He gave a quick glance at Janelle and tried to force a smile. "You'll be fine, Scrappy."

Scrappy, I'd forgotten that I used to call her that, too. Cordell stifled a sudden urge to laugh. How much more had he forgotten?

"I hope so," Janelle replied with a weak wink. "You owe me a *dance*."

The big grins that automatically broke out on Janelle and Cordell's faces weren't lost on Chyna. She could tell that there was a secret or a code that she wasn't privy to. "I never could dance as well as Janelle," Chyna said, struggling to add something to the conversation.

Cordell answered Chyna before Janelle could say anything, "No, you couldn't." He then turned back to Janelle and winked, too.

"Well, I couldn't have been all that bad," Chyna said, trying to act as though her feelings were hurt. "I wasn't exactly a wallflower when Janelle and I used to hang."

"That may be, but I was always better at *dancing* than you," Janelle said, weakly.

"Ahem," Cordell interjected. "Janelle, that's your baby sister. Be kind."

"Okay, enough with you two," Chyna said. "I know when I'm being played." She tried to smile. At that moment whatever Janelle wanted, Chyna would give her.

"Don't leave," Janelle said as she turned her head, again, toward Cordell. He'd already turned toward the door.

Her plea stopped him. "Okay," Cordell said as he came back and grabbed a second chair while directing Chyna to the one he'd vacated.

The three engaged in what they all knew was nothing short of a diversionary and silly conversation. And with each bit of laughter their common guilt grew instead of lessening.

After a while their back and forth of pleasantries was exhausted and silence cloaked the room. Several nurses entered and took Janelle's vitals while Cordell and Chyna stood nearby. Cordell had not told Chyna everything about his prior conversation with Janelle, but they'd made good use of the interruptions.

"I'm almost finished, Ms. Pierce," the nurse said as she placed a bandage over Janelle's latest IV insertion into a small vein on her hand.

Cordell and Chyna hurried their conversation along while trying to settle on a way to approach Janelle with any type of discussion at a later time. They'd not agreed upon much except that they weren't sure if Janelle would still exhibit some of the irrational behavior from before no matter what was said.

The seconds of silence that passed since the nurse left the room became too much for Janelle. The quietness came with the memory of her earlier conversation with Doctor Bayer. She didn't want to do that, but her discussion with the doctor came to mind despite her fighting it.

She was a fighter. She was fighting for her life. Of course, she had not shared that bit of bad news with them. Even with Doctor Bayer's earlier prognosis of the removal of her breasts, she wasn't ready to commit to it. So she'd approved the third biopsy, which they would do shortly. However, no matter what they found she would not give them permission to remove her breasts. On that, she was adamant.

"Can I get you a glass of water?" Cordell finally asked Janelle, as though those were the magic words to break the silence.

"She can't have anything to drink," Chyna said, quickly and without trying to hide her agitation. "They're going to give her anesthesia."

"Well awrighty, then, I guess that's that," Janelle added.

"I can't take this!" Cordell shot off his chair. He

stood in the middle of the room between the women. His face took on a determined look and the only thing missing from his Thorlike transformation was a hammer.

But it didn't mean he didn't have one.

"There's a connection between the three of us," Cordell said. "It's an unorthodox connection, but one nonetheless."

He nodded at each woman.

"What are you trying to say?" Chyna asked slowly. She was more than a little shocked. Had he begun to lose his mind, too?

"Just let me speak," Cordell said, even though he saw the warning look Janelle shot his way, he'd made up his mind to speak.

"No, Cordell," Janelle said. She wasn't certain where he was going with his sudden epiphany, but if it was to a place she'd not have revealed, there'd be no turning back. "I mean it!" She'd moved forward in the bed with indignation plastered on her face as she made her words more a warning than a request.

"Enough is enough," Cordell replied. "I can't sit here and pretend that I don't know that God is bigger than all of this."

"This? What do you mean, *this*?" Chyna's words were cautious. Too much was happening too soon and she'd had about enough.

"Chyna," Cordell said. "Earlier, at your house I shared something with Janelle that I probably shouldn't have. I should've come to you first."

"Not now, Cordell," Janelle urged.

Cordell ignored her and continued, "I know this is probably not the time or the place we'd have chosen to clear the air, but Janelle needs God to heal her body. We need to confess and get things out in the open so God can do a work."

"Not if it's going to hurt my sister," Chyna insisted. "Telling Janelle about the church's scheme to oust me will make her stop seeking God." She started to rise.

"Perhaps you didn't hear me." Cordell's voice was stern. "I've already started to share it with Janelle," Cordell said.

His voice became even more determined as he pulled Chyna back onto her chair. "Do I feel guilty? Yes, I do."

Cordell stopped long enough to look at Janelle. Her eyes twitched. The look she now had made it difficult for him to tell if she were becoming frightened or was just angry. Yet, he continued. "I'm not too certain that what I told her didn't have something to do with putting her in this hospital bed, but I've started it and I have to finish it."

Before Cordell could tell Chyna about the photos, Janelle began to struggle against the IV that held her arms and hand captive. "Cordell, please don't . . ." she said. "I should've told you everything back at the house instead of acting surprised. I was with her at the Sweet Bush. She didn't go to Cinnamon's bachelorette party alone."

Oh Lord, have mercy! He can't possibly know the truth about that time at the Sweet Bush and the stripper. Chyna's mind swung between the need to keep quiet and the need to keep Janelle's blood pressure down.

Janelle, even in her less-than-normal condition knew what Chyna was thinking. And so for a brief moment she donned her big sister gear. "Don't be too hard on him, Chyna. I only told him about the Sweet Bush thing because I was in one of my crazy moods, which you might interpret as a hissy fit or jealousy." Janelle frowned just a little before adding, "You're more churchified than me. Please forgive me."

"You were there, too?" Cordell asked, as though he'd not heard one word of the cover lie Janelle just gave. There it was. It was now out in the open except Janelle just added a piece of the puzzle that was new to Cordell. His mind was trying to process what she'd just revealed.

He'd already shared with her about the photograph Sister Blackstone sent and how he'd intercepted it and not told Chyna. He'd revealed everything during the moments after they finished crying out to God and had begun to laugh and reminisce. It was the way Janelle acted that gave him the courage to do it.

"You only seemed a little shocked, but able to handle things."

He stopped and turned to Chyna, who now looked as bad as Janelle had when they brought her to the hospital.

"How could you?" Chyna asked Cordell as she avoided Janelle's stare.

"I thought Janelle needed to know, and perhaps the three of us could fight those church folks together. Apparently, I was wrong."

"Get off his back." Janelle said as her voice seemed to grow deeper from the medication. "It was my idea to find the right time to tell you everything."

And then Janelle turned on Cordell.

"You're not all that innocent. You tried to play hero out of guilt and I knew that. I didn't tell you everything about the Sweet Bush episode with Chyna because I just didn't want to. It's as simple as that. But it don't mean I wasn't going to do it later."

Cordell was hanging between confusion and anger. "And when were you going to do that?" He'd finally realized Janelle was talking in code, which meant there was something more he didn't know.

"I was going to say something about how wrong those damn church folks was—and you, too, as soon as I woke up from passing out!"

And now they were where they were and in no better shape.

Chyna stood up and went to stand beside Janelle and kissed her gently on the forehead. "I've definitely placed too much on both of you. I'm sorry. From now on I'm handling my own affairs alone. I am a grown woman, after all."

She was a grown woman who still didn't know Cordell had the so-called proof from the board.

"So from this point on, we will not cause my sister any more pain," Chyna chided. "Besides, I thought you needed to 'clear the air' so we could pray?" Her tone turned a notch above serious into almost threatening. "You're supposed to be this big man who knows how to teach folks to keep their lives in order. Yet you show up and bring nothing but disorder to my sister's life."

Cordell felt instantly diminished. *What just happened?* He truly thought he was clearing a pathway to the altar by putting their sins out there. He, too, wasn't blameless. He'd already decided when it was a better time that he would confess to Janelle as to the why and the how of his marriage to Chyna. How did all this turn around on him?

As much as prayer was needed in that room, it wouldn't be done at that moment. There was too much anger, too few excuses, and not enough forgiveness.

And prayer wouldn't come on time outside on the street in front of the hospital. Prayer was substituted for accusations and revenge as Sister Blackstone and Deacon Athens continued to argue.

But prayer always had the last word; and it had it when Deacon Athens tried, in vain, to pull Sister Blackstone back onto the curb, a second time, and out of the way of a careening car.

"Jesus!" He'd yelled out. But his prayer came too late to save them.

Chapter 37

At the same time, upstairs in Janelle's hospital room the conversation and finger-pointing between Chyna and Cordell had escalated. Every time Janelle thought Cordell would reveal the existence of the damaging photo, she'd interrupt with a fake pain or whatever it took to bring the attention back to her. There was so much confusion in the room that none of them heard the urgent call for medical attention to the emergency room. And, of course, not one of them gave a thought to the whereabouts of Sister Blackstone or Deacon Athens.

Janelle finally took a stand. And despite the return of her pain and her need to protect Chyna, she realized she needed to protect herself as well. The only way she could do that was for Cordell to shut his mouth.

"Chyna," Janelle called out. "I need to speak with Cordell, alone."

"I'm not leaving him here with you to get you all upset before you go into surgery."

"It's too late for all of that. Right now I need to speak

with Cordell," Janelle hissed. "And I need to speak with him now."

Chyna knew her sister well enough to realize there wasn't any use in arguing. "I'll be right outside this door. If I hear so much as a syllable raised, I'll be right back in here."

"Why don't you pray while you're out there?"

The question stopped Chyna cold and it raised an eyebrow on Cordell as well.

"Stop acting like I can't ask you for prayer," Janelle snapped.

It wasn't like Chyna couldn't pray; she could. With all the baggage she carried, how could she go to God on Janelle's behalf with any success? She still needed to get her own house in order.

Before today, Chyna felt as though she'd made some headway in her repentance, but then Janelle's jealousy made her tell Cordell about what had happened when someone drugged her at Cinnamon's bachelorette party. And she also realized that the only way Janelle could've known for sure that something embarrassing happened was if she were sober enough to see it. Janelle had never confirmed anything.

In her mind, at that very moment, she felt that even if God had forgiven her, she just couldn't forgive herself. How could she when the shame she'd felt before increased in the past hour?

Chyna glanced over at Cordell, who seemed to look straight through her. She was his ex-wife, and he looked as though he didn't know her at all. She'd been wrong to expect his help.

"C'mon, Chyna," Janelle pleaded. "I really need to speak with Cordell, alone. We'll talk later."

"Say what?" Cordell asked. "What are you talking

about?" He was concerned that her meds had kicked in again. She made no sense to him.

"You just stick to dancing," Janelle quipped with a devilish grin.

"I'll be outside." Chyna left the room feeling somewhat better that her sister had signaled her allegiance, but it wasn't by much.

Before the door closed an inch behind Chyna, Janelle lit into Cordell. At that moment she felt she had nothing to lose and a lot to gain.

"Let me tell you something," Janelle said between clenched teeth. "I'm fighting for my life. Do you really think that you telling my sister about that damn photo, and her going to pieces, is gonna help me get better?"

The only things holding Janelle down and keeping her from railing further were her IVs.

Now it was Cordell's turn to say what he truly felt. Obviously, Janelle was in better shape than he knew if she could jump on him in such a vicious and unfair manner.

"I came back when I didn't have to do it. I could've kept that picture of *your* sister . . ."

"Don't you mean your ex-wife?" Janelle shot back.

"I married her, so I know exactly who she is and what she was!" Cordell fought the urge to just rush over and shake some sense into Janelle. He was determined to have his say, so he continued. "Finding you naked and in a condition I'd never seen you in before floored me. Hearing you praying before I'd even entered your room spun my whole sense of you out of whack."

"Say what?"

"Shut up, Janelle!" Cordell's hands were almost shaking but not from fear. He must've truly loved her to be so angry.

"Did you just tell me to shut up?" Janelle shot back.

"Let me say it again. Apparently, you don't hear too

well." He came closer and barked, "Shut the hell up, Janelle."

Janelle did.

Instead of fuming while waiting around for Janelle to finish discussing whatever it was with Cordell, she'd visit the hospital admission office. In their rush to get Janelle started with medical care, she hadn't finished the admission paperwork.

Chyna took the elevator down to the first floor. No sooner had she stepped off the elevator she was swept up and almost physically carried by a pool of news reporters and several camera crews. She almost panicked as she quickly relived the media circus surrounding Grayson and the Sweet Bush.

Instead, the press continued down the corridor, leaving her backed against the wall. She was bewildered until she saw Detective Gonzalez. *That's the same detective that interviewed me after Grayson's suicide.* She also remembered that he was the same married detective that Janelle slept with.

Chyna quickly moved a few feet, praying that she'd be able to turn the corner before the detective spied her. It turned out it just wasn't a day for her prayers to be answered, because she ran right into Detective Lavin.

Chapter 38

Chyna felt trapped. The throng of people seemed to suck up the very air she needed to breathe. It was too late to pretend that she'd not recognized the detectives, especially when Detective Lavin stopped and spoke.

"You are Mrs. Grayson Young, am I correct?" Detective Lavin asked while looking past her and nodding toward his partner to join him.

Detective Gonzalez swam through the mob of people to reach where Chyna and his partner stood. "Lavin," Detective Gonzalez said and then nodded at Chyna. "Sorry to have to see you under these type of circumstances again, Mrs. Young."

"Circumstances, what are you talking about?" If she'd been confused before, she was totally out of the loop now. She took a moment to size them up before speaking, again. "I'm at a loss."

Both detectives gently guided Chyna away from the crowd and over beside a wire-mesh-covered window. It was Detective Lavin who spoke up first.

"I'd assumed you were here to see about . . ." He

stopped and flipped open his pad. His eyes scanned the sheet and then he added, "A Mr. Athens and Ms. Blackstone."

"Do you mean Deacon Athens and Sister Blackstone?" Chyna replied. "What's wrong with them?"

Detective Lavin adjusted his coat and motioned for Detective Gonzalez to step to the side. When they were just a few feet away, Detective Lavin whispered, "Do we need to involve her just because they all go to the same church?"

"Probably not; we can just inform her as to what happened, as a courtesy, and get back to questioning the driver of the van." Detective Gonzalez looked over at Chyna.

From the way he ogled her, it was apparent that he'd lost none of the appreciation he had for the beautiful young woman when he'd interviewed her after her husband's death.

Chyna's eyes widened with every bit of detail the detectives shared about Deacon Athens and Sister Blackstone.

When they finished, Detective Lavin shoved his pad into his coat pocket and added, "Wasn't Ms. Blackstone one of your husband's personal assistants?"

"She's dead?" Chyna couldn't answer the question because she was still in shock. It was the third time since she'd asked the detectives for confirmation. Each time, they answered, "Yes," she felt as though she'd been gut-punched. There was no way the detectives knew she'd once tossed the old woman out of her house and even at that moment was trying to feel some sympathy.

"They're still working on the old man, Mr. Athens," Detective Lavin informed Chyna. "They're not giving him much of a chance, either."

"You're still the First Lady of New Hope Assembly, aren't you?" The question came from Detective Gonzalez, but he'd asked as though he'd be surprised if she still were.

"On paper, I am," Chyna replied. The last thing she wanted was to get caught in a stupid lie. "Is it important?"

"Some of your fellow church board members have gathered in the hospital chapel. I thought you might want to join them, since you now know what's happened."

Just then one of the elevator doors opened and Cordell stepped out into the same fray. He raised one arm as if to ward off something evil. It was apparent that he'd tried to get his bearings. Seconds later more people dashed past, not caring if he were in their way. "Watch it!" He snapped.

"Cordell," Chyna yelled. "Cordell, come over here."

Finding the direction of her voice was no easy task. Hospital or not, there was still quite a bit of noise in the corridor. When he finally saw her, he was surprised to see her with police detectives.

As Cordell approached, the detectives nodded and moved on.

"What's going on?" Cordell asked.

"Both Sister Blackstone and Deacon Athens were hit by a car after they left us upstairs," Chyna replied. Without inhaling she quickly asked, "What's happening with my sister?"

She hadn't meant to sound so cold, but too much had happened and she was overwhelmed by her choice of priorities.

What Cordell said aloud had nothing to do with what he was thinking at that very moment. "They've taken Janelle into surgery. I'm sorry. I couldn't use my cell phone to call you, and I didn't think to have you paged."

However, what he thought about was the mess he'd made upstairs. He'd taken it upon himself to tell Janelle about the explicit photo of Chyna and he'd come very close to divulging all of Sister Blackstone's plan to bring Chyna down. Now Janelle was sick and in surgery. He couldn't tell Chyna the truth, because he'd promised to keep it until Janelle could tell her sister. And now the very woman who'd held the ammunition to assassinate their character and worse was in a morgue.

God, what are you doing? Cordell thought as he guided Chyna, who'd started crying, to an empty seat. Whether his next move was done out of a sense of duty, a Christian act, or whatever, he wasn't certain. He tenderly pulled Chyna's head into the fold of his arm and cradled her as her sobs grew louder.

And, of course, while he had his arms around her, some of the church board members looked on, disapprovingly, from the doorway of the hospital chapel.

Chapter 39

There were two factions within the New Hope Assembly's Board of Trustees. There was one most often led by Deacon Athens, which included the two old forgetful deacons, the brothers Adam and Lucius. They'd fortunately forgotten about the old plans Sister Blackstone had to unseat and embarrass their First Lady and weren't privy to the new plan. And then there were those who simply thought their duty was to vote, every so often, for some project or personnel replacement.

However, only one of the board members, Deacon Pillar, knew for certain that the Deacon Athens who lay near death never wanted to go along with dismantling the church.

Before coming down to the hospital chapel to meet up with the other church members, Deacon Pillar was upstairs in ICU to see his old friend.

Deacon Pillar got off the elevator on the seventh floor and shuffled, with his shoulders stooped and hands wringing, quickly toward the nearby nurses station.

"Athens," he announced to one of the nurses bent

over a computer. The nurse never looked up and instead told him as well as pointed to where the deacon needed to go.

He slowly opened the door after donning a gown and paper shoes. There was nothing welcoming about the hospital room. The walls were a drab gray with sanitation warnings and shelves with several items for emergency use. The two windows were long and narrow. They were covered with matching drab grayish-green curtains. If Deacon Pillar had been in a joking mood, he would have reminded Deacon Athens that the décor wasn't all that different from his own studio apartment.

There was nothing to joke about. Within the last few days it seemed that everything was serious. The fight for restoring the church was serious. The method of doing it was serious. Preventing Sister Blackstone from demolishing the church was extremely serious.

Finding the courage needed to attend to his friend didn't come easy, especially when he saw Deacon Athens lying in the hospital bed. "My God," Deacon Pillar's eyes went wide as he tried to understand how his old friend could've survived what'd happened earlier. "God truly is a wonder."

He began to wring his hands, wishing he could touch Deacon Athens and wake him to chat. *Hey there, old friend, you know I need you to pull through. I can't handle those reprobates by myself.*

Deacon Pillar's thoughts seemed to drift off as he walked over to one of the windows. He was glad that the deacon was in a private room. *Man, you should see the crowds down on the street. It looks like the television folks down there talking with some of them. I heard a whole bunch of folks lifted that van off you.*

Deacon Pillar's shoulders seemed to droop a little. He nodded his head in disbelief as he looked again outside and then back at Deacon Athens.

Walking back over to the bed, he sighed again. There didn't seem many places on the old deacon's body that weren't bruised, bandaged, or hooked up to some type of equipment.

Even as messed up as you are, you're still better off than Eartha. I don't know if you've heard or not, but she didn't make it. He stopped speaking to himself, as though he were waiting for Deacon Athens to join in the conversation.

Some of the members downstairs had informed him that Deacon Athens had been placed in an "induced coma," rendering him unresponsive to any stimuli. The old deacon was single and with no family nearby that he'd claim. However, at least he had the presence of mind to have a prepaid medical and accidental insurance plan on record with the church.

While Deacon Pillar sat next to the bed of his old friend and prayed, the detectives entered the room.

"Sorry," Detective Lavin said. "Please, don't get up." He strolled over to the bed and shook Deacon Pillar's hand. He then looked around and added, "I was looking for one of the doctors on duty for this patient."

"I recognize you," Deacon Pillar said, softly, as he rose and indicated by pointing toward the door that they should step out of the room. On the way, he then turned and nodded toward Detective Gonzalez, who had just walked in. "No one has come in since I've been here."

Deacon Pillar took one last look at the motionless body of Deacon Athens before stepping out of the room. He was immediately joined by the detectives.

"This is such a tragedy," Deacon Pillar said. The wrinkles in his brown face seemed bloated with stretch marks that made him look like a peach pit. He wrung his hands and started to pace.

Deacon Gonzalez nodded in agreement before checking his watch. "We've got to go. Hopefully, we'll find the attending physician. If you see him before we return, please let the doctor know we need to speak with him." Detective Gonzalez didn't wait for a reply. He tapped his partner on the shoulder, and the two men walked away.

Stepping onto the elevator, they immediately moved to the back, allowing the other two people that came behind them to enter. Neither detective noticed Janelle, heavily sedated and lying on the gurney.

Meanwhile Cordell and Chyna managed to get to the hospital cafeteria without being seen by the press. They had, however, seen several of the board members, who'd immediately asked Chyna what to do about Sister Blackstone.

"We hope this doesn't bring back too many bad memories for you," one of the women said. Chyna recognized her from the choir.

"Let's take care of one situation at a time," Chyna replied. She realized that none of those standing around probably knew about Janelle.

Cordell stood behind Chyna and watched. It was as though she'd been attending church every week since Grayson's death, and everything was just fine. They were a sad-looking lot and they all seemed to look to her for guidance.

But then he turned around and looked over at the cafeteria entrance. He saw several more members. He recognized two of them from the board and they didn't look happy. Not that he expected them to look like they'd had a Holy Ghost–filled time, with all that just happened, but he detected something different about their attitudes. He was picking up a spirit that was disturbing and very sinister. It was just that strong.

Cordell waited and watched. He almost marveled at how Chyna appeared to take control. He also wondered how long it would last. He looked back toward the door, where the other members had not moved. *It is not gonna last long at all*.

While Deacon Athens lay comatose in his room, Janelle remained in the recovery room. She'd been there for almost three hours before she awoke to find both Cordell and Chyna staring down at her. It was almost midnight.

"Hey, gurl," Chyna whispered. "Thank God everything is all right."

Janelle didn't respond. She was too busy trying to gather her thoughts, which were foggy and disconnected. With only one hand free she used it to touch her chest.

Before Chyna could say another word, Janelle started to sob. Chyna didn't know how to respond, and of course, Cordell at that moment, was useless, too.

Chapter 40

It was almost daybreak. She'd stood by the last table against the hospital cafeteria's back wall praying for a miracle. Everything happened too fast and Chyna needed to get a moment of peace. It wasn't going to happen, at least not then.

Chyna was still surrounded by several of the church members who'd hurried to Downstate Medical once they heard about the accident. She scanned their faces; some she knew and many she didn't.

Chyna's mind swirled with contradictions. She tried to console while she, too, needed consolation. "God's going to bring us through this. I know He will." She accepted greetings from the members with a smile, knowing full well that some, if not most, were halfheartedly offered.

One of the young women from the ushers' board stepped forward and surprised Chyna by tapping her lightly on her shoulder to get Chyna's attention. "First Lady," she said weakly while using a tissue to wipe tears from her reddened face. "Sister Blackstone was an usher for a short while. Should we do something special for her?"

Chyna took the young woman's hand in hers and then took a moment to think. She'd almost forgotten just how long the old woman had been a member of New Hope Assembly and just how many boards she sat on and the number of auxiliaries she'd belonged to. "Let me speak with some of the other board members and get back to you," Chyna replied. She added, "Once I get this together, can I count on you to delegate it to?"

At that moment, with everything so chaotic, Chyna would've delegated anything to do with funerals or important decisions to any of the children from Sunday school.

The young woman gave a weak smile and indicated that she would do whatever Chyna needed. Of course, she was one of the ones who knew nothing about the plan to unseat Chyna.

Cordell was about to walk to the door where he'd seen some of the board members when he spied Deacon Pillar walking in the same direction.

"Praise Him," Cordell said while extending his hand to the deacon. "I guess you've heard."

Deacon Pillar gave a weak handshake and shook his head showing his disbelief. "Brother DeWitt, right? You're a good friend of the First Lady?"

"Yes, I'm sorry. I should've introduced myself."

"It's no bother. I just left Deacon Athens's room." He pulled Cordell over to an empty table. He sat down and indicated that Cordell should do the same.

"Listen," Deacon Pillar said. "This may not be the right time, but you and I need to chat." He gave Cordell a pained look before continuing, "I know what you know." He let his words hang in the air.

Cordell studied the old man's face. He saw the wear and the tear that sometimes occurred when one tried to work with a lot of "church" folks. "I'm not quite sure what you mean," Cordell replied. "Could you be more specific?"

"Play games if you want to," Deacon Pillar said as he slowly rose from his seat. He pointed a finger, crooked and bent, no doubt from arthritis, toward the cafeteria entrance. "They don't play by the rules."

Cordell's eyes followed the deacon's gaze and it fell upon the remaining church board members who'd, again, gathered in the doorway.

"—and those scallywags don't take prisoners, either." Deacon Pillar mumbled over his shoulder, as he ambled toward the other board members. "Praying time is here."

Cordell sat down again. He became angered as he thought about how much of a problem some church members could become. He saw Chyna and motioned with his finger for her to come to him.

Chyna didn't try to hide the look of relief that came over her face. She was grateful to Cordell for giving her a reason to walk away from the members. They'd pulled and tugged upon her almost nonstop, as though she were on a greeting line after service.

"Let's check in on Janelle again." Cordell said, once Chyna reached his side.

"Sure."

"After we see her, I need to talk further with you. I've some new and unfinished business to discuss."

"Now—?"

"Yes," Cordell answered while holding the elevator door open for Chyna. "I wish it could be some other time, but it can't wait."

They stepped off the elevator and were fortunate to

run into Doctor Bayer. Cordell knew the routine and took the opportunity to step aside so Chyna could discuss Janelle's condition.

"I'm remarkably surprised that Janelle's condition hadn't worsened as much as I'd originally suspected."

The doctor also used the opportunity to remind Chyna that Janelle's medications needed to be monitored more closely. "Emotions play just as big a role in a patient's recovery as the medication itself." Doctor Bayer admonished, "Janelle is a long ways from being in remission."

Cordell watched Chyna alternately nod and speak. He imagined Chyna was getting as much information as possible to take care of Janelle.

Chapter 41

While Janelle remained hospitalized, at home Chyna was tossed to and fro by one piece of drama after another.

During the last two weeks Chyna fought against an in-her-face pushback from some of the church board members. She was surprised when they even griped about how she oversaw Sister Blackstone's small funeral. In all their complaining, there wasn't one member who gave a suggestion as to what they would have done different.

She'd done the best she could. After all, there wasn't much that could be done for the old pastor's aide. Single and living alone, Sister Blackstone had done what most of the senior members of the church had; she'd given a power of attorney document to the church to dispose of her remains.

It was actually Deacon Pillar who'd talked her into having Sister Blackstone cremated. "When we get back her ashes," Deacon Pillar crowed, despite remembering how Reverend Young perished, "give 'em to me so I can have the ashes burned, too." He'd been quite adamant about knowing that Sister Blackstone wouldn't want a fuss.

The truth was that if the deacon hadn't suggested the cremation, Chyna would've found a way to have the old busybody burned.

She'd also designated the homebound and missionary board auxiliaries to stay close and attend to Deacon Athens. He was still hospitalized and comatose, and if no one else appeared at the hospital, Deacon Pillar always did. He saw to it that his friend was always comfortable.

Sometime later on in the week Cordell received another urgent call from Deacon Pillar. He'd resisted meeting the old deacon, because looking after Chyna and Janelle completely wore him out. As a relatively young man in his forties, he was feeling particularly tired lately. And then, Deacon Pillar said the words Cordell feared, "I've seen the picture of the First Lady. Now we can do this the easy way and avoid all hell breaking loose or you can sit on your behind and let that church board take her down."

"Where and when?" Cordell replied.

That was yesterday. Today, Cordell would find out exactly what the old deacon knew. He found a parking space inside the municipal parking lot on DeKalb Avenue in downtown Brooklyn. The weather was quite warm, and for that he was grateful. If his suspicions were right it was certain to be a coldhearted discussion.

Cordell walked through the glass doors of Junior's Restaurant. It'd been at that same spot on Flatbush and DeKalb since 1950 and was famous for its decadent and delicious cheesecake varieties. He spied the old deacon, who had his back hunched over and his head bobbing as he devoured his meal.

Cordell offered Deacon Pillar his hand before sliding back a chair opposite him and sitting. "Sorry I'm running a little late," Cordell apologized. "We brought Janelle home from the hospital today. I see you found something to do until I arrived." Cordell's attempt at humor was poor, but it was the best he could do to break the ice.

"It's not a problem," Deacon Pillar said. "I'm about finished with my cherry cheesecake." He slid the remaining gooey pie filling off the folk with his tongue. "If you ain't ordering, we can get right down to business."

"It's early," Cordell replied, "barely five o'clock, but I think I'll order something to drink."

"Suit yourself." The deacon leaned back and adjusted his suspenders before shaking the toothpick holder on the table. He managed to get out enough to put into his top shirt pocket for later use before actually putting one in his mouth. He didn't think of it as stealing. He thought of it as one of God's divine blessings, because he didn't have a lot of money to waste on buying toothpicks.

Cordell gave the waitress his drink order, a glass of seltzer water with lime, and then nodded toward the deacon. By the time the deacon finished telling Cordell all that was truly happening regarding Chyna and the evil parts he, Sister Blackstone, and Deacon Athens played, Cordell cancelled the second seltzer and ordered a Nutty Angel. "Double down on that vodka," he called out.

"My God," Cordell barked. His voice rose and he was about to lose control. "All of that because y'all thought the church wasn't holy enough?"

"It's not so much that too much secular stuff was going on, and that the church wasn't holy enough for the congregation," Deacon Pillar repeated, in exasperation, "it just wasn't holy enough for most of the board. After all, some of us tossed the first brick into the foundation." He leaned forward and almost whispered. "Now the destruction of the First Lady's life was all Eartha's doing. She just wasn't gonna have people associating what the reverend did with the church every time the First Lady came through the door. She claimed she had shaming information about Chyna."

"Okay, so it seems that we have pieces of this puzzle spread between us," Cordell said slowly. "And now I know that the picture of the First Lady was taken when she was drugged at a bachelorette party that just happened to have been at the Sweet Bush, too. So now, what do we do next?"

"Hell if I know," Deacon Pillar shot back. "You the one traveling around the country fixin' church mess. I was hoping you'd tell me."

"Do you know where Sister Blackstone hid what she had?"

"All I know is that on the same day that Athens was hit, he'd called me. He said that he and Eartha got into it and that he'd snatched a shopping bag from her that had some kind of book in it. She claimed the book had a whole bunch of stuff not only on the First Lady but also on Pastor Grayson and some of the other church members."

"Are you serious?" Cordell swigged down his second Nutty Angel, and wasn't feeling a thing. So he ordered another.

"As a heart attack," Deacon Pillar replied. "That picture you got, as far as I know, wasn't nothing compared to the smut that Eartha claimed she had."

"And you saw the other pictures?" Cordell asked.

"I only saw the one that was passed around at one of the board meetings," Deacon Pillar said and then, seemingly without thinking, he added a weak wink. "It didn't make me think any less of the First Lady. It made me think even higher of her. She should give some of those old biddies a few lessons. Maybe there wouldn't be so much creeping on the high and the low going on in the church."

The two men kept talking and tossing ideas around. It wasn't until Cordell was on his fourth Nutty Angel that he somehow remembered that Deacon Athens's car was still parked in front of Chyna's. He also remembered that Deacon Athens yelled out to Sister Blackstone that he had her shopping bag.

"I think I know where the book at," Cordell's words sounded thick and unsteady.

"That's good," Deacon Pillar answered. "Do you also know where your car is at?"

Deacon Pillar finally got the whereabouts of Cordell's car as well as retrieving the parking ticket from Cordell's pants pocket. He knew he probably looked a bit lecherous as he picked through Cordell's pants pocket in front of folks, but it couldn't be helped.

"Okay, Mr. Famous Leader and Know-It-All," Deacon Pillar teased. "Let's get you to your car. It's good that I grabbed a cab to get here. I'll be doing the driving, thank you."

Back at Chyna's, it'd started to get dark. She checked the clock in the living room. It was almost eight o'clock. Where was Cordell? He'd promised to stop by.

She picked up a tray she'd carried before stopping to turn down the radio in the living room. She was just about to continue down the hallway to the back bedroom when she heard the moaning.

Barely hours had passed since Janelle was released from her two-week hospital stay. Yet, every time she'd moan, groan, cough, or sneeze, it caused Chyna to rush to her sister's side. When she wasn't doing that, she was shadowing the woman she'd hired to clean her huge home. Janelle needed a sterile environment. Of course, neither sister was much into domestic house duties, but they weren't into filth, either, at least not when it came to where they lived.

Chyna raced toward Janelle's bedroom. "I'm coming!"

A glass dropped off the tray but Chyna ignored it as she raced inside. She looked over toward the bed.

Chyna was definitely worried now. All her talk about not needing anyone, Cordell in particular, was just that.

From her bed Janelle moaned again, unknowingly accompanying Chyna in a familiar tune that was now their number-one song, "Where is Cordell?"

Chapter 42

It was well after eight o'clock when Deacon Pillar pulled up in front of Chyna's with Cordell finally beginning to sober up. For the umpteenth time since they'd left Junior's Restaurant and hit the highway, Deacon Pillar put the gearshift in the wrong position to stop the car. The car yanked and hit the curb and almost snapped the head off a pigeon that'd played chicken with the car.

"Hey," Cordell snipped. "Whatcha doing?" That last lunge finally brought him around.

"This doggone thing ain't nothing like my old lemon." Lemon was what he called the old tractor trailer he'd driven for years and it had about ten different gears. "You lucky we made it."

Deacon Pillar unsnapped his seat belt and looked over at Cordell. "Good thing you're not witnessing to nobody about Jesus," the deacon chuckled. "You look like you should be somewhere in an A.A.A. meeting."

"That's for cars," Cordell said. Even partially drunk, he knew that.

"No, that's for your arse because you about one and a half times as drunk as a Christian oughta be."

Cordell flipped the mirror on the overhead dash. One look at his reflection was enough to give him a hangover even if the Nutty Angels hadn't. He grabbed a wet wipe from the passenger-side pocket holder and began to wipe his face. "Not too bad," he remarked when he finished. "But that's if nobody sees me in the light."

Both men exited the car and headed straight for Deacon Athens's car. Cordell was surprised to see Deacon Pillar pull out a heavily loaded key ring.

"That's the church's Seniors van. Athens was about the only one that drove it, though," Deacon Pillar said as he separated the keys on the ring. "There's about four of us with keys to it. We decided to keep copies 'cause old Athens kept forgetting where he laid 'em."

Both men noticed the lights were on in Chyna's living room but said nothing. Their main focus was on Deacon Athens's van.

One thing was in their favor. Deacon Athens kept the van spotless and uncluttered. Although the van was a bit dusty from just sitting for the last several weeks, inside was spotless.

"It's a good thing First Lady lives in this part of Brooklyn," Deacon Pillar noted. "Just about anywhere else they'd had this ole boy stripped down to the paint and one wheel spoke."

Cordell kept his eye on Chyna's house. The motion detector was too far away to shine the light on what they were doing. He checked his watch. "It's almost eight forty-five. Do we take a chance and go back to my hotel or should we at least check in on the women?"

"That's probably why you haven't gotten further along than you have," Deacon Pillar said with a short chuckle as he removed the bag from the van. "You don't ever let your left hand know what your right hand is doing." He quietly closed the door to the van and added, "You can get cut like that."

Deacon Pillar handed the bag to Cordell. He immediately went to the passenger side of Cordell's car. "You look sober enough to drive," he said as he slid in and began to buckle his seat belt. "I'm tired. All this plotting is wearing me out."

"You've never plotted before? That's not what you told me earlier," Cordell said as he, too, fastened his seat belt and started the engine.

"Oh, I've plotted before," Deacon Pillar replied. "But not with an amateur like you." That time he laughed loudly, "Hell, you ain't never plotted until you've been a part of the church board."

Inside Janelle's bedroom, Chyna thought she'd heard a car's engine through the open window. By the time she went to check it out, there was nothing but darkness.

"I'm sorry about this mess," Chyna told Janelle. "I guess I'm just trying too hard."

"I truly wish you'd stop," Janelle pretended to scold Chyna. "You're making me sick. Actually don't take no offense, but you working a girl's last good nerve." It took some effort, but she withheld any sign that she was still in pain. "By the way," Janelle said slowly, "I wasn't moaning."

"You weren't?" Chyna asked. She neared Janelle's bed and leaned over to fluff the pillow and tidy up her sister's bed. "I'm sorry if I heard wrong."

"You just oughta be," Janelle said. She was almost back to her feisty self, "I was singing."

The sisters laughed. Chyna finished cleaning up the mess and sat in the recliner opposite Janelle's bed. It took another few minutes before Chyna finally answered Janelle's unspoken question.

"I imagine that Cordell's conference earlier today went a little longer than he'd imagined. It's not quite nine o'clock, so he may still stop by to check in on you." Chyna automatically fidgeted with the television's remote control. She really didn't want Janelle to see the doubt in her eyes.

"He didn't have a conference today," Janelle replied. "That's not until next Saturday." She smiled slightly because she knew Chyna was still uncomfortable talking to her about Cordell.

During the time that passed, Janelle and Chyna did everything possible to avoid the conversation that needed to take place. It wasn't until a segment of the local news came on that there was no choice left. It was a news update. Deacon Athens had died.

And then there was one, Deacon Pillar.

Deacon Pillar and Cordell were almost to Cordell's hotel room when the deacon's cell phone rang. The color from the deacon's face drained quickly as his hands began to shake to the point where he almost dropped the phone.

Somehow Cordell knew. He didn't know how, but he just did. As soon as Deacon Pillar hung up the phone and turned his head to look out the passenger side window, Cordell whispered, "He's gone, isn't he?"

Cordell couldn't remember seeing an old man cry like Deacon Pillar. The man looked as though the entire world had crushed him.

Before Cordell could turn his car around, like the deacon's, his cell phone rang, too.

"I just heard," Cordell said softly. "In fact, I'm with Deacon Pillar." He said nothing for a few seconds as he appeared to listen intently to the caller. He sighed and finally added, "No, tell her I'll see her in the morning. Whenever he's ready, I'm going back to the hospital with Deacon Pillar."

Cordell hung up the phone. As he drove along Linden Boulevard on his way to Downstate Medical, he looked up in time to see the outline. The Sweet Bush stood in stark contrast to what it'd been. To add to its shame, it still hadn't been rebuilt or attended to since Grayson's melee. Its burnt-out shell reminded Cordell of all that had been destroyed within the past six months or so. He hoped the lives of those involved would fare better than that building.

Chapter 43

Shortly after Chyna had called Cordell about Deacon Athens's death, she'd anxiously paced across the deep brown carpet of her bedroom as her mind rambled.

Janelle had just drifted off to sleep when the telephone rang. Chyna grabbed the cordless phone and slipped out of Janelle's room in time to receive more bad news.

The telephone call, from one of the church members informing her of Deacon Athens's death, had sickened her, again. "Thank you for calling, but I just heard about it on the news." It was too much: too much like a sneak punch to her rekindled faith.

There was a war waged between her mind and heart. Deacon Athens was gone and now she hadn't expected to feel as guilty as she'd become about Sister Blackstone. Even before Grayson's death, she'd not been particularly close to the elderly woman. She kowtowed to Grayson sometimes like a pastor's aide, but at other times she seemed more like she was his mother. There never appeared to be room for Chyna in that relationship.

Chyna found herself almost in a daze as she looked out into the darkness from her bedroom window. "Jesus, you're the light of the world," she suddenly started to hum "You're the light, Lord." She'd sung that song more times than she could count, so why was she still stumbling around in spiritual blackout?

Chyna felt a chill even though the night was very warm outside. Clasping the collar of her housecoat, she shuddered and turned from the window. That's when she realized she still held the cordless phone in her hand. She was supposed to call one of the members of the bereavement auxiliary.

But she still hadn't. She'd chosen to call Cordell. After all, he'd returned into their lives bringing some of the calm and judgment they'd needed, along with some unnecessary drama, too. Of course, she also realized after a while that Cordell, her ex-husband, was still in love with her sister, his first love.

As much as she needed to call someone from bereavement to begin to take care of the funeral plans for Deacon Athens, she instead took another moment to recall the earlier conversation with Cordell.

The exchange between the two had presented more questions than answers. Chyna was truly puzzled. She went into the kitchen for a cup of tea. While she waited for the water to boil, her mind carried on with its quest to understand what was going on.

What was he doing with Deacon Pillar? I wasn't aware that they were particularly close. If not for Janelle's sake, why didn't he rush over and see about her?

She sat at the kitchen table and while dunking a teabag into the boiled water, she continued to search for anything that would make sense. And then the big question. *Is Cordell tiring of me and Janelle's dramas? Am I overly depending on him?*

Just as she was about to sip from her cup, Chyna's

thoughts were interrupted by a noise coming out of Janelle's room. She'd had an intercom installed in Janelle's room that was hooked up practically all over the house. Chyna could be at her sister's beck and call within moments of any distress or need.

The teaspoon was still in her hand as she raced into Janelle's bedroom. "You okay?" Chyna asked as she tried to figure out why Janelle stood naked in the mirror.

"It's working," Janelle said with a forced smile. "It's working." She turned slowly and pointed to her breasts, which she always referred to as "the girls." "The cocoa butter you prayed over has practically erased the scar from the biopsy." She turned around, again, and with apparent pain, she placed her hands on her hips. "Look at that. You've got to get another jar and quick," she laughed, still unashamed of her nudity. "The girls are back."

Chyna forced a smile. She was truly happy for her. "You're truly gifted in that department." She walked toward Janelle, stopping only a moment to grab Janelle's robe from the bed.

"Okay," Chyna teased. "I'm sure those girls are more modest than you, so you might want to cover them."

Janelle took the robe from Chyna's hands. She was beginning to tire, so she couldn't argue.

Chyna's smile began to slide. Janelle believed in the prayer that covered that jar of cocoa butter and lately, her prayer life had really taken off in earnest. So how could she take away that moment of gratefulness by telling her that the man who'd prayed over that jar of cocoa butter almost a year ago was now dead?

And Janelle hadn't mentioned Cordell, not once.

Chapter 44

The outline was barely out of sight. "Don't let your mind go there, young man," Deacon Pillar warned.

Cordell hadn't said anything aloud, but Deacon Pillar saw the grim remains of the Sweet Bush as well. How could anyone connected with either New Hope Assembly or the First Lady not be affected by that reminder?

"You're right," Cordell replied. "In about fifteen minutes we'll be at my hotel room."

"Sure wish Deacon Athens could meet us there," Deacon Pillar mumbled. He was still trying to hold it together for the sake of his old friend. It wasn't easy.

"It's too bad the deacon didn't have any family," Cordell said. He'd really said it just to have something to talk about. He saw the struggle that Deacon Pillar waged with his emotions.

"He wasn't totally alone," Deacon Pillar said. "He had a niece and a no-good nephew that live right here in Brooklyn." He turned to face Cordell, who had stopped for a traffic light. His eyes grew wide. "Well, Suh!" Deacon Pillar exclaimed, "Speaking of the devil."

"What are you talking about?" Cordell asked as he slowly moved across the light and began to turn.

"There's the no-good bum now."

Deacon Pillar pointed a gnarly finger toward a group of about four or five young men standing under a streetlight. Each man stood shuffling, heads swinging side to side, sizing up any random opportunities to rob or do anything sinister. But one of them stood out from the rest.

"See that one with half a shirt on and younger than the others," Deacon Pillar acted like he was about to spit. "The one with those demon tattoos."

"They all look about the same to me," Cordell responded. He'd almost stopped to a crawl to get a better look without inviting trouble. It was dark, so how could the deacon be sure of what he saw?

"It's no matter," Deacon Pillar said as he urged Cordell to drive on. "That damn Hard Life ain't gonna amount to crap in a cow field. That's one of the reasons why Deacon Athens never had much to do with that punk or his mama, Cinnamon."

"Cinnamon," Cordell said in surprise. "I once knew a Cinnamon. She was a longtime friend of Chyna."

"That would be the one," Deacon Pillar said, angrily. "I never could understand First Lady being friends with the likes of someone like that."

"Really, I'm surprised."

"Well, that was until I saw the picture," Deacon Pillar said. "But I still believe the First Lady has more class than that trash."

Cordell parked his car and took the deacon up to his hotel room. After offering the deacon something to drink and taking an aspirin himself, he went into the bedroom and retrieved the envelope.

"Still don't know why you told Janelle about some of this," Deacon Pillar said as he waited for Cordell to sit.

"Well, I did," Cordell answered. "I didn't plan on learning as much as I did, though."

"I'm not following you." Deacon Pillar said and then added, "Do you mind if I use your phone? I need to find out if they've removed Deacon Athens's body yet." No matter what was discussed that night, it always led back to his dear old friend.

Deacon Pillar called a few people. When finished he excused himself again and went into the bathroom. Stressed as he was, he still couldn't stop the tears from flowing, again, before he made it to the doorway.

While the deacon was in the bathroom, prayerfully trying to gain composure, Cordell went through Grayson's journal. By the time the deacon returned, Cordell had read enough. He was livid and completely sober.

While Cordell tried to comfort Deacon Pillar at the hotel and keep evil thoughts at bay, Chyna and Janelle watched television at home.

When Chyna saw Janelle tiring, she helped her sister back into bed. Tired as Janelle felt, she didn't want to sleep—not yet, anyway. So the sisters chatted about nothing in particular. It was apparent that each was skirting something.

It took an hour or two, but sleep finally hit Janelle. As she dozed off, it looked as though she smiled. Her hands lay protectively about her breasts while she slumbered. And, whether she meant to do it or not, she even mumbled, "Thank you, Jesus."

At the hotel, after much debate, Deacon Pillar and Cordell were totally in agreement upon one thing. The church should become more conservative in its policies but definitely not by including Chyna or her past indiscretions in the process.

"I'm gonna have to take your word for it that First Lady hasn't shown any signs of ever being involved in a scandalous situation again," Deacon Pillar said, cautiously. "I know she hasn't been around for quite some time since she was told to take time off to grieve. I've nothing to go on but your word and my friend Athens's belief that her character shouldn't be assassinated."

Again, at the mention of Deacon Athens, Deacon Pillar began to choke up.

"Are you sure you're gonna be all right by yourself?" Cordell asked and then added, "You are welcome to spend the night here if you wish to wait to go to the hospital or when you're done there."

"I'm not sure about . . ." Deacon Pillar's voice trailed.

"Please. I'm not sure I trust myself to be here alone with my anger. I need your counsel," Cordell interjected. He really didn't need it as much as he'd said, but he was really too tired to drive the deacon home after they went to the hospital and he sure could use a prayer partner that night.

Deacon Pillar looked at Cordell and then over to the radio, where the illuminated dial showed it was after eleven o'clock. He really couldn't remember the last time someone requested his counsel. And for certain no one on the church board had asked for it. There were probably more times that he and Athens bucked Sister Blackstone and hatched their outlandish plans than they'd agreed. But Athens was gone. It always came back to that.

Deacon Athens was in his eternal sleep now, but those on the other side of the grave found sleep evasive.

The moonlight shone bright on Janelle's face. She'd awakened a bit fuzzy. It wasn't an unusual feeling after taking her medication. She ran one hand through her hair, noting that the scarf had come off. Realizing that no hair fell when she did so helped her to gather her wits.

Janelle smiled and immediately grabbed the television remote control. She was about to roll out of bed and head for the bathroom when scrolling text across a news channel caught her attention.

"Mr. Earl Athens, the second Downstate Medical Center hit-and-run victim, succumbed earlier to injuries suffered almost three weeks ago. . . ."

Janelle didn't remember screaming. Apparently she had, because Chyna was helping her back onto the bed.

Chapter 45

The telephone in Cordell's hotel room emitted a stubborn ring. Even in the deep recesses of Cordell's sleep, he heard the phone's assault.

He almost tripped over Deacon Pillar, who'd let one leg fall off the pullout sofa, to grab the phone off the desk. He'd purposely put the phone far from the bed. He didn't want to fall into the temptation of using it when he should sleep.

By the time Cordell hung up the phone, Deacon Pillar was up and almost dressed.

"Didn't mean to listen in, but I couldn't help but overhear," Deacon Pillar offered. "I imagine that First Lady needs a friend. You can just drop me off at home on your way, if you don't mind."

"A change of plans," Cordell said rushing around to put on his clothes. "I'm gonna need you to come with me."

"Why is that?"

"Janelle has found out about Deacon Athens passing."

"What's that to her?" The deacon hadn't meant to

sound so cold, but it wasn't a secret that Janelle never hid her distaste for anything or anyone religious. Some, however, would also argue that Janelle told the truth more than most in the church.

When Cordell and Deacon Pillar arrived at Chyna's Highland Park home at around three in the morning she was on her second cup of tea. Her nerves were frayed. She'd no idea of how hard the deaths of Sister Blackstone and Deacon Athens impacted Janelle.

Chyna related what had happened and what was said when she found Janelle sobbing in her room. When she, too, had caught the scrolling news of Deacon Athens's death, earlier, she'd not told Janelle. She'd raced, as usual, into Janelle's room and found her crying.

> *"Why me, why am I living?" Janelle cried. "God could've taken me. I'm the one with the cancer and He let me live. I don't understand. That old man, Deacon Athens, prayed over a jar that's healing my scars and God just snatches him up."*

Janelle could hardly breathe, she was so upset.

Finally, she'd fallen back to sleep. She'd also tired from arguing with Chyna, who'd wanted to take her back to the hospital.

When Chyna finished relating what'd happened to cause her to call Cordell, he got up and left the room.

While Cordell went into Janelle's room, Deacon Pillar sat opposite Chyna in her living room. Like Chyna, he gulped tea and tried to decide how much he should tell her, if anything. While he contemplated what to do, he looked around and admired the décor of the room. It sure made his small apartment look like a hovel. Yet, he wasn't upset. He was happy to learn that despite all the church board had done to retrieve gifts and other items that she still maintained a sense of style.

Chyna also watched Deacon Pillar while she sipped her tea. There were several things she wanted to say, but she didn't know where to begin. Did he, too, know the entire truth about the Sweet Bush? She'd not forgotten the outburst from Janelle weeks ago when Cordell started to mention some type of file or something. And now it seemed that Cordell and the deacon appeared to be closer than she'd known.

"Can I get you another cup?" Chyna asked.

"No, thank you, First Lady." Deacon Pillar replied. "This is just fine."

"I guess there's no good time to express my sympathy. I know you and Deacon Athens were longtime friends."

"That's true. We've been under three pastors together," Deacon Pillar said before misspeaking his opinion. "Of course, Pastor Young would've made the fourth had he lived and served more than ten years." No sooner had he said it, he downed the remaining warm liquid. He'd done it quickly for no other reason than to have his mouth occupied, so nothing else stupid would come out.

The beginning of dawn had begun to cover the darkness of Janelle's room. Cordell debated whether or not to wake her. He decided not to do so. With his hands clasped, he chose to just sit in a chair and watch her.

Cordell was struck by how many times he'd visited Janelle in that very room and never paid attention to its layout, the furnishings, or anything other than her.

Soon, the brightness of the sun entered Janelle's bedroom window. It, too, seemed determined to fill in the blanks in Cordell's mind with everything he'd missed about the room. It didn't take but a moment or so before he saw it.

Cordell smiled. Why he'd not noticed the big sombrero that hung on a far wall he didn't know. What he did realize was that it was a gift he'd given Janelle more than fifteen years ago. He rose and walked over to it. He allowed his hands to run over the frayed strawlike material. He'd bought it for Janelle when they'd taken a trip to Cozumel, Mexico. Some of the memory was a bit hazy except the giddiness she showed about something so small and not all that expensive, he recalled.

Then he heard her almost childlike giggle before he had time to process the memory and all it meant. He spun around. He was embarrassed because he'd taken the sombrero off the wall. Frayed pieces of straw dangled from its tips as he'd tried to adjust it to fit his head, which was definitely bigger than Janelle's. He was about to destroy the hat by trying to wear it.

"That's all I have remaining from the last time we danced." The giggle turned sour fast. "You left the dance floor to dance with Chyna."

Chapter 46

Of course, while Cordell was in the room with Janelle, neither of them realized or remembered that Chyna had an intercom installed. So while the two sometimes laughed, and other times argued, every word filtered into the living room.

At that moment eavesdropping proved to be a good thing. It certainly changed the mood inside Chyna's living room. After Deacon Pillar's unintended reference to Grayson's death, Chyna was happy to change the subject.

"They used to dance together?" Deacon Pillar asked. "Was it ballroom dancing? They seemed too old to do that hippity-hoppity demon stuff."

Chyna said nothing, because she knew from the last conversation with Janelle and Cordell that whatever the dance was, she wasn't a part of it.

The silence of the intercom might as well been a clap of thunder the way it hit Chyna and Deacon Pillar at the same time. They lifted their heads and looked quizzically at each other.

"What do you think happened?" Deacon Pillar said,

"I don't hear nothing." He rose off his seat as fast as he could. He was about to bounce from the living room as though he owned the house.

In fact, he did just that with Chyna right on his heels. The problem was that Deacon Pillar wasn't certain which room was Janelle's until Chyna almost knocked the old man down as she pushed him aside and entered Janelle's room.

With Deacon Pillar catching up in time to look over Chyna's shoulder, he did what he should've done earlier in the living room. He quickly placed his hand over his mouth and stifled a surprised laugh.

Chyna and Deacon Pillar watched in fascination at the sight of Cordell and Janelle lying side by side across Janelle's bed. And, of course, Cordell looked ridiculous in a sombrero that looked like a horde of locusts had gotten to it.

Janelle looked up at the surprised looks on her uninvited guests' faces. "You might as well come on in."

Cordell looked sheepish and rightly so. He'd kept his clothes on, but one look would've told anyone who knew better that he was definitely ready to *dance*.

The laughter, again, broke the tension.

"Okay, you've all had your laugh." He did all he could to keep a serious face. "Let's get out of here and let Janelle get a little more sleep."

"Mind your own business." Janelle's word's seemed almost foolish despite her effort to stifle a yawn and rebuke Cordell at the same time.

Neither Chyna nor Deacon Pillar or even Cordell said another word. They simply looked at Janelle's half-closed eyes and left to return to the living room.

It was already close to eight o'clock in the morning.

"It's not my kitchen," Cordell said, "but I can stand to eat a little something."

"Stay right where you are," Chyna rose, "I remember how well you cook, but I'll fix something for all of us."

"Do you think Miss Janelle might want a little something to peck on?" Deacon Pillar, forever the thoughtful one, really wasn't comfortable with the young woman being alone in her room while they chowed down.

Chyna pointed to the intercom. "She's still sleeping and usually it's only oatmeal she eats. It coats her stomach and it's easy to keep down."

Deacon Pillar was certain he'd never look at oatmeal the same way again.

Around nine o'clock someone from the bereavement auxiliary returned Chyna's call. She'd just turned off the stove after cooking a big breakfast for all of them.

The discussion with the young girl she'd delegated to handle the home going covered some of the things necessary for Deacon Athens's funeral and the big differences in how it would be carried out compared to Sister Blackstone's recent home going.

After she'd hung up the telephone Chyna sat at her desk and scratched off a few things on a sheet of paper. It was the form that the church used when planning a funeral to make sure that all the bases were covered. It seemed unreal to her that a little more than six months ago, it was Grayson's death that pushed her out of her church duties as the First Lady. Now, it was the untimely deaths of Sister Blackstone and Deacon Athens that brought her back.

This must be an act of God, because I wasn't really fond of either of them. But then I could've said the same thing about Deacon Pillar twenty-four hours ago.

Chyna replaced all the pieces of paper in a folder and set it aside for someone to pick up.

Chyna returned to the kitchen and found that Janelle had awoken while she was on the telephone and managed to get to the kitchen. She'd joined the others and Cordell had made her a bowl of instant oatmeal.

"Good morning, my dear sister," Chyna placed her arm around Janelle and hugged her gently. "I'm glad to see you up. You look good."

"Chyna, please cut it out. My oatmeal is sweet enough so you can cut back on the syrupy words. You're about to turn me into a diabetic with your sweetness."

Everyone laughed at Janelle's usual rebuking and feisty demeanor.

"I truly like you, gal," Deacon Pillar said. "You tell it like it is and not like it was."

Another round of laughter and then the silence took a seat at the kitchen table. For a few uncomfortable moments, silence moved everyone's thoughts around like food on a plate.

Preferring not to repeat the funeral plans, Chyna poured herself another cup of tea. With steam rising from her cup, she sat, sipped, and waited to see where the conversation would go or at least start.

It went straight to the subject of Deacon Athens. That time, though, it wasn't about his death. It wasn't even about the fact that neither Deacon Pillar nor Cordell ever went to the hospital to see the body.

Apparently, while Chyna was out of the room Cordell, along with Deacon Pillar and Janelle decided it was time to call a spade a spade. There had to be a reason why two people who held the reins to the peace and destination for their lives had recently passed. Was God removing obstacles?

Chapter 47

Only a few moments had passed inside Chyna's kitchen when Deacon Pillar spoke up first. "I'm ready to get this over with," he said, leading the matter.

"I've made certain that the arrangements are taken care of as we speak," Chyna said. She just couldn't understand the sudden rush to bury Deacon Athens.

"That's wonderful," Deacon Pillar said with bushy eyebrows raised. "However, trust me with those two now gone, there'll be no stopping the craziness from the other board members unless we start putting out fires."

"I'm certain you're right," Chyna nodded, and then added, forcing the television image of the Sweet Bush fire to the back of her mind, "God is not the author of confusion." She wanted to ask the old deacon if he was talking about the same thing she was, but she didn't.

"Well, God certainly got my attention," Janelle said, softly. She could almost read Chyna's confused mind and she quickly changed the subject back to the matter at hand. "It took Him a while, yet, I don't think He needed to be so dramatic about it." Janelle let out a nervous laugh as she, subconsciously, touched her chest before continuing.

Cordell knew the discussion was needed, but he also needed to be a bit more ready to participate. He pushed away from the table. He reached for the coffeepot and refilled his cup. His face looked almost solemn as he struggled to voice his thoughts, "Okay, if there's a spiritual reason I can't think of one. Perhaps it was just their time to go."

"Cordell, please. You're not at one of your sessions. We're trying to be serious here." Janelle laid her spoon aside. "I may not be all up there with God like some of you . . ." Janelle stopped and eyed Deacon Pillar, letting him know he might not be one of the ones she were mentioning, "but even I know that God must've had a hand in all of this."

Disregarding Janelle's silent rebuke because he deserved it, Deacon Pillar stroked his chin and added, "I've thought about it, too. They were the power brokers on the board." Deacon Pillar said, firmly, "I'm wondering." The deacon's voice rose as he realized they'd all suddenly looked to him as their elder and said aloud the question on their minds, "I'm wondering if God removed what He saw as obstacles?"

"I've thought the same thing," Chyna echoed. "I've wondered if this was an act of God, although I hadn't thought of Deacon Athens as being that big of an obstacle." Chyna added, "So Deacon Pillar, why would you say such a thing?"

It was just the lead the deacon was waiting for. Without ceremony Deacon Pillar nodded toward Cordell, indicating he wanted the journal and everything placed on the table.

Chyna's eyes grew wild as her insides churned. She recognized Grayson's journal. He'd always taunted her with it but kept it out of her sight.

As for Janelle, she knew about the picture and if the journal were on the table, then the picture wasn't too far behind. She looked at Chyna sadly, because as much as she wanted to protect her younger sister, at that moment, she was helpless to do so. But then Janelle looked in Cordell's direction with her eyes blazing a hole through him. He'd not completely leveled with her. Why would he tell her about a picture but not about the journal?

"Let us pray," Deacon Pillar's commanding voice took over. He wasn't where he probably needed to be in God, at that moment, but he still knew spiritual confusion. He didn't wait for the others to comply. He dropped his head and began to pray.

"Heavenly Father and Most Precious Lord," Deacon Pillar pleaded. "We've come to you in the name of Your son Jesus. We've come to you with repentance in our hearts and on our lips. . . ."

With all hearts and minds purposed to set things in order, Deacon Pillar's prayer set the tone. However, even the most ardent of prayers didn't prepare the deacon for the confessions that would pour out.

Cordell, who was eager for quite some time to put things in order between he and the sisters, leaped in as soon as the "amen" was pronounced.

At first he turned to Janelle. She stared back with both horror and interest. He supposed she was horrified that Chyna would finally find out that Grayson had somehow gotten ahold of a picture of her more-than-exotic poses from Cinnamon's bachelorette party and it had landed in the hands of Sister Blackstone. He quickly decided to start with Chyna.

"Chyna," Cordell began. "The deacon has prayed and opened a door that we need to drag all our baggage through." He stopped and reached across the table to take Chyna's hand. She didn't resist, so he continued, "There's no use in pretending that our marriage was anything more than a matter of convenience. If you'd not gotten pregnant we wouldn't have married."

"I know," Chyna replied. "I know."

Cordell looked to Janelle to see if she were about to go into distress or worse before he continued. She didn't seem to be, so he then looked at the deacon, who said nothing but continued to keep his hands clasped. He looked like he was still in silent prayers.

"I could've asked you for a divorce when you miscarried because the reason for marriage was taken away, but I didn't. I didn't because I was still trying to punish Janelle. I truly believed that Janelle cheated on me."

"I sure found out about that the hard way," Chyna said. "Janelle almost beat me to a pulp."

"Beat you?" Cordell said, cautiously, "I never knew you two fought."

Janelle eyes became watery. "Let me interrupt right now," she said. "I know Chyna will never tell you everything no matter how hard this deacon prayed." She looked at Deacon Pillar and gave him a soft pat on his hand to show that she meant no disrespect.

"It's not necessary," Chyna urged. "Janelle, please, it's okay and in the past."

"It may be," Janelle said as she pulled a napkin from its holder and began to dab at her eyes, "but it's no sense in keeping it a secret. Secrets have nearly destroyed us."

"Cordell," Janelle began. She turned away to avoid Chyna's still-pleading eyes. "I did fight with Chyna. I fought because I'd discovered why you slept with her. I was angry with you because you should've come to me instead of sleeping with my sister. I was angry with Chyna, because even if she didn't know about you and me before the two of you got together, she was still carrying your child. I wanted to carry your child."

"What are you saying, Janelle?" Cordell asked the question even though he was sure he already knew the answer.

"Chyna lost her baby—your baby—because of me."

"Have mercy, Father," Deacon Pillar thought aloud. He then slouched and started muttering what everyone assumed were more prayers.

Cordell didn't know what to think or to feel. He hadn't felt particularly angry that Chyna had lost the child. Fact was, he was almost relieved. "I can't keep up this pretense, not even after all this time. The truth is that although we were so much in debt from me losing that disc jockey job and other stupid involvements I still wouldn't have divorced Chyna."

"Say what?" Janelle shot back.

"She was making more money than me and I needed to stay to survive. I'd lied when I told her I'd graduated from college. I hadn't."

"Are you still ignorant with a degree or without one?" Deacon Pillar asked the question in a way that most men would've known to just shut up.

Cordell wasn't most men. He kept the shovel in the hole and kept digging.

"I could've left and I didn't. I told myself that I was punishing Janelle and Chyna for being two women that brought me down. But neither of you told me to take that payola from the record company. It was all me. And a baby was the last thing I really wanted."

Chyna hung her head. She couldn't look Cordell in the eyes. She'd carried that burden for years. She had no way of knowing that, like Cordell, she'd not felt the anguish she should've when she lost the baby. There'd been a selfish sense of relief because she'd not wanted a child at that time, either. It was why she'd never become pregnant while married to Grayson, too. She never felt worthy to be a mother.

"I'm truly sorry," Janelle said. "I've apologized to Chyna a million times but never to you."

"I guess I've always needed my sister more than I needed a baby," Chyna interrupted. "She's always been first in my life. She's all the family I've had since my youth."

Cordell started to say more about the baby, but another question popped into his head. "When you met Grayson," he said to Chyna, "did you sleep with him to get back at me?" The thought always haunted him, but he'd preferred to believe that she'd just fell out of love with him and in love with Grayson.

"Yes, I did," Chyna confessed. "I did love him after a while, but not at first. I was impressed with all he had, but there was something else, too."

"What?" Cordell asked. He let go of one of her hands because she'd let her head drop. He lifted her chin, "What else was there?"

"I thought you'd go back to Janelle," Chyna said. "I really believed that once you knew the truth and that she hadn't cheated that you'd have gone back to her."

Cordell was shocked and Janelle became livid.

Chapter 48

Revelations poured fast, deep, and mostly angry around the kitchen table among Cordell, Janelle, and Chyna.

Meanwhile, Deacon Pillar listened intently. He'd read a lot of Grayson's journal and noticed that the confessions that went back and forth between Cordell and the women didn't apply to what was written in the journal. Perhaps, this was a bit more than he needed to hear. Yet he was fascinated. And the fascination wasn't felt in a bad way. He was consumed by the way he'd heard the hand of God played between the three. Their lives seemed intertwined, woven in a way that only God could fashion.

"Okay, this ain't got nothing much to do with me," Deacon Pillar finally said, "but let me sum it up based on some the half-truths y'all done told around this table."

"Excuse me." Janelle said as much for the rest as herself.

"Woman, please." Deacon Pillar gave Janelle a look that explained all that was necessary.

And Janelle backed down and the others knew better than to come forward.

"Y'all played each other and the game of life like amateurs. The only way things could've ended was bad and it did. All of y'all was committing adultery and sinning in each other's beds." Deacon Pillar then turned a little in his chair and took direct aim at Cordell.

"Now I ain't known you but for a little while, and we've been on speaking terms, less than that." He turned around again because he was partially blocking Chyna and Janelle's view of whatever look was certain to appear on Cordell's face. "Excuse me ladies, be patient, 'cause y'all up next." He turned back to Cordell.

"Brother Cordell, you jumped into relationship ministry, according to our brief chats, partially because of the mess you'd made of those two sisters sitting there, and taking money from Reverend Young to take First Lady off your hands. And, of course, you'd also felt God had forgiven you. Now what you haven't told these ladies is that you also thought more back then of your own ego. Even with debts covering your behind like acne, you could've divorced her for free."

Chyna was the first to drop her coffee cup. Janelle was a little more direct, "Cordell, you lousy son of a—"

"I ain't finished yet," Deacon Pillar cut Janelle off.

"You was the worst sort of coward back then." Deacon Pillar continued as he turned back to face Cordell. "I should know. I could've taught Coward 101 back in my day to a certain degree, but we ain't talking about my day. We're talking about yours."

"I've had enough." Cordell finally found a voice. Deacon Pillar wasn't finished.

"You loved that woman, Miss Janelle, sitting over there. She done been to some hell and back. I could take one look at her even before she got sick and see she was fighting for her life even back then."

And that's when Janelle's dam built of self-defense

broke. "Damn you, Cordell." Janelle was still fighting for her life and she left the kitchen table with Cordell insisting on helping her. She felt completely wiped out.

"I'm sorry, baby." Cordell whispered as he gently placed his strong arms under hers to help her walk.

Janelle didn't bother to respond. Both her emotions and her physical health seemed to turn on her when she needed to stay alert and involved in the confessions. She had to wonder if she'd brought on a new bout of nausea and weakness in order to keep some secrets just that . . . secret.

As soon as they entered the bedroom Janelle spied the intercom. There was still a way she could still listen in to whatever was going on in the kitchen.

Janelle ordered Cordell to return to the kitchen. It was useless for him to stay in the room with her. She really didn't want him there, anyway. She was in turmoil. She'd not wanted him to love Chyna, but when she found out that he hadn't, it angered her. Chyna was her blood and he'd been and still remained her heart. Didn't a heart need blood?

After Cordell closed the door behind him, Janelle placed the intercom box next to her pillow.

Cordell returned to the kitchen and found Chyna and Deacon Pillar sitting and sipping tea as though nothing had happened.

"She'll be fine." Cordell said as he stood by the door. He hadn't taken a seat because he still wasn't sure if he was welcome to do so.

"That's good." Chyna's answer was short, but the anger was still there.

"Take a seat, young fella," Deacon Pillar said, "Now I know I'm a guest here, and I've probably said a lot more than I should've—"

"Oh, you think so." Chyna said again, keeping her anger contained in a short reply.

Deacon Pillar as usual ignored the obvious and continued, "Listen, the hour is growing late and I'm growing tired. But, there's still some things that need to be said."

And he chose to begin the conversation with a bomb.

"You know," Deacon Pillar started off slowly and with his hands still clasped, "the way you two and Sister Janelle tell it, you'd think y'all was the only ones that ever used, abused, or done anything scandalous."

"I'm sure we've embarrassed you to a fault," Chyna said. Her tone was nonapologetic and followed by an insincere "I'm so sorry."

"Oh chile, please." The Deacon laughed a little before continuing, "What y'all have done is childish compared to some of the stuff Earl, Eartha, and I have committed, and we were up there praising God almost immediately afterward."

"What are you talking about?" Cordell asked as he sat and turned to face the deacon.

Janelle may have been in her room lying down, but she almost bolted straight up. She pulled the intercom box to her ear. She didn't want to miss a word. The old man sounded like he was about to admit to something outrageous. She'd repented, but not changed a whole lot, and the anticipation returned some of her strength.

"I hardly know where to begin," the deacon said almost cheerfully. He then caught himself and suddenly made a concerted effort to sound a bit more repentant, to add to the seriousness of what he was about to say.

"I'll begin it this way," Deacon Pillar said. "Eartha Blackstone used to be a stripper!"

Even the air conditioner in her room stopped running. Janelle dropped the intercom box and almost fell off the bed. Cordell and Chyna pushed their chairs in closer and propped their chins up in their hands.

"That's right," Deacon Pillar continued. "That's how me and Earl Athens first met her."

"When was that?" Cordell asked feeling he needed to say something.

"Oh well, I don't rightfully recall but it was way before the Sweet Bush was the Sweet Bush. In fact, I believe she stripped when it was called High Times." He suddenly leaned back in his chair before continuing. "Her father was the pastor back then at New Hope."

"I do remember hearing something about that," Chyna blurted. "I'd forgotten all about that her father was a pastor."

"Yep," Deacon Pillar said, "Eartha was the biggest ho in the church and her father once got mad and called her a Temple Ho."

Back in her bedroom, when she heard what the deacon just revealed, Janelle almost fell off the bed again. She was so shocked she didn't realize she was hanging on by clutching the sheets.

"Of course, we were a whole lot younger back in those days," Deacon Pillar exclaimed. "But just like we were taught by our parents, we still attended church on Sundays." He suddenly chuckled, "I remember one time me and Earl came to testimony service just an inch shy of being totally smashed." He stopped and looked toward the ceiling. His mood quickly turned somber. "That old rascal. I'm gonna miss him."

"Amen," Cordell whispered. It was more out of habit than anything else.

"Anyway, Earl started testifying about how he was so sorry that he'd disappointed God." Deacon Pillar started turning his head from side to side. "It would have turned out fine except someone called out, 'God forgives.' And, that was all Earl needed to hear. By the time he finished putting our business along with Eartha's on the front step of the church altar no one was certain there'd be any forgiveness."

"Why didn't her father try and stop her?" Cordell asked.

"He couldn't. He'd been going there on Wednesdays pretending to reach out and touch some poor souls. He'd caught Eartha stripping. Now I can't prove it," Deacon Pillar conspired, "But I wouldn't be a bit surprised if that old Pastor Blackstone hadn't reached and touched Eartha a few times. I imagine that's why she turned so damn mean."

"Really?" Chyna asked.

"First Lady," Deacon Pillar said. "If Pastor Blackstone touched anything outside of the church, it was probably a breast or something lower."

Deacon Pillar would've kept talking, but Janelle appeared suddenly in the kitchen doorway.

"Don't let me stop you," Janelle urged. "Oh, please do continue." The drama was too much to hear over an intercom. She wanted a front-row seat.

And they still hadn't touched on what was in Grayson's journal.

Chapter 49

It was now well after noon. The confession had gone on a lot longer than any of them anticipated.

After Deacon Pillar's revelation on the explicit and shameless exploits committed by Deacon Athens, Sister Blackstone, and himself during their heyday, the kitchen suddenly became ghostly quiet. No one knew what to say or to make of what he'd revealed.

As for Deacon Pillar, he seemed to be relieved. He even looked a bit younger and he didn't slouch so much. It was as though the weight of years of pretense had lifted and he was freed.

Finally it was Cordell who spoke up. "Deacon Pillar," he said. "Can I speak to you in the other room?"

"I don't see why not," Deacon Pillar replied. "I need to use the bathroom first. I try not to drink so much tea while out in public." He winked, thinking they knew what he meant.

Ten minutes later they did. Chyna didn't want to embarrass the old deacon, so she politely took the Febreze deodorizer and sprayed it heavily throughout the house to mask the odor coming from the bathroom.

Deacon Pillar returned to the living room smiling. He certainly looked relieved and didn't mind showing it. "What's up?" he asked Cordell.

"Have a seat," Cordell said as he sat opposite the sofa and waited for the deacon to sit. "I've turned off that intercom so we can talk freely." He pointed to the unit on one of the living room tables and clasped his hands. "You and I know a lot of what's in Grayson's journal would probably do more harm than good. Do you agree?"

"No doubt about it," Deacon Pillar replied. "What do you have in mind?"

"Let's burn it."

"Burn it?"

"Yes, burn it." Cordell leaned in closer before continuing, "Other than a couple of the board members, who has seen it or knows anything about it?"

Deacon Pillar thought for a moment before answering. He scratched his head and started to count on his stiffened fingers. "Well, there are about four others who now know about that picture. I can't recall any of them knowing about the journal. I didn't even know about it until Earl mentioned it."

"Okay, they've seen a picture of Chyna in a compromising position. What harm can that do if we handle things correctly?" Cordell asked.

"Oh, I beg to differ," Deacon Pillar said. "That may be the only picture you've seen. I can tell you that Eartha claimed to have seen another."

"Another one?"

"Yes, indeed," Deacon Pillar said, and gave a conspiring wink. "And, trust me brother. According to Eartha, First Lady looked spectacular and very skillful."

All Cordell could do at that point was sigh and fall back onto the sofa. So he did.

While the men were in the living room Chyna and Janelle sat for a few minutes, each with her own thoughts.

"Did you really forgive me for the loss of your baby?" Janelle finally asked, softly. "I really am sorry. I don't know what was wrong with me back then."

"You were angry and you were in love. That's a lethal combination," Chyna said before adding, "But yes, I forgave you."

"Why?"

"Because in my own twisted way, you did me a favor. Like I said before, I never wanted to be a mother. It sounds horrible, but I'm about telling the truth. Perhaps that's why I'm being punished."

"Well, I've got another confession to make, too," Janelle said. She hesitated and took a deep breath before she continued. "I knew that it was possible that your drink was drugged at Cinnamon's that night and didn't say anything."

"What?"

"Let me finish," Janelle said, cutting Chyna off. "I really didn't want you to be a First Lady, or a lady for that matter. I believed that Cordell found you to be better than me because I was such a freak with him. That and the fact that I thought you definitely had more education and class. After all, you went to college and I didn't. All I ever did was work temporary jobs, travel, and use men after Cordell dumped me."

"A freak?"

"Yes," Janelle replied realizing that Chyna cared nothing about the other part of her confession. "Cordell and I used to call it *dancing*."

Janelle and Chyna continued their discussion. They'd

been together in everything but truth. The two sisters' love and jealousy grew side by side. Like weeds, one emotion had to kill or choke the other.

Chyna was about to say something more when she heard her front door close. She got up and left the kitchen to see what was going on.

Janelle turned and looked out the window. She was surprised to see the old deacon and Cordell walking away from the house, and again without so much as a good-bye.

And when Janelle looked over to the far side of the house, in the daylight, she was even more surprised to see a tow truck preparing to tow away a strange van on the street. The van was only a few feet away from Chyna's house.

Chyna flung open her front door. She wasn't wearing shoes and hesitated to walk outside. Then she saw Cordell and the deacon speaking to a tow truck driver. She still hadn't seen or paid attention to the van that was parked a few feet away from her front yard. It took her another moment or two to realize it was the church van. It was the same van that Deacon Athens was driving when Sister Blackstone showed up unannounced on her doorstep.

She still hadn't made the connection between Grayson's journal and Sister Blackstone's shopping bag that was in Deacon Athens's possession.

Chyna waited at the front door for Cordell and Deacon Pillar to return.

"Someone called about the church van being abandoned. We got it straightened out," Cordell offered. "But you'll probably have to pull it off to the side of your driveway until someone comes and drives it back to the church."

"Can't you do it?" Chyna asked Deacon Pillar.

"Sure can't," he answered. "I'm a stick shift kind of fella."

While the others were chatting about the van and anything further to avoid getting back to the task at hand, Janelle dressed.

She'd put on a red cotton pantsuit that hung on her frame.

"I like that outfit," Cordell lied as he and Chyna entered her room. "The only thing missing is that crazy sombrero."

They all laughed. Cordell managed to lighten the atmosphere, and for that they were grateful.

Turning to Chyna, Cordell said, "I've got to get the deacon here back to his house."

"Not a problem," Chyna said. "I'm going to get Janelle settled and run by the church to check up on the arrangements for Deacon Athens's services."

"No!" Cordell and Deacon Pillar said, loudly and almost at the same time.

"What's up, Cordell?" Janelle asked. She knew a deception when she saw or heard it. Those two were up to something.

"I meant I didn't want Chyna to leave you alone," Cordell said, sheepishly.

"And what did your 'no' mean?" Janelle said turning to face Deacon Pillar.

"Errr . . ." He couldn't think of a lie to save his lying behind.

"He's lying," Janelle told Chyna. "Cordell's lying, too."

"I know," Chyna replied. "But I'm still going by the church." She gave the men a defiant look before turning to Janelle. "Do you wanna come with me?"

"Why not," Janelle replied. "I'm dressed for church." She laughed a bit and added, "Who knows? We may arrive in time for the hoochies rehearsal."

"Today is choir rehearsal day," the deacon blurted with a straight face.

"That's what I meant," Janelle said, struggling to keep a straight face, too.

Chapter 50

Cordell tried hard to pitch reasons for Deacon Pillar to carefully drive away the church van, but his arguments fell on deaf ears. The deacon would have no part of it. He was a stick shift guy and he would not budge.

Cordell, instead, turned over the van's keys to Chyna. And then he made sure that there was nothing left inside the van that would either further incriminate her or impede what they'd planned.

"Do you really figure we can disarm those board members who won't go along with keeping their mouths shut about bringing down the First Lady since they've seen the pictures?" Deacon Pillar asked as he and Cordell drove along Grand Central Parkway toward the church.

"Yes," Cordell replied. "But we need to go back through the journal. There are some things that don't need to be revealed."

"So let me understand this," the old deacon pondered, "we're gonna pull a spiritual blackmail on the board?"

"Pretty much." Cordell answered.

"Oh, I can't wait to see how this works." The deacon looked at the passing scenery as they drove past Shea Stadium. "I betcha we'll go into overtime with those dimwits."

"We'll do what we must do."

It'd taken Chyna more than an hour to place phone calls, get dressed, and head for the church. She'd also made sure that Janelle would be able to make the trip.

Except for twice-weekly visits to her oncologists, nutritionists, and other physicians, Janelle rarely left the house. However, after the soul-cleansing that went on in the kitchen, she was ready to take on the church and whoever. It seemed that a fight that didn't involve her health was welcomed.

While Janelle chose a red outfit that fit her sense of style, Chyna chose yellow. Chyna loved any shade of that color because it was always one that gave her hope.

It was almost six o'clock by the time Chyna and Janelle reached the church. She saw Cordell's car parked off to the side so he'd made it there, too.

"Are you going straight to meet with the bereavement committee?" Janelle asked. "I think I'll just sit somewhere in the back of the church and wait for you."

At that moment, several of the members arrived. A few acknowledged Chyna and most looked at Janelle as though she were an untouchable.

Sensing the vibe as being none-too-sociable and not wanting to cuss someone out, particularly since she'd been seeking a closer relationship with God, Janelle announced, "You know, sis, on second thought perhaps I'll just go into the library and wait. Maybe I'll find something interesting and inspiring to read to pass the time."

Chyna and Janelle entered the church. After reminding Janelle where the library was, they went their separate ways.

The pastor's study upstairs on the second level, again was hot from heated discussions. Several of the board members sat strewn around the study in various stages of pain, anger, and downright indignation. They'd been fighting for the better part of two hours. The tag team of DeWitt and Pillar, armed with tasty and alarming tidbits of information from Grayson's journal, had them TKO'd on a spiritual canvas.

"How much evil do you want to continue in this church?" One of the board members asked of Deacon Pillar. There was venom in his voice as he tried to show righteous indignation.

"Well, let me see," Deacon Pillar replied. "Are you gonna stop fornicating?"

Deacon Pillar was on a roll. He'd look at a page in the journal and then share what was written about a particular member with the entire room. When he'd finished, the guilty looked prepped and ready to be shipped straight to hell from the sanctuary.

Another TKO.

A momentary quietness fell over the room. No one else dared ask another stupid question.

With resignation a vote was taken. And all the dirty hands raised were in agreement that the information held on the First Lady and each of them would remain unspoken.

However, there was one question that had to be raised and solidified in the minds of the board members.

"How do we know if this young man will keep his word?" The question was voiced aloud even though it was still silently shared by the others. "He's not a part of this church."

Cordell used that opportunity to say a few things he'd wanted to say but didn't feel he should've. "Most of you have heard me speak here on more than one occasion. I've ministered on every kind of relationship. However, there's one thing none of you can deny. Haven't I always spoken about keeping the Word: the Word of God, your own word, and particularly words that would destroy?"

Heads nodded in agreement around the room.

Cordell continued, "The power of life and death is in the tongue. Isn't that what the Word of God teaches?"

"And, don't forget it is also in the journal we have of the late Reverend Grayson Young," Deacon Pillar added. Unlike Cordell, he knew those scallywags too well and they needed to be reminded just in case some hadn't read that part of the Bible.

"Now we can still bring this church back to its glory days. There's an opportunity for us to do it without tearing down some of the good work the younger members have brought about," Deacon Pillar continued.

"Imagine how much more the youth will be inclined to participate if you'd give them guidance instead of judgment?" Cordell asked. "Remember the Word also said that God calls the old because they know the way and the young because they are strong."

Just like Deacon Pillar figured, there'd always be one that would buck no matter how legit the argument. And the bucker sprang from one of the corners of the room.

Deacon Duke Brown rose. Unlike some of the others, he was one of the newer members of the church board. Fact was that there wasn't one mention of his name in the journal, but he didn't know that. It didn't mean his hands were clean; it only meant that the others didn't know his dirt. He'd decided at that moment to use his lack of complicity and separate from the other sinners.

"I think we need to rethink a few things," Duke said. "What if we keep this information and later find out that there are others that know the truth? How will it make us look?"

It was a legitimate question. The members all turned to Cordell and Deacon Pillar for a response.

"Just because everything ain't written in this journal don't mean I don't know about you and two of the ushers—"

Deacon Pillar never got a chance to finish. The slapping sound of Duke's butt hitting the leather seat beneath him interrupted the deacon's flow. It also didn't go unnoticed that Duke's surrender came with a gaped mouth.

Cordell looked over at the old deacon and wondered exactly what he knew, when he knew it, and how much. A smile broke out across his face while he shook his head. He had a newfound respect for the old man.

In another part of the church Chyna fared much better. The funeral arrangements made by the bereavement committee didn't need many changes. The young woman Chyna had given the task of pulling things together worked out better than Chyna could've known.

"We're so glad that you'll be more involved," one of the bereavement members offered.

It was just a sample, a welcome sample, of the well wishes that were to come Chyna's way.

Chyna left the meeting feeling perhaps God was working on her behalf. Her guilt was still hounding her, a little, even as she entered the small office that she'd sometimes occupied while waiting for service to start. It was also the office where she used to go over correspondence. She'd also used it as a changing room between services. There lay in a corner a couple of large hatboxes. She walked over and lifted up one of the covers.

The hat was a burnt orange with a yellow-tinged small floral and laced border. It flipped upward in the back and sloped downward just a bit to the side. It was made and presented as a gift to Chyna on her birthday by the pastor's aid auxiliary.

Chyna gently replaced the hat in the box. Just remembering that it was the same pastor's aid auxiliary headed by Sister Blackstone suddenly made the hat less attractive. But then she remembered that during her birthday ceremony that it wasn't Sister Blackstone that gave the presentation. Chyna was now certain that even back then, Sister Blackstone harbored unwarranted dislike for her.

Chyna wondered how long the old woman detested her. What had she done to deserve it? She was certain there'd never been a cross word between the two of them. Was she aware of the sometime over-the-top adoration shown toward Grayson by his chief pastor's aide? Yes? At that time she'd found it cute the way Sister Blackstone fussed over Grayson like an old mother hen.

Chyna left the hatboxes and decided to make use of her visit to the office. She went to the desk and found several piles of what she thought were items set aside for when she'd get to them. Her eyes fell upon a mound of mail that looked like postcards, greeting cards, and other miscellaneous correspondence that were probably old invites for her to attend a banquet or such. She looked over at the closet where some of her outfits still hung. There were also several unopened boxes. More gifts, perhaps.

With all that her eyes found to see what actually kept her attention were the questions caused by Sister Blackstone's hatred of her, and also what about Deacon Athens? She'd never had a problem with him. He was a bit bossy, or so it seemed, but not nearly as clingy to Grayson as Sister Blackstone had been.

I need to read that journal, Chyna thought as she swept the unopened mail into a small wastebasket. She suddenly remembered that when Cordell and Deacon Pillar left her kitchen they'd had the journal. When she saw them return from dealing with the tow truck driver, she didn't remember seeing it. Where was the journal?

On the other side of the church Janelle waited for Chyna to return. She watched some of the church members milling about the library. Although several people had come and gone during the time Janelle waited at one of the tables, not one came over and showed any interest or greeted her. It wouldn't have been too insulting had they not greeted one another with loud "Praise the Lords" or "God is good." Where was the Christian love for her or her sister?

Janelle was also starting to feel a little discomfort from the return of an ache under her left armpit. She'd forgotten to take her medication before she and Chyna left the house. Of course, she didn't carry the expensive prescriptions with her, either.

Janelle was absorbed in her thoughts and trying to minimize her pain through a breathing exercise. It was a technique she'd learned from one of her pain-management classes. She'd closed her eyes and while tuning everything out, she didn't hear Cordell approach and call out her name.

"Hey there," Cordell said as he pulled up a chair and sat down next to Janelle. "Are you okay?" He tried hard not to let any undue anxiety coat the question.

"I'll be okay," Janelle said as she looked up. "How did you know I was in the library?"

Cordell indicated with a nod of his head towards

some of the members, who had grown in number even during the few minutes he'd been there. "In this church if someone dropped a rock from their hand on the second floor, everyone on the first floor would know about it, before it hit the floor."

Together they shared a muffled laugh and tried to look innocent despite the automatic and disapproving masks upon the faces of the others.

While Janelle and Cordell were in the library, Chyna hurried from the other side of the church in their direction. She'd barely gotten a few doors from the library when she ran into Deacon Pillar. She almost knocked him down by accident.

They apologized to one another.

"You seem different," Chyna offered. "Why is that?"

"What do you mean?" Deacon Pillar replied. Inside, his heart and mind jumped for joy. He and Cordell had shut down the board. He was sure they'd eventually come up with some craziness, but for the moment things were good.

"You look like you just came out of a revival," Chyna answered. "It's almost like someone laid hands on you."

"Let's just say that when God is in the mix and you go down in battle . . ." He stopped and planted his feet apart and stood like a boxer. "You're coming up a winner. You definitely will have a glow."

"A battle?" Chyna asked as the two started walking. She wasn't sure where he'd been headed, but he didn't seem to mind walking with her.

"Guess what?" Deacon Pillar conspired with a wink. "Nobody will mess with you."

"Mess with me?" Chyna said with surprise. "What do you mean?"

And that's when the deacon realized he'd said too

much. He'd almost blown the reason why he and Cordell ambushed and blackmailed the board in the first place.

He immediately excused himself to use the men's bathroom. Without waiting for her to reply he rushed off. He angrily pushed through the bathroom door. *This is a fitting place, since I almost pissed everything away.*

Chapter 51

In another time or place Chyna might've followed Deacon Pillar into that men's bathroom. He'd just given her more angst that she didn't need.

Who, other than she, Janelle, the deacon, and Cordell were aware of the woefully sinful acts that were confessed at her kitchen table? She'd not wanted the deaths of Sister Blackstone or Deacon Athens, although she had to admit she wasn't upset that secrets died with them; or so she'd been led to believe. And just who had led her to that conclusion? "Cordell," Chyna hissed.

Chyna didn't try to hide her anger, not even when several of the other members who'd not seen her since Grayson's memorial tried to stop her to chat. Their "welcome back" greetings fell upon her deaf ears and her actions of not acknowledging their words pounded it home.

Chyna headed back toward the library to get Janelle. She needed to be talked down before she said or did something that would surely lead to fallout. She certainly didn't need that. And then she was going to get Cordell.

She needed the whole truth and not his edited version. There was no way that Deacon Pillar misspoke.

As Chyna neared a few doors down from the library, she was surprised to hear loud voices. The library was usually very quiet,

Carefully Chyna opened the library door. Her eyes swept the crowd of people inside. There were as many there as sometimes in the small sanctuary on Sundays. It sounded as though there was some type of meeting going on. She recognized several members from various auxiliaries in attendance. Then she heard a loud voice. It came from a table in the front of the room.

"In the Old Testament," Chyna heard a voice ring out almost preachy in tone. She recognized Cordell's voice.

Chyna made her way through a crowd gathered in the center and stood next to one of the congregants she'd known since arriving at New Hope.

The woman was dark-skinned with a pointy chin. She also looked about as wide as she was tall and about Chyna's own age. "They're all a bunch of hypocrites," the woman muttered before slapping at the meaty part of her hips with both hands.

Chyna didn't know what was said before, but the woman wasn't trying to hide her annoyance. In fact, the woman spun around and almost stepped on Chyna's foot, her wide hips parting the sea of onlookers as she left.

Chyna quickly stepped forward and occupied the space the woman left. She saw Cordell standing behind the speaker's podium. Janelle, looking more nervous than sick, was seated beside him at a table. Janelle had a book open, but what it was she'd been reading Chyna was unable to see.

Over the hissing or echo that emanated from a high Plexiglas podium Cordell leaned over and spoke into the microphone. Whatever he'd said before the crowd now caused many responses and some of them were as angry as the words said by the woman who'd just left.

"That's some cold stuff."

The words were said low and voiced by a young man who stood to Chyna's right. He was thin and dressed in all blue, including a blue bandanna that covered an almost oblong-shaped head.

Without responding, Chyna leaned in, prepared to ask what was happening when the young man murmured again.

"This is a hard room to work," he followed with a little laughter until he swung his head in Chyna's direction, and realized who he stood next to. "Oh, Praise the Lord, Sister Young," the young man whispered and then turned his head as though he were ashamed.

"Oh, we know the charge," Cordell blew each word out followed by an exhalation of air as though each were precious. He let his words linger in the air as he waved a hand. It was the first time Chyna noticed he'd still worn the large diamond-encrusted pinky ring sparkling as his hand swept across the audience. *Why hadn't I remembered that ring? He bought it just before our divorce was final.* Yet as quick as the question entered her mind she dismissed it when she saw that Janelle really looked sick; truly sick. She wanted to make a move toward her sister but found she couldn't.

With the library guests fully captured by the tenor of his speech, Cordell continued pointing accusingly at them. "God said that zeal without knowledge is a dangerous thing. And yet, when it's partnered with judging, prejudging or otherwise, you do so at your own peril."

Echoes of "Amen!" automatically rang out. It wasn't clear if they'd understood or were locked into their churchy "call-and-response" modes.

Cordell, still fueled by his indignation, ignored the false agreements and continued. His voice continued to rise almost to the point where he wouldn't need the microphone.

"Read what I just gave you, Sister Janelle!"

"Sister Janelle," someone, an elderly female, it sounded like, off to the side, tried to whisper a response laced with indignation, "Oh, it's Sister Janelle, now?"

That time there were no "amens" or replies from the crowd. At the very least some reasoned that perhaps they just needed to shut up even if they disagreed. It didn't stop some from turning their heads toward the woman who'd just issued the indictment. Several shook their heads, signaling that she really didn't have a leg to stand on when judging someone. The brown-skinned woman's complexion turned red from the silent rebuke.

Cordell continued from where he left off. He looked again at Janelle. With what Chyna thought sounded a lot like pride, he repeated, "Read where I've marked off, Sister Janelle."

Janelle's hands shook. Whether it was from having a Bible in her hand, which she was definitely not accustomed to, or anger from the confrontation that brought them to this point, she wasn't sure. However, she'd decided when Cordell came to her defense that it was good enough for her. She'd not let him nor God down at that moment.

"Matthew seven, the first paragraph," Janelle said as Cordell extended the microphone so she could be heard.

"First verse," someone called out correcting her. "Don't she know nothing trying to read God's word like that?"

Cordell's head shot up. Chyna's head turned in the direction of the reproach. Not one person moved and the person who had spoken had by then shut up.

But just as Cordell and the others heard the none-too-polite correction of what she'd said, so did Janelle. And that's when the real Janelle stood up. She did just that.

Her legs felt a little wobbly. It wasn't out of nervousness but because she was truly feeling a little weak. But not weak enough to have any of those sanctimonious, thin-skinned religious nuts make her feel ashamed.

Janelle acted as though she was born for that moment. She started from the beginning and spoke as though she'd not erred. "The book of Matthews, the *first verse*," she said, calmly. "Do not judge, or you, too, will be judged." She stopped and as if she were preaching, she allowed her eyes to settle on a group of board members who'd approached her earlier when Cordell left her side. He'd gone to the bathroom and that's when the mob decided to test her. "For the same way you judge others, you will be judged, and with the measure you use, it will be measured to you."

Janelle tried to sit down, but ended up almost collapsing instead. But she pulled it off true Janelle style and adjusted her seat as though nothing happened.

Meanwhile as Janelle read the scripture, Cordell held up Grayson's journal. No one in the crowd knew what it was other than perhaps another Bible. However, Duke Brown and the other board members knew exactly what Cordell held in his hands.

"I knew they'd try something crazy," the voice whispered to Chyna in a matter-of-fact manner. It was Deacon Pillar.

She hadn't seen nor thought about him. At least not since he'd fled to the men's bathroom after he'd blurted out something she was sure wasn't for her ears.

"Say what?" Chyna urged. "Repeat that."

"Damn," Deacon Pillar said. He'd not realized he was

standing next to Chyna because his mind was totally on what was happening at the podium.

Deacon Pillar excused himself silently by racing away, again.

Chyna just shook her head and returned her attention to Cordell and Janelle.

Cordell had taken the Bible from Janelle's hands. He realized she was just too weak to continue. He wasn't, so he did. "Verse two," Cordell said before adding, "I'd ask you to pull out your swords but if I said, instead, that most of you came into this room with speculation and judgment and not the Word of God, then I'd be judging, too. I won't do that." He stopped and flipped the page from the Bible. "I'll let the Word speak for me.

"Why do you look at the speck of sawdust in your brother's eye," he stopped and pointed toward Janelle. "In this case your sister's." He returned his gaze back to the Bible he held. "In your sister's eye and pay no attention to the plank in your own eye?"

Cordell closed the Bible. He turned away from the crowd who stood there, muted and condemned, and said to Janelle, "This part of God's Word is for you, my sister. I can recite it from memory."

"Do not give dogs what is sacred; do not throw your pearls to pigs. If you do, they may trample them under their feet, and then turn and tear you to pieces."

Cordell stopped talking and lifted Janelle's face by her chin. "God is doing a wonder in your life." He then turned toward the crowd, now speaking to Janelle and the crowd. "No, you do not have HIV as some in this room accused you of. They would have you believe, even if you had that dreaded disease, that by your mere presence you could spread it to them. In their ignorance and self-righteousness, instead of welcoming you to God's house, some blatantly and without an ounce of compassion had the gall to turn on you, a guest here in God's house, with their stupid accusations and no proof."

Cordell didn't try and hide his disapproval that time when he asked, "And what if she did? What if she did have HIV, AIDS, or even leprosy? None of you did what Christ asked of us. What if God turned his back on you? You don't think your sin is just as repulsive as any disease that you can think of or have?"

Cordell didn't wait for an answer, nor did he really expect a response from the crowd. Instead, he quickly returned to the podium with the microphone still in one hand and Grayson's journal held high in his other. "I imagine that most of you will be returning to your glass houses now."

As if still under his spell, most of the crowd, including the church board members, turned and headed away in all directions.

"I almost forgot, please forgive me," Cordell added, which caused some to stop in their tracks. "Deacon Pillar has something he'd like to announce."

Cordell stepped to the side and the old deacon ambled over to the podium after taking the journal from Cordell's hand. He held the journal not up high but just high enough for those who knew what it was to see it. Although he would speak to the crowd, he looked specifically over toward the church board. They still stood together like a clutch of eagles. "Let us be mindful that Deacon Athens's home going service will be tomorrow morning at eleven o'clock." Deacon Pillar said and then with as much respect as he could muster, he added, "And be prepared to eat and have a good time in our deacon's honor. He ain't gonna be burnt up like Eartha Blackstone, so we'll need a few cars to head out to Long Island's Pine

Grove Cemetery. Y'all bring your best rides and offer a ride to those who don't have transportation."

Deacon Pillar gave a wide and satisfied grin before saying, "Oh, and now y'all can return to your glass houses."

Chapter 52

The ride back to Chyna's house was just too quiet. Again, she'd not been able to get Janelle to go to the hospital, and she'd beat up on herself for not remembering to bring her sister's medication. Her lack of focus caused too many repercussions and she couldn't accept that.

If Janelle knew her sister's discomfort and thoughts, she was too tired to show it. She was also too happy to care. Cordell had come to her defense and as bad as she was sure she looked, he protected her as though she were a beauty queen.

"I see you must be feeling a lot better. You're grinning like the cat that'd eaten a canary," Chyna said after glancing over at Janelle.

Janelle didn't answer. She winked at Chyna and returned her gaze to looking out through the car's window.

"You know I'm not falling for that silent treatment you're trying to pull," Chyna chided. "I need to know what happened back there."

"Why?" Janelle finally asked.

"Why shouldn't I?" Chyna urged. "You're my big sister, and it looked like they were in the mood for a good stoning. It was about to get ugly in that library."

"Yeah," Janelle laughed slightly. "There was some ugliness in that library. Did you see what some of them wore?"

"You can do better than that. I know you." Chyna intended on getting more than her sister offered at that moment.

Janelle struggled against the seat belt to turn toward Chyna. "You know," Janelle said, slowly. "For someone who is the First Lady of a church, albeit a freaky one at one time, you don't know a lot." Janelle saw the change in Chyna's face at her reference to Chyna's sexual activities as well as felt the temperature within the car drop. "I'm just saying that you're so caught up in regret, remorse, and whatever other condemnation you've drummed up for yourself that you can't tell that God's forgiven me. Fact is, you can't even see that the young man you had in the hotel room hasn't even so much as dropped a dime to call you."

And that's when Chyna realized that he hadn't. Had God fixed that, too?

If at that moment they hadn't pulled up in front of Chyna's house, she might've had to pull over on the highway. She was just that stunned about all that was happening.

Chyna gave Janelle a strange look as she helped her from the car.

"Now what?" Janelle asked, as she returned Chyna's stare, "What did I say that was stupid? You're looking at me like those other church folks."

"There is nothing wrong," Chyna said. "I'm just adjusting to the change in you."

"A change in me?" Janelle replied as she stopped walking and faced Chyna. "How is it a change in me? I've been praying for weeks for God to forgive me. You'd have known it if you weren't so wrapped up in your own remorse."

There it was. Janelle had spit out what she'd held in for quite some time. The decision to take care of her personal needs hadn't come easy.

As they started to walk up the path toward the house, Janelle's thoughts struggled between her allegiance and self-preservation. Now, her life hung in the balance. In her mind, the mother of all attacks stepped in and broke her stride: breast cancer, the disease that'd killed their mother. The prospect of losing a breast and coming to terms with the loss of her beautiful hair, her svelte figure, and her quality of life had set her onto a path where she had to look out for herself. She was doing a very poor job.

Chyna stopped and gave Janelle a chance to catch her breath. She'd seen her sister walk slowly and took it to mean that she was overdoing things.

Back at New Hope, the drama continued, and Cordell, along with Deacon Pillar, renewed his attack.

"I normally don't swear on a Bible," Cordell said sternly to a few who'd not left to return to their glass houses. "But so help me, this time I am." He then took the Bible from the hands of Deacon Pillar. He laid one hand upon it and held up the journal with the other. "So help me, if another one of you tries to attack either Sister Young or Sister Pierce, as God is my witness, there won't be a secret left untold."

"Amen to that," Deacon Pillar added. "And y'all know it ain't gonna take me that much to tell it. I've done wrong, too, but, according to this here book, some of y'all done a lot worse."

Even the threat based on a promise on God's Word still didn't go without challenge. There were mumblings and grumblings. Some of the so-called righteous who were exposed feigned indignation toward those who believed their lying eyes and ears.

After they'd decided that the show of strength and power was over, Cordell offered the deacon a ride home. They'd been together more than twenty-four hours. It was more time than they had spent in conversation during the months since Cordell returned to Brooklyn.

"Do you believe they'll act like they have some sense now?" Deacon Pillar asked. "They're even feistier than I gave them credit for."

"As long as they believe that journal cover still had Grayson's evidence they'll keep quiet. They won't like it, but they'll do it."

"Yeah," Deacon Pillar said almost laughing. "If they'd been really smart they'd have asked to see the evidence a second time."

After Cordell and Deacon Pillar confronted the board members the first time, they'd left and went outside to the back of the building. It was while they were there that they'd decided to burn most of the journal. Cordell would've burned the entire thing, but it was Deacon Pillar who convinced him that for a backup they needed to keep a few sheets and its cover. Of course, the old deacon was right. Just the sight of the journal kept the church board mutiny in check. The pages they'd saved really didn't amount to much, but the other members didn't know it.

"I'm glad that's pretty much finished," Cordell said as he reached the deacon's block.

"Me, too," Deacon Pillar replied. He didn't feel a need to share that he'd almost messed things up when he informed Chyna that she had nothing to worry about.

"I'll see you at the funeral tomorrow," Cordell said after the deacon got out of the car. "Get some rest, old soldier."

"I'm gonna try my best," Deacon Pillar said. "I sure

wish I could chat with Earl, though. I know he'd get a kick outta how we outwitted the board."

"He probably would."

"Although, I gotta tell you." Deacon Pillar said smiling, "Earl Athens wouldn't have been so stupid as to fall for everything we dished out without tasting the fruit first."

Chapter 53

The next day the funeral for Deacon Athens didn't take too long. Most of the folks kept theirs lies and near-truths to the three-minute limit.

It wasn't until the drive back in the funeral limousine from Pine Lawn Cemetery, that Chyna finally had a chance to relax. She didn't have to worry about Janelle being back at the house alone. It was the day the house-keeper cleaned, and she had agreed to stay until Chyna returned.

Deacon Athens didn't have any close family ties. The only relatives anyone knew about really didn't have much to do with him. The reasons were never asked or explained. However, there was one particular relative, one of Chyna's best friends, Cinnamon. Cinnamon was still away performing on a cruise ship and wouldn't return, not even for the funeral of her uncle. Chyna tried her best when they spoke by phone to get Cinnamon to come home, but she wouldn't.

Chyna did, however, convince Cinnamon's son to be one of the pallbearers for his uncle. Chyna would never tell anyone that she'd paid the deacon's estranged teenaged nephew, Hard Life, to carry his uncle's body to and from the church.

The home-going service was wonderful, if such a thing were possible. It appeared that Deacon Earl Athens was very much beloved by most and feared by probably a lot more. However, even his best friend, Deacon Pillar, managed to contain his grief. It wasn't audible but the pained look on the old man's face spoke volumes.

Chyna still hadn't forgotten what Deacon Pillar said about her not worrying. Now was not the time for her to approach him about it. Perhaps it was better to leave well enough alone.

Chyna also thought about the preacher whom the bereavement auxiliary brought in to preach the eulogy. She knew the man, although not that well. The preacher, a powerful speaker named Bishop John Smith from the St. Paul's City of Lights Ministry, sometimes stood in for Grayson. It was during those times when the elderly preacher spoke that she actually saw a change in Grayson. It was too bad the Bishop hadn't been around often enough for Grayson to truly catch on.

"For every light that God puts out, a new one is lit. There is no big sin or little sin. Every sin is sin. Only man puts a value to it. Now I don't know why God is leading me to say this, but Earl Athens's light is out. He's gone, so I'm speaking to you, those who are still on this side of the grave. Get out of your own way and let God be God in your lives."

Chyna let her mind rest on those words spoken by Bishop Smith. He'd expounded a lot more and it only reassured her that as much and as often as she'd asked God to forgive her, she and she alone stood in the way of accepting it.

Since Chyna had promised the housekeeper that

she'd return as soon as the funeral was over, she had an excuse not to go back inside the church. She quickly got into her car and drove off without saying anything to anyone. There would be plenty of young ministers and other bereavement staff to take over and see to it that folks were fed and comforted.

While driving home, Chyna thought more about the changes that had come about since that night Grayson died. Earlier, before the funeral began, she was escorted to the chair she'd occupied while Grayson would preach. That was when she was actively the First Lady. But that day, too, there were some who treated her with the excitement of children who'd missed their mother. There were others who were more polite because of her title than sincerity. She was just glad to be there. But she couldn't lie to herself and say that while seated there at the funeral there weren't fleeting images of whatever happened with Grayson at the Sweet Bush. She didn't know when, if ever, the questions or images would stop. Perhaps they'd serve to remind her of the depths to which she and Grayson fell.

At least that's what she'd thought before the bishop spoke. As she turned in to the driveway, the words wouldn't leave her head. *Get out of your own way and let God be God in your lives.* . . .

Cordell's car was parked in front. She'd almost hit it when she made the turn. She hadn't thought about whether he was still at the church or not.

When Chyna entered the house, she found Janelle and Cordell in the living room. Janelle was still in her nightgown and seemed almost giddy. Cordell looked as though he were blushing or something akin to it.

"Okay," Chyna said as she laid her pocketbook on a chair. "Why do you two look like you've been caught with your hands in a cookie jar?"

"Who, me, take the cookies from the cookie jar?" Janelle softly sang the melody to an old children's rhyme.

"Yes, you took the cookie from the cookie jar." Cordell's melody was a bit off and he followed it with quiet laughter.

"You do know that there was a funeral this morning, don't you?" Chyna teased Cordell. She really wanted to blast him about being happy when they just buried someone, but she didn't want to upset Janelle.

"I guess you've forgotten that we are supposed to cry when someone is born and laugh when they leave," Janelle said in defense of Cordell. She knew exactly what Chyna really meant.

"Y'all wrong and you know it," Chyna accused. "But I guess it's all in how you take things to heart."

Chyna turned and left them in the living room. She was too tired to join them. She just couldn't wrap her mind around all the changes taking place in her life.

Chyna was also glad to see that the housekeeper had done the laundry. The woman didn't have to do hers, but she always did. Chyna usually paid her a little extra for doing so. Actually, it was Cordell who'd paid for the housekeeper, but she was instructed to never tell Janelle.

Chyna grabbed a pair of jeans from the pile of clean clothes and changed.

"Chyna," Janelle called into the intercom. "Can you come in the living room, please?"

Chyna came into the living room and found a seat. She yawned, indicating that whatever the problem was, she was just too tired to deal with it.

"Doctor Bayer called this morning after you left," Janelle said.

Chyna leaned forward and tried to read Janelle's expression. Her sister didn't look sad or upset. Weren't she and Cordell giggling like schoolchildren when she came in earlier?

"Well, what did she say?" Chyna asked.

"It hasn't spread to my lymph nodes," Janelle said lifting her arms. "It hasn't spread, period."

If Chyna could've thrown a party, she would've. Janelle's news caught her off guard, but it was welcomed. "So what exactly does it mean?" Chyna asked.

Janelle took Cordell's hand and placed it over her breast. She didn't appear ashamed because she wasn't. "It looks like the *girls* will be with me for quite some time."

"And you know how I love the *girls*," Cordell added with laughter.

"You two have no shame," Chyna said, struggling to maintain a straight face.

"Don't blame me," Janelle said, shyly. "Blame it on Deacon Athens. He's the one who prayed over that jar of cocoa butter."

"You're giving credit to Deacon Athens?" Cordell asked. "Seriously?"

"Of course not," Janelle replied. "I'm giving credit to God, who gave the gift to the deacon."

Cordell looked over at Chyna, who returned his look with a shrug.

"It's a start," Chyna said before adding, "We all gotta start somewhere on this journey."

"What are y'all talking about?" Janelle asked. She suddenly turned serious, as though she were annoyed about being a joke or something.

Cordell turned to Janelle. "Listen, honey," he said, softly. "It takes all kinds of faith to make this journey. No one person can say who God will use, because God uses whom He chooses."

"Amen," Chyna agreed. She didn't know if she'd have explained it like that, but she wasn't denying its validity.

"I don't understand," Janelle replied.

"Let me see if I can explain it better." Cordell stopped to think for a moment.

Chyna used the opportunity. She told Janelle, "Don't worry about figuring it out. Get out of your own way and let God be God in your life. Let Him be whatever it is that you need Him to be."

The conversation went on until Chyna excused herself again. It was still early, but her eyelids felt like lead. She really needed a nap. Just as she was about to rise, Cordell's cell phone rang out. She sat down again as she saw a change come across his face after he answered the call.

Cordell's change hadn't escaped Janelle either. She picked up on it immediately.

"I need to go to my car for something," Cordell said as a way of explaining why he was leaving the room. He still had his cell phone tight to his ear and he hurried out the front door.

"I wonder what that's all about," Janelle said, aloud.

"That would make two of us," Chyna replied. "I have no idea."

The sisters rose and went to the front window. Cordell said he was going to his car. Yet he was still talking on his cell phone. He became animated, with one hand flailing in the air as he talked. And he was nowhere near where his car was parked.

Chapter 54

The evening breeze tossed about flower petals and kicked up a little dirt outside Chyna's house. Cordell paced back and forth, continuing to bark into his cell phone.

From the living room window Chyna watched. "Janelle," she called out.

"Maybe you just need to mind your business." Janelle replied.

"Perhaps you're right." Chyna said. She didn't bother to add that Cordell had finally gotten into his car and drove off.

Chyna didn't have to tell Janelle anything. She felt something was amiss again.

"I'm growing tired of these games." Janelle complained. She waited a few minutes and then left the room. It was apparent that Cordell wasn't returning inside and yet he hadn't gone straight to his car, either. She couldn't stand the suspense and had gone into her bedroom to change. She was determined to see what was going on.

"Janelle," Chyna called through the intercom. "Are you okay?"

When Janelle didn't answer, Chyna raced from the living room to see why. Janelle was slowly slipping one foot into a sandal when Chyna rushed inside.

"He's gone," Chyna announced. "You don't have to rush."

"I'm not rushing for him," Janelle replied. "I'm rushing for you."

"What are you talking about?"

"We need to get some things straight." Janelle pointed toward a chair and added, "Have a seat, baby sister."

Whether it was the positive news from the doctor, the absence of Cordell, or the beginning of a faith walk, Chyna didn't know. All she knew was that Janelle looked like she meant business. Fact was, at that moment she looked and sounded just like the old Janelle. Chyna didn't know if that was a good thing or not.

"What's up with your grumpy 'I'm so Saved I just can't be bothered to be happy for no one else' self?" Janelle asked. Her voice didn't have its usual shakiness to it. It was definitely defiant and strong.

"Not now, Janelle," Chyna replied. "I just don't have the strength to argue."

"Get some!" Janelle sat on the edge of the bed and let one leg swing back and forth. She didn't appear to concede to what looked to be discomfort from the movement.

"I know there was a funeral today," Janelle started saying. "I get that funerals ain't pretty. They're not supposed to be for most normal folks. But you're acting like that deacon was the best friend you lost."

"Say what?" Chyna answered. "Now what are you talking about?" She was straining to keep a civil tongue, and Janelle wasn't making it easy.

"I'm talking about your funky attitude. Your wishy-washy mood swings. I'm talking about how you say one thing but you act another." Janelle stopped swinging her leg, and for whatever reason it seemed to cause her voice to rise.

"You need to get over it so you can get over," Janelle snapped. "It ain't always about you!"

"Where is this coming from?" Chyna asked.

"Apparently, it's coming from the Sweet Bush," Janelle said, coldly. "It's still burning inside you that I didn't help when I could've and I told when I shouldn't have."

"I don't need this bull!" Chyna jumped up and raced from the room. She was so enraged she hadn't seen Janelle leap off the bed to follow.

Chyna barged into the kitchen; her haven, where when things got hot she usually heated up something to eat or drink. When Janelle barreled into the kitchen, the temperature became scalding. She wasn't letting up.

"Why do you have to have all the attention?" Janelle asked, rhetorically. She didn't bother to wait for an answer. "You think I don't need or deserve attention."

"I didn't give you cancer!" Chyna snapped. "Don't blame that on me."

"You're such a fool!"

"I'm a fool?" Chyna said as she spun around. "You're the one standing in the doorway accusing me of craziness."

"Accusing you of craziness? Yes, I'm doing that. Accusing you of giving me cancer—no, I'm not doing that!"

Chyna could feel her head starting to throb. Her hands were sweating and she felt that if she didn't get somewhere peaceful real soon she couldn't be held responsible for her actions.

Chyna began opening and slamming the cabinet doors. She didn't bother to look inside any of them. She just used the actions to keep from slamming Janelle.

"Oh, that's good," Janelle taunted. "Slam those doors. We sure wouldn't want no more mishaps like the last time I grabbed your ass!"

There it was. The emotional floodgates had sprung a leak and it was Janelle that removed the dike.

"Oh, don't be so surprised at that word, it's in the Bible. You ain't all that," Janelle ranted. "Truth be told, you've never been all that."

Chyna threw a porcelain cup to the floor. It shattered much like she felt her relationship with Janelle would if the arguing continued. But she was helpless to stop because the truth, perhaps the ugliest parts, were about to come forth.

"You've always acted like you needed the love. Hell, when Mom and Dad died, you didn't think I needed the love, too?"

Janelle's anger pushed her and at the same time it was beginning to sap her strength. She fell onto one of the kitchen chairs, but her mouth had its own power and it went into full throttle.

"I've been carrying the blame for not stopping you when you first stepped out on your husband's cheating, now burnt-up behind. But it wasn't all that hard to convince you. How come you got into that game so easy?"

Chyna could say nothing. It was like every accusing word from Janelle's lips glued Chyna's mouth shut.

"Let me tell you what I've come up with," Janelle hissed, "I don't believe I had to drag you into nothing." Janelle leaned across the table and pointed her finger at Chyna. "You weren't in any better shape than me. But instead of sometimes showing me the love, you decided to show me every expensive little trinket Grayson brought you. You were so damn happy to shove it down my throat. When you did that, you snatched away some of me to go along with your privileged life."

Janelle was so into finally telling Chyna exactly how she felt neither she nor Chyna saw Cordell and Deacon Pillar standing in the doorway. Both men looked drained. How much had they heard? Janelle didn't know or care, because when she finished with Chyna there'd be plenty left over for Cordell.

Chyna's back was to the two men but they could see her shoulders heave. She hadn't said anything, but they knew she was crying.

"Janelle," Cordell called out. "What is going on? When I left you two were hugging and laughing."

"None of your damn business!" Janelle snapped. "You just wait your turn. I'm just getting started."

Chyna looked up at the sound of Cordell's voice. She suddenly felt embarrassed and struggled to use a tissue to dab her eyes.

"Oh, don't stop crying now," Janelle said as she watched her sister. "Get all the pity you can. It's the Chyna pity party." She turned and glared at the men. "Y'all come on in and join. Let me introduce y'all to Ms. Broken Chyna."

Not that they couldn't just turn and walk away, they could, but Cordell and Deacon Pillar did what they were told. They came into the kitchen. Each man grabbed a chair and waited for round two.

"What is going on?" Cordell's question poured forth again even when he'd meant to shut up.

"Little sister can't stand me having a little piece of heaven," Janelle snapped. "She thinks she's all saved from sin part of the time and when she don't think she is, she wants me to feel like I'm hellbound."

"When have I ever tried to make you feel like that?"

Chyna found her voice and she'd laced it with spite. "I've always tried to be there for you."

"No," Janelle shot back. "You've always tried to be there *before* me."

Cordell fell back into his seat. What had he done back then? The payback he'd sought to appease his anger at Janelle's alleged cheating was still thriving. It had grown and its tentacles spread into all of their lives, choking everything it contacted. He hung his head in shame. He'd truly hurt the two women to whom he felt the closest.

"I swear," Deacon Pillar said as he rubbed his shoulders, "Y'all some dumb kind of Christians." He stopped and turned to Janelle. "You probably the dumbest because you just accepted Christ recently."

"Say what?" Janelle said. She wasn't through, and the old man was throwing off her rhythm.

"Sit your dumb arse down, you giving Christianity a worse name than those other hypocrites at the church."

Deacon Pillar didn't care nor wait for a response from any of them before he continued. "We just buried my best friend today, and you living idiots are resurrecting a lot of crap that don't mean a damn thing. How long are y'all gonna let the likes of Grayson Young and Mother Eartha Blackstone control you—from the grave?"

"Hold on a minute, deacon," Cordell finally said.

"I ain't holding nothing compared to the grudges y'all are." He stood up and as though nothing cross had left his lips he asked Chyna, "Excuse me, First Lady. Can I get a glass of water before I teach this class?"

Deacon Pillar didn't have to get anything. Chyna was so stunned she rose and got it for him. She made sure the glass was a tall one and filled to the brim with ice before setting it in front of him.

"Thank you, First Lady. Now have a seat." Deacon Pillar took a sip and continued. "Much like our Lord did before he preached to those stubborn folks up on the

Mount of Olives or Moriah; my mind sometimes gets them mountains mixed up, he fed them some fish and bread." He looked again at Chyna and added, "Do Pizza Hut deliver around here?"

They were all in awe and stunned. Chyna, again, got up. She went over to one of the cupboards and took out a circular. She handed it to the deacon along with the telephone and sat back down.

"I fancy some extra cheese, myself. I see they got a special going on. You've got a choice between pepperoni, bacon, or pineapple." His eyes grew wide, "Who would put pineapple on pizza? That's sacrilege and dishonest."

Somehow the old man had taken over with wisdom and a choice of pizza. But they also knew that before he finished dismantling the problem there'd be a body count.

Chapter 55

An hour later the four were still seated in Chyna's kitchen. The pizza had been delivered. It was eaten by Deacon Pillar and picked over by the others.

The old man let out a belch without any sign of shame. He adjusted the waistline of his pants and leaned back after grabbing a toothpick from the holder. When he'd finished digging through his yellowed teeth for the last piece of stubborn cheese, he discarded the toothpick by flipping it into the nearby waste canister. He didn't miss. Of course, none of them knew he'd played basketball almost every day even into his forties.

Janelle let out a yawn and quickly covered her mouth. She looked around, but no one said anything, except the old man.

"Oh, don't get tired now, missy," Deacon Pillar rebuked. "Class is starting."

Deacon Pillar's face softened a bit. But his words kept their bite as he continued.

"I'll start with you, First Lady." He leaned back in his

chair and folded his arms. His eyes narrowed a bit before he continued. "You been a fool."

"Excuse me," Chyna shot back. She didn't think she needed to be spoken to in that manner, especially in her own home.

Chyna had lost the rights to her home when the old deacon finished his last bit of pan pizza. He was gonna have his say.

While the deacon gathered his thoughts to throw at Chyna, Janelle and Cordell had somehow managed to move their chairs closer together. Neither of them seemed to realize it, but the deacon did. He reserved that observation for later.

Deacon Pillar smiled. It was much like the same look of the shark in the movie *Jaws*. The smile only hid the bite.

"I say that you're a fool in the most respectful manner I can," Deacon Pillar said, warmly. "Your husband is dead. In fact, I suspect he and Eartha are probably in hell trying to figure out whose ash is whose." He stopped and laughed at his own joke.

The others didn't.

"Anyhow," Deacon Pillar continued. "Brother Cordell and I read every page of that journal. And before you go ape-crap, we've burned it, so there's no need. You just need to take our word for it."

Cordell was stunned. On the way back to Chyna's, he and the old man had agreed to never reveal what was written in Grayson's journal. Now, after a few bites of pizza, the old man's lips had loosened. One glance over at Janelle told Cordell he'd be lucky to leave that house alive. He couldn't do anything but place his head in his hands.

As though he read Cordell's mind Deacon Pillar tried to throw him a lifeline. "I made Brother Cordell promise not to say anything about the journal. But that was before we walked in here and found you two acting like y'all done lost your damn minds." He looked at Cordell and shook his head. "Alls them bets is off now."

"You had no right to destroy my husband's journal," Chyna said. "That was my property."

"No. You're wrong." Deacon Pillar explained, "You were the property."

"Come on, deacon," Cordell pleaded. "Enough is enough. None of this is necessary."

"You just might wanna mind your own business," Janelle barked. "Your behind still ain't safe."

"Now that's the Sister Pierce I've come to know and now respect. You handle that one there." He pointed at Cordell. "I'm gonna finish up over here," he added and pointed to Chyna.

"First of all, sometimes I do things that I think are right but perhaps for all the wrong reasons. It's much like you've done by your sister. Of course, I've come to find out that our beloved late Pastor Grayson always did the wrong things for the wrong reasons." Deacon Pillar leaned over and said as gentle as he could, "That idiot didn't love you. He didn't respect you. And most of all, if he had any self-respect he wouldn't have committed suicide. Murder perhaps; suicide . . . a no-no."

Deacon Pillar had their full attention.

"According to his own words, he planned on owning you from the moment you opened the door when you was married to Brother Cordell over there. He wrote that he liked owning and destroying beautiful things. That snake didn't care if it was day-old flowers or a twenty-something-year-old woman. He held them in the same class."

The deacon saw Chyna begin to weep, and it softened

his heart. So he turned to Janelle and started in on her. He'd come back to Chyna later.

"Sister Pierce," The deacon said. "I'm still gonna call you Sister Pierce even though you are a baby in Christ." He stopped and pointed his crooked finger at Janelle. "But you need to pull it together. Who the hell are you to dump on your sister? If you didn't wanna take care of her, you should've never started. You ain't her mama and you never could be."

Janelle started to say something, but her inner voice had better sense than she did. She stayed quiet.

"Don't think the reverend didn't play you, too. He took every piece of information he'd learned from his blabbermouth wife over here and turned it against you. It wasn't nothing personal. It was just the way he was."

The deacon stood up and stretched before going back at it. "I still can't believe how much power y'all giving that dead son of a . . ." He caught himself and added, "Lord, please forgive me. I can't stand no hypocrites."

All their mouths dropped open at the deacon's revelation.

"Sister Pierce," Deacon Pillar said. "Much of the stuff the reverend gave to your sister was just so she'd throw it unknowingly in your face."

Deacon Pillar suddenly stopped. He turned back to Chyna. "Oh yes, there's one other thing," Deacon Pillar told Chyna. "Those pictures."

"Pictures?" Chyna asked.

"Yeah," Deacon Pillar answered. "I'm talking about the nasty ones that Brother Cordell and I saw. Well, don't worry about nothing, because we burned them too." He started to smile a little and leaned toward her and said, softly, "You's about a talented First Lady, too. But don't ever let anyone make you feel lesser than what God feels about you."

The blood drained from Chyna's face. She looked to the floor, but there wasn't a crack big enough to hide her.

And then as if he'd just finished with the Sunday-morning announcements, he returned to where he left off.

Deacon Pillar continued quoting verse by verse of Grayson's devious plots and how the sisters and some of the other church members were involved. By the time he was ready to light into Cordell, the sisters sat stunned and started weeping.

"And now you, Brother Cordell," Deacon Pillar said as he turned to face him. "You already know what Grayson Young wrote about you, so we can rehash it or you can share it with the women when they're feeling better. It's up to you."

"I think you've said and done enough," Cordell said between clenched teeth.

"Well, so be it," Deacon Pillar remarked as he stood. "I'm plumb worn out. Putting y'all's demons to rest is tiring." He looked at his watch. "It's almost one o'clock. If Earl had been here we'd torn y'all behinds in less time." His voice grew sad. "I miss my old friend, Earl Athens. I'm never gonna have a friend like him on this side of the grave."

"Sorry you have to leave," Cordell said, sarcastically. "This has been a lot of fun."

"Well, I suggest you leave, too. I'm gonna need a ride back home, unless you wanna hang around here and get your butt burned like that journal."

Cordell rose and led the old man from the kitchen.

Chapter 56

Janelle was up before eleven o'clock that next morning. She'd slept poorly because Deacon Pillar's revelations worked better than a dose of No Doze.

Janelle was still in her bedclothes and still pissed off. She was in the middle of letting Chyna know just how much when she'd heard the doorbell ring. She'd opened the door and found two middle-aged women with pamphlets in their hands along with wide smiles.

They might as well have been bill collectors. There wasn't an ounce of concern in Janelle's voice. "Take a damn day off sometime," she'd barked. "Just because you ain't knocking on a door at sunrise, it don't mean it is okay to be a pain in the middle of the day, either."

The two women apologized for the interruption; they'd only wanted to talk with her about God. Janelle slammed the front door in the middle of their sentences.

Before the interruption Janelle had just begun her second or third rant against Chyna. She'd only opened the door because she'd stood in front of it so Chyna couldn't escape.

"You need to explain it to me, plainly. Why did Cordell take money from Grayson?" Janelle threatened. "I don't think I quite understood what you meant."

"Look, I told you from the beginning that I didn't want to have this conversation with you," Chyna replied.

"You told me a lot of stuff lately that you should've said before," Janelle hissed. "Now you ain't leaving here until we get things straight."

"You need to calm down," Chyna warned. "It's not worth your health."

"Oh, now you're a doctor?" Janelle replied. "Don't be so concerned about my health. You be concerned about your own."

Janelle pushed and shoved Chyna figuratively and physically that morning. She just couldn't let things continue the way they were. She'd found it hard to look at Chyna without wondering what Chyna knew and wasn't telling. The spirit of suspicion overtook Janelle to the point where she momentarily didn't care about her health as much as her need to know everything.

However, Janelle got more than she asked for. She'd cornered Chyna at a moment when Chyna was dealing with her own revelations.

Chyna was happy that God was making things clearer for her and now Janelle was beginning to cloud things up. Perhaps, she needed to just put it all out there. Let the chips fall where they may so she could reclaim her God.

"I don't know another way to put it," Chyna said. "We were at a bad point in the marriage. Truth is, there was never a good point, but then Grayson came along. I didn't know for a while just how much in debt Cordell was and by the time I found out he'd already accepted the money from Grayson to divorce me. It's pretty much the way Cordell explained it."

Janelle stood with her arms still folded against her

chest. The pain in her face made her look old. The angrier she became, the older she looked.

Without saying anything more, Janelle turned around. She moved quickly down the hallway from the living room and slammed the door behind her when she entered the bedroom.

Chyna couldn't move. Through the intercom she heard Janelle sobbing. It broke her heart, but Janelle asked for the truth. Chyna couldn't lie anymore. Every secret she held despite her reasons for doing so built a wall of distrust. Brick by brick she was trying to tear the wall down. It seemed that with every brick she removed she was hitting Janelle hard with it.

It hadn't been but a few hours since Chyna thought God was giving her a new understanding of His plan. Had she misunderstood? Had he not fully forgiven her?

It took a moment before Chyna, now fully absorbed with trying to understand what she once thought was true before she realized, again, there was no sound coming from Janelle's room.

Angry or not, as had become her habit, Chyna raced to Janelle's room. She'd just started to open it when Janelle rushed out.

"What are you doing?" Janelle asked. She'd changed her clothes and looked ready to step outdoors. "You can't knock? I know it's your house, but this is my room."

"I didn't hear you moving about," Chyna explained.

"So what if you didn't?" Janelle countered. "Do you need to be involved in everything I do? Do you listen in to hear if I'm pissing into the toilet, too?" Janelle didn't wait for Chyna to reply. Instead she raced back inside her room and grabbed the intercom.

"What are you doing?" Chyna asked.

"I'm doing to it what I feel like doing to you," Janelle threw the intercom down. The unit shattered as soon as it hit the floor. "You see that?" Janelle asked pointing to the floor. "That's you, Chyna. All broken into little pieces: a piece for me, a piece for Cordell, a tiny piece for God."

Janelle stepped over the busted intercom. She brushed past Chyna and without turning back she called out. "Why don't you just change your name? You can call yourself what I've come to call you, Broken Chyna."

However, Janelle no sooner slammed the front door behind her when she reentered. She hadn't returned alone. Cordell held her by the arm as she struggled against him.

Despite Janelle having argued with her, Chyna immediately started to come to Janelle's defense. The only thing that stopped her was the sight of Deacon Pillar standing behind Cordell.

"What do I need to do to get rid of y'all?" Chyna barked. Were they all moving in? It certainly felt like it.

Grinning like the whole world was okay, Deacon Pillar entered and immediately moved past Cordell struggling with Janelle. He went straight to Chyna. "Good afternoon," he said laughing. "Maybe we should start dating since I'm seeing so much of you." Deacon Pillar as usual started to laugh at his own joke.

"Speaking of dating," Deacon Pillar continued despite the look of annoyance on Chyna's face. "You got any of that pizza left or can we go get some?" He stopped and pointed toward Janelle and Cordell. "They need a timeout," he whispered. "Are they working your nerves as much as they are mine?"

Chyna was stunned. She didn't know how seriously to take Deacon Pillar. He always seemed to arrive at the right conclusion despite taking the long way through fantasyland to get there.

"I am suddenly hungry," Chyna said. She surrendered her home and left with the old deacon. She prayed

Janelle and Cordell didn't tear each other apart and that her furniture would be left intact, too.

Chyna and Deacon Pillar weren't gone long before Janelle found new strength with every accusation and hissy fit she threw at Cordell.

Cordell found that everything he taught or thought he knew about relationships didn't amount to a hill of beans when it came to Janelle. She was taking him to class like it was his first time. The way she went after him left no doubt that graduation was a long way off.

"You're doing all this ranting because Grayson paid me to divorce Chyna?" Cordell asked. "You didn't rant like this when Chyna and I mentioned it before." He'd kept repeating the question because he'd found it hard to believe Janelle's obsession with what he'd done to divorce her sister.

"You're truly stupid!" Janelle screamed. "How could you be such an idiot?"

"How could you believe that I could love someone else more than I'd loved you?" Cordell snapped. "Answer me. How could you believe that about me?"

"How could you not come to me when you divorced her?" Janelle was now screaming. "You were paid to get rid of her, but suddenly you grew a conscience and you couldn't come to me? Do you understand that the chances I took with different men were because I thought you didn't care about me and that I wasn't worth caring about? I could've been killed by some fool or disease!"

"She was your sister!" Cordell was seething. "She was your sister," he repeated.

"Fool!" Janelle replied. "She's still my sister!"

"I know that," Cordell said in defeat. "I know that."

"I never had arms around me like yours," Janelle blurted. "You were my first love. And even when you mar-

ried Chyna, I believed that there was still that part of you
that she couldn't have."

Cordell looked at Janelle and suddenly dropped his
head in shame. "She couldn't. That's why it wasn't that
hard to divorce her. I'd have done it for free."

"But you didn't," Janelle reminded Cordell. ░░ took
the money and you didn't bother to come back to ░░."

"I told you why I didn't. What more can I say?"
Cordell asked.

"How about telling the whole truth?" Janelle replied.

"What are you talking about?" Cordell looked up. He
didn't understand what more she wanted.

"You need to figure it out," Janelle answered. "We
can't *dance* until you do."

While Janelle and Cordell rode around and around
the truth, Chyna's ride to the pizza shop wasn't filled with
sage wisdom as she had figured it would be. The old deacon only talked about how much he loved pizza. When
they finally arrived at the pizza shop, Chyna walked a few
feet away from Deacon Pillar to read the menu board that
hung on a wall above the counter. They hadn't been inside
the Pizza Hut for more than a few minutes before he'd
started ranting about pineapple slices on pizza.

Deacon Pillar asked to speak with whoever made up
the pizza orders immediately after they'd arrived. For some
reason the Pizza Hut manager came out right away. He
thought the old man wanted to say thank you.

Instead, Deacon Pillar put in his order and started
right in on the poor man. "Do you know how many laws
of decency and cooking you've broken? How in the Sam
Hill can you call yourself a pizza maker and you putting
damn pineapple slices on the pizza? Do you make
pineapple sandwiches?" Deacon Pillar didn't wait for the
man to reply, he continued to light into him. "Of course,
you don't make pineapple sandwiches. So why would you

put pineapple slices on pizza dough? Ain't pizza made from the same dough as bread?"

By the time the old deacon finished with the pizza man, he'd received a promise that they'd never put pineapple slices on his pizza order again.

Chyna waited for Deacon Pillar to finish eating his personal-size pan pizza. She really didn't want him to eat inside her car, but it appeared that the pizza shop owner didn't want him eating inside the shop, either. She watched almost in fascination as the old man wolfed down his pizza.

"That was some good pizza," Deacon Pillar said while licking the sauce off his fingers. "The next time I think I'll make my order topped with some fried baloney."

"You'd eat fried baloney on pizza?" Chyna asked, wondering if the old man was serious.

"Yep, fried baloney on pizza makes sense." He turned toward Chyna and smiled, "You see, pizza starts with dough and so does bread. So if you can put fried baloney on a slice of bread it makes sense to put it on pizza."

Chyna decided that she just needed to keep her mouth closed and her sanity in check. She'd had enough craziness for one day and yet, she was beginning to feel a little comfortable with Deacon Pillar. Still she had to also admit that when he looked at her she wondered if he thought about the pictures from the Sweet Bush.

Deacon Pillar turned away from looking out the passenger-side window. He looked at Chyna and smiled. Somehow eating that pizza made him think of the pictures of Chyna at the Sweet Bush. Both were tasty images.

As they neared her house, the old man's cell phone rang. Chyna tried not to listen to the conversation. It was difficult because they were still in the car.

"No, don't give him the information," Deacon Pillar

snapped. "I told that boy to come by the church tomorrow. Don't let that man-child play you." The deacon snapped the cover to his phone shut and smiled.

"That was Sister Lawson," Deacon Pillar said.

"Sister Lawson, the church secretary?" Chyna asked.

"Yep. Earlier today I saw your friend Cinnamon's son. Hard Life, I think is what they call him."

"By the way, I spoke to Cinnamon, too. It was only for a few minutes earlier today because it was too expensive calling from a cruise ship."

Deacon Pillar, anxious to tell his part of the story, cut Chyna off, "Well, I told him about Earl leaving him some money, but he'd have to get all the particulars at church tomorrow."

"Why?" Chyna asked.

"Why not?" Deacon Pillar replied. "It ain't like the jail cell ain't gonna wait for him. He can spend a little time in God's house before they ship his sorry butt to the big house."

"You think God will touch him if he shows up, don't you?" Chyna laughed. Deacon Pillar was always trying to use more manipulation than faith.

"I hope so," The deacon replied. His mood turned serious suddenly. "I'm so tired of seeing these young men piss away their futures on some dumb crap."

"Why are you so hard on the young folks?" Chyna wanted to ask him that question before. Now seemed just as good a time as any to ask.

"Because I care about the young people," Deacon Pillar replied. "They's an ignorant bunch nowadays."

"Why do you keep saying that?"

"Because look at me. Look where I live and what I do. I was once an ignorant something, too. All I did was run the streets, run my hos. I'm sorry I meant ladies who like to work on their backs." He stopped and started singing, "Oh if it had not been for the Lord . . ."

Chyna pulled up to a stop light and looked over at the deacon and smiled. "You know what, Deacon Pillar? A very wise man just told me as recently as last night that I ought to be ashamed of myself."

"What are you talking about, First Lady?"

"The wise man reprimanded me for thinking lower of myself than God did."

Deacon Pillar let out a howl. "I did say that, didn't I?"

"Yes, you did."

"Damn, I'm smart."

And just that quick the old man's mood changed, and Chyna fully understood. Both needed constant reminders that their salvation was battle-tested daily, but with God on their sides the victory was theirs for the asking.

"How long have we been gone from your house?" Deacon Pillar asked. "I need a toilet break."

"I guess about an hour," Chyna replied. "We should be at my house in another five minutes."

"Well, hopefully those two ignoramuses will have their acts together. I'm tired of playing referee and cop. Ain't you?"

"It is like a second job," Chyna laughed. "I don't need nor want a second job."

"I know that's right," Deacon Pillar said. "I just hope those two don't make me lose my testimony."

"Me, too," Chyna added.

"I'd love to hear your testimony sometime," Deacon Pillar gave Chyna an impish grin. "First Lady, I betcha your testimony is one for the records."

For whatever reason, Chyna wasn't embarrassed that time. And she was beginning to learn that the reason the old man kept reminding her of what she'd been in the past was because she shouldn't be ashamed. She just needed to get out of her own way, accept God's forgiveness, and move on.

"You know, talent recognizes talent," Deacon Pillar said. The comment seemed to come from out of nowhere.

Chyna was afraid to ask, but felt she had to do it. "What are you talking about?"

"Keep up," Deacon Pillar answered. "I'm talking about Eartha Blackstone. I recognized it in her from the moment I lay eyes on her. I suspected her daddy did, too."

The Deacon laid his head back against the headrest before continuing. "Not sure if you are aware of it or not. I know Reverend Young was. Eartha was a lot like her father Reverend Richard Blackstone. He had to be one of the funniest pimps we had in New Hope Assembly's pulpit."

Chyna almost ran a light. "You already mentioned that, except the pimp part."

"Oh yeah, I did, didn't I? Well, I ain't got nothing more to say, 'cause I need to use your bathroom. You might wanna hurry up a bit. Pizza causes strange reactions in me."

"I remember," Chyna said as she pushed down on the car's accelerator.

Chapter 57

"**Y**'all keep on doing what you're doing. Don't mind me." Deacon Pillar dashed through the living room, nearly toppling a table on his way toward Chyna's bathroom.

Right behind the old man Chyna emerged through the front door. Like the old deacon, she paid no attention to either Cordell or Janelle. If she was bothered by the sight of the two embracing, she didn't show it.

Cordell's arms were stiff. He hadn't realized that he was still holding Janelle. They'd argued and said a few things that'd been held in for far too long. She'd even cussed him out.

"Janelle," Cordell whispered. "Wake up."

He shook her gently, and when that didn't seem to work he began to tickle her. He'd almost forgotten how sensitive she was to that. So the more she moved about and tried to avoid his moving fingers the more he played with her.

By the time Chyna and Deacon Pillar returned,

Cordell and Janelle were giggling like they were still in junior high school.

"You two are working my last nerve," Deacon Pillar remarked. "Get a room." He stopped and laughed as usual at his own joke.

Janelle wasn't embarrassed and didn't try to pretend that she was.

"Where's Chyna?" Janelle asked the old man.

"She's where she's supposed to be," Deacon Pillar replied. "She's fixing a real man some coffee."

"Does she know that it's what she's supposed to do?" Cordell added. "That doesn't sound like the Chyna I know."

"Actually," the deacon laughed, "she's supposed to be getting ready to go to a meeting at the church."

"Then why is she in the kitchen fixing you a cup of coffee?"

"Y'all dumber than dirt," Deacon Pillar huffed. "I haven't told her about the meeting yet." He tried to wink, but it appeared that his winking muscles seemed a bit too relaxed. He looked more like he was fighting sleep. "I'm gonna go with her back to the church. You two stay here and keep out of trouble."

"What's going on?" Cordell asked. He didn't recall anything about a meeting when he and the old man chatted earlier. He was beginning to think that the deacon's mind took far too many mental breaks. He seemed to enjoy manipulation.

"It's time for the annual vote for new programs. Since she's still on paper as having a vote, they can't do nothing until she tosses in her two cents."

"What-about-those-special-changes?" Cordell asked, slowly. He hoped the old man knew what he'd meant, but he felt he needed to explain further. "I'm talking about the ones that Sister Blackstone and Deacon Athens were working on."

"You do understand that the woman you all cuddled up with and trying to catch a feel ain't as stupid as you? You do know that?" Deacon Pillar sat down and sighed. "I swear, young man, you're sapping all my wisdom. Catch a clue and tell Sister Pierce everything. Stop making me out to be the Grinch every time I visit over here."

Deacon Pillar rose. "I'm going back to the kitchen and find out what is taking First Lady so long to bring me my coffee." He walked a few feet and turned around. Looking at Janelle, he added, "You might wanna whup his behind instead of letting him feel all over yours. He ain't telling you everything."

"Oh, is that a fact?" Janelle asked, "What do I have to do to get all the truth out of you, pump Sodium Pentothal up your behind?

Cordell's head dropped in defeat like a two-ton boulder. At the rate Deacon Pillar kept tossing him under the bus, there'd be nothing but skin and tread marks by the time he finished. He could hear the old man cackling as he walked down the hallway.

Chyna bustled around in the kitchen. The coffee she'd made for the old man had already cooled by the time she'd finished putting aside what she wanted to cook for later. She almost dropped a cake pan when she turned around and found him standing behind her.

"Deacon Pillar!" Chyna wanted to blast the old man but found she couldn't. She was finding it very hard to stay upset with him, because he usually came at her from left field. By the time she would figure out what he meant or what he was up to, the old man was on to something else.

"Is everything okay with those two in the living

room?" Chyna asked as she placed the cold cup of coffee into the microwave to reheat it.

"Oh, everything will be fine with them," Deacon Pillar answered, "Why you trying to kill me?"

"Excuse me?" Chyna remarked as the ringer on the microwave rang out and she retrieved the steaming cup of coffee. She sat it down in front of Deacon Pillar.

"I'm not drinking that!"

"Why not?" Chyna asked. She could feel her nerves suddenly rising to the same temperature as the coffee.

"You trying to introduce nuclear waste into my body through that damn machine over there." He pointed to the microwave. "You can't trust them things. Don't you know the government didn't introduce that gadget until the 1970s when the U.S. Census found that there were too many black folks still living?"

"Huh!"

"We've been acting crazy and committing extra crimes every since we started microwaving stuff. We've become too lazy and impatient to use good old ovens and stovetops." The Deacon took a napkin and gently pushed the cup aside as though radiation were on the cup's handle, too.

"You do know that it's not just black folks that use microwaves, don't you?" As soon as Chyna asked the question, she was sorry. She should've just made him another cup and left things alone.

But she hadn't.

"First Lady, you know I love and have come to respect you and your extra talent, but you don't know nothing about what makes folks tick." The old man suddenly looked tired so he found a seat at the kitchen table. "Listen here," Deacon Pillar continued. "It's like anything else. The government ain't gonna do nothing until it affects white folks, too. That's why they ain't making too many microwaves now. Instead, they're selling toaster ovens."

Deacon Pillar stopped and grinned. He was so proud of his knowledge and he didn't mind showing it. He clasped his hands together and with a nod of his chin toward her stove, he'd indicated to Chyna to get busy and bring him another cup of hot coffee.

"You might wanna hurry up with that," Deacon Pillar said. "We gonna be late for that meeting I forgot to tell you about."

Several hours later, a downpour started. It wasn't enough rain to stop the board members from showing up for their annual meeting. When Chyna and Deacon Pillar arrived at New Hope Assembly, they were informed that the others were all upstairs in one of the study rooms.

Once he'd calmed her down because he didn't tell her about the meeting, Deacon Pillar went to work on schooling her. Deacon Pillar had already told Chyna what to do and how to do it. He'd shared with her what she needed to say and how to say it. And, finally, before they went upstairs, he led her into the sanctuary for prayer. When they neared the front, he picked up a Bible that lay on one of the pews.

"I ain't got my cheaters with me, so I can't see too well," Deacon Pillar said. "So I'll do the praying and you do the reading."

Chyna took the Bible from the old man's hands. "I'm assuming you have a particular scripture in mind?"

"Be ye always ready," The deacon laughed, softly. "That's a freebie so you don't have to look it up. I'm good for that one." His tone turned serious. "We getting ready for a fight. And since these is church folks you got to have a special wind at your back. I need you to read and understand a verse or two from the book of Ephesians."

"Which verse?" Chyna asked as she began to thumb through the Bible.

"You need to pay closer attention. I said, 'verses.' You think them demons upstairs gonna be put to flight by just one verse?" He didn't wait for Chyna to answer. He continued, "I want you to read from verse eleven through seventeen." He moved over a bit on the pew so she could sit while he struggled to get down on his knees.

Chyna began to read aloud. "Ephesians, starting at the sixth verse. Put on the whole armor of God, that ye may be able to stand against the wiles of the devil.

"For we wrestle not against flesh and blood, but against principalities, against powers, against the rulers of the darkness of this world, against spiritual wickedness in high places . . ."

Chyna read down to the seventeenth verse: "And take the helmet of salvation, and the sword of the Spirit, which is the word of God."

"Amen." Deacon Pillar said when she finished. By then he'd made it to his knees and so he began to pray. "Heavenly Father, we are dressed for battle. Help us slay them devils. Amen."

And then the old man rose. He took the Bible from Chyna and placed it under his arm. "Let's go, First Lady. We are now officially blessed demon slayers."

Deacon Pillar and Chyna heard the board members as soon as they reached the second floor. Opening the door to the room, they found them spread about the room in cliques. Like bees in a hive there were pockets of buzzing, insinuations, finger-pointing, and a short testimony or two going on.

Deacon Pillar saw Deacon Duke Brown standing up surrounded by four of the members. "There's the main culprit right over there," Deacon Pillar said, pointing quickly at the man.

"Where did all these other folks come from?" Chyna asked. She didn't remember there being more than twelve at any of the few meetings she'd attended with Grayson.

"You've never been to the annual meeting. These are all the main and alternate board members. Just keep your wits about you. Once we slay that ornery dragon Duke Brown, the others will lie down and play dead."

Chapter 58

Janelle had thrown the last one of Chyna's expensive copper-bottom pots at Cordell. All she needed was one more to toss at him so he could have a matching nick on his neck.

"You're lucky I don't believe in violence!" Cordell said, rubbing what was sure to leave a scar. His mind whirled as he tried to figure out a safe way to pass Janelle, who stood looking buck wild and crazy as she blocked the only way out of the kitchen.

"You're the one that's lucky," Janelle snapped. "'Cause if I had a gun, I would've shot you."

"Oh, God must be so pleased with you," Cordell replied.

Like a serrated sledgehammer head, no sooner had the words left Cordell's mouth than they returned slicing him up and down and side to side. Who was he to judge her? All she'd wanted was the truth and he kept deciding what was true and how much he should dole out.

"I'm sorry," Cordell whispered. "I'm so sorry."

Janelle said nothing. She simply moved aside to give

him room to leave. She waited a moment, and when he didn't move she turned and left the kitchen.

Whatever skills he had at relationship counseling, again, seem to fail when it came to him and Janelle. Why couldn't he pull it together, he wondered.

While Cordell stood in the kitchen trying to figure out what to do next, Janelle returned.

That time she came back waving the sombrero. She flung it at him, hitting him in the chest. "Dance by your damn self."

She seemed to vanish like a vapor. Were it not for the frayed Mexican hat lying on the floor in front of him, he couldn't be sure if she'd actually returned.

Cordell kicked the hat aside and stepped into the hallway leading from the kitchen to the living room. "I don't need this drama," he muttered.

"What do you need?" Janelle stepped around the corner. She'd not gone far after tossing the hat. "What do you need?"

At that moment she seemed to change. Cordell didn't see the short hair or the motley complexion and gaunt body. He didn't see the woman who'd a moment before had said she'd shoot him if she could. He also didn't see a woman who held his heart for years even as he tried to piece it out to others. While he looked at her, he finally saw things for the way they were and not for what he wished.

His usual methods for dealing with relationship issues hadn't worked with Janelle, because she was the original model that'd shaped his thinking. Janelle's body, attitude, her heart, and her mind were always present whenever he gave out advice. But he'd built his practice on an old model. She'd grown and he was still stuck in the past.

Cordell looked at Janelle, who still stood with her

arms crossed in defiance as though challenging him. He'd never felt so inadequate as he did at that moment. She'd flung a hat and mentioned a dance as an answer to him questioning her relationship with God.

Cordell looked at Janelle, again. She still hadn't moved. "I'm sorry," he repeated.

"You just oughta be," Janelle said, while keeping her arms crossed. She might've hit him again if she didn't keep her hands constrained.

"You seem to know more about my relationship with God than I do," Janelle said. "Why is that?"

Cordell shrugged. He couldn't find a reason and he didn't want to make up one.

"Just so you don't think that I spend my days watching soap operas and Oprah, check this out." Janelle came closer so she didn't have to speak louder. She could also feel her usual tiredness coming on but she was determined to speak her mind. If she passed out then she just passed out. "You're always telling someone what to do. Perhaps you need to read more of your Bible and less of the word according to Cordell. You might wanna try and do what it says in the book of James. I believe it's the fifth verse: 'Even so the tongue is a little member, and boasted great things. Behold, how great a matter a little fire kindles.'

Janelle's hands reached out for the wall behind her. She tried to do so without letting Cordell know how weak she felt. "Now use that tongue and chew on that." She wanted to leave, but by then it was the only the wall that supported her body. Her feet wouldn't move.

However, Cordell wasn't entirely stunned by her Bible knowledge. He'd watched with great appreciation of how she'd committed the verse to memory. And its connection to what they'd discussed wasn't lost on him, either. But he wasn't about to let her get away completely.

At least not at that moment, when he saw she was weakened.

"Check this out," Cordell said as he rose and walked toward Janelle. "Proverbs eighteen and twenty-one: 'Death and life are in the power of the tongue: and they that love it shall eat the fruit thereof.' "

He caught her just as she was about to collapse. He also brought to life the words he'd just quoted. Cordell kissed Janelle hard. He kissed her as though he were giving up his own breath so she would live.

And the only response Janelle had was a fountain of tears.

Chapter 59

The curtains in the upstairs room at New Hope Assembly were drawn together. The only light in the room came from several overhead fluorescent bulbs. The Christian lights that should've come from the church board members were turned off due to lack of Christian participation. Just about every board member, the main ones as well as their alternates, were cutting up and acting the fool.

Chyna was in shock. She knew that some of those same members had an idea that she'd fallen from grace. By their actions, they'd fallen, too, and weren't trying to hide it.

"We ain't gonna get rid of the Christian nightclub," one of the board members said, adamantly. "It brings in a lot of money every fifth Saturday."

"It's also bringing in the wrong element," another voice from the back shouted out. "We ain't that kind of church!"

"He's right," Deacon Pillar interjected. "We ain't that kind of church. But we're sure that kind of board." He stopped and placed one hand in his pocket before continuing. "We ain't fit to tell those young folks nothing. We too busy trying to one-up each other, thinking God won't know no better."

"You need to keep quiet." The command came from Duke Brown. "You're just trying to impress Sister Young."

"I ain't got to impress the First Lady," Deacon Pillar shot back. "Y'all got to impress her, unless you've forgotten she gets the deciding vote around here."

All eyes fell upon Chyna. She'd hoped to remain in the background and leave without having to say a word.

"Oh, don't get me started," Duke Brown said as his blue eyes grew wide and his complexion reddened.

"Go ahead and start it," Deacon Pillar warned. "But you better believe I know how to stop it!"

From inside his shirt Deacon Pillar pulled out the journal. He felt secure that the others hadn't caught on yet that the journal only had a lot of gibberish on some pages. He'd not only been an avid basketball player back in the day but also, when he wasn't ushering on Sunday mornings, he was playing poker on Saturday nights, and winning, too.

"I'm gonna change the order of things," Deacon Pillar said suddenly. "We gonna vote on eliminating one of the board member seats. I think we got one too many knuckleheads on it." He looked over toward Duke, who stood dumbfounded.

"We got anybody willing to second the motion?" Deacon Pillar asked.

Hands flew up all around the room.

Deacon Pillar looked directly at Duke Brown and without blinking announced, "Come to think of it, we got more important decisions to make. Perhaps, if we need to do so, we'll get back to this particular issue."

Checkmate.

Chyna watched in amazement. For the next hour or
so Deacon Pillar moved the members and issues around
like a puppeteer. Every dissent was met by him waving
around the journal. It was a good thing that none of the alternates were needed to vote. None of them had a clue as
to what was going on. But they were certainly impressed
with the old man. An overwhelming vote moved to have
Deacon Pillar step into the shoes of the late Deacon Earl
Athens.

I'm gonna do right by you, old friend, Deacon Pillar
thought as he accepted the position. He wasn't nervous
about it. After all, he'd been at the side of the best and
wisest church board member there was at New Hope Assembly; Earl Athens would never be duplicated, but Deacon Pillar would give his best imitation.

"And, now for the last little piece of business," Deacon Pillar announced. "We need to vote on returning
some items to the First Lady, here. We was wrong to go to
her while she was in bad shape and mourning the loss of
her beloved—" He stopped, thinking perhaps he might've
been going a little bit overboard. He corrected what he
wanted to say. "This lady, our First Lady of New Hope
Assembly, was treated badly when Reverend Grayson
Young died."

"Don't you mean committed suicide?" The question
rang out from somewhere in the back, but no one stepped
forward to own it.

"Is he any less dead?" Deacon Pillar slammed the
journal on the desk. "Well, is he?"

No one responded, so the old man continued. "Just
like I was saying, I'm calling for a vote to return whatever
properties, real and paper, that was taken from the First
Lady to be returned as soon as possible."

Deacon Pillar watched for any dissenters. He didn't

get a sign from anyone, so he continued. "Let's get this motion seconded and passed."

Chyna was in shock. God had begun His restoration of her life. All she'd needed to do was to move out of her own way.

None of the other new church business took long and so, without hanging around, which usually led to more unwanted drama, Chyna and the old deacon left.

The trip back to Chyna's was filled with laughter. Every time she'd catch her breath or stop at a light, the old man caused her to howl as he imitated each of the board members as they caved in. Chyna and Deacon Pillar smiled so much they looked like matching smiley faces when they entered her house. She'd brought the old man back with her to Highland Park, despite him saying that he wanted to go home.

She called out for Janelle as soon as she came through the door. There wasn't an answer. She looked inside Janelle's bedroom, but no one was in it. She looked all through the house and it wasn't until Deacon Pillar said that Cordell's car was gone that she became worried.

Chapter 60

Chyna had torn Janelle's room apart. She saw her pots strewn about the kitchen and pieces of straw from Janelle's sombrero were in the living room.

While Chyna looked around outside her house Deacon Pillar kept hitting redial on his cell phone trying to reach Cordell. It'd been at least an hour and a half since he'd started, and it kept going directly to voice mail.

Chyna was near tears as she stood on the sidewalk in front of her house. She was frantic. She saw an unmarked police car that was moving slowly in her direction. She waved at it and indicated that she needed help. She shook her head in disbelief when the car stopped and the men got out. *There must not be any other policemen in Brooklyn.*

It's Detectives Gonzalez and Lavin. "What's wrong?" Chyna called out as the detectives approached. She hadn't called for the police, but she was about to do so.

"How are you, Mrs. Young?" It was Gonzalez; she'd remembered him from when Grayson died and at the hospital when the hit-and-run happened. She also remembered that Janelle had been real friendly in the biblical sense with the man.

"I was just trying to find Janelle," Chyna replied. "She's not here and she didn't leave a note."

By the time the other detective, Lavin, walked up, Deacon Pillar had come outside.

"Mrs. Young, how are you?" Detective Lavin asked. "Is everything okay?"

Both detectives smiled as they watched Deacon Pillar approach.

"Hey there Deke," Detective Lavin said as he held out his hand. "What's happening, old G?"

"I'm fair to middling," Deacon Pillar replied. "How's your mama doing?"

They traded pleasantries for a second and then went back to the issue at hand.

"I didn't know you hung around these parts," Detective Gonzalez told Deacon Pillar while laughing.

"That's because you don't know jack squat and you still trying to figure out if I'm your real daddy." Deacon Pillar seemed to forget that Janelle was missing. He started laughing as he turned to Chyna and added, "I used to date his mama, too."

"I still need to find Janelle," Chyna said, harshly. She could care less about any of the other craziness they discussed.

"Oh, yeah," Detective Gonzalez said. "She's fine."

Chyna looked at the detective like she wanted to take his gun. "How do you know?"

"She and her friend, Cordell, are over at the Kings Highway Mall in Flatbush."

"Say what?" Chyna replied.

"Yeah, she's over there. My wife is over that way, too. I think the three of them are having something to eat at Applebee's."

The only reason Detective Gonzalez spoke casually about Janelle and his wife being together was because Cordell was with them, too. He was certain Janelle wouldn't do anything stupid with Cordell there; at least he hoped she wouldn't.

They continued standing on the sidewalk in front of Chyna's, chatting for a few more minutes before the detectives returned to their car. Chyna discovered that they were actually going through her block to somewhere else that had nothing to do with them. However, she was glad that fate stepped in. But it didn't mean that she wasn't going to blast her sister when she returned. She also felt sorry for Cordell. The way the old deacon was ranting, Cordell's butt would probably be safer in a snake pit.

The tiredness from not having a good night's sleep was taking its toll on Chyna. But she wasn't going to leave the old deacon in the living room alone and she wasn't going to close her eyes until Janelle came home. She'd also discovered why neither Janelle nor Cordell were picking up their cell phones. They'd left them on vibrate, on a table by the sofa.

However, try as hard as she could, Chyna finally gave in to sleep. And she wasn't alone. While she nodded off on the sofa the old deacon was sawing logs with his mouth wide open as he lay back in the recliner.

The sun had already set when Chyna and Deacon Pillar woke up. It only took them a moment to realize that neither Cordell nor Janelle had returned.

"Can I get you something to drink?" Chyna asked the old man and then added, "I promise not to nuke it."

"You'd better not," Deacon Pillar replied with a grin. "I'll haunt you when I die if you do."

Chyna shook her head and laughed. He was really beginning to grow on her.

Five minutes later the two of them sat in what was becoming their "spot," the kitchen.

"What else you got to eat?" Deacon Pillar asked.

"Well I took out some chicken earlier, but it hasn't thawed out completely."

"Do you season yours with a little salt, pepper, garlic, and paprika?" Deacon Pillar's eyes grew large as he swept his short tongue across his lips. "Those are God's seasonings."

"I sure do," Chyna replied. "After I season the chicken parts I grab some flour and pour it into a jiffy bag to coat the chicken."

"A damn jiffy bag?" Deacon Pillar snapped. "Do you know that those plastic bags was made with stuff specifically to kill off black folks?"

"Say what?"

"Don't you young people know nothing?" Deacon Pillar said as he got up from his seat. "If you want to safely coat a piece of chicken with flour, you got to use a paper bag, a plain brown paper bag. You can't use one of them with them fancy words or pictures on it."

While the old man ranted on about his latest theory of why the government wanted to get rid of black folks, Chyna held her head in her hands and prayed for Janelle to return. At that moment she'd have even given Sister Blackstone a hug if she came back.

Chyna peeked through her fingers. The old man was still ranting about how to coat and fry chicken. She put her fingers back together. She wasn't even surprised when he started to wash his hands and then run water over the partially thawed chicken to hurry it along.

"And where's your iron skillet?" The Deacon asked, sharply. "Please don't tell me that you cook in one of those Teflon pans. Don't you know the government designed Teflon to kill black folks?"

*   *   *

An hour or so later Chyna let out a loud belch. She had to admit it. That was some of the best chicken she'd ever eaten. She couldn't tell the old man how good it was with words, but her continuous belching made him feel proud.

Since he'd done the cooking Chyna got up and started to fill the sink with dishwater.

"What's wrong with you?" Deacon Pillar asked, suddenly. "You done let all my good cooking drive you crazy?"

"What's wrong now?" Chyna asked, slowly while removing the dishes from off the table.

"You have a dishwasher. Why don't you use it?" The old man rose slowly and went over to stand by the dishwasher. "You putting your lovely hands into some old greasy, nasty dishwater. Don't you know it was a black man who invented the dishwasher? He done it so he could outsmart the government who wanted you to stick your hands in that nasty dishwater." He pressed the lever to open the dishwasher door. "Keep up with the times. If I'm gonna spend time over here you got to be a bit more modern for my taste."

Chyna suddenly started laughing. And when she did it caused the old man to start chuckling, too. She'd never met a character such as him and yet, she'd been the First Lady at his church all that time. It was at that moment Chyna realized just how isolated Grayson kept her. Beyond a hallelujah or two she really didn't know the congregation. That would change.

The hour was growing very late and Chyna still hadn't heard from Janelle or Cordell. The old deacon had kept her so busy with his left-of-center moments until she hadn't worried about them at all. She finally told him to get ready. She'd drive him home.

Whether out of more fatigue or what she didn't know, but the old man kept drifting off while she drove him across town to his apartment. She hadn't realized how close he lived to the Sweet Bush until she hit Linden Boulevard. She could almost feel the shift in her attitude as she saw the burnt skeleton still lording over the neighborhood.

"Deacon Pillar," Chyna said, softly. "You're almost home."

The old man stirred a bit before fully opening his eyes. "Oh my goodness," he said while yawning. "I'm sorry. I didn't mean to blank out on you again."

"It's not a problem. You've done so much for me. I know I've worn you out."

"Well, you haven't. But I betcha back in the day you could've." Deacon Pillar gave a chuckle, slapped his knee and rebuked himself. "I'm sorry," he said as serious as he could. "I just can't help myself sometimes. I don't mean no harm."

"No problem," Chyna lied. It really did bother her, but she was certain he was harmless. At least she believed he was.

When a police car with its siren blasting flew by she was reminded of the detectives that dropped by earlier.

"Did you really date that Detective Gonzalez's mama?" Chyna asked.

"Why? Are you jealous?" The old man could hardly stop laughing at the absurdity of the question. When he finally did, he added, "Yeah, I dated his mama. I also paid child support for his half–Puerto Rican butt until he was almost eighteen. They didn't have no Maury shows back then and DNA were just letters in the alphabet."

"I'm sorry to hear that. I imagined you probably wanted children," Chyna said softly as she pulled up in front of his building.

"Oh hell naw! I didn't want no brats. I was having too much fun." Without missing a beat, the old man flexed his shoulders as they'd stiffened while he'd dropped off.

"Well, Deacon Pillar," Chyna said. "You get upstairs safely. I'll probably see you at church tomorrow. I plan on coming to the second service at eleven."

"You need to be there for the first service," Deacon Pillar said as he reached for the door handle. "You've got a lot to thank God for and you just might wanna get started early."

"You're probably right," Chyna replied. "I've got to get it together."

"Well, maybe you can sleep a little better tonight knowing that you ain't got nothing to worry about."

"I certainly do thank you and Cordell for destroying Grayson's journal and those pictures and giving me support," Chyna said.

"What the hell you wanna thank that knucklehead Cordell for? He ain't the one that took care of that little video situation that was left over."

Chyna reached over before she could think about what she was doing. She grabbed the old man by the shoulder to keep him from leaving the car. "What video?" Chyna demanded, "What video?"

"You's feisty, too, and loaded with all that talent. I like that," Deacon Pillar said as he pulled his stiff body back onto the car seat. "But don't ever lay a hand on me again if we ain't in a prayer service."

Chyna didn't realize her hands were shaking until one accidentally hit the car's horn. The quick blast made her jump.

"Listen," Deacon Pillar said. "You got to stop worrying about every little thing. I told you the other day I took care of things. That bouncer was right about everything and he also had shown a little video he'd taken with his cell phone when the reverend did his thing. Last thing the church needs is some video resurfacing and regurgitating that scandal."

"But how—?"

"Chile, your dumb questions about to make my blood pressure rise. Listen, because I'm only gonna say this once."

"Okay."

"I slept with Gonzalez's mama, I told you that, right?"

"Yes," Chyna said, softly.

"Would you please stop interrupting so I can tell you this and take my tired butt upstairs to bed." Deacon Pillar didn't try to hide his annoyance. "I stopped paying child support, but I never stopped being that man's daddy. Now you connect the dots, 'cause I ain't trying to cause him to lose his good-paying job and me start back to loaning him money. You a big gal, you can figure out how I would get a video from a man I paid child support for despite his lying sorry-arse mama."

The deacon didn't wait for a reply and he didn't look over to Chyna to see whether she understood or not. He lifted his butt off the seat and got out the car. Just as he closed the door, he remarked, "But you sho' nuff talented. I'll see ya at church in the morning."

Chapter 61

At around five o'clock in the morning, Chyna heard the slight creaking sound of the front door opening. She could hear the announcement from the alarm near the front door sound off, "Please deactivate your away code." She'd set the alarm before she went to bedroom.

Chyna could've left the alarm unarmed, but she was a bit miffed with Janelle. Janelle had to know that she'd left her cell phone and hadn't bothered to call Chyna. It was almost as though Janelle were declaring her independence.

Chyna heard the sounds of footsteps on the living room carpet. However, as she listened closer, she made out the sound of footsteps that sounded a bit heavier as they hit the wooden floor in the hallway. She wasn't certain if she should've been annoyed or not, especially since she knew without a doubt that Janelle was not alone.

Chyna heard a light tap on her bedroom door. She took her time responding. "Yes," she said finally. "What?"

"I'm home," Janelle said, softly. "I hope I didn't worry

you none." She tapped softly again, "Did you hear what I said?"

"I heard you the first time you said it." Chyna turned over and much like a little child readying a temper tantrum she pulled the covers over her head.

And that's when another level of hell broke out.

"Did you just get snippy with me?" Janelle pushed open the door and blasted Chyna quick and hard. "I can't go out? I can't have a life unless you approve it? You need to get over yourself. I thought I'd straightened you out about that." Janelle was becoming winded. "Guess what? I had a ball!"

As soon as Chyna yanked the covers off and turned over, Janelle had disappeared. It was as if she'd been an apparition. Even Chyna wasn't too sure if she hadn't dreamt Janelle's presence.

Chyna rose from bed and went to her door. She was about to open the door when she heard loud voices. They weren't screaming, but the words were somewhat heated.

Obviously, Janelle was arguing with Cordell. After hearing several choice words thrown about, Chyna decided that perhaps Janelle wasn't totally wrong about her minding her own business. "Whatever," Chyna murmured. "She's a grown woman. She's a doggone sick woman, but she's still grown."

Chyna was now fully awake. She grabbed a robe from the foot of the bed before deciding to boldly step out of her bedroom to get something to drink.

Chyna slowly opened her door. A light filtered in from Janelle's bedroom. Chyna had just closed the door to her bedroom as quietly as possible when she heard it.

"Yes, yes, yes." Every yes word grew louder as Janelle cried out.

I know that skeezer ain't having sex in my home.

Chyna thought as she neared Janelle's bedroom. She had no reason to go in that direction because the kitchen was the opposite way.

"Thank you, Jesus," Janelle called out. "Lord, I praise your name."

"She has no shame," Chyna muttered.

Chyna was livid. Even if she had to pull Cordell off of Janelle, she would. Never mind that Cordell was her ex-husband and even less than that he'd been Janelle's first lover; Janelle's soul mate, as she'd called him.

The scampering of feet caused Chyna to stop cold.

Janelle flew out of her bedroom and almost knocked Chyna down. "Look at this!" Janelle squealed, "Look at it."

Cordell had followed and leaned against the door frame like a rat that ate the last piece of cheese.

"I'm gonna be getting married," Janelle blurted. She was giddy. "Cordell asked me to marry him."

Chyna was stunned but not jealous. "Is that why you were yelling out 'Thank you, Jesus'?"

"Why else would I?" Janelle asked, quickly. The question was followed by a look of understanding that spread fast from her to Cordell.

"C'mon, Chyna," Cordell said, finally moving away from the wall. "That's just tacky."

Chyna felt more embarrassed than she probably showed. "I'm happy for your good news," she said with a smile. "I'm truly happy for your blessing."

"Oh, and I'm keeping these here," Janelle said pointing at her favorite body parts, the girls.

"That's right," Cordell added. "Janelle and her *girls* are in remission."

Chyna grabbed Janelle and hugged her. "I'm so happy for you." She kissed her sister on the cheek. "I truly mean it."

"I know you do," Janelle replied. "And, I'm sorry that I put you and Cordell through so much. I needed to know that y'all loved me regardless. I needed to know it was love and not pity."

Cordell put his arms around Chyna's shoulders. He laughed. "I think folks will probably pity me and Chyna. We'll have to put up with you."

"Oh, y'all ain't gotta do a da—" Janelle caught herself. "I gotta work on this cussing. Probably the less time I spend around y'all the easier it will be."

"Then you might wanna stay away from the morning service," Chyna warned.

"Why?"

"Deacon Pillar threatened to be there."

"Oh, damn," Janelle blurted. "This is gonna be tough."

Chapter 62

The New Hope Assembly choir was hot! There were two lines going around the block for the eight o'clock first Sunday service. The weather was extremely warm for that time of the morning, so all the air conditioners worked overtime

And the hats! Designer hats were worn by women of all shapes and sizes. The men, short and tall and many of another persuasion, were fabulous. Looking over the crowd from the windows in the overflow section all the church attendees looked like multicolored jelly beans.

Inside the New Hope Assembly, Deacon Pillar strutted up and down the red plush-carpeted sanctuary. He was peacock proud in a striped zebra-skin hat, jacket, and pants. He wore a black shirt with a polka-dot bow tie. He stopped and shook hands with folks he wouldn't spit on if they were on fire. He wanted them to get a close look at his new outfit that cost every red cent he had. His lights were going to be turned off the following Tuesday, but that day, he was looking sharp and wasn't shy about it.

"I ministered First Lady and prayed with her," he

boasted to a crowd of folks that really weren't paying the old man any attention. "It was me and my commitment to the Lord that she found strength in to return and sit among y'all heathens."

Deacon Pillar kept repeating his mantra, row by row. He was determined to make things correct for *his* First Lady. In his mind he was doing just great. He wasn't one to accept public opinion that his mental and emotional health were questionable. In his world, where he was very well known, all his ideas pivoted between senility and the present, touched the sides of stubbornness and indignation, and finally collapsed upon his faith. He'd worked hard for his delusion.

Chyna was in another part of the church. She was nervous and her palms were sweaty. She wasn't supposed to say any more than a few words of appreciation. Her outfit, which was First Lady–appropriate, fit her to a tee. It was a deep purple long waistcoat dress. The color symbolized, in her mind, belonging to the royal priesthood and priestesses of God. The white tassels that hung from a white, gold, and purple wide-brimmed hat allowed her large brown eyes to peak out and appear wise beyond her thirty-something years.

She took another look at her outfit in a long mirror that hung in the room she'd used as a dressing area. She shook for a moment. Her mind quickly dismissed the memory of Grayson, who'd have stopped in with something negative to say if he wasn't the one who'd bought the outfit. But that was back when she attended services regularly.

Chyna heard a knock on the door. She looked at the clock. It was just about fifteen minutes before the start of the first morning service. She quickly rechecked her outfit, hat, and makeup before permitting entry.

"Oh, you just look talented no matter what you got

on or don't." Deacon Pillar's grin was both mischievous and contagious.

Chyna laughed. "Deacon Pillar," she teased, "are you ever gonna quit?"

"Not until they throw the last grain of dirt on me. And depending on what day they bury me I just might flick a grain or two back at 'em."

"Has Janelle showed up yet?" Chyna couldn't get Janelle to promise that she would. Janelle and Cordell stayed up long after Chyna had lay down to catch some sleep. She imagined they stayed up discussing wedding plans and praising God for the good news from Doctor Bayer.

"You thinking about your sister and that ex-husband of yours that you used to sleep with before you married that pickled puss Reverend Young, ain't you?" Deacon Pillar asked—or rather told—Chyna what he felt she was feeling.

"You know I loves you like a southern daughter," Deacon Pillar said, exasperated. "But your crazy mood swings are wearing me out."

He looked at her and let his shoulders slouch a little. "Chile, your burden is making me old. Now listen, I keep telling you that you can't think no less of yourself than God does. I know you making Him mad 'cause you pissing me off."

Chyna looked at Deacon Pillar and burst out laughing.

"Oh, I'm glad you think it's so funny," Deacon Pillar said as he tried not to laugh, too. "It's almost eight o'clock. Don't make sense to go into the pulpit late when you only twenty feet away from it. C'mon and bring your lil talented tail on."

Deacon Pillar took a quick glance in the long mirror.

He adjusted his polka-dot tie and straightened his zebra-striped jacket.

Chyna turned her head away quickly after catching the sight of his mixed patterns reflected in the mirror. All those dots and stripes clashing together had the possibility of kick-starting someone's dormant epilepsy.

There were two rows of pews that looked like long stair steps. They were separated by a short wall. That was where the church board members sat every Sunday looking high-minded and judgmental. While preachers preached, shouters shouted, and ushers snatched envelopes of money, they watched and made policy.

Unfortunately for the church board on that particular Sunday, Cordell sat holding Janelle's frail hands not five feet away. He watched them and they watched him. If one of the board members so much as looked like they were going to say something about the low-cut black dress Janelle wore with her *girls* on display and swaying to the organ music, he was ready. And he also had his backup, his new homey, the Deacon Pillar riding shotgun and seated on the other side of Janelle.

Janelle couldn't stop smiling. She'd even smiled while she slept for about an hour before she decided that she wanted to attend the service. She'd picked out the outfit and probably guessed it was somewhat inappropriate. Knowing Janelle, she wouldn't have worn it if it wasn't. Yet as sexy as Janelle thought she looked, Cordell had no doubts about his appearance. He looked a mess because he was still wearing the same clothes from the day before. There hadn't been time to stop by his hotel to change.

Cordell could've said something to Janelle about the low-cut dress and the above-the-knee hemline, but he didn't. One thing he was always sure of was if he caught a soul he didn't have to clean them. Cleaning was God's work, not his.

Chyna approached the podium when called upon. She graciously accepted the flowers presented heralding her return to New Hope Assembly. She thanked the members and as though she'd never missed a service she read the welcome address almost by heart.

As was her good fortune, it turned out that the Bishop John L. Smith from St. Paul's City of Lights Ministry was the guest speaker for that morning service. And he didn't disappoint.

He was a senior citizen, but he always carried himself like what the old folks used to call, "A somebody or a suchie muchie." He looked well rested from preaching the eulogy from the funeral a few days before. And although he was probably in his early seventies and had preached in the area for the better part of the past forty years, no matter which borough anyone went to they'd never hear a cross word about him. He believed in staying humble and available for God's service.

The Bishop John L. Smith, with his white robe swirling about his ankles, walked calmly to the pulpit. He smiled a smile that immediately put everyone at ease. There was no judgment in it; just the love of Jesus. He nodded toward where his personal organist sat down; it was a signal for the man to begin playing. And so before opening his Bible to preach, he sang a verse or two of a song called "I Won't Complain."

"Come go with me to the book of St. Matthew," The Bishop said slowly, as he turned the pages in his Bible. "Signal by saying 'amen' when you get there. If you have not found it or cannot find it, just say, 'Hold up, Bishop'."

Voices rang out saying, "Hold up, Bishop" peppering the sanctuary. It caused some to laugh. Deacon Pillar just looked around and shook his head in disgust. "It's the first doggone book of the New Testament," he muttered.

"Lay your eyes on the nineteenth verse," the Bishop

said and paused. He took a deep breath before he continued. "My subject for today is, 'Are You a Hooker?' "

"I swear I love to hear that man preach!" Deacon Pillar said a bit too loud. "Bring it, Bishop."

"Before y'all start to stampede for the door or think you've been called out, please allow me a moment to bring this word."

The phrase quiet as a cat jumping on cotton took on a new meaning. Folks were too afraid to even say amen for fear of having their business out in the open.

Bishop Smith continued, "Simon Peter and his brother Andrew were professional fishermen. And that meant that they knew every nook and cranny of the rivers and if there was a fish to be caught those brothers caught it.

"They'd fished all night and were preparing to clean their nets when Jesus appeared. Now, cleaning a net meant that the fishing or lack of fishing was over. It wasn't no use in lowering the nets again because if Peter and Andrew hadn't hooked a fish there weren't none.

"But you see they hadn't met the master fisherman. They didn't know nothing about the man who knew where every inch of their flesh led. They hadn't seen the likes of this man Jesus who taught fishin' 101. Those brothers, as skilled as they were, didn't know nothing until Jesus turned them into hookers. Can I just keep it real?"

"As real as Kraft Macaroni and Cheese," Deacon Pillar hollered. "You go ahead and break it down." He was about to say something else when he spied Cinnamon's juvenile delinquent son, Hard Life. He'd forgotten that the thug was supposed to show up to get the information about the money Earl left for him.

"Thank you, Brother Deacon. Now how did Jesus do that? Jesus told the brothers it didn't matter how long they'd fished. It mattered less how deep they'd dropped their nets. What mattered and would make them successful was their faith. They were going to learn to use their faith to hook fish they'd not seen.

"Has God called you to drop your net and by faith follow Him? Has He reminded you that it don't matter how far you've fallen or how much you think you know that until you know God and use your faith then you can't hook a soul, you can't hook a job, you can't hook a career. You can't be a hooker without faith. . . ."

The bishop continued delivering his sermon. Deacon Pillar grinned and hollered "hallelujah" just about every time the bishop mentioned the word hooker.

Nudging Janelle, the old deacon whispered, "Now what other church can you go to and get permission to be a hooker?"

Chapter 63

The way the people milled around the outside of New Hope Assembly, it wasn't clear whether the service was just starting or ended.

Everyone had an opinion about the relevance of Bishop Smith's sermon to their lives. And there were also some who just wanted to make sure that the term hooker and their names weren't one and the same with something sinister or illegal.

Deacon Pillar ran around the church feeling a spirit or something akin to it. There were several folks in the congregation that he'd always felt were hookers of a different sort.

However, for the most part the church got it. They understood that what the bishop meant was that each was supposed to live a life that would automatically hook someone and bring them to Christ. But that wasn't dramatic enough for some. They preferred giving it a more "worldly" connotation.

Chyna was running a little late when she finally met

up with Cordell and Janelle. She'd remained in the pastor's study to discuss a few things with the bishop. She actually seemed happier than she'd been in months when she came out of the office.

She'd decided not to tell Janelle all that was discussed with Bishop Smith. She was about to begin a journey of rediscovery and the less known, at that moment, the better. Her soul was at stake and she didn't have the luxury of trying to parse words or figure out what folks meant to say or entertain any other devices that could hinder.

She also found out that she didn't have to reveal to the bishop much of what was shameful and loathing in her heart. It seemed as though he came pretty much prepared to tell her only what "thus saith the Lord." He wasn't one to rely on a Bishop Smith's Revelatory Handbook for Christian Zealots and Dummies; the dummy part was redundant.

She'd gotten the message to come to the pastor's study almost immediately after the benediction was said. After giving and receiving the obligatory greetings, she'd left the main sanctuary.

"I'm so glad you stayed to chat," Bishop Smith told Chyna after she was escorted inside the pastor's study. As hard as he'd preached, he didn't have an ounce of perspiration showing. He looked almost angelic and perhaps a bit too confident in how he'd moved the people of God as he slowly removed his preaching robe.

He was just as methodical as he handed the robe to his aide, by the neck of the material, and watched the young aide grab the bishop's satchel and leave. "He's been with me for almost ten

years." Bishop Smith said with pride after the
young man closed the door behind him. He then
took another moment to smooth a wrinkle in his
suit jacket before putting it on.

As if she'd waited the sufficient amount of
time for his counsel, Bishop Smith looked at her
without smiling. His face looked part fatherly
and part politician.

"Are you gonna let God be God?" he asked
without any previous conversation or set up.
"You can't let anyone make you think less of
yourself than God thinks of you."

How many times do I need to hear that? Chyna
thought as she remembered his words. Her mind raced
while her eyes revealed warmth, and a peaceful understanding if nothing else.

Outside, while she waited on Chyna, Janelle questioned the validity of any preacher calling someone a
hooker. "Now had that been me—"

"That was you," Deacon Pillar argued. "But you were
a different kind of hooker."

"Deacon Pillar, please do not start." Cordell's pleas
fell upon deaf ears. His brown skin was turning beet red
from embarrassment. Janelle and the old deacon were
gonna set his reputation back to pre–Christ acceptance
status. He couldn't even pretend their back-and-forth ora-
tory was a joke. The best Cordell could hope for was that
the loud Sunday-morning quarterbacking of the hooker-
themed sermon wouldn't draw a bigger crowd than what
had already gathered about them.

"So you'll agree that every time you open your big
mouth and follow it up with some kind of Christian act
that somebody wants to follow that you're a hooker?"

Deacon Pillar asked in exhaustion. "'Cause if you don't,"
Deacon Pillar added, "there's another name I can have
folks call you that'll make you feel less of a spirit-filled
woman and more like a garden tool."

"Deacon Pillar," Cordell finally interrupted. "That's
my future wife. You can't talk to her like that."

"Cordell, mind your business," Janelle said as she
moved closer to the old man. "He knows stuff—" she
winked at Cordell, thinking the deacon didn't know she was
teasing.

Deacon Pillar gently removed Janelle's hand from his
shoulder. He straightened his polka-dot tie and said
sweetly, "I know enough about your business to bring
along volume two with me on Judgment Day. And you
best remember that God only has volume one."

Deacon Pillar, moving past Janelle who stood in
shock and embarrassment, whispered to Cordell, "And
you know that—man!"

Picking her jaw up carefully off the ground, Janelle
glared at the crowd, daring someone to say something.

No one did.

"Come on let's go to IHOP or somewhere and get
some natural food," Cordell urged as he took his future
bride by her arm. He steered her toward the car, which he'd
smartly parked on a side street instead of in the church's
crowded parking lot.

By the time Chyna exited the church's side door, she
looked younger. Almost so that Deacon Pillar had to take
a double look before he realized who she was despite her
outfit.

"I didn't realize you'd be waiting," Chyna said, apolo-
getically. "I was inside talking."

"You wasn't inside talking," Deacon Pillar said as he
took a large bag with flowers and other gifts from Chyna's

hands. "You was inside with Bishop Smith getting your hooker props."

Chyna didn't mean to laugh as loud as she did. She grabbed Deacon Pillar, who stood just a bit taller than she did even in her high heels. She hugged him and gave him a kiss on the cheek.

"Deacon Pillar," Chyna said, "You are a God-send. And I love you."

Deacon Pillar for the first time didn't have a smart comeback prepared. He suddenly looked as though it were the first time someone had said the words "I love you," and meant them. He could feel his staunch outer shield of protection weakening. And just that fast, he lit into Chyna.

Pushing her off just a little, the old man spoke only so she'd hear him, "Look," he said, "I've got a reputation. Don't ever be up in this church or area hugging up on me."

Chyna's jaw dropped. Any offense she'd felt was evident by the shocked look and anger spreading across her face. "What did you just say?"

"Oh, please, First Lady," Deacon Pillar reprimanded. "Would you please catch a clue?" He tapped her quickly on her finger to prod her along the path to the church parking lot. "You can't be all warm and fuzzy with the likes of me. I'm what these folks call in polite company, crotchety. I've worked hard to maintain that reputation. If these folks see me going all soft, then it'll make my work much harder."

"What work?" Chyna was still a little miffed, but she was intrigued by the way the old man's mind worked.

"My work for you," Deacon Pillar replied. "I got to keep these folks in check while you prepare yourself to get about God's work."

"God's work?" Chyna said, as she finally approached

her car. "What do you know about what work God has for me?"

"I know about as much as Bishop Smith does. I betcha he told you a few things from his Thus Saith the Lord handbook."

Chyna felt if there were such a thing as the *Twilight Zone*, she was in it.

"You look like you need something to eat." The old man started to snicker. "Just 'cause you a hooker don't mean you can't eat." He stopped and took her car keys dangling from her hand. "Here, let me open the door for you."

Chyna didn't fight the old man. She gave him the keys and watched him open the trunk of her car and put in the bag he'd carried.

"I am a bit hungry," Chyna finally said.

"I knew you would be," Deacon Pillar said. "Man or woman can't make it on bread alone."

"I believe God meant spiritual bread," Chyna said, suddenly proud to contribute to a spiritual part of the conversation.

"Yep, that's what God meant," The old man chuckled. "But I'm talking about something else. I meant bread like what I use when I make a sandwich."

"Oh," Chyna responded.

"Well, what are you waiting for now?" Deacon Pillar asked as he gave her the car keys through an open car window. "I'm hungry. How many hints do you need? I can stand on this sidewalk and regale you with the story of the five loaves and two fishes, or we can go and sit in Kyeon's and Frieda's Fried Fish House. We could be sucking the hot sauce off some of them catfish, or bottom feeders, if you nasty."

"Get in, Deacon," Chyna said, laughing. "Lord, have mercy."

She wanted to tell him again how much she'd come to love and appreciate him, but he'd already warned her. So she kept quiet as they went to eat.

Chapter 64

The following Friday, Cordell's car idled at the curb. It was almost seven o'clock in the morning and it had begun to rain. It was a gentle rain at first, but as the skies darkened, the rain came down harder.

There were raindrop stains on Cordell's powder-blue shirt and navy blue pants as he struggled with the idea of leaving Janelle behind. He was on his way back to Los Angeles. The time to tape more television episodes for his relationship series had arrived. He'd been fortunate that there were enough already in the can, which allowed him to have stayed away for so long.

"I really wish you could come with me back to L.A.," Cordell whispered.

"I wish I could, too," Janelle whispered back. She'd had a night that was very uncomfortable. Although she was in remission, she still had several more radiation sessions scheduled. There'd be one later that day, which couldn't be rescheduled. Neither could the taping of the show, so they were where they were.

"I need you to promise that you'll not overdo things. Can you behave for the next week?"

"Do I have a choice?" Janelle teased and pointed back inside the house. "You've left me here with Dudley Doo-Right and Sweet Polly Purebred."

"Don't you give them a hard time," Cordell said as he squeezed her hand gently.

"I think you ask too much."

He took another look at Janelle. She was starting to put on weight. It was subtle, but he noticed. Even her hair had thickened and she no longer wore a wig. Leave it to her to get the latest chic haircut and kick it up a notch.

Cordell spent another few minutes repeating a list of do's and don'ts. He'd already accepted the fact that when he wasn't around Janelle he felt like steel. It was a trait he'd been proud of for most of his career, but that came after he'd divorced Chyna. Yet as soon as he would come around Janelle, he'd change. Janelle had the power to bend his steel will like it was putty. He loved her that much.

"Unless y'all living in a barn," a voice called out from inside the house, "close the doggone door."

Deacon Pillar shuffled to the doorway and stood behind Janelle. "Listen, Brother Cordell, I was up real late last night fixing that plumbing downstairs. You got all that book learning but not the sense to know a hot from cold water pipe, even when it's got a tag on it.

"And don't let me start in on you, Missy Pierce." Deacon Pillar narrowed his eyes as a warning. "I ain't but one finger off a telephone button to call First Lady and tell her you standing in the rain."

"I'm not standing in the rain," Janelle barked.

"I didn't say nothing about telling her the whole

truth. Don't you know your Bible, yet? You supposed to prophesy in part and lie about the other part."

Before Cordell or Janelle could say a word, the old man disappeared back inside the house.

"I've got the car running," Cordell whispered. "I'd better get to the airport. I'm heading out of JFK," he reminded her. "So I'd better get started."

"I know," Janelle sighed. "It's still not easy seeing you leave."

"We've never had it easy," Cordell replied. "It's helped to make us who we are."

The couple spent another moment or two saying good-bye. They'd been apart a few times over the past several months since they'd become engaged, but never for a week.

Other things had changed, too. Chyna spent a lot of time away from the house. She'd begun working with Bishop Smith and his wife, Lady Laura, pushing their Neighborhood Empowerment project into the political arena. She was the liaison between New Hope Assembly and the City of Lights Ministry. Chyna loved it.

At first she'd felt guilty leaving Janelle so often. Between her and Cordell's absences, Janelle had become quite independent. Sometimes too much for her own good, but that's where the Deacon Pillar stepped in.

Every time Janelle wanted to take on another project that involved the church, Deacon Pillar would investigate first. As he often told her, "You can't just walk into a snake den all willy nilly. You'd better be prayed up and carry a gun."

"Are you gonna try and eat these boiled eggs or what?" Deacon Pillar yelled out from the kitchen. "Come on, Sister Pierce," Deacon Pillar urged. "I've got some other chores I need to finish before First Lady gets back from her trip."

"You'd better go inside before that old man tries to spank you," Cordell teased, sort of. With Deacon Pillar he was never sure he wouldn't follow through with his threats.

The week had gone by rather quickly with drama taking a holiday. But for Janelle that next Friday hadn't arrived soon enough. Janelle's strength had returned better and faster than usual. She was glad that she had enough time to get her hair wrapped and curled at her favorite Dominican hair salon and her nails polished, and take in one of her sexy outfits.

Of course, Janelle still had to contend with Chyna and Deacon Pillar's overprotective mood swings. She'd learned to navigate through their various guards by just agreeing with everything. Chyna usually fell for it. Deacon Pillar, not so much.

Janelle was also glad the house was empty. The alone time was welcomed and allowed her to primp and prep for Cordell. She'd gotten permission from Doctor Bayer to drink just a little wine if she could tolerate it. She'd tolerated it the other night to the point of almost passing out.

After checking herself out again for the umpteenth time, she went into the living room and sat by the window to wait for Cordell's arrival.

Two hours later, she was still waiting. Everyone but Cordell had called. She'd really gotten annoyed with Chyna when Chyna insisted that perhaps she needed to return home from the church to wait with Janelle. "Please," Janelle insisted, "I'm not a baby. I can wait for my man by myself." She realized too late that she probably didn't have to remind Chyna about Cordell when she'd added a little emphasis on the "my man" part.

Janelle didn't know when she'd dozed off. She awoke to find it dark outside and Cordell wasn't inside.

Chapter 65

Traffic that early evening along the Belt Parkway in Queens was backed up for almost a mile. Not that the traffic was ever light, but the highway rush hour usually wasn't as bad as it was then. Chyna, forced to drive at a snail's pace, was ready to pound on her horn, but it'd make no difference. It wasn't her normal route to get to her home but she'd been on that side of town at a meeting with Bishop Smith.

"Why today, Lord?" Chyna murmured. "Why today?"

She didn't really expect God to answer her, but she wasn't really surprised to hear her cell phone ring again.

Chyna's cell phone lay in a space beside the gearshift constructed specifically for it. The buzzing sound of its vibrator setting blasted an old Chaka Khan hit, "I'm Every Woman."

She meant to replace the tune with something more appropriate when it'd gone off at one of the church meetings. The disapproving looks from the other members told her that they were familiar with the melody, but she wasn't at the club.

Chyna reached over and checked the caller I.D.

"It's Janelle," she said, hurriedly. "This is probably the fifth time she's tried to reach me. I can't keep dodging my sister."

"Is stupidity freely dispensed in your family?" Deacon Pillar, firmly planted in his regular passenger side of the car hissed and sucked his teeth. Without asking permission, he quickly reached over and turned off Chyna's cell phone. "I should've done that the first hundred times that damn thing rung."

Fifteen minutes later they'd only driven about another half a mile. "This is not going to work, Deacon Pillar," Chyna said. She seemed almost ready to surrender to the traffic. "We're not going to make it to Janelle in time."

"So what if we don't?" Deacon Pillar asked. "She ain't going nowhere. Brother Cordell, for sure, ain't going nowhere. We'll get there when we be there." He quickly turned his head back to looking outside the car window but not before promising, "If this family doesn't hurry up and get truly saved, I'm going back to being alone. I swear, y'all about to make me lose my testimony—harrumph."

"Say what!" Chyna snapped. Her nerves were already frayed and that ungrateful old man was gnawing at her last one. She was about to say something to him before kicking him out of her car when he turned around and winked at her.

"You know what, Deacon Pillar?" Chyna said, trying her best not to laugh, "One day . . ."

Deacon Pillar snapped his fingers indicating that she turn her attention back to the traffic. "Will you please stop pretending you upset with me and drive? You're about to rear-end somebody and make some day, today." He started laughing. "Now that was a good one. I know you can't say that one wasn't funny without lying."

The sound of a cell phone ringing rang out again. That time it came from Deacon Pillar's phone. He pulled it out of his front pocket and looked at it. "Excuse me, First Lady, I need to take this."

Turning his head slightly the deacon spoke rather hastily, "Sister Pierce, stop all that blathering, I can't understand much of what you're saying." He listened for a few more minutes and turned to Chyna, "You may wanna answer your phone that's been turned off. Your sister is trying to get in touch with you."

Leaving Chyna gape mouthed, the old man went back to speaking with Janelle. "Now listen, we are stuck in traffic but we've been trying to get there to get you." He paused and then added, "We trying to get to you so we can take you to Brother Cordell, so get your drawers outta your ears and be ready when we get there."

"Deacon Pillar," Chyna said, slowly, "Are you crazy?" It was her time to ask him a question she'd been holding in for quite some time.

If the Deacon was insulted, he never showed it. He simply smiled and said, "I'm no crazier now than I was nine months ago when y'all started sapping up the little brains I had."

Chyna surrendered and decided to change the subject. "Why did you take Janelle's call and wouldn't let me?"

"You is a grown woman. How could I tell you to do something you didn't wanna?" He winked, again, knowing it always disarmed her. "She'll be all right. We didn't have a good connection, but it appears that she's concerned about Brother Cordell. She hadn't heard from him."

"I figured as much. That's partly why I didn't want to answer my cell phone."

"No, you'd rather blame me for it," Deacon Pillar interrupted.

"Perhaps we should tell Cordell to call Janelle. Things are getting out of hand and we don't want her getting sick with worry."

"Will you please let Sister Pierce handle her own business," the deacon replied, harshly. "If Brother Cordell wanted the plans changed, he would have called her yesterday when he got back. Your part in this scam is to pick up your sister and deliver her to the engagement party. I wished you'd stick to the plan." He pushed his seat back a little and added, "Back in the day, before Christ entered my life, you could've never ridden with me. You are a little too skittish for my taste."

Chapter 66

The lighting was perfect. The decorations were lavish. The food was prepared by the best cooks in Brooklyn, the New Hope Assembly mothers board. Those old women, five in all, raced back and forth bringing out oversized aluminum pans of perfectly seasoned delights. Steam carried the tasty aromas of fresh collard greens and smoked turkey necks, curried chicken, apple spiced pork chops, peas and rice soaked in coconut milk, a ton of cheese and bits of macaroni. That's how the mothers board rolled.

Cordell's pacing seemed almost identical to the old women's except they were supposed to rush about and he was not. He was quickly becoming a nervous wreck. "Why did I let that old man talk me into giving him my cell phone?" Cordell murmured. At the time he thought it was a good idea, because then he wouldn't be tempted to talk to Janelle. He knew once he heard her sweet voice he would have told her about the surprise engagement party.

Cordell already knew that Deacon Pillar and Chyna were stuck in traffic on the Belt Parkway. He was trying his best to figure out a way to get things moving. It wasn't easy getting all the people together for the surprise. A lot of the church folks still hadn't accepted Janelle, but the old deacon had quickly whipped them in line with a Bible verse here and there followed up by plenty of cussing and threats. By the time Deacon Pillar finished his task, there would be more than sixty people promising to attend. However, from the looks of those who were already there and the steady stream of others coming in, there'd be a lot more than sixty. For certain there'd be no food left to secret away in plastic bags and pocketbooks.

Back at home Janelle's eyes were red as beets. She'd never felt so abandoned. She finally turned off the television. The bad news was that a plane skidded off of a runway. The good news was that it wasn't Cordell's flight, and no one was seriously hurt.

So where was he? Why wasn't he picking up his phone?

Janelle washed her face for the third time. She was still trying to pull herself together. Surely if there were a problem, the old man would've said so.

The thought of Deacon Pillar almost caused Janelle to smile. He was such a character. He was a straight, no-chaser kind of grandfatherly type. She and Chyna had often admitted secretly that they were glad he was in their lives. He'd been the closest thing to a father or grandfather that they'd had since being teenagers. He certainly didn't take any crap and she liked that.

However, the thoughts about the old deacon were quickly replaced by her concern for Cordell. She'd already gotten over her anger about Chyna's cell phone being turned off.

"Janelle!" Chyna raced through the door and went straight to Janelle's bedroom. "Janelle," she called out and through the open bedroom door.

"I'm in the bathroom," Janelle answered. "Come here."

Chyna hurried to the hallway bathroom. "I'm so sorry. We were stuck in traffic."

"I know. Deacon Pillar told me. . . ."

Chyna cut her off. "You need to hurry and change."

"Why?" Janelle asked, cautiously. She began to get nervous. She didn't like the way Chyna burst in and was hurrying her to get dressed.

"Tell Sister Pierce to just throw on a clean dress over them drawers and let's get moving," Deacon Pillar yelled from the living room.

There was a questioning look spread over Janelle's face.

Chyna cut Janelle off before she could ask. "Don't ask," Chyna pleaded. "Please don't ask."

Chyna helped Janelle to dress while trying her best to avoid Janelle's questions about Cordell.

"Have you heard from him?" Janelle asked.

"Doesn't he always call?" Chyna kept replying by turning the question back onto Janelle.

"Where are we going?" Janelle asked Deacon Pillar, since she'd not received a straight answer from Chyna.

"None of your business," Deacon Pillar answered as he gently shoved Janelle out the door. "You are one nosey child, Sister Pierce." He kept urging her to walk faster toward the car. After opening the backseat door for Janelle to enter, he leaned and whispered, "You keep cutting up and you gonna make me not want to have any children."

Deacon Pillar closed the car door and laughed at his own joke as he got into the front seat.

"What's so funny?" Chyna asked as she started the engine.

"Mind your business," Deacon Pillar teased. "Me and

Sister Pierce trying to have an adult conversation. All you need to do is hurry up and get us to that engagement party."

Janelle's ears perked up. She sprang forward against her seatbelts and tapped Chyna on her shoulder. "What did Deacon Pillar just say?"

Deacon Pillar turned his head to avoid Chyna's glare.

"Oh, damn," he whispered.

By the time Chyna, Janelle, and Deacon Pillar arrived, folks were already seated and eating. They were almost two hours late and Cordell looked a mess when he finally saw them.

They could've saved their apologies. Most of the guests didn't care what time the honoree showed. They were facedown in plates of soul food and that trumped everything else.

"So when's the big day, again?" The question was asked about a dozen times despite the announcement that the wedding would be later, sometime in March.

Toasts were made by a few that truly meant well wishes to the engaged couple, and just as many were obligatory from the church board members.

Chyna and Deacon Pillar sat at the head table and watched the board members pop up and down, one at a time, giving words of advice and encouragement. Every time one of them ended with a short prayer, Deacon Pillar would tap Chyna's knee under the table. "Did you hear that hypocrite?" Deacon Pillar would ask. "I can't wait until they ask me to say a few words at their funeral."

"That's not nice or Christian." Chyna said, rebuking him without laughing at his crazy observation of things.

"You need to make up your mind," Deacon Pillar whispered.

"What are you talking about?" Chyna asked.

"Make up your mind whether you want me to be nice or Christian-like. You're making this southern father-daughter thing hard to figure out."

Chyna started laughing and couldn't stop. She'd only recently found out what the deacon meant when he said, 'southern father-daughter' relationship. He'd sat her down one morning and forced her to watch an episode of *The Jerry Springer Show*. She'd kept a cautious eye on him ever since then.

It was almost midnight when the engagement party was over and the fellowship hall cleared and cleaned. Chyna and Deacon Pillar remained to help despite being told there was no need.

They didn't stay out of a need to be helpful but more out of a need to give Cordell and Janelle some privacy.

By the time they were finished Chyna and Deacon Pillar were exhausted.

"Do you want me to drop you off at home or are you coming back with me?" Chyna asked. She really didn't feel like making a detour, but she would.

"You gonna have these blabbermouths biting at the bit if you keep bringing me home with you." Deacon Pillar laughed, but it wasn't his usual hearty one. It was more forced.

Chyna picked up on his mood change almost immediately. "What's wrong?"

"Just a bit tired," Deacon Pillar replied. "I'm doing too much with too little."

"I'm sorry. I didn't mean to put so much upon you," Chyna said, sadly. "Sometimes I imagine I just don't think about others like I should."

"Have mercy, First Lady," Deacon Pillar said. He let his shoulders stoop a little more than usual before he continued, "My world is not built around your little talented self."

"Excuse me?"

"It ain't always about you. Why do you keep making yourself lower than God does? How many times do I have to remind you of that?" Deacon Pillar took Chyna's hand. "Come on let's get to the car. I can chastise you while you drive."

And the deacon kept his word.

On the way back to Chyna's house, Deacon Pillar fought to keep his tired eyes open. He was determined to have his say despite dozing off every now and again.

"I'm surprised that a woman, a talented woman such as you, can't see what God has done for you." Deacon Pillar's head bobbed for a moment before he continued speaking.

"God has taken you from the depths of being a freak to the heights of being His woman. It's just like he did for that gal in the Bible that was caught in bed doing the nasty. Them church folks wanted to throw rocks at her, but Jesus wouldn't let 'em."

The deacon's head bobbed again before he recovered. Chyna kept driving in shock. She was listening but she was also grateful he'd never been asked to teach a Bible class.

"Jesus also used that talented woman named Mary." Deacon Pillar continued as though he hadn't stopped, "According to some she was about as talented as you seemed to be; I'm sorry. I meant to say that you were. I mean I'm sure you ain't lost your talent you just ain't using it like you used to do."

Deacon Pillar suddenly lifted his head and pointed his finger at Chyna, "You ain't been in no talent contests since the bachelorette party, right?"

Chyna almost plowed her car into one that stopped for a stop sign.

"Anyway, God used them women even when others

tossed them to the side. First Lady, I'm gonna tell you for the last time, I hope. If God thinks high enough of you to put you in a league with one of the most reputable of bishops, the Bishop John L. Smith, then you need to give yourself more credit. Stop tearing your building down when God is trying to add another floor."

Chyna never felt so convicted. The old deacon had broken it down without sermonizing. He'd met her on her level and in no uncertain terms lifted her at the same time.

"When you get a moment," Deacon Pillar said. "You might wanna read about Lazarus."

"I know about Lazarus," Chyna replied. "Jesus raised him from the grave after three days."

"And what else happened?" Deacon Pillar asked.

Chyna tried to recall the story. "I remember that Jesus was friends with Mary and Martha, who were sisters."

"Go ahead. What else?"

"When they asked Jesus to come and heal their brother Lazarus, Jesus put them off and by the time he arrived, Lazarus was in his grave for three days already."

"In his grave and he was stinking like a week-old dead crab," Deacon Pillar added. "What else?"

"Mary and Martha were upset with Jesus and accused Jesus of not caring enough to get there in time to save their brother."

"Bingo!" Deacon Pillar shouted. "Lord, I feel my help coming on."

Deacon Pillar ignored the shocked look on Chyna's face and spoke. "Let me make it plain," Deacon Pillar said as if he wouldn't. "If Jesus had come when those two sisters first asked him then they'd never have seen Jesus raise their brother from the dead." Deacon Pillar smiled. "Now do you see?"

"I'm not sure." Chyna admitted slowly.

"First Lady," Deacon Pillar snapped. "Lazarus had to die!"

He held his head in his hands and murmured, "Lord, why do you keep placing these crazy women in my life?"

"First Lady," Deacon Pillar continued. "You had to go through what you did at the Sweet Bush and even that crazy wannabe pastor husband. Just like Lazarus, you had issues that had to die. And Janelle had to go have her Lazarus moment, too. God let all that stuff happen and yet look at the two of you; God resurrected a new Lazarus in both your lives."

"My God," Chyna said, softly, "my God."

"And just to show you what a sense of humor God has, it looks like your sister's wedding is on the same date the Sweet Bush burned down. Ain't that just like God?"

Chapter 67

By the time the wedding arrived many things changed. The Sweet Bush was finally torn down. There was a much-needed supermarket built in its place.

Janelle insisted that when the day came for her wedding, the sun would shine. Whether due to prayer or Janelle's tenacity, March didn't arrive roaring like a lion. It purred, instead, like a pussy cat. The wedding and the reception took place at the New Hope Assembly Church. Of course, it wasn't totally acceptable to some, but Deacon Pillar had taken care of that. He started pulling tales of indiscretions from the deep recesses of his memory. Some he'd made up, but they were close enough to the truth to stop any revolts.

That sunny day also had just enough wind to tease Janelle's carefully coiffed hair that had grown down past her shoulders. The pearl-laced tiara sparkled every time she'd turn her head, denying any thoughts that she wasn't queen for that day.

Her wedding gown was, of course, a Janelle special.

She'd designed it on a whim. It was taupe-colored instead of white and it was, naturally, low cut. Not too low cut, but just enough so her *girls* could witness the wedding, too.

Chyna stood beside her sister. Her deep blue gown was as about as matronly as Janelle would allow. Chyna had insisted that as the maid of honor she be allowed some dignity. Janelle finally gave in and permitted Chyna to wear something that wasn't see-through and had a high neckline.

Of course, Janelle's wedding wasn't complete until the third member of their group had finally arrived back in the United States. Cinnamon's run on the cruise ship ended just in time for her to participate in Janelle's wedding. Her son, Hard Life, hadn't splurged as she thought he would've with his uncle's inheritance. He'd paid for her ticket to fly back to Brooklyn. Cinnamon wore a mauve colored off-the-shoulder, formfitting gown with a plunging neckline. It wasn't that way when Janelle had her fitted despite the three women being almost the same size in everything. Just like Janelle, Cinnamon liked her girls on display.

Cordell stood at the altar petrified. He looked like a man that was about to fight Mike Tyson and Muhammad Ali with gloves made of cotton. He kept fishing through his tuxedo for the vows he'd written.

"What you looking for, Dummy?" Deacon Pillar muttered with his tired eyes now blazing and shooting darts. "I sho' hope it's not an escape route. Me and First Lady got security all around the church."

"I can't find my vows." Cordell whispered to his best man. His hands kept fidgeting under his jacket as though ants attacked him.

"You still can't muster your manhood together. You

don't need no piece of paper." Deacon Pillar murmured, "Speak from your heart, coward. I didn't know being your best man was gonna be so tiring."

Cordell really didn't have a choice. As soon as Deacon Pillar stopped his scolding, Cordell felt and then saw Janelle's eyes. Her eyes had narrowed and her jaw was set. She was mentally cutting and slicing him from his head to his toes.

Chyna was unaware of the impending problem, so she watched in horror as Janelle suddenly started plucking blooms from her bridal bouquet. As soon as she followed Janelle's eyes and saw her sister was watching Cordell, Chyna became nervous. *I don't know what Cordell did, but he'd better fix it. Janelle looks like she's about to kill him before they even say "I do."*

Deacon Pillar saw it all and he did everything not to laugh. He'd watched Janelle pluck the flowers from her bouquet almost down to the stems while Cordell stood sweating. *Have mercy, that woman has scared the crap out of him. Janelle's more dangerous than that Bobbitt gal.*

Bishop Smith had counseled Chyna and Janelle to a point where the two sisters would at least promise to work out their issues. He was pleased with the progress and even more so when Janelle asked him to officiate at her wedding.

So while Bishop Smith continued with the wedding ceremony, Deacon Pillar took a moment to straighten his favorite polka-dot tie. He'd decided that no matter what Cordell said, he wasn't wearing a monkey suit. It'd taken quite a bit of arguing, but he finally got Chyna to side with him. So while the bride and groom along with the others in the wedding party were pretty much color coordinated, Deacon Pillar was not. He was the consummate example of every "don't" in the fashion handbook. Mister

Blackwell would've been lost for words to describe the mess the old man wore.

Chyna looked over at Deacon Pillar and smiled. She watched him as he straightened his polka-dot tie. She winked at him as he straightened his suspenders over a pair of beige khaki pants and that's when she realized the buttons on his red silk shirt were misaligned. However, all in all the old man looked a lot better than he would have in his favorite zebra stripes. That's what he'd originally wanted to wear.

Janelle had finished destroying her bouquet and whatever was left of Cordell's manhood. She'd have remained upset, but then Cordell began to speak when it came his time. She was almost giddy as she listened to Cordell recite his wedding vows. And then it was time to hear the words she'd waited a lifetime to hear.

"I now pronounce you man and wife. Now you may kiss your bride." Bishop Smith announced.

Cordell gently took Janelle in his arms and kissed her. They kissed so long and so deep until it was amazing they hadn't started to *dance* right there in front of all the guests.

The reception hall was beautiful. Chyna had recruited some of the ladies from the bereavement committee who knew a thing or two about coordinating an event. The reception started on time and went without a hitch. Even the church board acted like they had a semblance of sanity and Christianity. Of course, Deacon Pillar had brought his fake copy of the journal along just in case the hypocrites needed a reminder.

An hour or so into the reception, Chyna finally had a chance to sit. She'd been so busy helping Janelle to plan the wedding and all the chaos that went along with it, she hadn't a chance to relax in weeks.

"How are you doing, First Lady?"

Chyna looked up to see Deacon Pillar. "I'm doing just fine. Please sit with me."

Deacon Pillar pushed back a chair and sat down. He loosened his tie and let one suspender fall off his shoulder. It was as though half the weight of the world was lifted when he did.

"So tell me something," Deacon Pillar said with a tired twinkle in his eyes, "Are you going to continue working in that women's shelter? I hear Bishop Smith set it up for you."

"I love it." Chyna answered. "I truly believe that God took me through all that I've done just so I could help others."

"And what was the other reason He took you through?"

Chyna smiled and leaned closer. "So I would never think less of myself than He does."

"I'm glad you learned something I taught you." Deacon Pillar said as he patted her hand. "By the way, have you given much thought to what I asked you before?

"You want to discuss it here and now?"

"We might as well. I've already told Cinnamon about it."

"You told Cinnamon? Why?" Chyna was trying to sound annoyed and doing a very poor job of it.

"Oh gal, please," Deacon Pillar said as he finally let Chyna's hand go and the other suspender fall off his shoulder. "You know I can't keep nothing. I was telling her about Earl and reminding her of how he'd rest a lot better in his grave if she and that scandalous piece of flesh she birthed did something with their lives."

"I'm sure she must've loved hearing that." Chyna replied. She could only imagine how Cinnamon must've felt. When she had a moment she would talk to the old man about diplomacy. He apparently had never made its acquaintance.

"Look at them two over there cutting a rug on the floor." Deacon Pillar pointed a finger at Cordell and Janelle.

"I really wished she'd take it easy. She's been in remission less than a year."

"When are you gonna let that grown woman be an adult?" Deacon Pillar scolded. "You just need to mind your own business or I just might forget about becoming your spiritual daddy."

"You're right." Chyna said, "You're absolutely right."

"Of course, I am. And just to show you how I don't hold a grudge, I'm going to accept your apology and your answer."

"My answer, I didn't give it." Chyna reminded the deacon.

"So, you don't want me?" Deacon Pillar started to rise.

"You know I do." Chyna laughed. "When are you going to stop teasing me?"

"Never," Deacon Pillar said and added, "as long as you remain talented, the teasing will continue." He started to giggle like a young schoolboy. He really loved the idea that she didn't try to change him even when he'd remind her of her past when he called her talented. "Listen, daughter–First Lady," Deacon Pillar said as he took Chyna's hand, again. "Cordell and Janelle will be leaving for their honeymoon soon. Are you sure you want me to stay at your house? What about the rest of your reputation?"

"Deacon-daddy," Chyna replied.

"Deacon-daddy," Deacon Pillar interrupted, "I like that. I'd like it even better if you called me Big Poppa."

He took a moment and started slapping his knee as he laughed at his joke.

"Don't push it." Chyna scolded and laugh. "Yes, I need you to stay there while I'm away. I'm only going to the women's conference for a few days." She said. "I don't care what these people say."

"And, why is that, again?" Deacon Pillar said as he pointed around the hall at various ones. "Tell Deacon-daddy why you don't care."

"Because I know God would be angry if I thought less of myself, than He does."

"Damn right." Deacon Pillar exclaimed, "I'm glad you keep remembering that. I was about to turn stupid, myself, from trying to explain it to you."

Chyna and Deacon Pillar continued chatting. Of course, Deacon Pillar fancied that he knew about as much as she did about dancing. He got up and proved it by doing an old dance called the Huckle Buck. Chyna thought the old man was having seizures. He sure looked like it.

When it was time for Janelle to toss her bouquet, pandemonium broke out. She became upset because there wasn't one woman who thought it was good luck to step forward. None of them wanted to catch a bouquet of stems.

Well wishes were spoken along with video congratulations. When it came time for the reception to end, it was Deacon Pillar who suggested to Cordell that he might want to pack a little something to eat since they really hadn't touched the food during the reception.

"Good idea," Cordell said. "Let me get my bride. We need to say our good-byes and catch a plane."

"Where are you going for your honeymoon?" Deacon Pillar asked. "I sure hope it's not that Sandals place in Jamaica where all them naked folks be prancin' about."

One look at the happiness sliding quickly from Cordell's face told the old man that he was right. "You idiot," Deacon Pillar snapped, "What the hell is wrong with you?"

"I forgot," Cordell said, "I truly forgot."

"Damn, I wasn't even there and didn't know your dumb butt when you married the first lady. So how come I remembered that you two spent your honeymoon there, and you didn't?"

"Gotcha!" Cordell said as he laughed, "you fell for it."

"Yeah, okay I'll give you that one," Deacon Pillar said before adding, "Your dumb butt needs an excuse for why you and your soon-to-be-another-ex-wife won't be leaving for your honeymoon, tomorrow, don't you?"

"I honestly forgot," Cordell whispered as beads of perspiration broke out, "Janelle wanted to go there and I said yes."

"Do you always say yes to Janelle?"

"Yes."

"You really are whupped. I know she can't be more talented than First Lady. I mean, I saw the pictures of the First Lady. Frankly, I don't think I want to meet a woman that is *that* talented anyway. Too much pressure for one man," Deacon Pillar remarked as he took an envelope from his pants pocket. "Here, idiot."

Cordell took the envelope and felt its weight. He opened it, and after getting over the shock, he began to laugh. "Deacon, what would I do without you?"

"That's why I'm your best man at this here travesty of a wedding."

"How did you know?" Cordell asked.

"Because that bigmouthed bride of yours, she mentioned it to the First Lady." Deacon Pillar answered, "And, since the First Lady had never told Janelle where the two of you went for your honeymoon, Janelle had no idea."

Deacon Pillar stopped suddenly and whispered, "First Lady also said that she was the one that paid for y'all honeymoon back then. How long you been triflin'?"

"Thank God the old me has passed away and, today, I'm a different man. That's all I can tell you."

"Well, I'm sure you'll find a way to make her think it was your idea to surprise her with a honeymoon in Hawaii instead."

Cordell put his arms around the old man's shoulders and gave him a hug. "I love you, Deacon Pillar." Cordell suddenly became somber. "I never knew my father, and you've become the closest thing to one I've had. I thank God for you."

"Get your paws off me." Deacon Pillar said as he struggled to hold back his tears. "I'm already trying to be a sugar daddy to the First Lady, and now you trying to get in on the action."

"Huh?" Cordell was a bit surprised. He hadn't expected the old man to react the way he did.

"Gotcha," Deacon Pillar said before hugging Cordell. He gave him a quick slap on the back.

From across the room the men saw Chyna, Cinnamon, and one of the catering people trying to calm down Janelle.

"Something's wrong." Cordell said as he started to walk away quickly.

"I'm right behind you." Deacon Pillar said.

By the time Cordell and Deacon Pillar reached the other side of the hall Bishop Smith had Janelle by one of her arms. Janelle was flailing with her other one.

"What's wrong?" Cordell said as he approached. "Janelle, are you all right?"

"Hell no, I ain't all right." Janelle snapped.

"You can't use that type of language." Bishop Smith said before he stopped. One look at the anger coming from Janelle had stopped the powerful man of God right in mid sentence. "Although, Peter cussed too."

Deacon Pillar tapped Chyna on her hand. "What's up?"

"There's been a little mixup with the special menu Janelle ordered for their honeymoon snack." Chyna answered.

"I'm so sorry." The woman's white chef hat was bobbing while she wiped her hand on her apron. She tried desperately to be both professional and apologetic. It was becoming harder because Janelle looked like she wanted to take the argument outside.

For the caterer's safety, Bishop Smith, Chyna, and Deacon Pillar took her aside. In the meantime, Cordell continued to calm Janelle down.

"Sweetheart," Cordell said sweetly, "This is our wedding day. Please don't be upset over something as small as a food mixup. It'll be okay."

"Oh no, it won't," Janelle said sadly. "That woman forgot to make the most important dish I'd asked for.

"Which was what?" Cordell asked. "Whatever it is we can pick it up on the way. I've got two bottles of champagne. Our flight won't leave until tomorrow morning. We'll stop by KFC or somewhere."

"Cordell," Janelle replied. She tried to calm down and make her words sound as sweet as his. "I'm not worried about the champagne—"

Chyna saw the expression on Cordell's face change. He and Janelle were both coming toward her and neither looked any happier than before. She was glad that the caterer had decided to leave when Bishop Smith did.

"Okay," Deacon Pillar said, "I don't like being left out in the dark. What the hell is wrong with those two?"

"You wouldn't understand." Chyna said. "The woman didn't make the chitlins."

"Chitlins?" Deacon Pillar answered, "so what?"

"Janelle likes to have chitlins and champagne, together. She says they're like an aphrodisiac."

"Damn, I didn't think too many people knew about that." Deacon Pillar said. "I used to serve that to some of the gentlemen that called on my ladies. I made a ton of money when I served that concoction."

Just as Chyna was about to pick her jaw off the floor Cordell and Janelle appeared.

"I guess by now you know what's wrong?" Cordell said to Chyna.

"I do, but I don't believe it. In all my life I've never heard Janelle say anything about champagne and chitlins."

"I didn't have to share all my secrets with you." Janelle said. She sat down and it was as though she'd given up on her marriage before they'd left the reception.

"You know, y'all ignoramuses gonna kill me yet," Deacon Pillar said. "Y'all tell Cinnamon and that future serial killer son of hers good night and let's go."

"Where?" Cordell asked.

"Back to my place." Deacon Pillar answered.

"Janelle and I don't want to put you out," Cordell said, "It's our wedding night. We'll be okay."

"Do you want just 'okay' on your wedding night or do you want your world rocked: your toes lit up, your blood vessels poppin', and your head kissing your own knees?" Deacon Pillar said as he inched his way toward the door, pulling up his suspenders as he went. "If you do, then follow me."

"Why?" Janelle asked.

"Have mercy! Y'all make me sick," Deacon Pillar said as he reached the door. "I just made a pot of chitlins last night. I just can't remember if I left a window open."

From *Sister Betty Says I Do*

Available now wherever books
and ebooks are sold

Prologue

A year ago . . .

"Sister Betty," Trustee Freddie Noel whispered, his bony, hairless chest pushing in and out. Adding to what was apparently a moment of uncertainty, he swallowed hard, nearly tripping as a leg hit the edge of the ottoman.

Feeling somewhat embarrassed from the near fall, he bit his bottom lip before announcing, "I need to say something." He fumbled around inside the pocket of his suit jacket and retrieved a small box tied with a blue silk ribbon. "You know I ain't the most romantic being on the planet. . . ." Freddie quickly lowered his eyes. His shoulders slumped as he took a deep breath, while at the same time raising his free hand and pulling at a small sprig of silver hair that resembled a Mohawk in training. It was a nervous habit formed twenty-five years ago, when he turned forty-five.

His cheeks, turning almost a bright red, contrasting sharply with his lemon-yellow complexion, slowly began shrinking, freeing the air seconds ago trapped inside his lungs. Now, with the untied box in hand, Freddie's fragile body knelt at Sister Betty's feet. He slowly raised his head. His tired and now tearing brown eyes, embedded in deep sockets, began darting between the opened box and the huge fourteen-carat, pear-shaped diamond ring he now held between two trembling fingers. "Betty . . . Sarah . . . Becton, would you pretty please marry me?"

Sister Betty, almost a foot shorter than Freddie, could feel a hot sensation flooding throughout her small brown-skinned body. She felt as though she'd suddenly turned into the head of a lit match. If that was the case, then her sudden rush of tears would quickly douse its flame.

"Yes," she replied, smiling, then giggling like a child who received what she'd always wanted on Christmas morning. She allowed him to slip the diamond engagement ring upon her finger. And, just as the man kneeling before her had done moments ago, she quickly took a deep breath, struggling to form the words through her smile. Finally, she added, "Yes, Freddie, I will marry you."

That was late spring of 2010. It was a first for them in marriage, and as far as carnal matters went, perhaps for Freddie more so than for Betty. She'd lain with a young man once in her youth, an ill-advised sexual act committed inside her parents' South Carolina barn that ultimately produced a stillborn son. Freddie, on the other hand, had had several missteps, which had caused most women seeking fulfillment to shun him. He ultimately learned to do without the pleasure of a woman.

They were overjoyed now, having lived into their twilight years, to finally jump the broom. Their future looked so bright, they'd begun wearing sunglasses every day.

"Honey Bee, what do you think about honeymooning in Aruba?" He'd not bothered to tell her that it was a place he'd always dreamt about going. He could've gone more than a year ago, when he won over a hundred million dollars from South Carolina's Mega Millions lottery. Instead of traveling and living the high life, he'd given most of it to the beloved Crossing Over Sanctuary Church, where he and Sister Betty attended, because it was in deep financial trouble.

He didn't wait for her to answer before laying out upon her living room coffee table several brochures detailing cruises and land vacations in the Caribbean. "Just take your pick," he told her. "Anywhere you wanna go . . . And if none of these tickle your fancy, we can visit a travel agent and see what else there is."

On that beautiful sunny day, when all things seemed possible, the date was set and the wedding planning was about to go into full swing.

Of course, ole Satan wasn't on the guest list but decided he'd send a gift or two, anyway.

Grab the Hottest Fiction
from
Dafina Books